DARKENED SKIES BOOK THREE

AMID TWISTED CHAOS

H.E. BAUMAN

First paperback edition February 2024

Cover design by MiblArt

Map by Cartographybird Maps

Jeanine Harrell of Indie Edits with Jeanine

ISBN 979-8-9888024-3-3 (paperback)

ISBN 979-8-9888024-4-0 (hardcover)

ISBN 979-8-9888024-2-6 (ebook)

www.hebauman.com

CONTENT WARNING

Thank you for picking up *Amid Twisted Chaos*, the third book in the Darkened Skies series. If you have not read *Under Darkened Skies* and *Into Whispering Shadows* yet, you will need to do that before you read this book. The series must be read in order.

The story includes themes and events that may not be suitable for some readers:

- Fantasy and magical violence, including on- and off-screen character deaths

- Mentions of blood and injuries

- Stalking and threats

- Several open door sex scenes

- Nightmares, anxiety, and PTSD symptoms

- Mildly disordered eating (not descriptive, related to grief)

- References to torture (past), parental death, mild alcohol consumption, current war, historical wars, and rebellion

Please take care of yourself as you read.

THE NORTH SEA
TALMARIS
GRAND DUCHY OF NOVARIA
ZINDIR
THE ZAIKUD EMPIRE
MACADIAN MOUNTAINS
POSAN
FORT AVALON
NARIZON
FORT BLACKROCK
CORSYCA
FORT IRONWING
KINGDOM OF DELIA
SAPOI
CAPITAL CITIES
CITIES
NOTABLE TOWNS
FORTS
MEMATOS
ILESOURIA
THE WESTERN SEA

IRVINA
THE LOST ISLES
MANTARES MOUNTAINS
THE HELOSIAN EMPIRE
THE EASTERN SEA
REPUBLIC OF TORNAMA
THE BADLANDS
RING OF FIRE
TINALE BAY
KALAMA
SEZIA
THASIA
KATAVENA
TAIPOLI ISLANDS
THE SOUTHERN OCEAN

To those trying to reclaim their power

CHAPTER 1

The last three weeks had been quiet. Too quiet for Astrea Sovna's comfort.

She'd been in hiding in northern Novaria for weeks. There'd been no dreams planted by Nazarov. There'd been no void mages finding and attacking the estate. There'd been no hint of The One or the Paragon. There'd been no assassins sent by the Helosian emperor. Nothing.

Astrea didn't trust quiet.

A gull cried out overhead, bringing Astrea back to reality just in time to dodge Commander Lucian's punch. Starlight sparked past her head as she dipped to the right.

"You're distracted," Lucian said as he followed her. The wind played with a few strands of his long, dark hair that had escaped its usual bun.

"Sorry."

"Just focus. Don't apologize."

Another punch, this one without magic. Astrea dodged again. She was getting better at that. Adi came at her from her left with chunks of earth. One slammed into her upper arm. Hot, bright light whizzed past her as she stumbled back two steps.

"Where's your shield?" Lucian barked.

"Which one?" Astrea's breath came in quick bursts as she pivoted again. Another chunk of grassy earth shot past her.

"Both of them."

Trying to pull her mental barrier around herself and summon a shield of light proved to be an impossible task. It was too much for her to focus on at once.

Still, Astrea pulled her emotions back toward herself, closer and closer until the world around her was quiet and dull. No whispering focus from Adi. No heavy wall from Lucian. No colors or tastes or sensations dancing over her skin. It was almost sad.

Light swirled around Lucian's raised fists. Astrea tugged at the energy buzzing under her skin. She'd seen Lucian make this shield a hundred times in the last month, and she pictured it in her mind now. It was as wide and tall as she was. Her magic roared to life, weaving itself tighter and tighter until the light was a dense, glimmering wall. It blocked Lucian's blow, vibrations rippling through Astrea's bones. How did he not break his hand using that much force?

"Keep it up," Lucian ordered.

He punched the shield again. Astrea's entire body vibrated. She gritted her teeth.

"Hold it, Az!" Adi called from somewhere behind her.

"Do not let it fall," Lucian warned.

Astrea's arms trembled as energy coursed through her. She was either going to let the light shield or her mental barrier fall. Astrea had no choice; she simply couldn't hold both. Awareness exploded over her senses again as Lucian's kick connected with her shield. Pain erupted in Astrea's chest, and her light faltered as she sank to the ground.

"Fight it!" Lucian called. "Fight back!"

Looking up through the tears clouding her vision, Astrea searched for the emotions that had to be floating around the commander. There were none. No colors. No energy for her to grab. Sweat beaded on her forehead.

"How will you fight the void mages when they have no emotions for you to pull on?" Lucian taunted. He plucked at her anger, making her chest burn hotter.

He'd promised she would someday be able to do that, too: hold her own barrier while reaching beyond it to pull on others' energy. At this rate, Astrea wasn't so sure. Someday seemed very far away. No matter how much she practiced, no matter how much she learned, it never seemed to be enough.

"Commander!" Adi called.

"Fight back," Lucian whispered, his midnight blue eyes locked on Astrea's. "You know how."

"Commander, that's enough!"

Astrea's lungs squeezed, a sputtering cough building in her throat. Her mind threatened to drag her back to that dark, awful place even as Adi yelled at the commander again. *Not there.* Her fingers dug into the grass. *Not there.* Though Astrea barely managed to get her hand off the ground, starlight blasted Lucian square in the chest. He stumbled back, teal approval sparking against the gray sky. His leather armor smoldered.

"*There* it is," he said, grinning even as Astrea coughed and wheezed. "Good. Again."

Astrea pushed to a stand and tugged at her armor, the same set Jin had so carefully fitted to her body weeks ago. He'd insisted it was good for her to wear while training. "I don't want to do it again," she said as Adi stalked closer.

"The Paragon didn't give you a choice," Lucian snapped.

"I *need* a break."

"The Paragon didn't give you a break from the blue lotus when they held you under that house. Victor Nazarov didn't give you a break when he—"

"Enough," Adi barked. "She told you she needs a break, so she's getting a break."

"That's not fair, Commander," Astrea muttered as she pulled her mental barrier back around herself. It was no good taking chances around Lucian.

"I'm here to prepare you, Astrea, not to be fair."

"I just need five minutes!" Five minutes to calm down, to ground herself in reality and pull her mind back from those tunnels and that house. Was that really so much to ask?

"You're the one who asked to run this drill." Lucian crossed his arms. "There are no breaks. You know that."

Astrea turned on her heel, marching through the empty yard of the old military base they'd been hiding out at. There wasn't much for comfort here, so far away from civilization, but there was a garden—if a few rose bushes and trees could be called a garden—at the back of the small compound. She hurried past the gray brick building that once housed Novarian military officers, ignoring Lucian as he shouted for her to come back to the yard.

Commander Lucian could be kind. He had helped watch over Astrea and her friends for the last month. He *was* teaching her about the magic they shared. But the last time he'd truly been kind to her was that night after she'd escaped the Paragon. The night he'd healed her. In the weeks since, he'd become rigid. Unyielding. All she needed was a little patience from him.

Behind the house was quiet. A space for her to be alone. The only other way to get there was from the door that led into the kitchen.

She dropped onto a wrought iron bench nestled between two massive evergreens and took her hair out of its braid. Her whole body ached; it always did after a lesson with Lucian. Going inside and taking a shower sounded better than sitting out here, but since leaving Talmaris, Jin had only become more attuned to her mood. He'd be able to pick up on her frustration in a heartbeat.

It was nice to be so well understood, but Jin and Lucian had been butting heads since the moment the commander got to the base. They disagreed about a lot of things, but they especially disagreed on how intense Lucian's training tactics were. The commander was pushing all of them to their limits, but Jin especially didn't like how aggressive his Lightbringer lessons were.

In fact, Astrea had broken her wrist two weeks prior during a similar exercise to the one they'd just wrapped up. She'd thought Jin was actually going to punch Lucian. He hadn't but only because Adi stepped in. Now Jin's team trained in the afternoons while Astrea worked with Lucian, and sometimes Adi or Marko, in the mornings.

Astrea flexed her wrist—long since healed by her magic—and sighed. She understood why Lucian was doing what he was doing. She did. He was right, after all. The Paragon wouldn't be patient. They wouldn't give her breaks. Hadn't given her breaks when they'd held her under that house for days. Neither would the Helosians. Astrea needed to be stronger. She needed to keep pushing herself.

Sitting around and ruminating on it wasn't going to help. Besides, even if she needed to push herself, Astrea truly needed a break. Just the mention of blue lotus made her skin crawl. If Lucian really wanted to make her go back out into the yard and keep practicing, he'd have to drag her out of the house kicking and screaming.

She'd just started through the home's drab halls when a throat cleared behind her.

"Done with training?" a rough voice asked.

"Why do you always do that, Marko?" Astrea mumbled as she climbed the first few stairs. Unlike the grandiose guest house back at Grand Duchess Ysabel's palace, this house was utilitarian. No soft rugs. No sweeping staircases. No chandeliers or fancy dishware. And that was all fine by Astrea. She just hated how the stairs squeaked.

"Do what?" Marko asked from just behind her.

"Approach so quietly. Just say you're there."

"I wasn't sure you would want to talk to me."

"And why would you think that?"

"Because you look angry."

"Maybe I am angry."

"The commander again?"

"You know," Astrea said as they reached the top of the stairs, "you sure do ask a lot of questions for someone who once claimed to have a morbid lack of curiosity. Don't you have a gate or a front door to watch?"

"Ouch," he said, fake hurt laced into his voice. "Is that really what you think?"

"Right now? Yes."

When they'd first arrived in the Novarian capital of Talmaris, Astrea hadn't been so sure about Marko. He'd been polite enough, if not a bit aloof. And he'd seen her at her worst since then, that night she finally got away from the Paragon. But in the last month, he'd proven to be a decent companion and competent guard. He was funny and got on well with both Adi and Jin.

Commander Lucian had assigned Marko to be Astrea's personal guard after everything that had happened. Though the Paragon could jump anyone between locations with their void magic, the group had agreed it was best for Astrea and Jin to never be alone. That way, if the Paragon did come, someone else would be there to assist. Since coming to the estate, Marko had started giving her more space, mostly because someone else *was* always around. If Jin was busy, Adi was around. If Adi was also busy, Lennor or Civan—the twins on Jin's team—were around. And Lucian was usually somewhere nearby.

Marko lifted one lean shoulder. "Just doing my job."

"Well, I'd like to take a shower alone," Astrea said. "Unless that's unacceptable." She knew she shouldn't be giving him an attitude. He'd done nothing wrong. But Astrea just wanted to be alone for a few minutes.

"Completely reasonable."

"Great. So you can go back to whatever you were doing before."

"Are you sure you don't want to stay outside for a bit longer?" Marko asked. "Otherwise Lucian's going to come inside and drone on about skies knows what."

"I'm sure."

"Fine," Marko said with a sigh. "I'll be around."

"And I'll be upstairs."

As Astrea started up to the third floor, she couldn't help but notice the house was surprisingly quiet. Jin's team's preferred method of communication was shouting to each other from different rooms; she didn't understand why they couldn't just stand up and walk to the other room to chat.

She'd almost thought the house was empty until she opened the door to the bedroom she was sharing with Jin. He sat cross-legged in the middle of their bed, an array of papers spread out in front of him.

As soon as she walked in, he looked up and smiled. "There you are."

"Here I am," she muttered as she unlaced her boots.

"That doesn't sound good."

"I'm fine." Astrea picked up her boots and carried them toward the wardrobe.

She was about to ask Jin what he was doing when the door that led to their small balcony creaked open. Civan walked in, then hesitated when he saw Astrea. "I'll go wake Len," he murmured before hurrying out into the hall.

Astrea shook her head. Civan was still a mystery to her, so silent that sometimes she forgot he was in the room. As soon as the bedroom door was closed, Astrea tugged off her body armor, then tossed it on the ground next to her boots. Moving into the bathroom, she started the shower first, then went to the linen closet for a towel. When she turned, Jin was standing in the doorway, arms crossed over his chest. Like her, he was wearing his training clothes: thick black pants and a black shirt.

"So, you're not fine," he said.

"Just annoyed with Lucian."

"He didn't break another of your bones, did he?"

"No. He just expects more of me than I'm capable of giving." She pulled her shirt over her head and tossed it on the tile floor. "He thinks I should have more stamina by now."

It was frustrating. Embarrassing. Astrea hated it. She hated that she wasn't stronger in a fight. She could do so much more when she healed. Back in Talmaris, Adi had theorized that maybe her Lightbringer magic didn't respond the same way because it wasn't meant to be so aggressive. Lucian didn't seem to have that issue, though. *Maybe I'm just weak.*

"Lucian's a fool if he expects you to be at the level of one of his people who's been training for years," Jin said. "You've only been training for a few weeks. Cut yourself some slack. No one in the world is going to master their magic in that time."

Astrea wiggled out of her pants as she said, "If you count my sessions in Talmaris, I've had almost six weeks."

"Right, because almost six weeks is *so* much more time. The perfect amount of time to master your magic and learn self-defense. Silly me."

"You're annoying when you're sarcastic," she said over her shoulder. She stuck her hand under the water, but it was barely tepid.

"And you're too hard on yourself." When she glared at him, Jin raised his hands up in surrender. "I thought we were just stating the obvious."

"Annoying," she said again, but she couldn't help but smile when he grinned at her.

Jin was good at that. He was good at breaking her out of her bad moods.

"I need to finish reading up on what Ellie sent over last week," Jin said. "Then I have to go work with Civan and Lennor."

"That's the third time you've read Ellie's report."

In the weeks they'd been away from Talmaris, communication with the palace and the rest of their friends had been beyond limited. Just one delivery had come: a restock of supplies and a single thick folder of information from Eliana and Grand Duchess Ysabel. Astrea hadn't read the report for herself, but Jin, Adi, and Lucian had pored over it multiple times. It detailed what information Ysabel's people had been able to gather about Kalama and Emperor Aelius's plans, which all seemed to point back to Corsyca and the war effort. Nothing about pursuing Eliana and Jin.

Jin lifted one broad shoulder. "I just want to make sure I didn't miss anything."

"I doubt you have if you've read it so many times," Astrea said. "You said there's barely anything of use in it."

"That's the trouble. My father's never so slow to respond. The fact that he hasn't even *tried* to come after us doesn't sit right with me. We've been away from Kalama for nearly two months. He should've reacted by now."

It didn't sit right with Astrea either. None of it did. Emperor Aelius's uncharacteristically slow response. The Paragon's apparent retreat. Being away from Kalama for nearly two months.

"And you think Ellie's report is somehow going to reveal your father's grand plans?" she asked.

"I'm just thinking there may be something I'm not seeing." He sighed. "I don't think I'll be done until dinner."

Some days they barely saw each other. It was selfish, but Astrea wanted to spend every second she could with Jin. Being here, removed from Kalama and Talmaris, was nice. Even with his team, Lucian, and Marko around. It was nice to be able to pretend for a little while that they lived a quiet life by the ocean. That they weren't the targets of some ancient organization. But today wouldn't be that way. Today was about business.

"Then I'll see you at dinner," she said. Finally, Jin crossed the bathroom and pulled her close. "You'll get all sweaty if you do that."

"I don't care." He leaned in, kissed her gently, then pulled away. "I'm about to become far more of a mess than you." Jin's fingers trailed to the waistband of her bloomers, and he barely pulled the fabric away from her skin. "See you at dinner."

As Jin left the bathroom, Astrea finished disrobing, then stepped under the warm water. She enjoyed Jin's attention, but she needed to focus. There were chores to be done, and if she wasn't going to be training for the rest of the day or helping decipher Emperor Aelius's inaction, she needed to find a way to make herself useful.

CHAPTER 2

Astrea slid the dishes into one of the kitchen cupboards, then closed the door. Everyone on the base had chores to do, partially as a way to keep the house running and partially to alleviate boredom. There wasn't that much else to do, really. Astrea had already taken the laundry off the line, and now that the dishes were put away, she was done until dinner.

"Feeling better?" Marko asked from where he stood near the back door that led to the minuscule garden.

How does Ellie do this all the time? Astrea wondered. Never being alone was exhausting. With Jin's team running through another set of overly complicated drills in the yard—and Lucian being with them—Astrea had hoped to at least pretend she had time to herself. But Marko took his job of watching over her very seriously.

"I guess." Astrea circled the large worktable in the middle of the kitchen, then stopped in front of the counter anchored to the back wall. She'd started brewing coffee while Marko stepped out for a moment, and by the looks of it, the drink was done.

"Am I allowed to ask a question?"

"Sure." Astrea lifted the pour-over contraption off the carafe now holding the most important thing in the world: Kalamian coffee. Not the weaker Novarian variety. The stuff from home, the stuff Zephyrine had sent them off with. "Ask away," she said as she put the contraption in the sink.

"My sudden curiosity doesn't offend you?" Marko asked.

"Is that your question?"

Marko huffed, but Astrea swore she could hear his smile as he said, "Have you ever considered telling the commander how you feel?"

What a novel idea. But she held her tongue. Marko was just trying to help. Instead, she poured coffee into two mugs and said, "How I feel doesn't matter."

"That's bleak."

"It's true." She turned and set one of the mugs on the central work table, then nudged it toward where Marko stood with his arms crossed.

He watched her for a moment, gray eyes discerning. Moving slowly, he first brushed a lock of shoulder-length blond hair from his face, then reached for the drink. "Thank you for this."

Astrea still didn't know how Marko had gotten the scar that marred his cheek, nor did she know much about him at all. But she knew one thing. He liked Kalamian coffee as much as she did.

"I'm sorry for snapping at you earlier," she said. "You're just doing your job."

"I know." Marko lifted the mug to his thin lips, and as he took a sip, he groaned. "How do you all manage to make this so good?"

Astrea half smiled. She had no answer for that question; the intricacies of coffee production wasn't a topic she was well-versed in. "I'll leave the rest if you want it," Astrea said as she picked up her own mug. "I'll be in the library."

Even as she left the kitchen, barrier pulled tight around herself, Astrea knew Marko would be following her. She tried to ignore that, instead focusing on the dark wood floors stretching down one hallway, then another. This part of the house was quiet, the library on one side of the hall and a small parlor on the other. She supposed even the military officers who used to live there would've required such things, especially at such a remote location. The decommissioned base was in the far northern reaches of Novaria, just a mile from the ocean and hidden among the thick northern woods. The perfect hiding spot for her and Jin.

She opened the pocket door to the library. It was nothing compared to the Great Library back in Kalama, but here, Astrea felt just a little bit at home. Two short sofas occupied the middle of the room; a narrow coffee table separated them. Nestled behind one sofa was a writing desk made of gleaming wood. Built-in bookshelves lined the wall opposite the door, and that was it. Simple. Small. Safe.

Astrea had taken organizing the library upon herself. Not because it was a useful task but because she didn't know what else to do with her time. Besides, haphazardly arranged books had always bothered her. She'd tried several times over the years to organize Saros's office in the observatory, but he'd always made a mess of it again. A little clutter was fine, but she didn't know how he found anything.

Organizing a collection of this size should've taken her a couple days at most. But she'd also been hoping to find something related to the so-called Stargazer's prophecy the Paragon had told her about. The chances of that were impossibly small. Practically nonexistent. But if she could just find *something* . . .

Cressida was back in Talmaris, combing through palace and city archives with Mariya, the grand duchess's Stargazer, and Tomas, the grand duchess's librarian. Astrea had also left Mattina's journal with them, along with the other few scraps of evidence they had about the Paragon.

In the sole report Eliana had sent to the base—the one Jin kept rereading—Tomas had been kind enough to send some notes from his research. He, Mariya, and Cressida had been going through the books that Professor Kostas Shalysko, the Paragon sympathizer who had fooled them, had given Tomas just before the palace attack. Just before he died.

Though Tomas's notes had been difficult to read, the trouble had been worth it.

They hadn't uncovered the prophecy the Paragon followed, but they had learned more. Tytas Ramkas had been the first One, or the first ruler of the Paragon, during the Great Wars. Dreamwalkers were revered among the early Paragon, and Astrea already knew from Ninette that they had always been in charge of the clandestine group. Tytas Ramkas's void mage army had terrorized both the early Novarians and early Helosians, as well as other rulers in the areas surrounding the Macadian and Antare Mountains. The Paragon's civilization had been semi-nomadic, always on the move throughout the mountains as war raged on between other armies. And while the book had been helpful in filling in some of the details, it barely mentioned void magic at all.

Besides, none of that answered their questions about the prophecy or where the book Emperor Aelius wanted was, but Astrea could hazard a guess about what information it contained. Surely that lost book said something about void magic and where it came from. Maybe it would even answer questions about why Emperor Aelius had been interested in Tytas Ramkas. At least, it seemed he was since his government had purchased that bust of the old Paragonian ruler. Maybe the book even held the key to restoring balance. Maybe that was why the Paragon wanted it so badly for themselves.

Astrea returned to the shelf she'd been working on the day before and sighed. So much for being organized. *Adi must've picked through the stacks again.*

Footsteps shuffled in behind her, and Astrea loosened her tight hold on her magic. Marko and his wavering wall. She peeked over her shoulder at him.

"Are you just going to stand there, or would you like to help me?" she asked.

"I've never been one for books," he replied dryly.

"Yes, well, you don't have to like them to help me organize them."

With a small grunt, Marko set his mug down on the coffee table and joined Astrea. "Why're they such a mess?"

"Adi," Astrea said. "He's been dying for something new to read, but none of these suit his tastes."

"And what are his tastes?" Marko picked up a thick brown tome and read the title aloud. "*Zaikudi Battle Tactics During the Early Great Wars.*" He scoffed. "That doesn't suit anyone's taste."

"He likes romance novels," Astrea said, "and none of these come close."

"Huh."

"What?" Astrea asked, taking the brown book from Marko and bringing it to the section she'd assigned to similar topics.

"I didn't expect him to enjoy those."

"Why's that?"

"Just didn't seem like the type."

"I thought you'd never been one for books," she quipped as she joined him and took the next book he handed to her. The gold font stamped into the blue cover mentioned something about geography. "How would you know the type?"

"Because my former partner was the type, and Adi's nothing like him."

"Oh? Were you married?"

"No," Marko mumbled as Astrea slid the geography book in place. "Let's just move on, shall we?"

Astrea accepted another book from Marko, another about geography. "You know, I don't really know much about you, Marko."

"Nor I you. Sometimes it's better that way."

"You know plenty about me." Astrea wedged the book into place. "You know I'm Novarian but grew up in Kalama, that I'm a Lightbringer, and that I'm apparently part of some prophecy. We spend so much time together; shouldn't we know each other better?"

"And yet I don't even know your favorite color," Marko mused as he turned another book over between his palms. When Astrea gave him a pointed look, he sighed. "My father was from central Helosia, my mother was from southern Novaria, and I grew up south of Talmaris. You already know I'm a Tempest. I'm part of no prophecies."

"And your favorite color?" Astrea prompted.

"Don't have one."

"Do you know Commander Lucian's favorite color?"

"No."

"Haven't you worked together for a while?"

"Years. Why does that mean I should know his favorite color?"

Astrea shrugged. She'd known those kinds of things about her colleagues back at the library in Kalama. "Sometimes it's nice to talk about things that don't revolve around safety or the end of the world." If Astrea could keep her mind from straying for five minutes, it was worth it. "My favorite color is purple."

"Noted."

"How old are you?"

A deep, rumbly laugh started in Marko's chest. "Why the skies does that matter?"

"I'm just curious." Astrea took two more books off the stack as Marko went to get his coffee. "I'm twenty-four."

"Twenty-nine."

"And you really don't have a favorite color?"

"No."

Astrea rolled her eyes, then shelved the next few books in silence. She hadn't realized Marko was part Helosian, not that it mattered. People traveled all over the continent and started families in other countries;

that wasn't really a surprise. Their few minutes of conversation, at least, had pulled her mind away from the Paragon and distracted her from the never-ending ache in her heart.

Soft footsteps crossed the floor to where she stood. Astrea glanced up at Marko; he wasn't much taller than Cressida, but he was still a head taller than Astrea.

"Here." He handed her another book. "And for what it's worth, I wouldn't say it's my *favorite* color, but I suppose green is nice."

Astrea smiled up at him. Maybe Marko's company wasn't so bad after all.

The sun had begun to set outside, painting the kitchen walls an array of pink, orange, and gold. A loud thud echoed through the room as Adi dropped a sack of potatoes on the center worktable.

"Peel eight of them, please," he said to Astrea.

"Where's the peeler?"

"You *still* don't know where the peeler is?"

"I haven't been helping you for that long."

"You've been helping me for nearly a month!" Adi laughed as he walked to a drawer on the opposite side of the kitchen. He returned with a peeler and handed it to her. "Wash them first."

Astrea took the peeler from him. "Don't worry, I remembered *that*."

She'd started helping Adi in the kitchen within a few days of getting to the estate. Astrea had never been one for cooking—Cressida didn't like to share the kitchen, and Saros didn't cook either—but she liked having something to do. And spending time with Adi was fun. He always kept her mind distracted when all it seemed to want to do was remind Astrea of all the bad things that had happened. Lennor joined them sometimes, as did Jin, but it was usually just her and Adi. It was also a good time for her to practice pulling her mental barrier around herself; doing so while trying to focus on a nonmagical task was getting less challenging.

"Did I ever tell you about the time I nearly burned down the kitchen at Fort Avalon?" Adi opened the refrigerator and started rummaging through it.

"That doesn't exactly sound like a fun story." Astrea began sorting through the potatoes Adi had given her to find the largest eight. She'd quickly learned that when feeding Jin's team, Marko, and Lucian, it was better to err on the side of making too much food. It always got eaten.

"Zephyrine didn't think it was too fun at the time," Adi said, "but we laugh about it now."

Astrea retrieved the colander and loaded half the potatoes in, then brought them to the sink and started the water. "What happened?"

"We actually had a night off and were going to listen to one of the pro sports matches from Kalama on the radio," Adi said. "I decided that popping corn would be a great thing to add to the night. We even had beer."

"Was that rare at the fort?"

"Rare enough."

Astrea turned the water off and switched the potatoes out for the second half.

"Jin, Dorin, and Rasa had brought the radio to the mess hall so I could listen while I cooked for us. I left the oil heating on the stove for too long without checking on it, though."

Astrea turned the water off again. She grabbed a towel and laid it over the sink's drain, then grabbed the peeler. "I thought you weren't supposed to leave oil unattended."

"You're not. I got cocky."

"And you almost burned down the fort."

He laughed. "I did. None of us remembered until Jin saw the smoke coming from the kitchen."

"I assume everything was fine," Astrea said over her shoulder.

"Well, I did have a Fireweaver and Tidebacker with me. They got the fire under control before anything important burned down."

"Then how is that almost burning down the fort?"

"Like you've never added a little dramatic flair to a story?"

"Not like that," she muttered, and Adi snorted.

"How are those potatoes coming?"

"Halfway done." She'd gotten good with the peeler in the last couple weeks. It was monotonous, easy, though she had accidentally cut her finger the first time she used the tool. "What do you want me to do when I'm finished?"

"Cube them, then toss them in oil. I'll set the spices out for you."

Astrea finished peeling the last of the potatoes. She set the final one aside, then picked up the towel with the potato peels still in it and took it out the door from the kitchen to the garden. She dumped the peels in the compost, then went back inside. Only now, the kitchen was empty.

Before leaving, Adi had set the spices out, as promised, but whatever meat and other vegetables he'd taken out of the refrigerator were still sitting on the counter.

Even when she'd cubed the potatoes, he still wasn't back. She loosened her grip on her magic and pushed her senses out; he was a few rooms over, or at least, she thought it was him. Astrea pulled her magic back to herself.

She needed a bowl, a large bowl, if she was to fit that many potatoes in it. She checked in the lower cabinets first, but there wasn't anything there. Civan was in charge of washing the dishes and putting them away, and try as Adi might, he couldn't get Civan to put things away in the same spot. Astrea checked four of the upper cabinets before she finally found the large white bowl she needed.

There was just one problem. It was high up on a shelf, higher than she could reach. She could just wait for Adi, but something made Astrea try reaching for it anyway. As her fingers brushed the smooth ceramic, a strong arm wrapped around her waist.

"I'll get it." Jin reached the bowl without issue, and he set it down on the counter in front of her. "Why didn't you call for me?"

"I thought I might be able to get it."

Jin's arm was still wrapped around her waist. He spun her around, then pulled her closer to him.

"What are you doing?" she asked.

"Is Adi behind me?"

When Astrea peered around him, all she saw was the empty kitchen. "No, why?"

"Good."

He pulled her closer still, his free hand moving to cradle the back of her head as he kissed her. A whimper escaped her as Jin pulled her lower lip between his teeth. This was how their time at the fort had been: morning training, slow evenings, stolen moments when the others weren't around. In moments like this, she could almost forget that they were hiding from the Paragon. She could almost forget that Eliana was preparing for Helosia's civil war. She could almost forget that she and Jin were just prisoners in a fancy house.

Almost.

But there were other routines too: her gloom, Jin's disagreements with Lucian, everyone's frustration at being stuck here at the base. Some days were good and Astrea barely noticed those things. Other days, she could barely function aside from training and chores. And sometimes, it was a miracle she got out of bed at all.

"I don't think that's sanitary for a kitchen," she said as he pulled away.

"Good thing all the food is over there, then."

Jin kissed her again as he backed her up against the counter near the sink. Astrea knew she should be working on dinner, as promised, but she didn't think she'd ever get sick of Jin kissing her like that.

She wrapped her arms around his neck, breaking their kiss just long enough to whisper, "You really shouldn't start things when we can't finish them."

"Oh, but it's so fun," Jin whispered against her mouth. "A preview of later."

"Are you here to help, Captain, or are you just going to distract my assistant?"

Adi's voice made Astrea break away, her cheeks heating. But Jin kept his gaze on her face for a beat longer, that secret smile of his returning.

"Put me to work," Jin said as he finally turned to Adi and began rolling up his sleeves. "I'll help make up for the time I distracted her."

Adi rolled his eyes. "Fine. You can help *me*. Let Az do her job."

As Adi went back to prepping the meat, Jin turned to Astrea, raising his eyebrows and mouthing, "Wow."

"Don't make me kick you out of my kitchen, Captain," Adi called without looking away from the spices he was rubbing on the meat.

"Well, you heard him," Astrea said as she reached past Jin and grabbed the bowl. "Get to work, *Captain*."

Chapter 3

Everyone was seated around the table in the estate's dining room, their knives and forks clinking against the dishes. Astrea forced herself to calm, though she wanted to twitch with every sound. It wasn't that they were doing it on purpose, nor was the noise unexpected. Between trying to mask her discomfort and pull her barrier around her mind, Astrea could barely focus on the conversation. Still, she tried.

"No chocolate cake?" Lennor asked, voice light. She tucked a strand of dark brown hair behind her ear. It was strange to see it out of her usual pigtail braids. "Don't think for a second that we forgot about that."

"Yeah," Adi said from Astrea's left. "Can't go back on your promise now."

"I'm not going back on my promise." Setting his utensils down, Jin leaned back and crossed his arms over his chest. "There's no chocolate left in the house."

Adi and Lennor looked across the table at each other, then at Civan.

"Nobody told me it was off limits," he murmured.

Even when Civan was guarding Astrea and Jin, he barely talked. He only seemed to when Astrea, Lucian, and Marko weren't around. Astrea had managed to catch a few conversations before she entered whatever room he was in, but even then, he was far quieter than his sister.

"Just teasing." Lennor shoved her twin's shoulder, then grinned at Astrea. "Have you ever had Jin's chocolate cake?"

Astrea pushed a few leftover potatoes around on her plate, trying not to scrape her fork against the ceramic. "No, I didn't realize he could bake."

Since arriving at the base, Astrea had learned that both Adi and Jin were actually decent in the kitchen. Adi more so than Jin, but they'd taken over most of the meal preparations. Apparently, back during their days at Fort Avalon, Adi had taught Jin how to cook.

Lennor and Civan had pitched in recently, too, and made Zaiku-di dishes several times. Astrea particularly liked the steamed vegetable dumplings they'd made the week before. Their father had been from Zaikud; Astrea had even overheard them practicing the language with Adi a few times.

"I wouldn't call it baking," Jin said. "That's all I can make. I'm not like Cress."

"Right." Astrea forced a smile, her heart aching at the thought of her best friend. Just months before, Cressida had been trying new tart recipes. Now she was stuck in Talmaris, helping Grand Duchess Ysabel's people search for answers about the Paragon.

Astrea stopped pushing the vegetables around her plate, instead reaching for her wine glass and leaning back in her chair. It was a red—her least favorite—and she didn't drink much of it, though she liked the feeling of the cool, heavy glass in her hand.

"Speaking of Miss Nikaphoros," Lucian said, "any update from Talmaris, Your Highness?"

"You got the same report as me, Commander," Jin said. "Nothing."

Nothing. All Astrea knew was that the Novarians had found no viable leads on the Paragon so far. No clues about the prophecy the Paragon were using to justify . . . well, whatever it was they were doing.

Lucian sighed.

What was he upset about? Jin was right. It was a silly question. There was no way for Zephyrine to give Jin secret messages, just like there was no way for Ysabel to give them to Lucian. Here, at the base, there was one phone and one radio, both located in the main hall. Neither had been used in all the weeks they'd been there except for once, to let Lucian know about the delivery. And there was only one road in and out of the property; nobody could get into the base unseen.

"Unfortunate," Lucian finally said. He twisted the stem of his wine glass twice, then stopped. "We'll just have to be patient."

Another fork—Marko's, she thought—scraped against a plate. That was it for Astrea; she'd officially reached her limit.

"I'll do the dishes tonight," she offered, already jumping out of her seat. She hated doing the dishes, but at least the sound of running water would drown out everything else. "Just bring them in whenever you're ready."

She picked up her plate and hurried out of the dining room, using the butler's pantry to get to the kitchen. Adi had already washed the pots and pans used to prep the meal; all she needed was whatever was on the dining table. As Astrea pushed up her sleeves and turned on the sink, Lennor walked into the room, several serving dishes stacked on each other.

"Do you need any help?" she asked as she set the stack next to the sink. "Civ and I always do this."

Astrea half smiled. "No, that's alright. I can do them."

Lennor hesitated for a moment, then nodded. "I'll get Civan to help bring the rest in. Just shout if you change your mind. We'll be in the parlor."

One member of Jin's too-helpful team down. When Civan showed up next, he deposited a stack of dirty plates on the counter near the sink and left with nothing more than a simple nod at Astrea. Adi, miraculously, didn't come into the kitchen, nor did Marko or Lucian. Astrea had just finished washing the serving dishes when Jin strode in.

"Len said you refused help," he said as he set a collection of wine glasses down next. "Put me to work if you don't want to ask the others."

"I can do it," Astrea said. "I just need a few minutes to myself. Haven't had much of that today."

Jin smiled gently. He knew her; he knew she needed time by herself. She always had, even when they were much younger. The first few times she'd retreated from their garden games, both Eliana and Jin had assumed something was wrong. But they'd caught on quickly and stopped worrying about it so much.

"Of course. I'll be upstairs if you change your mind. I believe Marko's going to patrol again for a while before Len and Civan take over for him."

Astrea flashed another of those weak half smiles at him. Jin brushed her shoulder with his hand, then headed out.

After feeding seven, getting the kitchen cleaned up could easily be a three-person job. Astrea had to turn the water off twice to dry and put away the dishes she'd already cleaned. But everyone actually left her alone, the house now quiet except for Adi's occasional laugh and the sound of the radio playing music several rooms over. Even that grated on her frayed mind, but it was better than how loud the room seemed at dinner. With the water back on, Astrea almost couldn't hear any of it.

She washed one of the wine glasses, then set it aside to dry after. Her fingers, slippery with soap and water, dropped the next glass she reached for. It shattered on the white kitchen tiles, a dozen shards glittering in the light. Swearing, Astrea turned off the water and crouched down to pick it up.

As her fingers brushed the first piece of glass, Astrea's stomach lurched. The kitchen lights seemed darker, the room colder. Goose bumps prickled her skin as her chest tightened painfully. Music still played in the other room, and Adi laughed again. Astrea's head swam as she tried to pick up the glass.

No, she heard herself think. She wasn't in those tunnels. But when she looked up, Astrea swore she saw Ninette's mask reflected in the window above the sink. Her hands shook.

She needed to leave. She needed to get away from the noise and the music that now seemed impossibly loud. Forcing herself to drop the shard, Astrea stood and walked on wobbling legs to the side door. It opened to the garden, and Astrea slipped into the darkness beyond.

Skies, it was so dark out. No moon tonight; too many clouds. *Maybe this was a bad idea.*

But it was quiet. So quiet out here. Astrea hadn't had quiet in days. Weeks.

She didn't venture far, only managing to walk to the tall oak tree a few dozen feet from the kitchen door. Then she sank down into the soft grass and leaned back against the tree's trunk, curling in on herself.

Her face heated. Burying her head in her arms, Astrea squeezed her eyes shut, trying to stave off the tears. Not now. Why was this happening now? She wasn't in that place anymore.

But she was. Here, in the dark, curled up like this. It was exactly how she'd been curled up in front of Nazarov before she used her magic . . . however she'd used it. It was exactly how she'd sat when Nazarov had said he couldn't kill her *yet.*

The knot in Astrea's chest tightened again as she held her breath, trying to stifle the building sob. The hold on her mental barrier was weakening; it slipped through her fingers, slippery like that skies damned wine glass.

No, she couldn't let her barrier fall. If she did, Lucian would feel it. He'd know, and he'd either come yell at her for not practicing or tell Jin something was wrong. Jin was already worried enough. He didn't say it, but he was. She grasped at her magic, trying to pull it back in, but it was so hard.

Astrea forced out a breath, but at the very end, she choked out a sob. She curled in tighter, trying to quiet her cries.

She missed Cressida. She missed Eliana. She missed Sarsali and Balthazar and Saros. She missed Raela and everyone at the library. Two months. Astrea had been gone from Kalama for almost two months, and she didn't even have anything to show for it.

She was supposed to be fighting back against the Paragon. She was supposed to be getting control over magic, over herself. Her barrier that she was fighting so hard to control rushed away from her, too fast for Astrea to grab again. She doubted she'd have the strength anyway.

What was it she was supposed to do now? Breathing or counting or something . . . She couldn't remember. Why couldn't she remember?

It wasn't supposed to be like this. She wasn't supposed to be losing control here, now, tonight. Dinner had been fine; it hadn't even been that loud. She'd just been enjoying listening to Jin and Adi's stories in the kitchen a few hours earlier. What was wrong with her?

"Astrea."

"I'm sorry," she whispered, barely lifting her head to look at Marko standing before her. "I'm sorry," she repeated, grabbing desperately for the barrier that just wasn't there. Not that Marko could see or feel her energy like Lucian could, but if her barrier was down, Lucian would surely know. He would know, and then he would lecture her about building her stamina. She was just so tired.

"Astrea." When Marko said her name again, it was gentle. "Stop."

"I'm sorry, I'm—"

He crouched in front of her, but he didn't reach out. "Don't apologize."

An ugly sound came out of Astrea as she tried to swallow another sob. Somewhere beyond her tears, she could see colors dancing around him. Blue. Sadness. Dark green. Concern.

What did he have to be sad about?

"Do you want me to get Ji—"

"No." Astrea swallowed hard, her throat tight and swollen.

"Why not?"

Why not go get Jin? Because Astrea had been trying to hide these episodes from him, from all of them. Jin had seen just one such breakdown, had found her curled up in the corner of their bathroom once earlier in the month. It had been too much for Astrea, too much for him. She knew it was. That torrent of concern and pain and sadness she'd felt from him had been too much. She didn't want him to ever feel that way because of her. Because she couldn't pull herself together.

"Just . . . please don't," Astrea whispered. "Please. Don't tell the others about this."

"Alright, I won't."

Astrea wiped at her eyes with her palms, her face warm and puffy under her touch. "Why are you here, Marko?"

A hint of a smile pulled at his mouth, making his scar pucker. "You are my charge," he said. "I went to the kitchen to check on you and saw the door cracked open. If you were trying to hide, well . . ." He motioned to the open garden around them. "This isn't much of a hiding spot." Then he actually smiled as he said, "Next time, you might crawl behind the rose bushes over there."

"What about the thorns?"

"Good point."

A choked laugh escaped Astrea, then more tears fell. She wiped those away, her mind suddenly exhausted.

"It's been a long day," Marko said. "Perhaps you should go to bed."

"I need to finish washing—"

"I'll clean everything up."

Astrea let Marko help her off the ground. Her joints cracked in protest.

It was too much like that night Jin had rescued her. Too much. She touched her arms, where all those void burns had long since healed. All she found was smooth skin slightly damp from her tears and dishwater. Her shoulder, where Nazarov had stabbed her, almost ached with the memory, but as Astrea ran her hand over the spot, that too was smooth. No blood.

Not real.

Astrea followed Marko into the house, wiping her wet cheeks as she stepped back into the bright kitchen. Adi's laugh echoed clear through the house again, Lennor's giggle joining it. The radio was still on, some big band tune floating through the main level.

As Marko moved toward the sink in silence, Astrea slipped back out through the butler's pantry, cutting through the now-empty dining room. If she could avoid walking by the parlor, she could avoid Adi, Lennor, and Civan.

She crept upstairs. When she finally made it to the third floor, the door to her and Jin's room was cracked open. Astrea smoothed her hair and scrubbed at her face. It would do no good; her pale skin always became blotchy and pink when she cried. She could heal it, she supposed, but that would require energy she didn't have. Maybe Jin wouldn't make her talk about it.

Entering the room as quietly as she could, Astrea closed the door behind her. And when she turned back to the bed, ready for a stream of questions, all she found was an empty room. Hadn't Jin said he was coming upstairs?

Astrea's mind hurt too much to try to focus on her senses to find him. He was somewhere in the house, that much she was sure of. She could feel six people, though their energy pressed painfully into her bones.

Pulling her magic back as much as she could muster, Astrea went through her bedtime routine—or most of it. She just wanted to sleep. She just wanted all of this to be over.

Someday. Someday her life had to go back to normal, right? Someday she would see her family again. And someday she'd be strong like she wanted to be.

CHAPTER 4

Astrea's boots pounded into the sand as she ran faster, faster, faster. Down the beach she sprinted, waves lapping to her right and Jin calling her name from behind.

She had to keep going.

Astrea pumped her legs even as a stitch formed in her side. Her breathing became ragged, uneven, desperate. Cool wind slapped her face as she veered left toward the forest's tree line.

Out here, she was as far away as she could get from Kalama. The opposite side of the continent. Practically a world away. And it didn't feel like she was far enough away from anything.

She hopped over a log, kicking up sand as she landed on the beach. The finish line Adi had set up was in sight. Lennor waved her arms in the air, cheering as Astrea drew closer.

Astrea's lungs burned. Her thighs burned. Every piece of her burned.

She was almost there.

They weren't exactly racing; Adi just thought running on the beach was a good idea. More difficult. Difficult was good. Difficult would prepare her. And she was beating both Adi and Jin. Marko and Civan, too. And Lucian? Well, he hadn't even bothered to try.

Astrea rushed down the beach, hopped over the long branch Adi had used to mark their end spot, and collapsed into the sand. Her breath came in heavy gasps. She thought she might actually be sick.

"Wow, I can't believe you beat Adi!" Lennor exclaimed.

Astrea forced her eyes open, squinting against the midafternoon sun. Lennor hovered over her, grinning from ear to ear.

"Is it . . . really . . . that . . . hard?" Astrea gasped between breaths even though she already knew the answer. She had never been faster than Adi, and she wasn't sure she could do it again.

"Well, he held the record for second fastest mile up at Fort Ironwing, so . . . it's pretty hard," Lennor said.

Adi and Jin crossed the line at nearly the same moment. Jin collapsed into the sand next to Astrea, and Adi paced in circles nearby. Civan came next, and finally, Marko joined them.

"You're fast," Marko said as he ran a hand over his hair. Astrea squinted up at him, but he didn't even look winded.

"And you didn't try," she said.

Marko shrugged.

Lennor opened her knapsack and pulled out canteens, then began passing them out. Lennor Rusas was a year younger than Astrea, petite, and a powerful Tempest. Astrea had spent hours watching Jin and his team train. The only reason Lennor hadn't run the course with them was because she'd re-injured her knee two days earlier. It was an old injury, one that had never healed properly and now never would. Magic had its limitations. So despite Astrea fixing it up for Lennor, the Tempest was understandably being careful with it for a few days.

The stitch in Astrea's side finally passed, so she sat up and took a canteen from Lennor. Then she shoved to her feet and meandered toward the water.

"So," Adi said, "you four up for some drills?"

You four, meaning Jin, the twins, and Marko. Astrea knew this routine and was fine with it. She liked watching them work, and their drills were far too advanced for her, anyway. She'd be on standby in case any of them got hurt.

Astrea continued walking the same short path near the ocean. Back and forth, back and forth, past seashells and chunks of seaweed. When she turned to start back the other way, she nearly bumped into Lucian.

He frowned. "Can we talk?"

"Sure." She didn't have much to say to him, but Lucian could talk. "About what?"

"Yesterday."

"I'm not going to apologize for taking the time I needed. I was having a—" She hadn't told any of them that her mind took her back to that house and those tunnels. Jin was the only one who knew, and he only knew that she saw it in her dreams.

"Having a what?"

"I was just having a bad day. Am I allowed to have those?"

"Everyone has bad days," Lucian said. "And I wasn't talking about training. I was talking about after dinner, though I assume that was also because of your bad day."

Astrea looked over at the others. Lennor was telling the men where to stand for their drill.

Of course Lucian had felt that slip in her control. And of course he was going to say something. He was strange that way, often swapping from aggressive to concerned. He'd done this back in Talmaris, too.

Astrea sucked in a deep breath, then let it out slowly. "I didn't mean to stop practicing. I'm trying hard to practice every day, so I can get stronger, like you said. I know I need the stamina for my lightbringing."

Lucian sighed. "When I said you needed stamina, I did not mean that you had to constantly practice."

"Well, your instructions weren't specific. If that wasn't what you meant, why didn't you correct me?"

"Because there are times I feel your barrier fall outside of lessons. I assumed you were practicing of your own desire, not my command."

"You made it pretty obvious what happens when I stop practicing," Astrea muttered as she crossed her arms over her chest.

"I would not attack you outside of a lesson, Astrea."

She kept her gaze glued to the rest of the group. Jin and Marko were battling it out while Adi and Civan attacked them as a team. *Complicated*. She said nothing even when Lucian sighed again.

"You shouldn't be keeping all of that inside. Just based on what I felt last night—"

"That's really none of your business," Astrea snapped.

"Maybe not, but I think it would be healthier if you didn't hide it all away. Give yourself some room to breathe. Besides, I could use the help keeping watch."

"I thought Jin and I weren't allowed to help," Astrea said.

Across the beach, Marko blasted Civan with wind so hard that he fell on his ass.

"Yes, well, I may not let you two tap in for nightly guard duty anytime soon, but that's not to say you can't help this way, especially during the day."

Lucian and the others had outvoted Astrea and Jin early in their stay at the old base. Because the Paragon were so keen on nabbing the two of them, everyone else thought it best for Jin and Astrea to not be on guard duty, especially after dark. Based on old patterns from Kalama and Talmaris, that seemed to be the Paragon's preferred time of day.

The only time Astrea really tried to keep her magic open to sense any void mages was when Lucian went to sleep, which he often did around midafternoon for a few hours.

"I will." Astrea wanted to help, even if it meant Lucian knowing just how much everything hurt. Their safety was more important than her feelings.

"And I owe you an apology," Lucian said. When Astrea started to speak, he held up a hand. "I'm sorry about what happened that night of the dinner."

Astrea stared up at Lucian, watching as blue sadness wavered around his entire body. That couldn't be right. Lucian, sad? Apologizing?

"I promised you and your friends that we could keep you all safe," Lucian said, "and we failed you. *I* failed you."

Lucian had indeed made that promise. He'd sworn void mages wouldn't get to the palace. But he'd also had entire teams of Lightbringers and other mages on the lookout. From what Astrea understood, the palace had been overrun by mages teleporting in. How were they supposed to prevent that?

"Why are you telling me this?" Astrea asked, watching as more colors spiked around him. Steel pain. Dark green concern. Deep blue regret.

"Because I need to say it, and you need to hear it."

Conversations with Lucian had been few and far between since leaving Talmaris. If they weren't working on her lightbringing skills, they pretty much stayed out of each other's way. If they were in the same room for more than a few moments, it was either for dinner or because Lucian needed to talk to Jin and Adi.

"And I'm sorry that I've been so harsh in our lessons that you felt you had to hide all the time," he continued. "That was never my intent."

Back at the training session, Adi had Jin flat on his back. Astrea's first instinct was to rush over, but she stayed put. Jin sat up, laughing and brushing sand from his hair.

"I don't really know what to say," she confessed to Lucian.

"Sometimes I cross lines, Astrea. I know that. And you don't have to say anything. I simply wanted to apologize." His barrier pulled back in, and the colors around him died. "Have you been talking to your friends about—"

"No." The word cut the air between them, harsher than she meant for it to be.

"Why not?"

Would Lucian understand? He never seemed to. He had a lot to teach her as a Lightbringer, but the commander was not soft. He was neither gentle nor particularly kind. How could he possibly understand what she was about to say?

"I don't like when I lose control," she whispered. Losing control just reminded Astrea of that dark place under that house. Reminded her of the way she'd been so desperate and scared. Just like how she felt the night before. How she almost always felt. It snuck up on her at the most random times during the day, this overwhelming feeling she was being hunted, watched, attacked. That she was just moments away from losing it again.

"Nobody does," Lucian said. "It's more manageable if you don't let it build up."

Right. Manageable. It was almost funny. How was she supposed to manage it when she was so afraid of the dark that she needed a light on to sleep? She'd told Jin about the darkness and how it scared her, and he'd moved a few things around in their room to make a night light for her. Just a lamp tucked in the corner on the floor, but it was enough to help. She loved him for the gesture, but she hated that he had to make it at all. Sure, she'd always been sensitive, but wasn't she stronger than this? Better than that?

She had promised herself she was going to fight back against the Paragon, but here she was, hiding on a beach and using nightlights despite being a grown woman.

"I'll think about it," Astrea finally said.

"I hope you do." Lucian headed for where Civan and Adi were a flurry of fists, water, and earth, shouting about wanting to tap in for the next drill.

Astrea fiddled with the end of her braid. She couldn't go far or find a place to be alone, but walking was better than standing around doing nothing. So she went back to her march, wearing the same path in the sand as the others went back to training.

Wave after wave crashed against the shore. High tide had come in, and while her companions wrapped up their exercises, Astrea had moved to a spot on the beach farther from the water. She tugged her knees up to her chest and stared out at the setting sun.

Sand crunched next to her, then Jin dropped to the ground. "It's pretty, isn't it?" he asked.

"It is," she said. "I've always liked the sound of the waves, but I never really loved the beach."

"Something about sand going in the wrong places, if I remember correctly."

Astrea half laughed. "The summer after I turned eighteen, Cress insisted I'd been spending too much time studying all spring for my exams. And I had. So we made a plan to do something different every single day for two weeks straight."

"You, not following a routine for two weeks?" Jin chuckled. "I don't believe that."

A wry smile pulled at the corners of Astrea's mouth. She had always loved her routines. Hated deviations from them.

"Well, I tried it," Astrea said. "We tried a number of new cafés before Cress agreed the White Lily really did have the best coffee in Kalama. We tried different Taipoli restaurants, then agreed Cress still made the best Taipoli food in the city. There were museum days, shopping days, and days we did nothing at all. Then there was the day she got me to the beach."

Astrea untied her braid, letting the breeze dance through her hair. "It was a perfect Kalamian summer day. The sun was out, the sea breeze kicked up in early afternoon, and every single other skies damned person was at the beach." If she closed her eyes, Astrea could actually imagine herself back on that beach with her best friend. "I'd agreed to try this new thing for Cress, so even though it seemed like the last place I wanted to be, I stayed. Both of us ended up getting hit in the face by kids playing with beach balls. Cress popped one of them, then bought the kid an ice cream because she felt so bad."

"That's not the *worst* day at the beach," Jin said. "Could've started raining."

"Oh, it did. And when we got home, soaked and covered in sand, I realized just how bad my sunburn was. If I hadn't healed it, I would've been red as a tomato for two weeks."

"I always wondered how you didn't burn."

"I really miss Cress," Astrea whispered as she reached for Jin's hand. "And Ellie."

She'd spent time apart from them before, of course. Eliana traveled for her father sometimes. Cressida and her parents sometimes went away on holidays. Sometimes they all just got too busy to see each other. But they'd always had ways to talk. Letters, phone calls, telegrams. Astrea hadn't even gotten to talk to her friends in weeks. Not even a small hello.

Jin twined his fingers through hers. "I do too. It's not forever, though. Just a little while."

That was the problem. Astrea knew just how easily "a little while" could turn into forever. Hiding her magic temporarily, until Saros could find another job in another country, had turned into fourteen years. It just had. Routines settled. Workloads grew. Holidays passed. And then Astrea had suddenly found herself in the middle of some conspiracy.

"I don't like just sitting around here," she said.

"We're hardly sitting. Training is important."

"I know, I know. I just mean that I want to do something more. Something to figure out where the Paragon are or what your father is doing."

Waves continued crashing, a welcome rumble in the background. Down the beach to their right, Adi and Lennor had started playing in the water. Astrea didn't know how; the water this far north was freezing.

Jin sighed quietly. "I don't know that there's anything we *can* do out here."

"I sat around hiding for years, Jin. Fourteen years. I don't want to hide anymore."

She peeked over at him. Jin was watching her in that way he did sometimes, gentle and curious. "Alright. So if you don't want to hide, what do you have in mind?"

"I was thinking maybe we could go to the eastern ruins we never visited. The ones we were going to go to originally. The professor . . ." She huffed. "The professor suggested they were important, and I think he'd be the one to know, right? So let's go. Let's see what we can find there."

A deep furrow formed between Jin's eyebrows. "The Paragon seem to have a connection to those places. It's probably dangerous."

"I know."

"It's breaking orders. Breaking chain of command. We rarely ever left Fort Avalon without getting direct orders."

"But it's war with the Paragon, right? So why aren't we doing more? Shouldn't we be proactive?"

Jin's expression softened. "There's a lot of sitting around during war, Az. A lot of waiting."

"But we have to try something!" She balled her hands into fists. "I don't want to just . . . sit here waiting for Nazarov to show up again. We can't do that. I can't do that."

With a heavy sigh, Jin stared out at the water. His wall was tight, impossible for her to reach past. His shoulders tightened.

"The ruins might tell us something," she said.

"I can't believe I'm going to say this . . ." He shook his head, but when he turned to her, he was smiling. The smallest, tightest half smile. "*If* we're going to do this, how do you propose we go about it?"

Astrea looked down the beach at Jin's team again. Lennor blasted Adi with air, drying him off. Then she blasted her brother, who hadn't even gone in the ocean. Near them, Marko and Lucian were in conversation.

Adi and the twins would agree to the plan, Astrea was sure. And she doubted Marko would really be an obstacle in all this. "I think the only one we really have to convince is Lucian."

"Then let's head back and talk to the team," Jin said. "And together, we'll find a way to convince the commander."

CHAPTER 5

Approval and anxiety washed over Astrea in wave after wave, filling the kitchen to the brim. Adi, Lennor, and Civan were all on board with the plan to go to the mountains. As she'd suspected, it hadn't taken any convincing at all to get Jin's team to agree.

"So, back to the ruins," Adi said as he poured another cup of coffee for himself. He'd brewed a fresh pot after dinner, though Astrea didn't know how he could drink the stuff so late into the night and still sleep. "What do you hope to find there?"

"You'll need to find something to convince the commander to go." Marko's rough voice drew everyone's attention to where he leaned against the kitchen doorway, arms folded loosely over his stomach.

Adi beamed at him. "And what am I if not convincing, Marko?"

"Many things, Adi."

"Like?"

"Overly confident."

"You say that like it's a bad thing."

"I certainly didn't say it was a good thing."

"And yet you're smiling at me like that. I can't be that bad."

Only a hint of a smile pulled at Marko's mouth, but for him? That was a lot. His cheeks flushed. Astrea bit her lip to keep from laughing, and Lennor ducked her head.

"And what do you think about this plan, Marko?" Jin asked. "I assume you heard everything."

"Of course I did." Marko strode to the kitchen island and took one of the empty mugs Adi had set out. He poured a cup of coffee. "I was just coming in for this since I'm about to meet Lucian for the night's rounds, but we're here now. You want to go out looking for the Paragon yourselves?"

"Not them necessarily," Astrea said. "Information."

"Information." Marko tapped his short fingers against the counter. His stormy gaze flicked to Jin. "You think defying orders is a good idea?"

It was exactly what Jin had been concerned about. Concerned about it, yes, but he also gave into the idea very quickly. Astrea was still a little surprised about that if she was honest with herself. She wasn't going to question it too much, though. She didn't want him to have a chance to change his mind.

"I think Astrea's right in that we can't just keep sitting around waiting for them to make the first move," Jin said. "We need to move while we have the chance. And that means a little risk, but the bigger risk is just sitting around doing nothing."

"Well, it *is* getting boring around here," Marko drawled.

"Then if you don't think I'm convincing enough, help us when we talk to Lucian," Adi said. "We already know he's the real obstacle."

"He seems to be in a decent mood tonight, so now's the time if you want to pitch it," Marko said.

"Right now?" Astrea asked.

"Why not?" Marko shrugged. "He's waiting for me in the yard."

"Ask him to come inside, then," Jin said. "Let's just get this over with."

Marko scooped up his coffee, then left the kitchen without another word. As he did, Lennor nudged Adi's ribs. "What?" Adi asked as he peered down at her.

"Nothing." Lennor shot Astrea a knowing look.

"What?" Adi asked again. He glanced at Civan. "Do you know what Len's on about?"

"I never know that," Civan murmured.

Jin cleared his throat, but even his lips were curving up into a knowing grin. "Let's just focus, shall we?"

The twins and Adi busied themselves with their coffee and small talk . . . well, it was really Lennor and Adi talking. Astrea barely touched her coffee, though she did keep her hands curled around her mug. When Marko returned a few minutes later, a frowning Lucian followed him into the kitchen. Astrea steeled herself. She knew this was the right course of action. Jin and the others thought so, too. She could do this. She could convince the commander.

"So," Lucian said as he stood opposite the team, "Marko tells me there's something we need to discuss?" If it weren't for the dark fatigues he wore, Lucian looked almost like a teacher at the front of a classroom.

"Yes," Astrea said. "I want to go to the ruins in the Antare Mountains, the ones we were supposed to go to before everything got delayed."

Lucian didn't move another muscle. Lavender surprise pulsed around him in bright waves. "You want to break the grand duchess's orders to stay put?"

Not this again.

"And you do remember what happened when we went to the western site, don't you?" Lucian continued. "Victor Nazarov dreamwalked to you."

"I remember," Astrea said.

"You do realize he could do it again, don't you? They seem to have a connection to these sites."

A painful knot lodged itself in Astrea's sternum. "I know that, but we can't sit around here forever while Tomas, Mariya, and Cress try to find *something*, can we? Maybe we'll be able to figure out where the Paragon disappeared to or what their prophecy is. Wouldn't the grand duchess be grateful if we did that?"

"We are neither archaeologists nor historians," Lucian said.

"So?" Adi asked.

Marko pinned him with a look. "How is *that* being convincing?"

Adi puffed out his cheeks. "I mean, it's not ideal," he conceded, "but it's our only option . . . unless you want to wait around until someone from Talmaris decides to head out to the ruins, Commander. This could give us a lead on where the Paragon went."

"We could find them before they find us," Jin said. "The longer we sit around this base, the more likely they are to track us down."

"Please, Lucian," Astrea said when he remained silent. "We have to do something. I know it's breaking whatever chain of command you have, but we can't just wait. I need to—*we* need to figure out something."

He scanned her frame, surely watching her colors. She almost reached for that barrier of hers, but what was the point? She'd already slipped up.

"Is this because of how you're feeling?" Lucian asked. "Or do you truly think it's wise?"

"It's not about that," she muttered.

"Really? Because we've *all*"—he looked pointedly around the kitchen—"been through a lot lately. We're tired. Overworked out here, just the seven of us. Scared, too. I want to make sure logic is driving this suggestion, not emotion."

Astrea sucked in a sharp breath. Lucian didn't trust her to be honest about her intentions? How could she be any more honest with him, especially with her energy right there in front of his eyes? Of course she was tired. Of course the team was overworked. And of course she was scared. But she couldn't let fear stop her in her tracks. Not anymore.

"Az?" Jin asked, like they were all waiting for *her* answer.

"Logic says we go to the other location the Paragon's own spy suggested we visit," she said. "It's a risk, but so is staying put."

"We can't afford to wait much longer," Marko said. "We've given the Paragon too much time to regroup, Commander."

"I don't love the idea either, Lucian, but Az is right," Jin said. "It's time to try something else."

With a sigh, Lucian pursed his lips. "Alright."

"Really?" Astrea asked. She'd expected him to put up more of a fight.

"Getting a lead on them is important, as Marko said. We've been here long enough."

"Should I call Talmaris—" Marko started, but Lucian waved him off.

"Don't bother. It's just going to cause us issues. I'll tell the grand duchess when—if—she needs to know."

Jin rolled his eyes. "Because that's going to go well."

"Sometimes it's better to ask for forgiveness than permission," Lucian said. "She'll understand."

"When can we get started?" Astrea asked.

Lucian smiled. Genuinely smiled. Astrea wasn't sure she'd ever seen that look on the commander's face before. "As soon as you like. How about Adi puts on another pot of coffee and we get to planning?"

By the time they'd finished a plan, it was well past midnight. Astrea was eager to put everything into action, but they'd need a day—a real, full day—to prepare.

The sound of running water echoed in the bathroom behind Astrea. She opened the wardrobe tucked in the corner of their bedroom, then wiggled out of her dress. She ran her fingers over the spot where Victor Nazarov had stabbed her in her shoulder. It still hurt sometimes, though she'd checked it over with her magic a dozen times in the last few weeks. There was nothing there but a faint discoloration now, just a pale, narrow line. Her magic could find no problems with the muscle or joint.

Her back had scarred, too. A week after they'd arrived at the old base, she'd made Jin hold up a mirror so she could see for herself. Three thick, jagged lines adorned the pale plane between her shoulder blades. Some days, if she caught a glimpse of her back in the mirror, she wanted to crawl out of her own skin. Some days, she wanted to regardless of what she could or could not see.

After hanging her dress up, Astrea slid one of Jin's spare shirts from a hanger and slipped it over her head. She padded across the room to bed, sighing happily as she climbed in and pulled the blankets over herself. Pushing herself on the beach and running that hard had really taken it out of her, more than she realized. Now that the energy of planning their excursion was running out, Astrea wasn't sure how long she'd stay awake.

The bathroom door creaked open as Jin returned to their room. Moving to the far corner of the bedroom, he crouched down to turn on the small table lamp he'd put on the floor. It didn't give much light tucked away in the corner, but it helped Astrea remember where she was when she woke in the middle of the night.

Jin turned off the dim overhead light, plunging the room into the low, warm glow of that little lamp. Then he joined Astrea in bed and groaned as he lay down. "I never used to look forward to bedtime, but now it's all I think about."

"Why?" Astrea sank farther under the blankets until just her nose and eyes were above them.

"Because I'm always tired," he said as he rolled onto his side to face her. "And because I like seeing you—just you—before going to sleep. No team."

"Right." She turned to face him, too, and offered a small smile. "I can help if you're that tired."

"That's alright. I was just spoiled those weeks I was back in Kalama and even Talmaris. Before my father made me return home, my team and I were rarely at Fort Ironwing for more than a day or two before we had to go back out. Got used to not sleeping much."

"Maybe that's why you're so tired now," Astrea offered. "You need the rest."

"Maybe."

"Are the others this tired?"

"Probably, but I doubt they'd tell me."

If she were honest with herself, Astrea wasn't sure she'd notice the team's fatigue. Her own mind and body were clouded with it these days. All she ever seemed to feel was tired. Besides, it was pointless. Unless they suffered a broken bone or other serious injury, the team wouldn't let her heal anything. And in the last few weeks, only Lennor and Adi had needed the extra help from Astrea's lightbringing. Lennor had re-injured her knee, and she'd suffered a deep cut on her arm after a nasty hit from Adi's earthmoving. Adi had needed healing after an icicle Civan shot at him grazed his leg.

"Is it selfish," Jin whispered, "that part of me wishes we could just run away?"

"It's certainly not prudent," Astrea said as she burrowed into the pillows. "Where would we even go?"

"Well, there really is no place we could go. I'm just so tired. Eight years. This summer was supposed to be a break from it all."

Astrea found his hand under the blankets and clutched it tightly. "I'm sorry."

"Don't be. You're not responsible for an ancient void army or my father."

Astrea swallowed hard. She was not responsible for those things, no. But she hated knowing Jin felt that way and that she couldn't actually help. "Do you think we're doing the right thing?"

Jin's whole body relaxed as he closed his eyes. "Going to the mountains?"

"Yeah."

"It's the right choice."

How did anyone ever know what the right choice was? Astrea disagreed with Emperor Aelius's politics, but how did he make decisions with such ease? That was how it appeared, anyway. Or was he like her, struggling with those decisions behind closed doors instead of letting his children and councillors see?

"My night light isn't keeping you awake, is it?" Astrea whispered. "That's not why you're tired?"

"No." Wrapping his arms around her waist, Jin pulled Astrea into his body and kissed her cheek. The faintest chuckle left him as he asked, "Have I told you about the smaller airships we were using for our missions to Corsyca?"

"No."

"Tiny, smaller than you can probably imagine." His eyes popped open, so close Astrea could make out the flecks of amber in his irises despite the low light. "No upper deck. No additional rooms. We had to sleep on the floor of the main cabin. So skies damned loud with the engines."

"That sounds awful."

"Yes, well, when you've been trekking through the muddy and war-torn Corsycan foothills for several days to hunt down a Zaikudi general or Delian sergeant, any safe space is enough to let you get some sleep, bright lights and loud engines be damned."

A knot bloomed in Astrea's chest. Jin had been through so much. So had Adi, Lennor, and Civan. An uncomfortable airship had definitely been the least of their worries.

"The light stays on for as long as you need it, Az," Jin murmured. "Besides, I have what I need to sleep."

"And what's that?"

"You."

Astrea almost rolled her eyes, but instead, she snuggled closer to him, reveling in the feeling of him next to her. Jin's fatigue pressed into her bones, heavy and oppressive, noticeable if she really tried to find it past her own exhaustion. But his peace and approval wrapped around her, too. They were gentle. Warm. She drank it all in. Eventually, Jin's breathing slowed, those steady feelings drifting away as he slipped into slumber.

Please let him be right, she thought. *Please let this be the right decision.*

CHAPTER 6

When Astrea had pitched the idea of going to the mountains two days before, she had imagined they'd already be on their way. Now, she sat in the old base's parlor, staring at maps that Jin and Adi had pinned to the walls.

"It was *right* here," Jin said, circling a section of the mountains with the tip of his finger. "I swear. I remember because it was due west of this river." He pointed again, then drew a line from the river to the mountains. "I know this was it."

"And I remember it being farther east," Lucian argued. Jin took half a step back as Lucian jabbed an unsharpened pencil at the map. "Right here."

"You're both wrong, but Jin's closer," Adi said, then pointed to a third spot. "It was here."

Astrea pinched the bridge of her nose. For the last day and a half, they'd been gathering all kinds of things they might need: food for the airship, sleeping bags, clean laundry, a way to brew coffee on the go. Maps, of course, and Astrea's notes from their time at the Talmaran palace library.

"You're all wrong," Astrea said. Everyone in the room turned to look at her, and she held up her notebook. She'd almost forgotten she'd brought it with her.

"Then would you care to show us where it is, Astrea?" Lucian asked with a small huff.

Astrea shouldered her way past Adi and Jin, then grabbed Lucian's pencil from him. She studied the map carefully for a moment, tracing the shapes of the mountains and foothills marking the border between Novaria, Tornama, and Helosia. She looked back down at her notes, then the map. There. Just south and west of the small river Jin had pointed out. She jabbed the unsharpened end of the pencil there.

"It's right around here," she said. "It's closer to this pass. Remember? The Path of Ruin. The void army used mountain passes to antagonize the other countries. Right here, just south of the pass and west of the river. That's it."

Lucian frowned, but Adi slung his arm around Astrea's shoulder and gave her a little shake. "Good thing you're good with maps."

"I'm good at keeping notes," she replied. "It might not be *exactly* there, but it's in that area."

Grinning down at her, Adi plucked the pencil out of her grip. "So if that's our target zone, we'll need a flight path."

"A flight path well away from prying eyes." Lucian pointed at their location on the map, right near the northern sea, then traced a line through the mountains that made up most of northeastern Novaria. "It will be slower, but we should avoid all air traffic. Nobody comes out here."

"And the base to our south?" Jin asked. "Won't they see us take off? Surely they're keeping an eye on the skies."

"Not if we go before first light," Lucian said. "It will take us all day to fly there anyway. The earlier the start we get, the better."

"Will we be ready in time?" Lennor asked from the back of the parlor. Astrea slunk away from the maps and dropped back onto the worn sofa across from her and Civan. "I don't think we've got enough food if we're going to be gone for more than a few days. And what if someone from the palace calls while we're out?"

Astrea hadn't considered that. Though communication with Talmaris had been minimal, there was technically a working phone and radio on the base. If Zephyrine or Ysabel called and nobody answered, would they fear the worst? Send a platoon out?

With her free hand, Astrea reached up to play with her necklace, a habit she'd started back in Talmaris. But her fingers found nothing except the soft fabric of her dress. She swallowed hard and moved her hand away. She did that sometimes. Still reached for the metal and stone she expected to be there even though Nazarov had stolen that necklace from her weeks ago.

Crossing his arms over his chest, Lucian ducked his head for a moment. "Varojin," he said, "I know the base commander personally. Perhaps we should tell her just in case something goes wrong."

"I thought we were doing this completely off the record," Jin said.

"Off the official record. Fay will keep everything quiet."

Jin scrubbed at his face and sighed. "And how do you know this Fay?"

"We go back many years."

"That's not very specific."

"Is it relevant how I know her?" Lucian asked. "I'd trust Fay with my life. We've been trusting her for the last few weeks. She knows *someone* is up here, though she doesn't know it's me."

"It seems relevant. We had no idea you had a connection to the neighboring base. I just want to know a little more about her before I start trusting her with more information. That's not unreasonable."

"You've asked me to put my trust into this mission," the commander said. "Trust me about this, Varojin. Fay will be an ally."

Jin gestured vaguely, as if for Lucian to continue.

Tilting her head back, Astrea stared up at the wood-paneled ceiling. Both men's annoyance scraped over her skin. Just when she'd thought Jin and Lucian were getting on the same page. Just when she'd hoped things would go off without a hitch. But Jin had a point. So did the commander.

Lucian huffed. "Fay and I grew up together just south of Talmaris. We served in the same platoon before I transferred to the palace."

"Commander." Marko's voice held a warning, but a warning of what? "Just tell them. We're wasting time."

Lucian huffed again. "There's nothing to tell." When nobody said anything, he said, "Fay and I were once engaged."

Jin let out a low, sardonic chuckle as whispers of surprise danced over Astrea's exposed arms. "I'm sorry. You want us to trust your former fiancée? I assume there's a reason the wedding didn't happen."

"Some things simply don't work out, Varojin," Lucian snapped. When Jin crossed his arms, Lucian said, "We wanted different things and grew into different people. We parted ways amicably. There are no hard feelings."

Across from Astrea, Lennor's thin eyebrows quirked up. Lucian, engaged? Astrea couldn't imagine it. He seemed like the last person in the world to have a romantic bone in his body.

"But Fay will not run to the grand duchess unless it's absolutely necessary for our safety," Lucian concluded. "I swear it. She won't interfere."

"I served under her before transitioning to the palace team," Marko said. "If that counts for anything. I would trust Fay with my life."

Jin looked first at Adi, then Astrea, then the twins. Rubbing his face, he sighed. "She really won't tell anyone else?"

"Not unless she must, Varojin," the commander replied. "I swear it."

"Alright," he said. "Get a note to her. Is there anything else we need to do before tomorrow?"

"Airship's loaded," Civan said.

"Laundry's done," Lennor said. "And we're mostly packed."

"I think all that's left is to chart our flight path." Flashing a smile at Astrea, Adi added, "And maybe fit in one more training session, if you're up for it."

Astrea nodded. She still needed to pack, but she could do that later.

"Good," Lucian said. "Let's reconvene after dinner for a final check."

And with that, they were dismissed.

Vibrations traveled through Astrea's body as Adi kicked her light shield. She dug her heels into the ground, legs tensing as she pushed back against him.

Bending her knees, Astrea braced herself just before Adi kicked the shield again. And again, she pushed back against him. It took every ounce of her strength; Adi was pure muscle and *heavy*. Her limbs trembled with the effort.

They'd been training for nearly an hour and running this drill for twenty minutes, repeating it over and over again. Adi would go through several attacks, sometimes with his earthmoving and sometimes without magic. Astrea had to block or dodge them; she was supposed to use both options at least twice, and then they'd reset. Her mental barrier kept falling in the middle of the drill, but Lucian wasn't around to yell at her. Astrea pulled it back whenever she noticed the lapse anyway.

"Good, Az!" Jin shouted from the sidelines of the sparring circle. "Again!"

As Adi reset his position, Astrea dropped her shield and gave her arms and legs a little shake. She was going to be obnoxiously sore later.

"You good?" Adi asked.

"Yeah, I'm good."

It was the most progress she'd made since leaving Kalama. Her training back at Ysabel's palace had been sporadic, some days totally eaten up with researching or something else. Here, in the northern reaches of Novaria, Astrea had all the time in the world to practice. She wasn't *great*, but she felt better about using her body and her magic.

"Alright, start!" Jin called.

Adi didn't even throw half of what he could at Astrea; she knew that from watching him train with Jin and the others. But even what he did throw at her was a challenge. Punch first, earthmoving included. Astrea's shield flared to life. Adi's dirt and rock crumbled and fell to the ground. She smiled, her shield faltering as she watched the projectile fall. Adi moved in, sweeping one leg toward her. Astrea pivoted in a rush, barely blocking him with her leg the way he'd taught her.

"Don't leave your face so open." Adi tapped her cheek with his palm. "You're too focused on what I've just finished doing instead of what I'm doing next."

"How am I supposed to focus on both?" she asked, fists already falling to her sides.

That was her next mistake, and Astrea knew it. Adi hadn't meant to have a conversation about it; it was simple instruction. She managed to dance out of Adi's reach just in time. He laughed.

"Thought we went over *that* lesson weeks ago," he said, circling left. "Don't drop your fists."

"You're annoying when you're in trainer mode."

He laughed again. "That's the point!"

Astrea loosened her mental barrier. A whisper of focus reached out, little more than a breeze on her skin. That always happened when Adi was about to strike.

He kicked at her midsection. Astrea forced as much energy into her shield as she could. The light flared brighter. When Adi's boot connected with it, she shoved back against him with the full force of her weight. He stumbled back, then fell on his back with a loud "oof."

"Adi!" She dropped her shields immediately, a dull ache radiating through her shoulders and back as she sank to the ground next to him. Jin strolled toward them, peach amusement bright against the late afternoon sun. "I'm so sorry!"

"Sorry?" Adi laughed, marigold excitement pulsing around his head. "Fucking skies, Az, don't apologize! That was great!"

Astrea's eyebrows drew together as she helped Adi sit up. "It was?"

"That's exactly what we've wanted you to do." He clapped her on the shoulder. "You're way stronger than I thought. I mean, damn." Rolling his left shoulder, Adi winced. "Catch someone off guard like that in a fight and you might do way more damage than you did just now."

Damage. She didn't want to hurt Adi. A Helosian assassin? Yes. A Paragon sycophant? Absolutely. But not Adi. "Let me heal it."

"If you want, sure."

Astrea laid her hand on Adi's shoulder. White light danced around her hand as she pushed her magic deep under Adi's skin. They both sighed, him in relief and her in pain.

"That was great, Az." Grass crunched under Jin's boots as he stopped next to them. The yard had grown brittle in the month they'd been using it for these kinds of exercises. "How do you feel?"

"Tired," she admitted as she pulled her hand away from Adi. He thanked her, then let Jin pull him off the ground. "I don't know how you two do this for hours every day."

Jin extended his hand to Astrea next, and she took it. "Because at first, we had no choice, and then it became a habit," he said. "You don't have to do it that much to improve, though. Can I show you one thing before we call it a day?"

"Anything," Astrea said quickly.

Jin and Adi took up the drill position again, Astrea standing off to one side so she could see what they were both doing. Jin angled his body farther away from her, his stance awkward.

"See where my feet are?" he asked, motioning toward the ground.

"Yeah," Astrea called back.

"That's what you're doing," he said, "and it's not going to make movement easier."

That must've been some cue because Adi kicked at Jin's front knee. Jin's retreat was graceless, sloppy, especially for him. Even Astrea could see that. The two men reset, and this time, Jin kept his body more centered.

"And if you do it like this . . ." As Adi kicked at Jin again, he danced backward more smoothly. Jin dropped his fists and shrugged. "Easier. Come try."

Astrea stepped back into their sparring circle, taking Jin's position in front of Adi. She planted her feet in the right position, left leg forward and right leg back.

"Better, but . . ." Jin's hands rested on Astrea's hips, his grip firm as he tugged them back gently and adjusted her angle again.

She was sure her entire face turned the color of a tomato despite the touch being entirely innocent. He'd tugged on her hips in a similar way early that morning, but that hadn't been for sparring practice. And that morning had been much more fun.

"There," he said. "Go ahead."

Once Jin backed up, Adi raised an eyebrow. "Ready?"

"You don't have to—" Astrea started, yelping as she dodged backward.

"See?" Jin said from behind her. "That was better."

It had been easier, even distracted. More fluid. Looser.

"I'll try to remember for next time," Astrea said. "Unless you think we should keep going today?"

Part of her wanted to keep going. Pushing herself past the limits of exhaustion was one of the few ways she could actually sleep at night anymore. But the other part of her wanted to reserve some of her energy for the rest of their flight preparations, not to mention the hike they'd surely endure on the way to the ruins.

"What do you think, Captain?" Adi asked as Jin rejoined them.

Jin's eyes raked over Astrea's form. "How does your body feel?"

"Like gelatin," she admitted.

"Then we're done for the day. You've put in a lot of work this week."

"I'll see you two for dinner," Adi said. "I'm going for a run before I head inside."

Before either Jin or Astrea could respond, Adi started off toward the base's gate. They usually went out in pairs or quads if they were leaving the grounds, but Adi typically just ran laps around the base's perimeter anyway. And besides, both she and Lucian were supposed to be keeping their senses open. Other than the seven of them, the base was empty.

"Stretch before we go in," Jin said.

Astrea groaned. She hated stretching almost as much as she hated running. While running was exhausting, this was just boring. Besides, she'd rather go get cleaned up and prepare for their excursion. "I was hoping you'd forget."

He dropped into the grass. "You're only going to be more sore tomorrow if you skip it."

Astrea sat next to him, sighing as she followed his lead and moved through a series of stretches. By the time they were done, Adi had returned from his jog and moved on to stretching on his own. Astrea and Jin had just entered the house when Lucian walked into the foyer.

"There you are," Lucian said, unusually chipper. "I made the call. Fay knows."

"So, we're ready to go?" Jin asked.

"All ready," Lucian said. "We leave before sunrise."

Chapter 7

Mountains stretched as far as Astrea could see. Dark clouds loomed to the south, the direction of the ruins. As Lucian had promised, the indirect route they'd flown had taken many more hours than a straight flight would've. But they'd never been followed and hadn't received any radio calls from Novarian forces or ships.

"Should be visible any time," Jin said as he looked down at the map he held, then back out the window. "Don't take your eyes off those mountains."

The airship began its slow descent. The towering evergreens and snowy mountain caps drew closer. Thankfully, despite the snow on the highest peaks, the rest of the mountains seemed to be clear. Astrea strained to pick out anything among the thick forest below. Any sign of the ruins. They had to be down there somewhere.

"There," Civan said, pointing. "To the southeast."

"Where?" Lennor asked, pressing her face against the window.

"Those black things. They look like towers."

Scattered among the forest were half-crumbling black towers, or so they appeared from the high angle. Astrea stepped closer to the window, her breath fogging the glass as she tried to get a better look.

"We think that's it?" Lucian asked.

"It's our best bet," Jin said. "Right on target for where Az thought they'd be. Good catch, Civan." He crossed the cabin in a few long strides and yelled directions to Adi and Marko, who were in the cockpit.

Another ten minutes of circling above the ruins, and Adi and Marko finally found a spot where they could safely land the airship. It was another fifteen minutes before they actually landed and powered the whole thing down. Astrea reached for her knapsack.

"Ready?" Jin asked as his hand brushed the spot between Astrea's shoulders. He leaned down and grabbed his pack from where they'd put their luggage in the far corner of the cabin.

Astrea shouldered her bag, then tugged at her body armor, ensuring it was secure. Everything was as it should be. "I'm just glad you're not making me jump out of the airship this time."

Jin chuckled and nudged her toward the exit. "No jumping, just hiking." Then he called out to the rest of the team, "Come on! Let's get going before the rain arrives."

Once Marko unsealed the door, they climbed down the airship's rattling metal stairs one by one. A damp chill immediately settled in Astrea's bones. She shivered. A sweater was buried at the bottom of her knapsack, under the rest of the supplies Jin and Adi had given her to pack. *Damn it.*

Taking the lead, Jin and Lucian set off through the forest. They'd landed downhill from the ruins, and the thick trees and rocky ground did little to suggest how far away they actually were. But Jin and Lucian were actually agreeing on which way to go, so Astrea wasn't going to complain.

"How long do you think it'll take to get there?" Astrea asked Adi, keeping her voice low. The twins were behind them, and Marko was bringing up the rear.

"Oh, based on what I could tell from above, maybe an hour." Adi shrugged as he stepped over a large, knotted root sticking out of the ground. "There's a bit of a climb, too."

"You could tell that from the airship?" Most of it had looked the same to Astrea, disorienting from the air.

"You start to learn what to look for when you're dropping into war-zones from high above."

"Right."

They continued on in silence except for the occasional chatter between Adi, Jin, and Lucian. Astrea let her senses spread as far and wide as she could, through the trees and in every direction. Aside from the occasional squirrel or bird, the forest lacked signs of life.

The farther they got from the airship, the darker the clouds above them grew. Goose bumps prickled Astrea's skin even under her thick shirt and armor. *This is the right choice,* she reminded herself as brush crunched under her boots. It was their only choice aside from waiting around for Grand Duchess Ysabel. Being so far away from the old base was just . . . different. And different wasn't bad. It just wasn't comfortable, either.

Rain began to fall slowly at first, then in heavy drops as the storm picked up. No lightning flashed, unlike so many storms back in Kalama. Astrea shivered. Civan created a watery shield over their heads. Wet mud squelched under Astrea's boots, and she slipped once as the terrain grew steeper.

"You know," Adi said half over his shoulder, "this reminds me of that time we deployed into Corsyca to find that Zaikudi spy. What was her name?"

"Skies if I know," Lennor said. "The one we took out after the Delian sergeant or the one after the Zaikudi captain?"

"After the captain."

"Civ?" Lennor asked. "Do you remember?"

"Why?" Civan didn't sound thrilled, but Astrea kept her gaze on the uneven ground instead of glancing back at him.

"Because you remember everything."

Civan huffed. "The one who infiltrated Ironwing? Her name was Seta."

"Yeah, that was her!" Adi said. "Skies, it rained just as bad that day. Awful mission. Nothing is worse than trying to hunt down your target in the snow, though."

"Oh?" Astrea asked.

"I don't know." Lennor hummed. "That sweltering summer heat . . ."

Adi shook his head. "Still not worse than snow."

"You really think the snow is worse?" Lennor asked. "Jin can melt it! We have no protection against the heat. All that sweat and blood mixing . . . nasty."

"Not to mention how bad you all smelled from no showers." Civan said it so quietly Astrea wasn't sure the others heard, but Adi laughed. Astrea laughed, too.

Ahead, Lucian and Jin slowed until they stopped completely. The forest around them thinned out, revealing a tall, jagged cliff face that rose up toward the sky. Moss, ferns, and other fauna trailed up the rock, poking out of divots and crevices.

"Is this what you meant by a bit of a climb?" Astrea asked Adi as she craned her neck. The rock extended a solid hundred feet in the air before sloping upward again. There wasn't even any way to climb it, no stairs or hand holes or anything. Rain beaded on its surface.

"It's not that far," Adi said. "Not with my earthmoving."

Astrea rubbed her forehead as she stared up at the cliffside. At Adi's direction, the group formed a tight circle at the base of the rock wall.

Civan's shield hovered over their heads, the strangest umbrella Astrea had ever seen in her twenty-four years of life.

"Hold on," Adi said. "Literally."

Bracing herself, Astrea held onto Jin's arm. The twins held onto each other, and Marko and Lucian steadied themselves. The earth rumbled underneath their feet before they shot skyward. Astrea's grip on Jin tightened. It was like an elevator, only without walls or pulleys or any kind of safety mechanisms. Rain pummeled their watery umbrella as they shot through the air and up the side of the cliff.

As soon as they reached the top, Adi said, "Off, quickly." His voice shook, and as Astrea peeked over her shoulder at him, she noticed his arms trembling. Just how much energy did that take?

Jin helped Astrea off first. There were no trees up here. No ferns or pine needles or dirt. Just slick rock for the next thirty feet, then another cliff face to ascend. *Shit.*

Civan and Lennor joined them next, then Marko. Lucian and Adi stepped off the earthen elevator at the same moment. The earth plummeted out of sight, landing with a softer thud than Astrea expected given the distance.

"Not so bad," Adi said as he started for the next cliff they'd have to ascend. It only rose two stories in the air, maybe less. "Just watch your—"

Pain exploded in Astrea's right knee, then her face. She stumbled, her boots sliding on the wet rock. Her death grip on Jin's arm was the only thing keeping her from faceplanting.

"Commander!" Marko called just as Jin cried, "Az!" Worry scraped her skin, rough like sandpaper.

Lucian wheezed as he said, "I'm fine."

"He's not fine," Astrea gritted out as Jin righted her again.

Behind them, Lucian was sprawled out on the ground, face down. His back heaved. Pain slammed into Astrea again and again and again.

Shit. Her head swam. She didn't let go of her death grip on Jin as they made their way to the commander. Marko helped him turn over on his back, and Civan's shield expanded over them as the rain began to fall even harder.

"Should've waited for the clouds to pass," Lucian muttered, squeezing his eyes shut.

"Too late for that, isn't it?" Astrea snapped as she squatted down near him. Up close, the bright red mark on his forehead became obvious. "I need to touch you, Lucian."

"Give me a moment."

"What could you possibly need a moment for?" Astrea asked. He was hurt. And judging by the pain pulsing brightly in her leg, he'd broken his kneecap. Why would he want to wait? "We need to keep moving."

"Commander?" Jin said when Lucian still didn't respond.

Lucian sucked in a deep breath. "I do not like being healed by others."

"Well, suck it up," Jin said. "Let Astrea do it, or fix it yourself now. We can't carry you."

"It's better if I do it, Commander." At least, Astrea thought it would be. Whenever she'd healed herself in the past, fatigue would linger as her body recovered from the mirror pain she reflected at herself. "Just get it over with, alright? We'll both recover more quickly."

"Fine," he said from between clenched teeth. Lucian hadn't opened his eyes, and his face had turned a bright shade of red. Magenta embarrassment tinged his aura, the first time Astrea had ever seen that color around the commander.

Sucking in a deep breath, Astrea placed one hand near Lucian's knee and the other on the side of his head. It took everything in her to summon her healing light. It tickled her palms, warm and gentle, as it pushed forward and into Lucian's body. Astrea tried not to curl in on herself as the pain in her knee and head doubled. It receded to a dull ache as Lucian let out a relieved sigh.

"We should get going," Astrea said. Sitting on a ledge near old Paragon ruins didn't seem wise. "Come on."

"Give me a moment, Astrea," Lucian said as he pushed himself into a sitting position. "Give yourself a moment, too."

"I'm fine." Astrea shoved to her feet. Jin steadied her as she swayed.

"Just ten minutes," Lucian said. "To compose ourselves. Please."

Astrea had never heard Lucian say please. Not once. Not in Talmaris. Not at the base. Not even at the dinner table, where manners would be very much appreciated. She stared down at him, mouth half-open. "What?"

"I know I've been harsh in training, Astrea," Lucian said, "but I think I finally understand the true need for a break."

Now Lucian understood the need for a break? He couldn't understand when she was having hard days, days when memories of the Paragon's tunnels overwhelmed her? Or when she kept getting knocked on her ass over and over again? But he could understand now that he'd broken his knee because he *slipped*?

Irritation flooded through Astrea, rough and cold. Yes, he'd apologized a few days before while on the beach, but now his excuse sounded ludicrous. Her jaw clenched.

"Come on, Az," Jin said as he tugged her away from the commander. "Ten minutes. We'll have some water, then be on our way."

They rejoined Adi, who earthmoved a chunk of rock out from the next cliff face to create an overhang to shield them from the rain. Astrea slumped down and rested her back against the wall as the rest of the mirror pain dulled into a low ache.

"You're not going to shove him off the cliff, are you?" Adi asked, voice low.

"No," Astrea muttered. "Just thinking about it."

"Think about it all you want," Jin said. "Let's just get up to those ruins in one piece, yeah?"

"Fine," Astrea said, and Jin actually smiled. "Are we close?"

"Almost there, I promise." With a quiet groan, he sat down next to her. "Twenty minutes, including our break."

Twenty minutes. Twenty minutes and they could figure out what Professor Kostas Shalysko and the Paragon were hiding out here.

As Jin promised, they didn't have to hike much farther once they ascended the second cliff face. The soaring trees returned, as did Lucian's brooding silence. The gentle slope upward eventually flattened out, and the trees began to thin. The rain began to clear out, too, though more dark clouds loomed to the south.

The ruins in the Macadian Mountains had been graying stone, discolored by the weather and elements over time. The ruins towering above Astrea now were dark, oppressive, and soaked from the earlier storm. Sun shone through a break in the clouds, reflecting off the water and lighting the ruins up like a beacon.

"Wow," Lennor breathed, lavender surprise spiking around her.

"What is this place?" Civan asked.

Unlike the ruins out to the west, these were more intact. Towers marked three corners of what could've once been a square structure. Three of the four walls were still standing and didn't even look like they'd been impacted by the elements, save the recent rain storm. Had Astrea not known these were old Paragon ruins, she might've assumed they were buildings still under construction. Strange buildings, anyway.

"I don't suppose your notes said anything about this, Astrea?" Lucian asked.

"No." The books hadn't been specific about the ruins, nor had Professor Shalysko. The only thing Astrea had known was that they were supposed to be here.

"Don't wander too far," Jin instructed as they started for the main structure. "Stay in groups. Do *not* go off on your own."

Lucian and Marko headed south while the rest of them focused on the main structure. Wide, shallow stairs led into the building. Without its roof, Astrea wasn't sure exactly how tall it once was, but the remaining towers were four stories tall. The building couldn't have been much taller than that, but that wouldn't make it very large.

"It's smaller than the site out west," Astrea said as she stepped into the middle of the empty space. Several large chunks of crumbling wall sat on the floor, which was mostly covered in fallen pine needles. "What do you think it was?"

"Some kind of fort." Adi gestured to the closest tower. "Look at the shape of the windows. One of those books we read talked about that."

Astrea shielded her eyes as more sun appeared through a split in the thick storm clouds. One book back in Talmaris had talked about geography and architecture in fort specifications during the Great Wars; Astrea hadn't paid much attention to it, as it hadn't seemed relevant at the time. But she remembered *something* about the topic, and she trusted Adi's memory. The windows were smaller than she expected; they were just long, narrow openings with no glass.

"And we thought this might be one of the locations where the void army attacked the armies crossing between east and west, right?" Jin asked.

"Right," Astrea said. Land to the east now belonged to Novaria, but before the Great Wars, it hadn't. "Let's see if we can find anything about Tytas Ramkas or that void language."

It was a lofty goal, one Astrea wasn't even sure was helpful anymore, but it was really all they could go on. Any evidence that lined up with the other ruins could be useful.

"Alright," Jin said. "Adi, take Len and Civan and go to the southern tower. You remember what the void language looks like?" When Adi confirmed he did, Jin asked him to tell Marko and Lucian to check the east tower. "Az and I will take the last one."

As the group split up, Astrea and Jin headed to the tower at the northern edge of the ruins. They circled around its base and found what had once been a doorway. Rusted, half-broken hinges revealed where a door would have stood. Now, the archway was empty. Inside, stairs spiraled up. With the narrow windows and the clouds returning, the inside of the tower was also dark.

"Well," Jin said as he motioned to the empty first level, "shall we?"

Astrea took a tentative step toward the wall, then another. Its black surface gleamed in the warmth of Jin's fire, metallic almost. He followed her, his boots barely making a sound on the stone floor. Unlike the walls at the western ruins, these ones held no strange symbols or languages. They were smooth and slightly worn, nothing more. And the farther inside they moved, the less Astrea could feel.

It wasn't quite like those tunnels the Paragon held her in. No, through those peculiar windows and the wide-open doorway, Astrea's magic squeezed out. But the rest of the structure blocked her from the outside world. If Lucian hadn't told her about the tunnels doing that, she might've never known. But here, now, it was obvious, like her magic wanted to find a place to go but couldn't.

"Jin, this place feels like—it *looks* like—" Astrea's fingers twitched at her sides as she explained what it felt like to her lightbringing.

"But you can still feel something?" Jin asked, swallowing hard.

"Some."

"Adi and the others?"

"Yes, mostly. The walls seem to be blocking a lot."

Frowning, Jin crossed to the nearest window and shouted, "Adi? Lucian?" The words echoed through the half-enclosed building between the towers.

"Jin?" Adi called just as Lucian yelled, "I feel it, too!"

"That answers that." Pressing his lips together, Jin turned back to Astrea. "Do you want to keep going up?"

Did she *want* to? No, Astrea didn't want to stay in this place any longer than she had to. Her earlier determination bled away as dread built in her bones. She nodded anyway.

You aren't there, she reminded herself as they began climbing the stairs. As she walked, Astrea examined the walls, searching for any trace of language. Still, they were empty. The second floor was as barren as the first save a few half-fallen ceiling beams. They resumed their climb. *You aren't there.*

Outside, rain began to fall. It slapped against the tower's exterior, and what rain managed to sneak in through the windows soaked sections of the tower floor. Astrea nearly slipped once as they circled the third level. Empty, just like the others. She started for the stairs to ascend to the final floor, only to find several beams blocking the stairway.

"Hold on." As Jin extinguished his flame, Astrea pulled on her light. It lit up the space around them, harsher against those strange walls than Jin's fire had been. He moved two of the beams, then helped her step over the third. "You alright?" Though Jin resummoned his flame, Astrea couldn't make herself dismiss her light. "You're white as a ghost."

"Fine," Astrea lied. "Tired. Cold."

"The weather's just our luck, isn't it?" he asked wryly.

If he knew she was lying, he didn't press, and for that, Astrea was grateful.

"Oh, shit," Jin muttered as he came to a stop at the top of the stairs.

"What?" Astrea asked, peering around him. The stairs were so narrow here that he nearly blocked the whole doorway. "Shit."

The small room at the top of the tower was not empty. Far from it. Dust, pine needles, and cobwebs marred the floor, but the walls . . . Those gleaming metallic walls were covered in writing, not just in Helosian, Novarian, and Tornamian, but that peculiar void language, too. Three words, repeated over and over again. *Chaos. Destruction. Balance.*

Astrea squeezed past Jin and brought her light to the nearest wall. The words were haphazardly carved, as if whoever had written them hadn't had the proper tools or time. Shrugging her pack off, Astrea opened the top and pulled out her notebook. After digging a pencil out, she squatted down to where she could look at the words more closely.

"What are you doing?" Jin asked.

"I want to copy this down." Astrea didn't know how to decipher an alphabet she'd never seen, especially one with no cipher, but someone in Talmaris would know how. Someone at the university . . . if they could find a professor to trust. "Bring your fire closer."

It took a few tries, thanks to her trembling hands, but Astrea got the void language copied down with what she assumed were the corresponding words. *Chaos. Destruction. Balance.* Those had to be what the void words meant.

Astrea closed her notebook, then reached for her knapsack. Once the book was safely tucked away again and hidden underneath her sleeping bag, she buckled the straps. She'd just moved to shoulder the pack when Jin reached for her hand.

"Az."

When she glanced up at him, she found the faintest sheens of yellow worry and blue regret circling around him.

"You're really alright?"

She half smiled. "No. But this isn't the time or place to get upset."

Jin studied her face. Astrea was sure he was going to press her about it, but he squeezed her hand, then said, "Let's go find the others."

As they returned to ground level and the original structure, Jin tucked Astrea against his side. It didn't shield her from the rain, but she was grateful for his heat and his touch. As the sky and clouds came into view, and as her magic could spread wide again, her limbs stopped shaking so much.

Lucian and Marko were already waiting, and Adi and the twins weren't far behind. Mint relief coated Astrea's tongue as they all reunited in the middle, and the relief doubled when Civan's makeshift umbrella covered their heads again.

"Anything?" Lucian asked. "Besides the obviously familiar nature of the stone."

"We found words," Adi said. "Chaos, destruction, and balance, in a few languages as well as that void one from the other site."

"That's what we found, too," Jin said. "None in yours?" he asked the two Novarians.

"Nothing," Marko confirmed. "Just many cobwebs."

It wasn't a cipher, but Astrea relaxed a fraction. They had three new words connected to the void language. They knew the ruins were made of the same stone—or similar stone—to the tunnels under the void house in Talmaris. It was plenty more than they'd had just a day earlier. Something to offer Tomas, Mariya, and Cressida.

"We should bring some of this material back with us," Jin said. "Get the sample to Talmaris if Ysabel will let us return."

Lucian ran a hand over his wet hair and stared back at the tower he'd just been exploring.

"We need to go back regardless of what the grand duchess will allow." Astrea swallowed hard. "We need to go back to that house. And we need to find someone who can translate an unknown language."

Jin's arm, still circled around Astrea's shoulders, flexed as he said, "She's right, Commander. We need to go back to Talmaris as soon as we can."

Silence settled over the group, the only sound the pitter patter of rain as it fell around them. Astrea was sure Lucian was going to protest, but he simply murmured his agreement.

"Do we have enough fuel to get back to the capital from here?" Lennor asked, half reluctant. "We're a lot farther from the capital than the base."

"We'll go back to the base first," Lucian said. "We'll get what we need, then we'll go to Talmaris. I'll radio the palace once we're en route."

Jin glanced up at the sky. "Then let's go. We might be able to make it back to the airship before nightfall."

Chapter 8

The hike back from the ruins to the airship the night before had left a permanent chill in Astrea's bones. Even now, in the relative comfort of the old base's house, she couldn't get warm. Astrea tugged on the one sweater she had before grabbing more clothes out of the wardrobe.

They were supposed to leave the base within the hour. It was just midmorning, but if they left soon, they could get back to the capital before midnight. Exhaustion pulled at the corners of Astrea's mind; she hadn't been able to sleep much on the way from the ruins back to the base, and after a quick shower to clean the mud off herself, she hadn't been able to sleep for more than a couple hours. There was too much to do. She'd sleep on the flight back to Talmaris.

Astrea finished packing her clothes first, then grabbed Jin's. He and Adi were down in the yard, trying to get the airship fueled up and ready to go, while everyone else finished packing up the old house. When that was done, she triple-checked that her notes were in her satchel. They were. She checked again, just to be sure.

Marko knocked on the half-open door, then nudged it the rest of the way open. "You almost ready?" he asked.

"Coming." Astrea slung her satchel across her body, then grabbed the suitcases. Jin already had their knapsacks on the ship. Marko took the luggage from Astrea, then they both headed downstairs. "Is everything ready to go?" she asked.

"Just about. Ship's all loaded except for this and the twins' belongings."

When they got out to the yard, Astrea didn't see Jin or Adi near the airship, though Lucian was visible through its windows, and the footsteps behind Astrea betrayed the twins before she felt their relief and fatigue. She followed Marko into the airship, then deposited her satchel with the other luggage.

"Where are Adi and Jin?" Lennor asked as she joined Astrea.

"Still outside," Lucian replied as he left the cockpit. "Apparently there's an issue."

"An issue?" Astrea and Lennor asked at the same time.

"I was just going out to see if I can assist," Lucian said. "Though I must admit, I'm not familiar with engines."

If Lucian wasn't familiar, what could he possibly do to help? Not that Astrea knew engines either. Nor was that going to stop her from at least going to ask what was wrong. She led the way back out into the morning sun, squinting as it appeared from behind the clouds.

"I just don't understand what happened," Jin said as he came around from the back of the airship. Adi was just a couple of steps behind him. "It worked fine last night."

"Sometimes things just break," Adi said. "I need more than twenty minutes to figure out what's wrong with it." He glanced at Astrea, Lucian, and the twins. "I don't suppose any of you know anything about mechanics?"

"Engine's running too hot," Jin said as Lucian began to ask a question. "Can't figure out why. We need some time."

"Not my specialty," Lucian said. "Though Marko had some training on it back in the day. Perhaps he can assist."

As Lucian stalked off, calling Marko's name, Astrea looked to Adi and Jin. "It's too bad Cress isn't here," she said. "She's great with this stuff."

"I know my way around motorcycle engines, some trucks," Adi said. "Not airships. This thing's way bigger than what I usually work with."

Astrea didn't know if Cressida had experience with airships specifically, but Lodestar Industries, her family's company, dealt with all manner of tech. And Cressida was a natural with such problems. It had always seemed to Astrea that Cressida could decode and understand technology in just a matter of minutes.

"We'll figure it out," Jin said. "Between the three of us, we should—"

Jin stumbled forward, crying out in pain. Agony flooded Astrea's body, piercing her right between her shoulder blades and spreading to every muscle and bone. That pain doubled as Astrea also collapsed to her knees.

"What's happening?" That sounded like Lennor.

Panic pressed into Astrea from every corner of the base as darkness clouded her vision. She couldn't speak. She couldn't breathe.

Not now, she thought. *Not now.*

Oh, it is now, *little Lightbringer.* Victor Nazarov's voice echoed through Astrea's mind, cold despite the sunshine she could still feel on her face. *And the gang's all here. What a treat this is.*

In Astrea's mind, she heard Jin ask, *What the fuck do you want, Nazarov?*

Shadows cleared from Astrea's vision, revealing images similar to what The One had shown her while she was with the Paragon. Kalama on fire, destroyed. The palace gone, replaced by something dark, like the ruins they'd just visited. But then it changed, three groups of soldiers fighting each other. Red Helosian uniforms, the blue uniforms of Delian soldiers, and the dark green the Zaikudi wore. Corsyca?

You know your father is using void magic too, don't you, Sunreaper? Nazarov asked. *Join me and we can put an end to him.*

You're not better than him, Jin snapped.

No? What makes you so sure about that?

Murdering people? What about all those dead mages in Sezia? You would kill your own?

That was not the Paragon, Sunreaper, Nazarov snarled. *I'm surprised you haven't figured that out yet. Maybe you're more useless than your little plaything.*

Then maybe it was you yourself, Jin said. *You did just kill your leader.*

Not me, princeling. Try again.

My father?

Silence buzzed in Astrea's ear before Nazarov snapped, *Lightbringer.*

When Astrea didn't respond, the image changed from the war to the observatory back home. Saros, in his office, hunched over some papers and an old coffee cup. Sarsali and Balthazar, there with him. The whole place burning to the ground.

What? she croaked.

The sun and moon will *help us restore balance,* Nazarov said. *We can do this the easy way or the hard way. Your choice, Astrea.*

Why do you think we'll help you destroy the continent? Jin asked.

Nazarov chuckled, and the image changed from Saros to the eldest Auris sibling. Apelo and two little girls—his daughters, Astrea assumed—were in the Helosian throne room. That familiar void fire, the hot and cold that The One had sent into her dreams so many times, licked Astrea's skin. She cried out, though she wasn't sure if that was just in her mind or if she'd actually made a noise.

I'll see you two very soon, Nazarov whispered.

The world rushed back to Astrea in a disorienting cacophony of sound, light, and emotion. Though she was already on her knees, Astrea lost her balance. She squeezed her eyes shut as she dropped her forehead to the ground. Not again. She'd had a month without one hint of dreamwalking. A month without so much as a whisper from the Paragon. And now here, at the base . . .

A sob built in her chest, but Astrea swallowed it. It came out as little more than an angry hiccup. Her magic spread wide, a net to find and catch the void. But there was nothing other than the pain and confusion of her team. Jin's rage. Adi's rage, a perfect mirror of Jin's.

And Lucian. Oh, Lucian was angriest of them all. Heat seared her skin as he stalked toward them.

"That was him?" Lucian asked.

Jin's hand pressed between Astrea's shoulders, warm and heavy, as she forced herself to sit up. Colors swirled through the yard, gray confusion and steel pain and crimson rage. Around her, Jin's entire team was on the ground, too, their breath coming in quick, shallow bursts.

"You saw it?" Astrea asked. Nazarov had only spoken to her and Jin directly.

"Oh, I saw it," Lucian said. Everyone else confirmed they'd seen the visions, too.

Would Lucian finally understand? Astrea was sure he could see the colors that must've been flaring in her own aura. White terror, steel pain, midnight blue grief. And anger. She was so angry.

Never mind how Nazarov finally found her. How had he dreamwalked to not just her but six other people at once? And why could he not just leave her alone?

"I can't feel him nearby," Astrea said, though she almost didn't trust herself.

"Nor do I." Lucian folded his arms across his chest. "But I trust he's not as far off as I'd like, either."

"We need to fix this ship," Jin said. "And we need to fix it now. We're not equipped to fight him if he comes with as many as he did last time."

"We still don't know what's wrong with it," Adi said. "Marko and I will need time."

"Commander." Marko's rough voice made Astrea jump.

"I know," Lucian muttered.

"What do you know?" Jin asked.

Lucian started for the house in the distance. "I need to make a call."

"A call?" Jin yelled after him. "What could you possibly need to call someone about right now?"

"Get to work on that engine!" Lucian called over his shoulder. "I'm going to call my ex-fiancée."

Astrea huffed. What were they going to do? Lead Nazarov back to Talmaris? Back to the palace and innocent lives? Grand Duchess Ysabel had sent her heirs off to other locations for the time being, but that didn't change the many civilians who would be put in harm's way.

But the fact still remained: they needed to get to that house. They needed to compare the sample from the ruins to those tunnels, and they needed to bring the new void words to Tomas.

The base had been safe for weeks, but now Nazarov was on the hunt again. Sitting around and waiting for him to show up wasn't an option. They needed to get moving and find their answers.

"Shine your light a little higher," Adi said as he leaned into a section of the engine he'd opened up. Astrea lifted her hand. "Good, hold it there."

Once Lucian had gone to call his former fiancée, Adi and Marko had gotten to work on the airship again. Astrea and the others had joined them, agreeing that now was not the time to split up. And Astrea's light could actually be useful as the two men worked.

Astrea had never seen an airship engine before. In fact, she'd only seen car engines because of Cressida and Balthazar. And this particular engine, Astrea imagined, was far smaller than the ones used for larger airships. It was all gray metal, tubes and wires, and dozens of pieces she didn't understand. But she didn't need to know what all of it did. She just needed to give light.

She peeked over her shoulder at where Jin, Lennor, and Civan all stood. The airship's engine compartment was cramped, dark, and smelled of oil and smoke. Pistons and wheels connected other pieces to the engine, and gauges and dials, large and small, decorated the walls. The door leading outside and a small window were the only places light came in. A ladder even led up one of the walls, to somewhere in the main cabin above them, Astrea assumed.

"It's the cooling system for sure," Marko said as he finally straightened. "There's nothing we can do until Fay gets here, unless we have a stock of airship coolant laying around."

"Don't know about any being around here." Adi wiped his hands on a cloth that was now more gray than white. "When was the last time this thing was serviced? Shouldn't even be an issue. Haven't flown that many miles."

"We should check for the coolant." Anxiety buzzed around Jin, bright orange against the dark walls. "Maybe the Novarians left some behind."

"We can go check," Lennor offered. "Maybe there's some in the old garage."

"You can check if you want," Marko said. "The grand duchess would've had this place cleaned out, though."

"Take no more than ten minutes," Jin said. "If you can't find it, we'll assume there's none. And where's Lucian?"

"Here," Lucian called, ducking slightly as he squeezed through the narrow doorway. "Fay said she can be here in less than an hour. I told her to bring whatever she could since we were still running diagnostics."

"Hope you told her we need coolant," Adi muttered.

"I did, among other things."

"Len, Civ, go check the garage just in case," Jin said. "Ten minutes, then come back."

"You got it, Captain," Lennor said. Lucian mumbled something about joining the twins, then followed them back out into the fresh air.

Adi fisted his hair, then shook his head as he paced down the narrow catwalk in the compartment. Anxiety grated across Astrea's skin, rough like sandpaper.

"How long will it take to get in the air once we get the coolant?" Jin asked Marko.

"Not that long," he said. "But we'll probably need another hour to make sure everything's working properly."

Jin huffed. "Two hours before we're in the sky?"

Astrea lifted her hand and put more energy into her light as she glanced at the engine again. "Why do we need the coolant?"

"We can't let the engine overheat," Marko said dryly.

"Well, *obviously*, but is there not another way to keep it cool? Water or something?"

"We're fucked if we only add water. The coolant has components to keep it from freezing over."

"Civan could keep the water from freezing, couldn't he?" Astrea asked. She swore she'd heard Balthazar talking about having one of his Tidebacker employees do something similar before. And Civan was definitely a talented mage.

"It gets very cold down here once we're in the air," Marko said. "He cannot control that."

Astrea stared at the engine, then the light pulsing faintly in her hand. Jin was right to be worried; two hours was a long time for them to sit around. At least if they could get into the sky, they could avoid Nazarov. That had to be their priority. "Jin could make it warm in here," she said. "Lucian and I could, too, if we have to."

"Hypothetically, that could work." Marko scrubbed at his face, fatigue rolling off him in slow waves. None of them had slept enough. "If we *have* to do it that way. I'd prefer not to."

"But Nazarov—"

"Did not give us a time frame. I'd prefer to do this the right way so we don't end up dying in an airship crash somewhere over the Novarian countryside."

Astrea blew out a sharp breath. Maybe Marko had a point.

"Az is right," Jin said. "So are you, Marko. We'll wait a half hour, and if this Fay hasn't shown up, we'll try it. We could at least fly to the other base that way, right?"

"If we have to," Marko muttered. "I suppose *that* won't kill us."

"We won't even need that much altitude," Adi said as he rejoined them. "We could make that much work. Flying there wouldn't take long at all."

A backup plan. This was good. The situation was far from ideal, but at least they could get to the other base if they had to.

"I'm going to sit outside if you don't need me," Astrea said. "It smells awful in here."

With a chuckle, Adi waved her off. Jin followed her without a word, sticking close as she wandered a few feet away from the ship and dropped into the grass. He sat down next to her, groaning as he did.

Reaching for Jin's hand, Astrea twined her fingers with his. He ran his thumb over the back of her hand in small, comforting circles. He didn't need to say it, nor did she. Nazarov had found them. Again. Had threatened their families, or at least, that was the implication of that vision.

Part of Astrea wondered if they should just wait for him to show up, but no. Last time, he'd shown up with a small army. Seven of them could not fight off a small army, not when Nazarov could jump Astrea and Jin away. They needed to focus on the new mission: getting this information back to Talmaris and figuring out how the tunnels and ruins were connected.

Astrea just hoped their airship could get them there in one piece.

As expected, the garage had been empty of any supplies they might use. And when the half hour mark passed, Lucian had insisted they wait ten more minutes. Ten more minutes, and then they could try the backup plan.

So when a new wall pressed in against Astrea's senses, she jumped up from her spot in the grass. Lucian, too, jumped to his feet.

"That's Fay," he said. "We need to open the gates."

Whoever it was, it certainly wasn't Victor Nazarov. No hint of that cold, wrong hollowness approached the base.

"We need to confirm it's her," Jin said.

Despite Lucian's exaggerated sigh, the group headed for the iron gate. Just outside, a dark green military truck sat idle. A woman waved from behind the steering wheel.

"That's her alright," Marko said.

Astrea's shoulders loosened. She stepped back from the gravel road and let the others pull the gates open. Fay drove inside, then stopped the truck next to the airship while the others closed and locked the gates again.

Watching Fay step out of the truck was almost surreal. Astrea hadn't known what to expect of Lucian's former fiancée, but it wasn't the petite, beautiful woman dusting off her midnight blue fatigues. Her dark hair was smoothed back into a bun that poofed out with her natural curls, and her deep umber complexion was flawless.

"Well, well, well," she called as she walked toward the group. "The great Lucian Astor needs my help not once but twice in a single week. And to think I hadn't heard from you in years."

"Hello, Fay," Lucian said.

"Luci, that's no way to greet your former betrothed." Fay smiled up at him, her dark brown eyes flashing with something warm.

"Luci?" Adi whispered as Lucian stepped forward and kissed Fay on the cheek.

Unexpected. Entirely unexpected. Astrea had never seen Lucian be . . . tender. Gentle. Peach amusement colored the air around the two. Whatever had driven them to separate, at least they seemed to be on good terms now.

"Let's just see what you've brought, shall we?" Lucian asked. "Marko says we need coolant."

"And lots of it," Marko said.

"Can't say I brought *lots*," Fay replied, "but we should have enough to get you back to Talmaris. No unnecessary flight paths, though, Luci."

"Are you trying to embarrass me in front of my colleagues?" Lucian asked.

"Of course."

Astrea didn't know what to say as Marko, Adi, and Fay unloaded the necessary supplies from the back of the truck. Marko was asking her about a few people they both seemed to know, presumably soldiers he'd served with. Light green pulsed around Adi, his attention focused on the engine compartment as he headed that way. Astrea hurried after him, already pulling on her light.

"What do you need me to do?" she asked once they were back at the engine. Marko and Fay's voices drifted through the open door.

"Just point that light where I tell you." Adi set down an unmarked black bottle. "Let's see if we can get this done sooner than Marko estimated."

Doing as he asked, Astrea focused her light on a specific container attached to the engine. Adi yanked its cap off just as Marko and Fay strolled inside.

"And you must be the Lightbringer Lucian said he's training," Fay said as she passed Astrea. "I'm Commander Fay Kalandi."

"It's nice to meet you," Astrea said. Both Novarians set additional black bottles on the ground right within Adi's reach.

"Hope he's not going too hard on you," Fay said as she unscrewed the top of one bottle. "He always had a way of being his worst self when he was in charge of someone's training."

Lucian really hadn't been his best self since that night Astrea had been rescued from the Paragon, but she wasn't going to tell his ex-fiancée that. There was no point, especially not when they needed to get airborne as soon as possible.

"Astrea's been handling him just fine," Marko said. "Is this really all the coolant you brought? This isn't even going to be half of what we need."

"It's all we could spare. Our supplies are running low, and we don't get deliveries out here that often."

"We'll just have to make it work," Adi said as he dumped another bottle into that same compartment. "We can get to Talmaris. We'll just push the ship."

"If we slow down, we might be able to take some of the stress off the engine," Marko said. "If Civan, Varojin, and the Lightbringers keep an eye on it, too, we should make it without overheating."

Lavender surprise flared up around Fay. "Smart."

"Yes, well, it's an emergency situation," Marko said. "Need to get back as soon as possible."

"I hope everything's alright," Fay said, her gaze darting from Marko to Astrea and back again. "Lucian did sound worried on the phone, and he's never worried."

"You're aware of the threat we encountered at the palace a few weeks ago?" Marko asked, and Fay nodded. "Well, it's related to that."

"Not here, I hope?" she asked. "My Lightbringers have sensed nothing out of the ordinary."

Astrea hadn't been expecting that, but she supposed she should have been. The entire Novarian military would be on high alert after the attack on the palace.

"Not here but coming, or so we think," Astrea said.

Adi finished pouring the last bottle into the compartment, then passed the empty bottle to Marko. Fay picked up the others scattered on the floor.

"Let's hope you're right, Marko," Adi said. "Thanks for the coolant, Commander Kalandi."

Dismissing her light, Astrea followed the commander and two men outside.

"All done, Luci!" Fay called. "I thought you would've needed more from me. That was almost too easy, at least when it comes to you."

Jin's eyebrows raised as he looked at Astrea. She just shrugged. Five minutes with Lucian's ex-fiancée wasn't enough time to judge whatever their relationship was.

"Trust me, Commander," Adi said to Fay, "there's nothing simple about what we need to do to get back." He fixed his attention on Jin. "We've only got half the coolant we need. We're going to need Civan."

"Just tell me what you need me to do," the Tidebacker said, his voice low and rumbling.

"Thank you, Fay," Lucian said. "I owe you."

"I believe you owe me a lot of things." No malice coated her words, and she flashed another brilliant smile up at him. "I'll just add it to your tab." She turned back to the rest of the group. "Good luck, and sorry I couldn't be of more help."

As Lucian escorted Fay back to her truck, Civan followed Marko and Adi to the engine room.

"Az, Len," Jin said, "go wait in the cabin. We'll be ready to go in a few minutes."

"Nothing you need us to do?" Lennor asked.

"Not right now. Let's just get out of here, yeah?" Jin said. "Time to go back to Talmaris."

Chapter 9

Cornflower blue, deep lavender, and violet painted the sky outside as the sun sank lower and lower below the horizon. They were somewhere above central Novaria. The trip was taking longer than it should've, but as Adi had reminded them all several times already, going slow would help ensure the engines didn't overheat.

Even with Civan's tidebacking to keep the diluted coolant stable and Marko monitoring the machinery, Adi didn't dare go faster. Though he was in the engine room below the main cabin, Civan's fatigue pressed into Astrea, making her eyelids heavy. Both Lucian and Marko were with him while Adi piloted the ship.

It would be another couple of hours yet before they reached Talmaris.

Astrea didn't know what to do with herself. Jin had laid his head in her lap about an hour before, and now, he was out cold. As he slept, she played with his curls, admiring the way the sunlight made the chestnut color that much prettier. He hadn't slept at all since they'd left the ruins. This was good. He needed this.

She glanced at the pile of their bags in the corner. Their sample from the ruins was there, as was Astrea's notebook with the void language samples. Tempted as she was to go grab her note to review again, that'd wake Jin. And besides, in just a few hours, they'd get that information into the hands of people who could help . . . or at least have a more solid plan to find people who could help.

Jin stirred. His arms twitched, muscles flexing. His eyebrows furrowed, then smoothed. "No," he whispered.

Astrea stilled.

"Stop," he whispered. "No."

"Jin?"

"Please, please . . ."

"Jin," Astrea whispered again, giving him a slight shake. "Jin, wake up."

He startled, eyelids flying open to reveal sleepy, worried golden irises. "I'm awake." Deep blue sadness and white terror fizzled out in his aura, there one moment and gone the next as he looked around the cabin.

"It was just a dream," Astrea said, smoothing some of his curls back. He'd done the same thing for her half a dozen times in the last few weeks. "Go back to sleep."

"Ship's alright?" he asked.

"Ship's fine." Astrea assumed as much considering the steady emotions of everyone else. Lennor had disappeared a couple of minutes prior to check on Civan. If something were wrong, Astrea would've felt it by now. Lennor was easy to read.

"You're alright?"

She nodded.

Jin's chest heaved as he settled back down. Lennor's dark brown hair appeared as she climbed up the engine room ladder. She shimmied out of the hole, then closed the hatch. When she turned, she shot Astrea a questioning look.

"I'll be right back," Astrea whispered to Jin. He lifted his head, and she slipped off the barely padded bench. When she peeked at him over her shoulder, he was already lying back down and closing his eyes. He relaxed instantly.

Astrea hadn't gotten to spend much time alone with Lennor the last few weeks, but she liked her. Lennor was kind, and she often had jokes or stories to share, especially when Adi was around. Those two got on like old friends, though it was Astrea's understanding that they'd only known each other for a little over a year. But, she supposed, serving together in war would bond people together quickly.

"How's Civan?" Astrea murmured to Lennor when she was close enough. They were on the opposite side of the cabin from Jin, whose heavy breathing suggested he was back asleep.

"Tired," Lennor admitted as she tucked flyaways behind her ear. "But he'll be fine. Marko said everything's good to go if Adi keeps us steady."

The Adi Astrea knew was steady. He'd been nothing but steady since leaving Kalama. Since she'd met him in Kalama, too.

"Well, that's good news, right?"

"Yeah." Lennor glanced at Jin, then back at Astrea. "How's he doing?"

"Tired, just like the rest of us."

"I bet." Lennor settled on the ground and leaned her back against the wall, then motioned for Astrea to sit next to her. When she did, Lennor continued, "It's funny. Before the war, Civan and I were trying to make it in the pro mage leagues."

"Really?" Astrea asked. She'd heard about athletes getting conscripted, but she'd only heard about that in passing. She'd never kept up with sports the way Balthazar and Cressida had. "Were you any good?"

"Well, it's tough when you don't have the resources to train like some of the others on the circuit. But yeah, we were alright. We were making progress."

"I'm sorry it got disrupted by the war."

Lennor shrugged a slender shoulder. "Not your fault and certainly nothing that can be changed now. I was just going to say that even though this was not the life I'd imagined for myself a couple of years ago, I'm really proud to be here. You know . . . helping Jin." Her cheeks flushed red as she added, "Doing something not for Emperor Aelius."

"Yeah . . ." Astrea paused. Jin had thrown one arm over his eyes, and the other hung off the side of the bench. It was hardly wide enough to accommodate him, but it was that or sleeping on the floor. As her magic washed over him, all Astrea could sense was the calm of sleep. "I don't know what Jin's told you about me, but this isn't where I imagined myself, either. Definitely not two years ago and definitely not two months ago."

"Funny how life changes sometimes, isn't it?"

"Yeah."

Astrea stared across the cabin at the windows. The sky grew darker, and the first stars began to glow. She plucked at her long skirt, a dozen questions building in her chest. Questions about Jin and Adi, about the war, about Lennor and Civan. But she didn't ask. Instead, she sat in the silence Lennor seemed fine with. Astrea leaned her head back against the wall, only perking up when Jin moved. His face contorted, then relaxed.

"I don't think I've ever actually seen him sleep," Lennor murmured.

"What?"

"Rarely saw him sleep when we were deployed. On flights into drop zones, he'd always be poring over intelligence reports. On flights back to base, he wouldn't sleep until the rest of us were settled."

That didn't sound healthy. "Do you think about the war often?"

Lennor shrugged again. "I'm pretty sure we all do. It's hard to forget that kind of thing."

"Right," Astrea whispered. Of course that would be impossible to forget.

Except for the slow rise and fall of his chest, Jin had gone completely still. No colors surged into his aura.

Astrea wasn't foolish enough to think the war—both wars that he'd fought in—didn't still affect him in some ways. That was clear, from how he didn't like splitting the team up to his promise to leave no one behind. But when they'd talked about his time at war before, he'd seemed . . . not at peace with it all, necessarily, but like he accepted those years for what they were.

Now, though, she wasn't so sure.

He twitched again in his sleep, whispering something too quietly for Astrea to hear.

Was he struggling, too? Not just with everything from the last eight years but from the last couple of months? She wasn't naive enough to think any of this had been easy on him.

No, the last couple of months had been so hard.

And she had the sinking feeling things were only about to get harder now that Nazarov had shown up again.

By the time they reached Talmaris, the sky was pitch black. Dark clouds rolled past the airship windows, obscuring the views of the stars and city. Rain splattered against the glass.

Astrea sat on the edge of one of the benches, bouncing her leg. Turbulence made the ship rumble. Astrea clutched the edge of her seat. She hated turbulence. Worse, the engine had finally started overheating.

"Ten minutes out," Adi's voice said over the crackling speakers. Astrea was sure the announcement was more for Civan, Lucian, and Jin in the engine room. "Palace is expecting us. Told us to go straight there, but they didn't sound thrilled."

Astrea wasn't surprised to hear the palace wasn't happy about their sudden arrival. After all, she hadn't been entirely sure Grand Duchess

Ysabel would allow it despite the information they needed to both share and gather. They'd come back to Talmaris against orders.

Turbulence rocked the ship again. Astrea clung to her bench, every muscle in her body tightening as she tried not to tumble to the floor. Ten minutes. They just needed to make it ten minutes.

"Is it wise to be flying through a storm like this?" Astrea asked Lennor as the Tempest joined her.

"No . . ." Lennor grimaced. "But we don't really have a choice, either."

Maybe they couldn't stop, but they'd be lucky if the storm didn't knock them out of the sky before they made it to the palace.

"Does he need help?" Astrea asked, watching through the cockpit window as orange anxiety pulsed bright and strong around Adi. Outside, blue lightning flashed across the sky, illuminating the towering storm clouds for half a heartbeat.

"Hope not," Lennor said with a tight chuckle. "I never learned how to fly."

One more bump in the air was going to make Astrea jump out of her own skin. It didn't help when Adi came back on over the ship's speakers and told the four in the engine room to get back up to the cabin.

Jin was the first to scramble up the ladder. He pulled Civan out next, then they made way for Marko and Lucian to join them. Heat and steam pushed out of the opening in the floor.

"You sure we're gonna make it?" Jin asked Marko.

"Adi can push it," Marko said. "We'll be fine."

Fine. Astrea wasn't so sure they'd be fine.

"You two better not get us fucking killed," Jin said as he pushed to his feet. Sweat beaded on his brow.

Civan's dark hair stuck to his forehead, long since matted down from the hours of work and heat. All four of the men were disheveled—especially Lucian, who rarely had a hair out of place.

"Have a little faith," Marko said as he started toward the cockpit, red determination spiking around him. "Adi knows what he's doing."

Lightning flashed outside the windows again. A deep rumble of thunder shook Astrea to the core of her bones. The ship surged forward. Rain pelted the glass harder, like pebbles clinking against the windows.

"Five minutes out," Adi's voice came over the speakers, barely audible over the rain and thunder. "Hold onto something. Bumpy landing."

Marko stood right behind Adi, pointing at something. As he did, Jin joined Astrea on her bench. Civan joined his sister. Lucian grabbed onto one of the thick metal beams near the edge of the rounded ceiling.

"Adi really better not get us killed," Astrea mumbled, and Jin actually laughed.

Five minutes turned to four, then three, as they sped through the stormy night. As they descended, turbulence shook the entire ship. Astrea held onto Jin with one hand and the seat with the other. Lights twinkled outside the windows, refracting on the rain. Three minutes turned to two, and the palace came into focus up ahead.

Lightning crackled. The airship frame creaked and rattled. They may as well have been a child's toy airship, being tossed around the sky during afternoon playtime.

Adi came on the speakers again. "Bumpy's turned to rough. Hang on."

The ship descended farther and farther, speeding past the palace and over the last trees of the garden. It scraped the branches and leaves before slamming down onto the ground.

Astrea fell forward out of her seat. Jin tried to catch her, but he followed her to the floor, swearing as they both hit the cold metal. Lennor and Civan were in no better shape, nor was Lucian. They all groaned.

Low, aching pain pulsed through Astrea's limbs. None of the pain was bad enough to suggest anyone was seriously hurt, though a dozen bruises may as well have covered her body. The neat pile of their suitcases had long since become a jumbled mess. Beyond the windows was just darkness and a fresh downpour of rain.

"You good?" Jin asked as he helped Astrea sit up.

"Fine, you?"

"Fine," he echoed.

"Everyone else?" Lucian called. "We alright?"

As the twins, Adi, and Marko all confirmed they were okay, Astrea loosed a breath. "What happened?" she asked Jin.

"Pretty sure something took out one of our rudders," Adi said as he climbed out of the pilot's seat. "And I'm pretty sure the engine finally gave up. Good thing you four weren't down there."

Emotions and walls penetrated the edge of Astrea's senses, then bright lights shone through the windows. Shouts followed as Lucian scrambled to the door and began unsealing it.

"My team," he explained before stepping out into the chilly rain. "It's just us!" he yelled. "It's us!"

The anxiety flaring outside settled as Lucian went to meet the Novarian guards. Astrea dug her hands into her hair and blew out a harsh breath. Everyone was okay. Everything was fine.

"Let's grab our things and go," Jin said. "Best not be out here too long. That surely drew some attention."

After gathering their luggage, they all headed for the door. Outside, rain continued pouring down around them, though Civan created a shield above their heads. Mud squelched under their boots. Lucian had met his team halfway across the small clearing the airship now sat in. Smoke and steam rose into the air.

The Novarians led them through the thick trees. Metal spikes glinted on top of the compound walls, towering high above them all.

Guards—perhaps soldiers, based on their plain blue uniforms—were stationed every dozen feet. Ysabel really was taking no chances now.

Lucian ushered their group through a gate Astrea had never seen before, then into a thick stone building that reminded her of the guard house on the opposite side of the compound. The air instantly warmed. Inside, electric lights glowed, though they did nothing to make the plain space welcoming. The interior matched the exterior, just gray brick walls and dark wood floors.

"We can get into the palace this way," Lucian explained as he led them down a long corridor.

A few turns, and Lucian had them in a room to clean the mud off their shoes. As if that were so important despite their news. Perhaps it was to Ysabel. Once he deemed everyone sufficiently mud-free, they continued on. And as much as Astrea wanted to deliver the information both about Nazarov and the ruins to the grand duchess, Lucian's new breakneck pace was almost too much.

"Come along!" Lucian called over his shoulder, the words echoing in the empty hallway. "Faster."

Nobody said a word as they went. The stark corridor eventually turned, then turned again, and the lights warmed and brightened. Carpets ran the length of the next hallway, simple in design but thick. Wainscoting lined the lower halves of the walls. A servants' hall, if Astrea had to guess. The deeper they went into the palace, the more familiar the views and the more heavily armed guards and soldiers they passed. It may as well have been a warzone.

The very first night Astrea and her friends had arrived in Talmaris, they'd been escorted to Ysabel's throne room. Tonight, though, they went past those grand double doors. The territory became unfamiliar again until finally, Lucian stopped in front of a set of much smaller double doors Astrea had never seen.

As soon as the doors opened, anxiety and relief pummeled Astrea, building to a crescendo as not one but two bodies practically tackled her. Eliana and Cressida threw their arms around Astrea, holding her upright as she stumbled. Despite her wet clothes and the audience, Astrea actually laughed.

"You're back!" Eliana cried in her ear.

"Hey, Ellie," Astrea choked out. She'd known returning to Talmaris meant returning to her friends, but after everything with Nazarov, she hadn't been able to really think about what it meant. Hadn't anticipated the relief and joy and anxiety all tangling together in her chest.

"Thank the skies," Cressida whispered. "This place is boring without you."

"Boring?" Astrea echoed. "I'm the most boring person here."

Cressida squeezed her shoulders. "Well, I like your brand of boring. Way better than anyone else here."

A throat cleared, and the girls finally pulled away from Astrea. Behind them, in the large meeting room, stood Grand Duchess Ysabel. Imperious as ever, with her dark blue dress and hair swept up elegantly on her head. Even at the midnight bell, she was intimidatingly put together.

"You're back, Commander," she said to Lucian. "Crashed an airship, did you?"

So much for our reunion.

"We hardly crashed it, though the storm took us by surprise," Lucian said. "And we had engine issues."

The grand duchess simply arched one eyebrow before looking at Jin and Astrea. "Welcome back." Icy was the only way to describe Ysabel tonight. "You have information?"

"I already told you that, Your Highness," Lucian said.

"And yet you did not tell me what it was."

"We have a lot to tell you, Ysabel," Jin said. "Probably best discussed in person anyway. Do you want to talk about this now or in the morning?"

"Now," Ysabel replied. "I'll have someone bring in coffee. We have a lot to tell you, too."

Chapter 10

Astrea curled her hands around the warm coffee cup one of Ysabel's staff set in front of her, letting its heat sink into her freezing hands. Getting rained on twice in two days wasn't doing her any good.

The long table in the meeting room was full: Jin, Cressida, Eliana, Nicos, and Adi, of course, but also the twins, Zephyrine, Marko, and Lucian. The guards and remaining servant left the room, though Astrea could still sense them in the hallway beyond.

"Let's get right to it, shall we?" Ysabel barely looked any of them in the eye, nor did she reach for her coffee. "What could possibly prompt you to come back to Talmaris now, Lucian?"

Jin stood and went to where they'd dumped their luggage on the floor. He rummaged through his knapsack first, then Astrea's. When he came back to the table, he set down her notebook and the piece of the ruins they'd brought back with them. The dark rock was as large as the palm of his hand, and it glinted under the chandelier's warm light.

Ysabel scoffed. "More rocks?"

"From the ruins out east," Jin said.

Surprise rippled around the table, doubling when Astrea added, "And we found new void language words, along with what we think are translations."

Jin explained their decision to go to the ruins, as well as its remote location and the differences in building material. As Jin passed the piece to Cressida, Lucian explained the way the ruins felt like the tunnels underneath the Paragon's hideout in Talmaris. He followed it up with an explanation of Nazarov's dreamwalking and a condensed explanation of their airship's mechanical issues.

"And you thought coming back to Talmaris was a good idea when Victor Nazarov has made contact again?" Ysabel's gaze darted to Jin, then Astrea. "Is this the only time he's contacted you, Miss Sovna?"

"The only," Astrea confirmed.

"We need to get back under that house, Your Highness," Lucian said. "The Paragon were going to find us one way or another. There's something strange about those locations, and we need to figure out what."

Warring displeasure and understanding moved across Astrea's skin in an uncomfortable dance. Ysabel took one sip of her coffee, then another. "And you still think going back to that house is a good idea now that Nazarov has reached out?"

Lucian's jaw tightened. "I think it's the only way, Your Highness."

"I agree," Cressida said as she set the sample down on the table. "That's meteorite, like what the emperor was looking into. We need to go under that house."

Astrea slumped back in her chair. How hadn't she made that connection? Sure, the ruins sample didn't look quite like the meteorite Cressida had stolen back in Kalama, but these days, Astrea's mind felt slow as molasses. She'd sometimes start one train of thought, only to forget what she'd been thinking about halfway through. Her mind often felt fractured, far beyond distracted. She'd never been like this before.

Not that there was anything they could've done with that meteorite connection had they figured it out at the ruins. Someone still would've had to go to the Paragon's hideout, and they still would've needed to get a sample to Talmaris. Astrea just hated feeling like this. It was different than not having answers, different from the way she'd felt all summer. It was like her mind didn't want to work at all some days, and that scared her.

"We've had the house under tight surveillance and security since Miss Sovna's rescue," Ysabel said. "But if you're going back, I'd like to still have a team sweep the tunnels and surrounding area to ensure it's safe."

"I can put together a team now—" Lucian started, already standing.

"Sit, Lucian," Ysabel said. "The storms are only getting worse overnight. Send a team when they're cleared, then go first thing in the morning."

"But—" he started, only to be cut off again.

"Not only am I unwilling to send teams out in such nasty weather," Ysabel said, "but it sounds like you've barely slept. A few more hours will change nothing. And besides, I've not even told you what we've learned."

A faint sheen of rusty annoyance flickered around Lucian's head, then disappeared. But the grand duchess was right; they were exhausted. Fatigue pressed and pressed against Astrea's body. A few hours of sleep would serve them better than running around Talmaris in severe storms in the middle of the night.

"And what have you learned?" Jin took a sip of his coffee, then grimaced.

Astrea only held onto hers for its heat. After weeks of Kalamian coffee she'd been brewing at the base, she had no desire for the weak Talmaran stuff.

"Miss Nikaphoros?" Ysabel prompted.

Cressida swallowed hard. "Well, Ellie, Nicos, and I have been helping Tomas look at every angle we could think of for the Paragon."

One of Ysabel's thin eyebrows quirked up. "So has Mariya."

"Right, sorry." Cressida cleared her throat. "Not just the Paragon itself, but the Great Wars, the mythology, the prophecy, all of it."

"And?" Jin asked.

"And we've found a couple things," she said. "It's been a lot of information to go through, but after the professor, well . . . we thought it best to keep things in-house for now."

Eliana flashed a tight-lipped smile. Astrea hadn't been expecting Eliana to help, not because she wouldn't be helpful but because Astrea simply assumed she would be busy working the grand duchess's council on the political front.

"And what I'm trying to say," Cressida continued, "is that we found a different prophecy about balance, as well as some more accounts of the Great Wars. Nothing to contradict what we were starting to learn through the professor."

A prophecy? They'd found a *prophecy*? Couldn't they have started with that news? Astrea's heart thundered in her chest as she sat up. "What did it say?"

"It said the earth and stars will restore balance. It's from a copy of a Stargazer's log, which was produced three hundred years ago, from just before the Rebuilding started."

The Rebuilding had come more than a century after the Great Wars ended, a time when society began to restore all that had been destroyed during the wars. Innovation had picked up, and governments and economies had begun to stabilize, leading into the start of the world's industrial revolution.

"The earth and stars?" Adi echoed.

Eliana cleared her throat. "We don't know for certain that it's at all related to the Paragon's so-called prophecy. But it seems likely, doesn't it?"

"It's got to be," Astrea said, realization washing over her in wave after wave. "It's balance."

"What?" Eliana asked.

"My uncle . . . the *Myth and Magic book* . . ." As gray confusion filtered around the table, Astrea said, "The magical elements balance each other out. Water, fire, earth, air. And now celestial and void." Months before, in Kalama, Saros had been telling Astrea that old stories centered on balance between the elements and even within the elements themselves.

"And the earth and stars, plus sun and moon . . ." Jin trailed off. "That has to be it. That has to be the whole prophecy. Split, for some reason, but the full one . . ."

Astrea folded her hands in her lap in a sad attempt to stop their trembling. Skies, she was cold. "Did it say anything else? Do you know who the Stargazer was? Or their actual vision?"

"No," Cressida said. "We only found this a few days ago, and it wasn't attributed to any particular Stargazer, though it claims the actual logs date back to the year 509."

If the copy of the logs were indeed authentic, that meant they were a little more than five hundred years old, from during the Great Wars.

"When they had me . . ." Astrea's voice shook, but she continued, "When they had me, The One told me I was meant to help them restore balance to the world and magic. That has to be what the Stargazer's log is referring to."

"It would be nice to know what this Stargazer's vision was," Lucian murmured.

"And without knowing who had the vision, we don't even know where to begin looking." Cressida shrugged. "Mariya's been focused on that the last few days. It didn't even say what country or court they were from. We're assuming Novarian for the time being but haven't found original copies of anything yet. We're trying."

Astrea stifled a sigh. One more half-useful hint. Why couldn't she have found something at the Paragon's house when she'd been trying to look around? Why hadn't The One told her more? He wanted her to understand, so why withhold information? To make her depend on him for answers?

"Go upstairs," Ysabel said. "Get some rest. You can head to the Paragon's hideout at first light."

Astrea knew she would have questions later, when her mind wasn't so fragmented and her body wasn't so tired. They could go to the Paragon's house, then talk about what else had been found while researching. None of the rest of the team argued, either. They all stood and began collecting their things.

"Lucian," Ysabel said, the word sharp. "Marko. May I speak with you two?"

"Of course, Your Highness," Lucian said.

Astrea followed her friends out of the meeting room, happy to let Lucian and Marko deal with their leader.

Though Astrea had thought she was going to get straight to bed at the guest house, that was not the way they went. Eliana and Cressida led everyone through the palace halls, down unfamiliar passageways and up several flights of stairs. Eventually, Astrea realized they'd gone into another wing of the building entirely.

"Well, here it is," Eliana said, motioning left and right at a junction. The corridor was filled with guards—some unreadable and some curious—and closed doors. "This is where we're staying now."

Astrea couldn't help but wonder where this kind of protection had been for her and Jin at the base. But of course, Ysabel was interested in protecting herself and also Eliana, the future Helosian empress. Jin may have been Ysabel's blood family, but Eliana's safety trumped that.

"Civan, Lennor." Zephyrine flipped her long braid over her shoulder. "Let me show you to your rooms, unless you need me, Jin?"

"We can talk later," Jin said before looking at the twins. "Get some rest. I need you there in the morning."

"Goodnight," Lennor called over her shoulder as she followed Zephyrine and Civan down the corridor to the right.

"Which means we can talk now," Eliana said, grabbing Astrea's hand and pulling her toward a door on the left.

Inside was a large sitting room, big enough for eight. The decor was the same as the rest of the palace: thick rugs, dark wood trim, muted wallpaper, elegant furniture. A fireplace stood on the far wall, and Nicos's fireweaving lit it up immediately. A doorway to the right led into what Astrea assumed had to be a bedroom.

As soon as the door closed behind them, a dozen questions flew through the air. Cressida, Adi, and Eliana began trading information and queries, impossible for Astrea to keep up with. She dropped Eliana's hand and sank into the tufted cream sofa.

"Skies, you three talk a lot," Nicos muttered, flopping into a chair opposite Astrea. "El, let them breathe. Let them sleep."

"I haven't seen them in a month, Nic." Crossing her arms over her chest, Eliana said, "That little meeting barely answered any of my questions."

"Nor mine, Ellie, but Nicos is right," Jin said. "It's a lot."

Astrea scanned Nicos, Eliana, and Cressida over as best she could. They seemed fine. A little tired, sure. None of them were as vibrant as they had been in Kalama two months before. None of them were hurt, though. Anxious, maybe. Astrea couldn't read Nicos, but Eliana and Cressida were wide open.

"I'm just tired, Ellie," Astrea said. "One question at a time. I'll try to answer them."

"Are you alright?" Eliana asked. "All three of you?"

"Fine," Astrea said, and Jin and Adi echoed her.

"Have you been eating?" Eliana asked. "You all look like you've lost weight. You look tired."

"Haven't lost any weight," Jin said. "We've been eating fine. Just been up for nearly two days straight."

They'd been eating better than Astrea had expected to out in the middle of nowhere. Well, the team had. Astrea had been forcing herself to eat. She'd barely had an appetite since the ordeal with the Paragon. She didn't think her body had changed, though.

As for not sleeping, Astrea didn't think she or Jin or any of the team had slept enough in weeks. Between rotating guard shifts, training, and Astrea's dreams, there hadn't been much rest.

Eliana pressed her lips into a thin line. "You really went to the other ruins?"

"No, we lied about that and pulled that rock from nowhere," Jin muttered. "Yes, we went to the ruins. It was fine until we got back to the base and Nazarov dreamwalked to us."

Huffing, Eliana said, "You don't have to be snappy about it."

"Sorry, not trying to be snappy. I'm just exhausted."

Walking toward the fireplace, Eliana kept her back toward the rest of the room. Rusty annoyance and mint relief spiked high around her, the colors so bright they made Astrea's eyes hurt.

"What's with all the guards?" Jin asked Nicos.

"Ysabel's new protocol. A guard or soldier at every junction and every door," Nicos explained. "All thoroughly reviewed by Lucian's second-in-command. At least a quarter of them are Lightbringers."

"That many?" Adi asked.

"Pulled in from other units and bases around Novaria where there were Lightbringers to spare." Nicos shrugged. "There's been no trace of the void since the first attack."

"Ysabel's really taking this seriously," Jin said.

"What did you expect?" Eliana asked as she turned back toward the group. "She was attacked just as much as we were."

"I didn't say I didn't expect it, Ellie."

Cressida shot Astrea a questioning look. She barely shrugged in response. The bickering was the most unexpected part of all this. Jin and Eliana usually got on fine.

"Maybe we should all just go to bed," Cressida offered. "That way we're ready for the morning."

"I assume you two are staying together," Jin said, motioning between Nicos and Eliana. Both of them flushed red, but Nicos nodded. "What about the rest of us?"

"You can all have your own rooms if you want," Eliana said.

"Jin and I will share," Astrea said. Weeks ago, that would've felt impossible to say out loud. Now, she offered a tired smile up at Jin as he settled his hand on her shoulder.

"I should go talk to Zephyrine," Jin said. "Adi?"

"Sure." Even Adi's usual enthusiasm was gone, replaced by heavy eyelids. "Twenty minutes, then I'm going to bed regardless of what she has to tell us."

Jin agreed, and then they were gone.

"Az, let us show you to your room," Eliana said, almost conspiratorially. Astrea held back a groan; she didn't want to move. "Me and Cress."

"El—" Nicos started, but Eliana waved him off.

"It's fine, Nic."

"Is it actually safe? For you to be with me, I mean." Astrea was sure the palace was just about as safe as anywhere else right now. But being in the same room as Eliana might put her at risk of dreamwalking or worse.

"It's very safe," Eliana replied. "Now do you want to go to bed or stay on that sofa?"

Astrea grabbed her and Jin's knapsacks, then her satchel, and let Cressida and Eliana take the suitcases. Guards watched them as they walked twenty feet down the hall to another door.

Opening it unceremoniously, Eliana announced, "Here we are!" The room was practically a mirror image of the one they'd just left, though this one had more blue accents.

"And I'm directly across the hall," Cressida said.

Astrea didn't know what it was, but as she walked from the sitting room into the bedroom, with her best friends right behind her, the tears started. She dropped her bags on the floor, then sat on the edge of the bed.

"Az?" Eliana asked. "What, has Jin been an ass or something?"

"No," Astrea said, half laughing and half crying. She wiped at her tears with the back of her hand. "I just missed you both."

Throwing the suitcases on the floor, Eliana and Cressida joined Astrea on the soft, oversized bed. Some distant part of Astrea's mind told her she should take off her shoes and clothes before ruining the grand duchess's bed linens, but she didn't really care. As she hugged Eliana and Cressida, their relief washed over her in cool waves.

Astrea had never been away from them for that long before. Sure, it had barely been a month, and both Eliana and Cressida had been on trips away from Kalama over the years. But neither had ever been gone at the same time. They weren't just her friends but her sisters. They were who she went to for everything, and the opposite was true, too.

But she'd survived that, just like she'd survived the last two months away from Saros and the Nikaphoroses.

"We missed you, too," Cressida said when Astrea finally loosened her tight hold on them. "It was shit not getting to talk to you."

"And imagine poor Az," Eliana quipped. "Stuck out there with Commander Lucian and my brother."

A choked laugh bubbled up Astrea's throat. "Jin's fine. Lucian's just annoying. Adi started teaching me how to cook."

"Oh yeah?" Cressida asked. "Burn the place down?"

Eliana snorted as Astrea answered, "He mostly just had me peel vegetables. Lennor and Civan are nice, too, though Civan doesn't talk much."

"I noticed that about him while you went to the Macadian Mountains," Eliana said. "So quiet you wouldn't know he was around."

"They were trying to make it in the mage sport leagues before the war," Astrea said, racking her mind for what else she had to share. "Oh, and I knocked Adi on his ass a few times during training."

Eliana snorted again. "Now *that* I would pay a thousand lire to see."

"Is there anything else I need to know tonight?" Astrea asked.

"Nothing we can't figure out tomorrow," Cressida said. "I think I've done you proud. I'm really learning my way around that card catalog in the library."

"Hey, I'm learning it, too!" Eliana protested.

"I'm very proud." Eliana had rarely visited the Great Library back home, and Raela—Astrea's old boss—had never let Cressida touch the catalog since she wasn't a librarian.

As Eliana and Cressida started filling her in on palace happenings for the last month, Astrea closed her eyes and leaned back into the fluffy pillows. Cressida lay down on her right, Eliana on the left. And it was there, cocooned between her friends and their happy chatter, that Astrea finally fell asleep.

CHAPTER 11

As she cracked her eyes open, Astrea couldn't remember when Jin had joined her in bed. She couldn't remember Eliana or Cressida leaving. But there she was, not in the muddy, travel-worn clothes but one of Jin's clean shirts, his arms wrapped around her from behind. There was even a small, warm light coming from the far corner of the room.

Her nightlight. He'd set up another nightlight for her.

"Hi," Jin whispered as she stirred.

"Did you sleep?"

"Yeah, only woke up a few minutes ago. We need to get ready to go soon."

"Sure." Astrea snuggled down into the pillows. And she would crawl out of bed in a couple more minutes, but for now, she pressed back into Jin's heat and sighed, content.

"Did *you* sleep?" he asked, his breath tickling her cheek.

"Yeah." Astrea may have slept, but it hadn't been a good night's rest. Dreams of fire and airship crashes and battle plagued her, though they were quickly fading to nothing but fragmented images in her mind.

Jin hummed his response, then pressed a kiss to Astrea's neck. Sparks flickered down her body. She turned in Jin's arms, and once they were face to face, he kissed the end of her nose. The short hairs of his beard prickled her lips as she pecked his chin. He caught her mouth with his as she pulled away, tart lust exploding over her tongue. But it died, replaced by sweet approval and heavy regret.

"I'm afraid there's no time for that," Jin whispered as he pulled away.

"Who said I'm trying to start that?"

"So much more responsible than me." He pulled her tighter against his body, then kissed her cheek. "Alright. Let's not be late."

Getting out of bed was the true challenge. Astrea's entire body protested as she scooted to the edge of the mattress and stood. It continued its protest even as she showered and even when Jin used his fireweaving to warm her tight shoulders. It only stopped its protest when she was finally dressed—body armor and all—and drinking coffee in the meeting room one of the many palace guards had escorted them to. Outside the looming windows, the sun had barely started to rise.

Tugging at the waistband of her pants, Astrea tried to focus on her mediocre coffee instead. She'd worn trousers more in the last couple of months than she had in the last decade, and she still didn't love them. But one of her flowy dresses certainly wasn't practical for the morning's mission.

Except for Astrea and Jin, the room was empty. He sat next to her, his body so tight he was like a spring ready to explode.

"Jin?" Astrea asked.

"Yeah?" He sipped his coffee.

"You seem tense."

"Just a bit worried." His fingers tapped the table. "About taking you back there."

"But I need to go to help—"

"I know," Jin said gently. "I know you do. I'm not asking you to stay behind. But I can't turn off the part of my mind that worries."

"I understand."

And she did. Astrea understood that better than anything.

She hoped she would be useful on this outing. So much of the time in that house was a blur. But she'd been in that house more than anyone. Knew the Paragon better than anyone. If there was a chance she could remember something, *anything*, then wasn't it worth going?

Cressida arrived first, dressed in her armor just like Astrea. It was still a foreign sight. She held the door open, and instead of Adi or Eliana walking in, a stranger followed. She had to be nearly a foot shorter than Cressida. Her terra cotta skin gleamed in the meeting room's chandelier light, and something in her cornflower blue eyes seemed almost mischievous.

"Hey, Cress," Jin said. "And good morning . . . ?"

The stranger waved at them with one hand, the other firmly planted on the shiny black cane she was using. "Mariya Halara," she said. "The Grand Ducal Stargazer."

"This is Prince Varojin Auris," Cressida said, "and Astrea Sovna, my best friend. They're—"

"Yes, yes, the two these Paragon are after. I know." Mariya moved farther into the room and sat in one of the seats opposite Astrea and Jin. "Sovna, eh? Are you related to Sar—"

"Yes," Astrea said with more force than she expected. "He's my uncle. Do you know him?"

"We trained together at university, but that was what, twenty years ago?" Mariya ran a hand over the tight coils of her hair, then shrugged. "I haven't seen him in many years. Didn't socialize all that much back in the day, your uncle. Such a quiet fellow."

It was strange, almost unreal, to have this tangible connection back to Saros. Astrea had a hundred questions for Mariya about her uncle, but would this Stargazer even know? She didn't seem to know Saros well. Maybe they could find time to talk another day, when the rest of the group wasn't strolling into the room. Astrea settled back in her chair and sipped on her coffee.

Eliana and Nicos walked in with little fanfare, and Eliana greeted Mariya as if they'd known each other for years. Cressida made introductions for the rest of the team when they arrived with Marko. But Lucian? Well, when he strode into the room and spotted Mariya, his eyebrows furrowed.

"Mariya?" he asked as he circled to the head of the oval table. "What are you doing here?"

The Stargazer scoffed. "What kind of question is that?"

"No one told me you'd be coming on this morning's mission."

"Sometimes plans must change, Commander."

"Has Her Highness approved it?"

"Her Highness told me to figure this out. And I think my coming on your outing will help," Mariya said. "Cressida was telling me about this meteorite you think is under part of Talmaris. I'd like to go examine it myself, in person." When Lucian turned to Cressida, Mariya added, "Oh, leave the girl alone. You know it's better if I join you."

"Maybe we can get answers that much faster," Jin said.

Lucian rubbed his forehead as if warding off a headache. "Fine." He cleared his throat, then said, "We'll be at the house within an hour. We'll take three trucks. We're going in, learning about those tunnels, and coming back. Strictly business. No pit stops. No delays."

"And here I was, wanting to stop for ice cream on the way," Cressida whispered next to Astrea. Lucian pinned her with a look.

"Marko, Adi, and the twins already know this," Lucian continued with one last pointed look at Cressida, "but someone must be with Astrea and Varojin at all times. Preferably two people, and two people who can fight in case the Paragon show up."

The Stargazer rolled her eyes. "Subtle, Lucian."

"What?" he asked.

"I can hold my own," Mariya said, "and you know it."

"And yet you've been out of practice for years. When was the last time you sparred?"

"Some of us have more important things to do than have pretend fights all day."

Astrea stole a glance at Cressida. She shook her head almost imperceptibly. What was this strange animosity between Lucian and Mariya? And why was warm amusement rolling off the Stargazer? Only the slightest pinch of annoyance joined the mix. Lucian didn't seem pleased at all.

Eliana cleared her throat. "Should they even be going if it's that much of a risk, Commander?"

"The site is locked down, Your Imperial Highness," Lucian replied. "We go, we take precautions, and we move quickly. Now, if there are no more questions, let's move."

After a quick goodbye to Eliana and Nicos, the rest of them headed outside. Even in the early morning light, the military's heavy presence was obvious. Ominous, really. The Novarian palace had been beautiful and serene once, but now, soldiers swarmed the grounds. Machine guns were mounted on top of trucks parked out front. Even many of the guards, who were surely mages, carried weapons. Astrea swallowed thickly.

Several large military trucks idled on the palace driveway. Zephyrine, Civan, and Lennor climbed into the one at the back of the line. Marko, Lucian, and Mariya headed for the first truck.

"I'm very glad we aren't going to be in there with them," Adi murmured as Jin led him, Astrea, and Cressida to the middle vehicle.

"What's Lucian's deal?" Cressida asked. "Has he been that grumpy the whole time you've been gone?"

"Pretty much." Astrea fiddled with the end of her braid. The commander was still a mystery to her, always running hot and cold. "But Mariya seemed to think the whole exchange was funny."

Jin helped Astrea climb up into their truck, which was definitely not made for comfort. Metal benches lined the two walls. The convoy rumbled down the palace driveway and eventually merged onto the quiet streets of Talmaris. Though there were no windows in the back to look out of, Astrea could see through the windshield. The view was mostly just tall trees, empty sidewalks, and the occasional building.

Astrea's fingers wrapped around the edge of her bench, her knuckles turning white with her tightening grip as she pushed past her friends' fatigue and kept her senses open. At the speed they were traveling, Astrea wasn't sure she'd even catch any voids, but as Lucian said: take no chances.

This was it. They were going back to the Paragon's hideout. *She* was. Astrea didn't know what she hoped to find. Ideally, Mariya and Cressida would figure out something about the tunnels. Maybe there'd be more evidence of the void language to add to their growing list. Astrea needed to ask Tomas about finding a linguist to work with when they got back to the palace.

The truck made its way through downtown Talmaris, then eventually onto emptier streets where the buildings were spread farther and farther apart. Astrea didn't recognize any of it. She wasn't sure she would. That night Jin and Adi had rescued her was fuzzy in her memory. She couldn't remember the drive from the house to the palace at all.

Eventually, the truck slowed, then stopped, as a large green house came into view through the windshield. Like the palace, soldiers swarmed the area. More military trucks were parked out front. It looked more like a war zone than an upper-class suburban home.

Jin climbed out of the back of the truck first, then helped both Astrea and Cressida on their jump to the ground. Adi followed, stretching as he stepped into the rising sunshine.

"It looks so normal," Cressida said as she stopped next to Astrea.

"Yeah," she murmured.

That was part of the problem. The house looked *so* normal. Dark green paint. Dark wood trim. Several stories rose into the air, and thick, towering trees surrounded the house. How had the Paragon been operating here, apparently unnoticed? The closest neighbors weren't terribly far away. Astrea could see the houses through the gardens and greenery.

"Well," Lucian said as he joined them, "shall we go inside?"

Jin's hand found the small of Astrea's back, just a light pressure through her armor as he nudged her forward. Sucking in one last deep breath of fresh air, Astrea followed Lucian toward the house. *Find the answers.* That's what she was here to do, and she would. She would find answers.

The interior of the house was only vaguely familiar at first. But those hardwood floors. The narrow hallways. Astrea had tried to run down these very halls. Had been stopped by Nazarov. It all came back to her in a rush.

"I know we need to go downstairs," she managed to say past the dryness in her mouth, "but can we go into his office, too?"

"My teams have already been over it," Lucian said, "but we can look again if you'd like."

"I think it's this way," Astrea said, nodding to her right.

"Mariya, Cress, how about you two go downstairs," Jin said. "Take Zephyrine, Civan, and Lennor with you."

"Marko, stay up here," Lucian said. "I'll go downstairs with the others."

Astrea started down the hallway toward The One's office. What was she looking for? She wasn't exactly sure. They were here for the tunnels, not this. But something carried her feet forward anyway.

On her left was that painting of the parents and daughter. She glanced at it only briefly, taking in the daughter's chestnut hair and soft brown eyes, the hard looks on the parents' faces. "It's just up here," Astrea said over her shoulder at the three men following her.

And there it was. The One's office door. Astrea half anticipated feeling those cold voids all around her, just like last time. But there were none. There were walls of many soldiers. Jin's, Adi's, and Marko's walls. The emotions of others. Worry. Boredom. Fatigue. But no voids. The house was full of life.

The door creaked as Astrea pushed it open. Inside was exactly as she remembered it from those few lucid conversations she'd had with The One. The desk. The chair they'd forced her to sit in. The mostly empty bookcases.

What she'd been expecting, Astrea wasn't sure. The One's dead body, perhaps. Some Paragon symbol etched into the wooden walls. Destruction, like the way they'd left the professor's office. Anything besides the silence.

"What are you looking for?" Marko asked from the doorway.

"I don't know," Astrea admitted as she circled behind the desk. When she'd last been here, Nazarov had stabbed The One. She'd heard his body drop. And yet there wasn't even a blood stain on the floor. "While I was here, I tried to look around, but they caught me before I got anywhere."

"The commander's teams have already swept the place. Perhaps we should join him downstairs."

"Just give us a few minutes, Marko," Jin said. "We'll be quick."

Marko grunted a response and took up a position just outside the door.

Staring at The One's desk, Astrea tried to pull forth some memory besides those of Tovan injecting the blue lotus and Nazarov burning her when she'd tried to fight back. As Astrea's hands trembled, she clasped them tightly in front of her.

There'd been something about this desk. The One had constantly leaned to his right. He'd fiddled with something on that side of the desk, too. One of the drawers, maybe? Astrea remembered him going for one of those drawers.

She reached for the top drawer and yanked on it. It stuck, barely moving from its position. That wasn't right. She would swear on her own life she saw The One open that drawer. She tugged again.

"Problem?" Jin asked as he rounded the desk to join her. On the other side of the room, Adi was examining the walls and a small beige credenza.

"He opened this drawer when I was here," Astrea said. "I know Marko said they swept the place, but . . ."

"Let me see if I can get it." Jin yanked on the drawer, too, but it didn't move. He sighed, then squatted down in front of it. "Sometimes these old drawers just stick. You're sure it was this one?"

"Almost positive."

Jin shrugged his knapsack off, then pulled out a series of narrow metal tools. They looked like lock picks, but the drawer wasn't locked. "Can I have some light?" he asked as he opened the drawer underneath the stuck one.

Astrea summoned a pinprick of light, aiming it at the empty area under the drawer where Jin was now looking. He hummed, then stuck one of the long pieces of metal into the gap. It scratched against what sounded like paper. With a little maneuvering, Jin yanked out an envelope. Its corner tore as he pulled it free.

"That'll do it," he muttered, holding the thick envelope in one hand and pulling on the drawer with the other. It moved easily on its track again, but when Astrea peered inside, it was empty.

"All good?" Adi asked as he approached the desk from the other side.

Astrea dismissed her light. "Fine. I'm sure whatever was in here, Ysabel's people already got."

Next to her, Jin had gone still. He still crouched on the ground, his tools clutched in one hand as he held the envelope in the other. In the top right corner—the one that was torn—was the beginning of a word: Sevi.

Jin glanced up at her, then Adi. He flicked his gaze toward the door where Marko still stood with his back to them. Then Jin slid his tools and the envelope back into his knapsack and buckled it up.

Why was Jin trying to hide that from Marko?

Then it washed over her.

Sevi. The torn corner. That very well could've said Seviya. Jin's mother's family.

But why would The One have a letter with Jin's mother's family name on it? They'd surmised Jin's connection to all of this was his intense fireweaving power, or as the Paragon called him, the Sunreaper. Had they been wrong?

"Later," Jin mouthed.

Later, indeed.

"Alright, Marko," Jin called out as he shouldered his pack. "Let's go downstairs. You were right. Everything here was cleared out."

They followed Marko back through the home's winding halls, Astrea stuck right between Adi and Jin. She had to shove the letter out of her mind, just as she had to shove down her fear as they crept closer to the basement door. The last time she'd seen this door, Jin had been carrying her, bloody and beaten. It was so unassuming now, just a regular oak door like all the others in the house.

Creeping down those steep basement stairs made Astrea's pulse double. The darkness surging in around her made her pulse triple. Jin's flame lit up the space, and after a few deep breaths, Astrea pulled on her light. Below, several Novarian guards in dark blue uniforms stood at attention, flashlights in hand. After getting directions from them about which way Lucian and the others went, Marko continued on down the long, dark corridor.

It's just the dark, Astrea reminded herself. *Nobody's here except your allies. The place is locked down.*

They may as well have been walking forever in that surging darkness. Despite Jin's flames and her starlight, and despite the fact that they actually didn't have to walk far, Astrea wanted to crawl out of her skin or sprint back up the stairs. Just as her steps slowed, voices and familiar emotions and walls came across Astrea's senses. Soon, the team was in view.

"And you really can't feel anything above us?" Cressida asked Lucian. "The same as at the ruins?"

"The very same," Lucian responded. "It is as Astrea and I explained. Something about this rock blocks our senses."

Cressida ran her fingers over the tunnel wall, marveling. Mariya tapped the wall with the end of her cane and shook her head.

"I can feel something is off," the Stargazer said, "but I would like to get samples from different areas to bring back to the observatory. Perhaps Cressida and I can run some tests there?"

"Way ahead of you." With a twitch of her fingers, a portion of the wall morphed and pulled away, forming a small chunk over Cressida's outstretched palm. "How many samples?"

"Perhaps we can get another one from this way," Mariya said, already heading farther into the darkness. Lennor scurried after her and Cressida, her flashlight bobbing up and down.

"Anything upstairs?" Lucian asked.

"Nothing," Astrea said, hoping he wasn't as good at spotting her lies as Jin and Cressida were. "Just a lot I vaguely recall. Marko said some of your teams recovered items from upstairs?"

"Barely any, last I heard before we went out east," Lucian said, arms crossing tightly over his chest. "It was nearly empty when we got here that night."

"Could we take a look at all of that when we get back to the palace?" Jin asked. "Assuming Ysabel allows us to stay. She didn't seem too keen on our presence last night."

Despite knowing the grand duchess wasn't thrilled to see their group, Astrea hadn't given much thought to going back to the old base. Once they had their information, they could go back to hiding out until something new came up. But going back to their former hideout didn't make sense. Nazarov seemed to know its location. Would Ysabel send them to a different base next?

"Can you blame her, Varojin?" Lucian asked. But even so, wariness prickled Astrea's arms. "There's no winning no matter where we go."

"You don't have to go with us, Commander," Jin said. "You could stay here and continue the investigation into the Paragon's disappearance. You'd probably be of more use here in the capital."

"And leave Astrea as the sole Lightbringer?" the commander retorted. "That's hardly fair to her or any of you. Two Lightbringers, minimum."

As a reply formed on Astrea's tongue, pain lanced through her back. She stumbled forward, falling to her hands and knees before she could steady herself. They slammed against the cold, hard tunnel floor as her vision clouded over.

So, you've returned, little Lightbringer. It wasn't Nazarov's voice but The One's. *I'm glad to see Victor didn't scare you off.*

The One. Not Nazarov. The One, dreamwalking to her, as he had so many times.

You're alive? she thought. She'd heard that body crash to the floor that night. She'd felt that pain.

A heavy hand settled between Astrea's shoulders, warm and familiar. Jin. Anxiety grated against her entire being, though she couldn't see any orange. She couldn't see anything. It was just darkness, that suffocating, all-consuming darkness.

Indeed. There's still much for you to—

Astrea couldn't stop the cry that left her as more pain seared through her body. Hot and cold pulsed in her bones, almost like the pain fought itself, swirling and tumbling through her. Dozens of tiny needles poked her mind. Her insides twisted.

I knew you weren't dead, Nazarov's voice cut in, *but you really think you're going to be the one to talk to Miss Sovna?*

Two? How were both of them dreamwalking to her at the same time? She'd just begun to ask when something sharp twisted in her shoulder, her sternum, her head. It wasn't unlike the ghost pain she felt from others, though it felt . . . heavier. Rougher.

What do you two want? Astrea managed to think. She wheezed, as if someone had punched her right in the stomach.

I wonder, The One drawled as the darkness evaporated, *if you'll miss your uncle just as much as you miss Roxana?*

A lake, stretching as far as Astrea could see. Rolling green fields and wildflowers. A garden so beautiful it could've been Sarsali's work. And the house she grew up in before Saros took her to Kalama, a modest thing of brick and wood. Then the house burst into flames, a woman's screams begging Astrea to run. It was not the first time the Paragon had shown Astrea a place from her childhood. It was not the first time they'd mentioned Roxana.

Help me and you won't have to find out, The One whispered. *Convince the Sunreaper to help us, too, unless you want everyone you love to suffer. You know how awful it feels. You know because you felt it when Victor did it to me.*

The image changed, morphing and shimmering until Kalama—home—came into view. The city was on fire, void flames snaking up building after building. And at the center of it all, Saros, Sarsali, and Balthazar lying prone on the ground.

Something sharp scraped against Astrea's sternum as pain overwhelmed her again. Her ribs throbbed. Her heart thundered. The image disappeared, almost like someone had switched off the lights. Astrea fell forward, but strong arms steadied her and that warm hand rubbed small circles on her back. Even with her vision dark again, the world around her seemed to twist and tilt.

What my colleague seems keen on doing is hurting you, Miss Sovna, Nazarov said, his voice smooth and false.

And you aren't? Astrea asked.

Nazarov chuckled, the sound like a lie. *Of course not. You're supposed to help me, remember? So let me help you. Let me explain.*

No.

So stubborn. Nazarov clicked his tongue.

He'd started to speak again when pain flooded Astrea's veins. Hot and cold burned through her, not unlike when The One had been stabbed. No voices came, but the agony continued, morphing into some sick tug-of-war in her mind. Though she was stone still, it felt like someone was yanking her back and forth.

What was happening?

Just when she thought she was going to be sick, the pain eased, and Nazarov cleared his throat. *Meet me somewhere away from all of the guards and police and soldiers. None of the grand duchess's lap dogs are allowed, including the other Lightbringer.*

What was that? Astrea asked. *What just happened? What did you do?*

Agree to meet me, then I'll explain it all.

I need to think about it.

And I need an answer now.

I can't think when you do this. It hurts too much.

Silence pressed in around her. What Astrea really needed was a plan. She wanted to meet Nazarov to try to get information about . . . everything . . . but she couldn't agree without a plan.

You can have one day, Nazarov finally said. *Talk soon, little Lightbringer.*

And just like that, the darkness receded, replaced by warm flames and starlight. Astrea choked out a cough and pressed her forehead against the cold floor, her limbs frozen.

"Az?" Jin asked gently. Anxiety pulsed so brightly through the tunnel, from every direction, that Astrea could see it even with her eyes closed.

"I think they're connected to this stone somehow," Astrea forced herself to say, her breaths starting to come faster. "Nazarov and the Paragon's leader were both dreamwalking to me."

"At the same time?" Lucian asked.

Still crouched on the floor, Astrea squeezed her eyes tighter. The pain of dreamwalking was gone, but she could feel those void flames on her skin. Where Nazarov had cut her. Where Tovan had fractured her ribs. The memories pushed and pushed against her until she couldn't breathe at all and her hands began to shake.

They're not here, she reminded herself. *They're not here. But they might be soon. Move.*

She did not move, but she forced her eyes open.

Lucian's light. Cress's boots. The walls.

Jin's hand. The cold floor. My armor.

There wasn't much of anything she could smell here in these tunnels, so Astrea simply sucked in one deep breath and held it. When she finally blew it out, she glanced up. The tight worry in Cressida's features. Mariya's furrowed brow. Lennor and Civan hanging to one side, unsure. Lucian, arms crossed over his chest. Astrea couldn't make herself look back at Jin, Adi, or Marko.

"At the same time," she finally answered Lucian. "The One started it, then Nazarov joined and seemed to . . . force him out somehow. I don't know exactly. It hurt."

"And what did they want?" Lucian asked.

"The One threatened my uncle and Cressida's parents if I don't get Jin to help him," Astrea said. "And Nazarov wants to meet me to talk."

"That's not going to happen."

"Why not?" Astrea asked, all too aware of the tremble in her voice. "You wanted to use me as bait weeks ago."

"And that was before we knew they had unhinged war plans!" Lucian exclaimed. His words softened as he said, "We can't just hand you over to them."

"He said he'll explain things to me if I meet him without the Novarians present," Astrea shot back. "We need information, so let me talk to him."

As Lucian began to protest, Jin said, "I don't think this is the place for this conversation, Commander. Let's think about it when we get back to the palace."

As Jin helped Astrea to her feet, she sucked in another deep breath. It didn't stop the energy buzzing under her skin, but it helped everything come into sharper focus around her.

"I . . ." Cressida hesitated, then rolled one shoulder. "Mariya and I really should take a couple of additional samples if there's time."

"Quickly," Lucian said. "Do not venture far."

"Len, Civan—" Jin started, but the twins were already following Cressida down the tunnel.

As Lucian and Marko began discussing something in hushed tones, she nudged Jin toward the stairs. "Let's go," she said. "I don't want to be here anymore."

Chapter 12

Astrea's fingers tapped against the top of the smooth mahogany table in the grand duchess's meeting room. The ruler herself wasn't present, nor was most of Jin's team. It was just their original group from Helosia, plus Lucian and Marko.

"Astrea, I realize you want to find answers. So do I," Lucian said, his voice almost empathetic. "But going to talk to Victor Nazarov is out of the question. It's very likely he simply wants to grab you and Varojin for whatever inane plan he has."

"Or maybe he wants to give me information," she replied. They'd been going round and round in this debate, just the two of them. Lucian started to say something, but Astrea cut him off. "Yes, I'm well aware of the fact that he may be manipulating me. I'm well aware of the fact that he might try to take me somewhere else. But you didn't feel what I did, Lucian. You didn't feel The One and Nazarov fighting inside my mind. Nazarov didn't kill the leader he was trying to depose, and now they're at odds."

"And you think this rivalry means Nazarov is suddenly on our side?"

"Of course not," Astrea said. "But I think it's worth taking a chance if it means we get the information we obviously aren't going to find on our own."

Lucian turned and paced toward the fireplace on the opposite wall, his shoulders tight. Annoyance and frustration rolled off him in waves of rusty reds and browns.

"We need a plan," Astrea said to the others. "Maybe we could meet him at the ruins. Lucian and other guards could stay on the airship nearby."

"Az . . ." Eliana heaved a sigh. "Are you sure it's wise? Going to meet him, I mean. Surely there are better ways. Or we could set some kind of trap."

"And have him jump away?" Adi asked. "You didn't see what they could do."

"There's no way to prevent it?" Eliana asked.

"Not that we know of," Jin said.

He'd said very little on the ride back to the palace, just held Astrea's hand. Though she'd managed to pull herself out of a panic while in the tunnels, the feeling had returned ten minutes into their drive. She'd sat frozen in place for another ten minutes before pulling herself out of it again.

"This meteorite doesn't stop them like it stops your lightbringing?" Eliana asked.

"No. They seem to be connected to it somehow," Astrea said. "Or at the very least, it doesn't stop them."

"If it stops *your* magic," Cressida said, "what if it enhances theirs somehow?"

Astrea chewed on her lower lip. It was possible, she supposed. Maybe meteorite—or certain ones, like what Saros had sensed—held special properties that interacted with void magic. Could that be why the emperor wanted more meteorite for himself? To create something for his void mages?

"Maybe I could find out if Lucian lets me talk to Nazarov," Astrea said, making more rust explode around the commander.

She didn't revel in the idea of going to meet Victor Nazarov. Her mind wouldn't let her forget all of the awful things he'd done, which were certainly on par with The One's endless dreamwalking and drugs. Worse, probably. But Tomas and Mariya's research was slow going. They still had to find an expert to help them begin building the void language translations. If there was even a *chance* Nazarov was willing to give them information, wasn't that worth taking?

"I think we should seriously consider what Nazarov is offering," Marko said. "He seems fixated on Astrea, yes, but if he's going against his own leader, maybe it's worth a risk. Maybe we can find a way to use the Paragon's internal schism to our advantage."

"He wants an answer tomorrow," Astrea said.

Lucian sighed heavily as he turned back toward the group. "Let me talk to the grand duchess."

"I'm going whether she allows me or not, Lucian." Astrea didn't know how she'd actually arrange the meeting or keep herself safe, but forcing the issue seemed to be working. "You can either be in on the plans or not."

"She's going, Lucian," Jin said. Lavender surprise flickered around the table. "We're both going, whether Ysabel supports it or not. I'll take my team, and we'll get it done if you won't."

With another sigh, Lucian pinched the bridge of his nose. "You won't be doing this alone," he muttered. "Just give me the night to work something out with her. Skies knows I'm going to need time to convince her."

Going back upstairs was the last thing Astrea really needed to do. She needed to go talk to Tomas and Mariya. She needed to see what Mariya felt with that meteorite. And she needed to keep training. She'd already missed two morning lessons with Adi. But as she sank into the sofa in her and Jin's sitting room, Astrea couldn't make herself get up.

Nobody else seemed keen on moving, either. Cressida plopped down on Astrea's right, Eliana on her left. Adi dropped into a chair across from them as Nicos fiddled with the door's lock. Jin opened his knapsack and pulled out the partially torn envelope.

"What's that?" Eliana asked.

"We found this in the Paragon leader's desk," Jin said, "wedged under a drawer. The full name was ripped off, but it could be my mother's surname."

"It was hidden?" Nicos asked as he stopped near the edge of the sitting area.

"Seems more likely that it fell and got stuck," Jin said. "I don't think anyone would try to hide it there. It almost didn't come out in one piece."

"What's it say?" Eliana asked.

"He hasn't even opened it," Cressida said.

Rolling her eyes, Eliana leaned around Astrea. "I know. I want him to open it."

The top of the envelope had already been torn open, likely some time ago. Jin pulled out the letter inside; it was several pages thick. The paper unfolded with a creak. As Jin began to read, wariness prickled Astrea's skin. A whisper of confusion followed, then dark green concern blossomed in his aura.

"Jin?" Astrea asked.

He blinked rapidly as he moved on to the next page, then the next. Dark gray hate bled into that green, overwhelming and making it impossible for Astrea to breathe.

"Jin?" Eliana asked. "What is it?"

With a heavy sigh, Jin tossed the letter onto the table. "Well, it's definitely about my family."

"What did it say?"

"Just read it, Ellie." Jin crossed his arms over his chest and stalked toward the fireplace.

Eliana reached for the letter, her short fingers leaving slight indentations as she gripped the old paper. Astrea read over her shoulder, skimming the pages as quickly as she could. As far as Astrea could tell, it was a personal letter, mostly about Novarian court gossip and business dealings. It was signed off by Lord Tanel Seviya.

"It seems irrelevant," Eliana said as she passed the papers to Cressida.

"Finding that in the Paragon's hideout is irrelevant?" Jin asked.

"No, I mean the *contents* seem irrelevant," Eliana said. "Why would the Paragon have a letter from your grandfather?"

Why, indeed, would The One have that letter? Astrea combed through her memories of those five days she'd spent with the Paragon. The One had mentioned Astrea's family. Had called Jin the Sunreaper. Had shown Astrea visions of everyone she'd ever loved. But he'd never, ever brought up Jin's family aside from the emperor, at least that Astrea could remember. Unless . . .

"Wait," Astrea barely whispered. Jin's gaze tracked right to hers. "Was your mother an only child?"

"Yes," Jin said. "Why?"

"The portrait."

"What?" he asked as confusion swept through the room like a breeze.

"The portrait in the hallway," Astrea said. "The family portrait. It was a daughter and her parents." That portrait had seemed familiar to Astrea somehow. She'd thought it was just the drugs warping her mind, but . . . "I think that was your mother's house."

Jin studied her as the others passed the letter back and forth. His wall had returned, heavy and all too familiar. "Can you describe it?" he asked. "I didn't really look at the pictures."

"The girl was maybe ten years old," Astrea said, trying to pull forth the image in her mind's eye. "She had a round face and loose curls. Her hair and eyes were both brown. She looked more like her mother. The father had paler skin and darker hair."

Jin's jaw muscles flexed, then loosened, then flexed again. "My mother had brown eyes."

"Lots of people have brown eyes," Eliana said, gesturing to both Adi and Nicos.

"Come on, El," Nicos said. He was the last to look at the letter, but his mouth was set in a thin line. "Jin's right. There's no way this is a coincidence."

"I was just trying to make him feel better," she muttered. "Of course it's connected."

"If I'd realized sooner—" Astrea started, but Jin shook his head.

"How could you have known what my mother looked like?" he asked. "I mean, I barely remember what she looks like after all this time."

"Nor do I," Eliana said. "Not that I ever saw much of her."

"Alright." Jin crossed the room to join them again, then squatted next to the coffee table. "So, if the Paragon were using my mother's childhood home as their hideout, is my family connected to the Paragon?" he asked. "Or is this just some kind of strange, sick joke the Paragon set up in case I ever went there? They've been trying to confuse Az . . . Maybe they're trying to confuse me?"

The Paragon may have been trying to confuse Astrea when she was their prisoner, but what would it accomplish if they played with Jin now? The Paragon couldn't even be sure he'd go to that house and find that letter.

"Or get Ysabel to turn on you if her people found it," Nicos said. "Maybe trying to break up our alliance."

"*If* her people found it," Cressida said. "And they didn't."

"They searched that house thoroughly." Nicos scratched his beard. "So why didn't they find it?"

"Why would the Novarians hide it?" she countered. "It wouldn't make sense to do so. And if the Paragon really did decide to conceal it in that desk . . . well, it's a piss poor plan if you ask me. Wouldn't it be easier to implicate Jin another way? Something more direct?"

Adi shook his head. "As if the Paragon are ever direct."

"I think Cress is right," Jin said. "It seems most like an oversight, just something that got missed."

"So it has to be one of the first two options," Astrea said, and Jin nodded.

"Surely Ysabel knows where her own cousin lived," Adi said. "Why is this only coming up now?"

"But why would she hide that?" Cressida asked. "She's been honest about everything so far."

"As far as we're aware," Nicos said. "We have no idea if she's actually been transparent."

Astrea plucked at the thick fabric of her black pants. No, they had no idea if Ysabel had been honest. Why would she hide Jin's family connection to the void if she knew about it, though? What could she possibly gain by withholding that information? Ysabel had spent weeks talking about building family connections and a future between Novaria and Helosia. Lying about this would just destroy the relationships she'd built with Jin and Eliana.

"Are we safe here?" Astrea asked. "Is Ysabel somehow—"

"I don't think Ysabel's connected to the Paragon," Eliana said quickly. "Truly. But I can't say whether or not she would've hidden the knowledge that the house had once belonged to your family, Jin."

Cressida pressed her lips into a thin line. "So, what, do we go confront her?"

"No." Jin's answer was quick, sharp. "No. I don't want her to know that we know something is wrong."

"But shouldn't we—" Cressida started.

"I'd just like a little time to figure out if Ysabel knew," he said. "Then I'll bring the information to Lucian. I trust him."

Trusting Lucian and liking him were different things, Astrea supposed. She trusted the commander, too, despite their differences.

"How much time?" Eliana asked.

"A couple of days," Jin said. "If I can't learn anything in that time, I'll go to the commander."

"And until then?" Nicos asked.

"We do whatever it is that keeps up appearances. Just lay low and do whatever it is that you normally do around here."

CHAPTER 13

Sitting around sipping coffee used to be Astrea's favorite way to start her mornings. Now, she fidgeted with the cup she held, barely taking a single sip as she watched Jin walk around their room, still preparing for the day.

After what had happened at that void house the morning before, Astrea had spent most of the remainder of the day resting. She'd spent some of that time with Eliana and Cressida; both eventually had to leave to do other things. Eliana, Ysabel, and Zephyrine had convinced the Novarian council to at least declare war on the Paragon privately, though they had yet to back Eliana. Cressida had gone to start testing the new samples with Mariya. Once they'd left, Astrea and Jin had fallen asleep and slept through dinner.

"Do you want something to eat?" Astrea asked Jin when he strode out of the bathroom. A tray laden with extra coffee and pastries sat on the end of the bed. She had yet to touch them. "One of the guards brought this."

The top few buttons of Jin's white shirt were still undone, revealing his tan chest and the gold chain she'd first seen him wear in Kalama. It was almost a strange sight. In the weeks they'd been at the base, he'd rarely worn anything other than his fatigues.

"I'd love some coffee." He sat down on his side of the bed and reached for the tray. As he began pouring the steaming liquid into a mug, Jin continued, "I need your help with something today."

"Sure. What is it?"

When Jin offered her one of the flaky raspberry turnovers from the tray, Astrea took it grudgingly. She knew she had to eat. She just had no appetite. Still, she took a bite and tried to savor the sweet, sugary filling.

"I want to talk to Tomas today and find records about my mother's family," he said. "It could be a dead end, but I want to learn what I can before I go to Ysabel or my cousins."

"Didn't she tell us your mother's parents were exiled from court?" Astrea asked, racking her mind for the conversation that had happened just weeks ago. It felt like a lifetime. "Would they have the records of an exiled family?"

"Maybe. I don't know, honestly. But Tomas likes you, and you know how to find information."

Astrea shrugged one shoulder and sipped her coffee. She'd been good at finding information once upon a time. Now, all she seemed to do was fail. She wasn't a very good detective, not when it came to the Paragon.

"I'll help ... I just don't know if I'll be able to actually find what you're looking for."

"It's worth a try, right?"

"Right." There wasn't much else Astrea could do that day, anyway, while they waited for Ysabel, Lucian, and Nazarov. Training didn't appeal to her, nor did watching Mariya and Cressida experiment with meteorite. "When do you want to go?"

"Let's finish breakfast." Swiping a pastry for himself, Jin stood and carried both his food and coffee to the narrow writing desk tucked in one corner of the bedroom. "Can't believe we slept for so long."

"Well, we haven't exactly been resting."

"No, I suppose not," Jin said. "And I suppose we should."

It just felt impossible to rest when they were so close to everything they needed. Astrea nibbled on her turnover, letting the tart raspberry jam explode in her mouth. She used to love that. Now, she rarely found pleasure in much of anything. She rarely felt anything other than grief, anger, or fear. She wanted to be happy. She wanted to enjoy things. But that seemed as impossible as rest.

Goose bumps prickled Astrea's skin. Nazarov had only given Astrea one day to mull over his proposition. She had no idea when he was going to contact her again. He'd always had the ability to just show up in her mind, she supposed, but knowing it was coming was almost worse. Why hadn't he been more specific? Why wouldn't he want her to be prepared for the meeting *he* asked for?

Jin's hand on her knee made Astrea's attention snap back to the room. He sat next to her on the bed. Yellow worry pulsed around him in quick, sharp beats.

"I'm fine," she said quickly.

"You're doing that a lot lately."

"Doing what?"

"Retreating. Getting unfocused."

She shrugged. What was she going to do, lie to Jin? Of course she'd been unfocused. Retreating into her own mind. Getting lost.

"That happened to me a lot after Ilesouria," he said gently. "It's not unusual. I've seen it in so many soldiers—"

"I'm alright," she said again. "I can keep working on this."

"I know you can, Az. I'm just worried about you." He nodded at the pastry still in her hand. "You haven't been eating much."

"Just haven't been hungry."

"And the nightmares?"

She shrugged again.

"What can I do?" he asked. Pleaded. That yellow vibrated around his frame, joined by deep blue regret. "I've been there, Az. I know what it feels like."

"I just need a distraction," Astrea whispered. "Maybe I'll go back to training."

"And I've been there, too." His words were so, so gentle. "Training because at least it's something to focus on rather than what hurts."

Astrea shrugged a third time. That was part of why she'd thrown herself into training the last few weeks, but more than that, she wanted to be prepared. Had to be for what was surely coming next.

Jin's hand found hers. "Distractions don't help you heal. It's like wrapping a bandage around a gushing wound . . . it's just not enough, even if it soaks up some of the blood."

Maybe it wouldn't heal her wounds, but Astrea didn't know what else to do. How did she heal from what had happened? How did she fix any of it?

"We should go," Astrea said.

Pressing his lips together, Jin watched her. Sure he was going to force the issue, Astrea braced herself.

"Alright," he finally said. "Let's see what Tomas has to say."

As soon as Jin stepped out of their room, a familiar feminine voice called out, "Oh, perfect! I was hoping to see you."

Peeking around his wide shoulders, Astrea found Eliana and Nicos loitering in the hall. The Novarian guards behind them watched on in silence.

"Just going to the library, Ellie," Jin said.

"Perfect," she said, "because I need to get out."

"We'll be fine—"

"Whatever it is you're looking for"—Eliana pinned both Jin and Astrea with a look—"I'd be happy to help. I insist."

That was the end of that. As the four of them headed through the palace, Eliana chatted with Jin, updating him on small, insignificant news. Nicos chimed in occasionally. Astrea barely heard any of it. Her body buzzed, not with excitement but dread. She forced herself to take a deep breath.

The professor isn't here. Another deep breath. *Tomas is our friend.* Another. *There are dozens of guards and soldiers nearby. And no voids.*

Pushing her shoulders back, Astrea followed her friends into the library. Its deep blue walls, dark wood floors, and mezzanine were exactly as they had been. There was no sign of Professor Kostas Shalysko anywhere.

"Oh!" Tomas exclaimed as he strolled out from one of the aisles. "Your Highnesses . . ."

"Hi, Tomas." Eliana flashed him a cheeky smile. "Busy?"

"Not for you, Your Imperial Highness." Tomas ambled to a nearby table and set down the armful of books he was carrying. "What can I do for you? I still haven't found any actual references to the Paragon. If they called themselves by that name in the past, it's been scrubbed from the history books. I'm trying to find some potential alternative they may have used, but . . ."

"Not here about that, actually." Jin tucked his hands in his pockets. With his slacks, wingtip shoes, and button-up shirt, Jin actually looked like a civilian for once. And it was a good look for him. "I was hoping to find out a little more about the Seviya family, actually."

"The Seviya family?" Tomas echoed, gray confusion bursting around him. "I haven't heard that name in . . . well, in a very long time."

Jin shared a look with Eliana. Then he leaned toward the librarian and murmured, "I don't know if Ysabel told you, but my mother was a Seviya."

Shock rippled out from Tomas, cold and sharp. Astrea took half a step back.

"Truly?" Tomas barely whispered. When Jin nodded, the librarian continued, "No, she didn't tell me."

"I don't know who is allowed to know," Jin said, "but I just wanted to learn a little more about where she came from. Where I came from. She died when I was quite young."

Tomas's expression softened. "Of course."

"And you'll keep this between us?" Eliana asked.

"Of course, Your Imperial Highness," Tomas said quickly. "Of course. Now, let's see . . . what exactly do you want to know?"

"Do you have any of their family records?" Jin asked as Tomas began scanning the aisles. "Maybe personal documents of some kind?"

"Certainly not in here. Although . . . I believe we may have some downstairs." The librarian gestured back to the books on the table and said, "I was trying to find more about the Paragon, but if you need me to stop . . ."

"That's alright," Astrea cut in. "If you show us where we need to go, I'm sure I can figure out where things are."

"Very well." After pushing up his glasses, Tomas motioned for the four of them to follow him.

He led them to the opposite end of the library, past the circular staircase he always ran up to get to his office, and to a narrow, unassuming door tucked behind it. Its dark trim and blue paint blended in with the walls, rendering it almost unnoticeable.

Tomas produced a small key ring from the pocket of his waistcoat, then unlocked the door. Once inside, he flicked on a light switch, and low, warm lights buzzed to life overhead. A cold draft prickled Astrea's arms as they started down the narrow hallway that turned into a set of narrow stone stairs.

"Here we are," Tomas said as they reached the bottom. Unlike the library back in Kalama, this basement had a low ceiling, old stone walls, and dust. So much dust. Jin sneezed. "Though it's a bit of a mess, as you can see. I've been meaning to organize things better."

Alcoves set within the walls at even spacing held long stone shelves packed to the brim with folios and books of every size imaginable. Astrea scanned the room. There seemed to be no filing system. *Wonderful.*

"And these are all . . . records?" she asked as she stepped forward.

"Indeed," Tomas said. He headed for one side of the room, and Astrea followed. "If you're looking for Seviya, it should be somewhere over here. The grand duchess likes me to keep family documents in that section"—he gestured to their right—"but obviously didn't want . . . *that . . .* mixed up with official documentation."

"Are these documents only about family?" Jin asked as he stepped up next to Astrea. "All of them?"

"Oh, no, no." Motioning to the wall behind them, Tomas said, "No, there are lots of things we keep down here. Old editions, books that need to be repaired, old family documents. Nothing too crucial and certainly nothing confidential."

"I should hope not," Eliana whispered.

Jin crossed his arms over his chest. "Do you know anything about the Seviyas? I only know what Ysabel told me."

Tomas fiddled with the keys still in his hand. "Well, Your Highness . . . nobody knows much about them. Most of that happened before my time. I'd just started my apprenticeship here when I heard that Lord Tanel Seviya had passed."

"And that was how long ago?" Jin asked.

"Oh . . . nearly three decades."

"You've been here that long?" Eliana asked.

Tomas chuckled and rubbed the back of his neck. "I started early, Your Imperial Highness. Just fifteen when I began learning the ropes here, and I of course took time off when I went to university. My aunt had been the palace librarian before me."

Eliana nodded, watching as Nicos examined a shelf filled with thick tomes that reminded Astrea of the encyclopedias in Raela's office back home.

"Well, thank you, Tomas," Jin said. "I appreciate your discretion."

"Of course, Your Highness. Family secrets often leave us with so many questions, don't they? In fact, in my family, my great-grandmother was . . ." Tomas chuckled awkwardly. "Well, let's just say my great-grandfather and her children didn't appreciate some of the confusion . . . though it all got sorted in the end."

"Oh," Eliana murmured, eyebrows raised.

"If I can aid you in your search for answers, I'm happy to help. Now, if you need me," Tomas continued, "I'll be upstairs. I'm trying to find a few things for Mariya."

"We'll be here!" Jin called as Tomas headed back up. After a few moments, the door at the top of the stairs clicked shut, and Jin turned to Astrea. "So . . . where do we begin?"

Astrea looked at the alcove Tomas had suggested as their starting point. Books, journals, and folios lined the shelves, some of them even left in stacks on the ground. "We start here."

A shiver danced down Astrea's spine as she sifted through another stack of folders. So far, they'd found information about other Novarian noble families. The Reminlos, Sarfova, and Yaneva families all seemed prominent; some had even married cousins of the grand ducal family. They'd also found information on the Kanirva family; Sinni Kanirva was one of the members of Ysabel's council.

Astrea shivered again as cold air bit into her skin. Just an hour down here and she was freezing.

"You good?" Eliana asked as she joined Astrea.

"Just cold." Astrea really wished she'd thought to put a sweater over her dress. The Great Library's basement back home was never so chilly. "Did you find anything?"

"No. I put that stuff in my 'irrelevant' pile. Anything else for me to look through?"

Astrea nudged a stack of folders toward her.

Jin, who had long since sat on the floor on the opposite side of the room, sneezed as paper rustled. "Could there be any more dust?" he muttered. "Or could they have cleaned up down here every now and again?"

"Doesn't seem like they use it much," Nicos said. "Some of this stuff is almost a hundred years old. I mean, why keep letters from so long ago?"

"You'd be surprised what gets archived," Eliana replied as she lifted her next stack and carried it off. "We have so much of this back home, too. I can't think of the last time anyone went through it."

It hardly seemed like a proper archive to Astrea, but maybe keeping up with it had just never been a priority, especially if it wasn't "crucial" or "confidential," as Tomas had said.

With the four of them working together, they were nearly through the first half of the section Tomas had guided them to. Astrea had just one more pile to sort, then they could move on. She picked up the folios and journals, then carried them to where Jin, Nicos, and Eliana had sat in a loose circle on the floor.

It was mostly boring work. She'd never realized how mundane the lives of nobility could be, but they were just like everyone else, just with more money and influence. Letters detailed affairs, divorces, birth announcements, business dealings. None of it seemed worth keeping, just as Nicos had said.

She'd just started on a letter from four decades prior when Jin let out a sharp breath. Astrea peeked over at him.

"Found something?" Eliana asked, not even looking up from the journal open in her lap.

"Yeah," Jin murmured as he scanned the page.

"Well?"

Jin went completely still beside Astrea. Hesitating, she set down the letter she'd been reading and faced him, watching as gray confusion and crimson rage battled around him.

"Jin?" she asked.

After sucking in a deep breath, Jin read aloud, "Caliste does not yet understand what it is we're trying to teach her. She will have to learn if she wants to make this family proud someday."

Astrea frowned. That didn't exactly sound like a supportive environment for a child.

"The Seviya line has been unappreciated for centuries. When she finally comes of age, she will realize her true purpose," Jin continued. "I have not yet shown her what belongs to her, what is her right as a descendant of the great Seviyas. If she does not understand these lessons, then she is not ready. But she cannot have forever to learn. The time is coming for us to reclaim our place."

"Who wrote that?" Eliana asked.

Jin's golden eyes hardened. "My grandfather."

What lessons had the Seviya parents been trying to teach Caliste? As far as Astrea knew, Jin's mother hadn't been a mage. That's what Ysabel and Jin's cousins had claimed, at least.

"Though I take her to the basement once a week, Caliste shows no sign of understanding," Jin continued reading. "It is disappointing to have such a useless offspring, but perhaps as she grows older, she will find a way to make this work." Sighing, he rubbed his temples. "He almost sounds worse than my father."

"I'm sorry," Astrea said. What else was there to say? Jin had told her once that nothing about his family truly surprised him anymore, that he'd seen it all growing up at the Kalamian palace. But had some small part of him, despite finding that letter at the Paragon's hideout, still hoped that his mother's family wasn't entirely awful?

"It's alright," Jin said. "They're all gone anyway. Whatever he was trying to teach her is more important than my feelings on something that happened four decades ago."

Was it, though? Yes, they needed to understand what was going on with the Seviya family, but Jin's feelings still mattered.

"I'd be upset if I were you," Astrea said. "It must be hard to read that."

"Is there anything else?" Eliana asked.

Jin flipped through a few pages of the journal. "It mostly discusses business dealings and his desire for the Novarian court to welcome his family again. Nothing that points to the Paragon or anything else."

Astrea bit her lower lip. "What was the Seviyan descendants right?" she asked. "And the true purpose for your mother?"

Nicos ran a hand through his hair, which was uncharacteristically loose around his shoulders. "Would the grand duchess know what this means? Maybe we need to ask her."

"I'd like to keep looking for anything else we can find before we approach her," Jin said. "Surely there's more."

Astrea looked back at the piles of documents still tucked in the alcove. There was plenty more for them to look through before the day was over, but she couldn't help but wonder if they'd get through it before Nazarov dreamwalked to her again. He'd promised her one day, so he'd have to be reaching out to her soon, and they still hadn't heard from Commander Lucian.

"I'll start sorting the rest," Astrea offered as she stood. "I'll bring it over to you when it's ready."

"Thanks, Az," Eliana said, already burying her nose in another letter.

Astrea went back to the untouched documents and put her hands on her hips. If there were answers for Jin, she was going to find them.

Chapter 14

There was just one thing Astrea was certain about: Grand Duchess Ysabel had to be frustrated with their group. That much had been obvious the night they'd returned from the old base, and it was becoming clearer the longer Lucian didn't show up at their door with an answer about their plan. What solidified it, though, was the fact that they hadn't been invited to dinner. Eliana *had* been invited to dine with the grand duchess, but the rest of them had not.

Now, Astrea sat curled up on her and Jin's bed as she leafed through a diary they'd found earlier that afternoon in the basement. It was one of the few items belonging to Jin's grandfather, Lord Tanel Seviya. Based on what was in the book, he didn't seem to be a particularly attached father or husband. Most of his notes on the first two dozen pages were about business affairs. Then there were the sections on minor court gossip and drama from decades prior—certainly more interesting than numbers. There were also some entries about personal travels, especially between his old estate and the Novarian capital.

And then there were the musings about young Caliste's tutoring and lack of magic.

Reading those felt like an invasion of the family's privacy. Lord Seviya always circled back to Caliste having some "purpose" to fulfill. He always circled back to familial pride and responsibility. It was a lot to put on anyone's shoulders but especially a child. He actually didn't sound that different than Emperor Aelius; he was always going on about Eliana's duty to the empire and Auris dynasty.

"So?" Jin asked from beside her. "What do you think?"

Astrea traced the slanted, slightly faded handwriting with her eyes. "I think . . ." She sighed. "I don't know what to think. It seems like he was an ass."

Jin smirked. "Besides that?"

They'd been trying to determine with absolute certainty whether or not Tanel Seviya had been connected to the Paragon. There'd been no hard evidence to support that, but . . .

"I really think it's unlikely the Paragon were just trying to create the illusion of a connection."

"Me too."

"So what do we do?"

"We tell the others," Jin said, "and then we ask Ysabel what she knows. Maybe she doesn't know they're connected, but maybe she can tell us more about them."

"She doesn't seem that keen on helping lately," Astrea muttered as she finally closed the diary and handed it back to Jin.

"Maybe not, but I have a feeling she's just anxious about having us back in the capital. I would be in her position."

"Then she should tell us to go away."

Astrea flopped back against her pillows. Though Ysabel hadn't invited them to dine with her, Astrea was almost relieved. She didn't think she could handle sitting in a dining room and pretending to care about formal manners.

The mattress shifted, then Jin draped his arm over Astrea's waist and laid his head near hers. He'd just started to ask her a question when a loud knock sounded on the door.

"That's probably dinner," he said with a sigh. "I'll get it."

As Jin crawled out of bed, Astrea forced herself to sit up. She needed to eat, yes, but she also needed to find Lucian and figure out what she was supposed to tell Nazarov.

"Hey, Az!" Cressida's voice drifted from the sitting room into the bedroom. "Dinner!"

Astrea climbed out of bed and smoothed the front of her dress before heading for the sitting room. There, she found not just Jin and Cressida but Adi, Lennor, Civan, and Zephyrine. *Unexpected.* A cart laden with covered dishes and carafes of water and wine waited near the door.

"Thought we'd get the outcasts together for dinner," Adi said as Cressida shuffled back toward the cart and began peeking under the lids.

"I'd hardly call us outcasts, Adi," Jin replied.

"Oh, excuse me," Adi said. "I thought those of us who were not invited to grace the grand duchess with our presence might spend the evening together."

Though Jin rolled his eyes, the corners of his mouth pulled up. Astrea was going to offer Cressida help, but Lennor had wandered over, green curiosity floating around her like mist. So, Astrea hung back, instead taking a seat on the sofa.

The sitting room could fit them all, but the coffee table wasn't large enough to accommodate all of the dishware and drinks. Eventually, they got sorted and all held their plates on their laps. The meals were identical, with crispy roasted potatoes, grilled red meat, and a variety of other vegetables on the plate. There was even fresh bread, still steaming as Cressida sliced it open.

"Not bad for not getting invited to the dining room," Adi said around his mouthful of potatoes.

"Well, I'm certainly fine with no invitation," Cressida said. She'd claimed the spot on the sofa next to Astrea, and Jin was on the floor next to Astrea's feet. "I've got to tell you, aside from Ellie, I am *not* cut out to deal with royalty all the time. So much tiptoeing, and for what? I haven't been able to relax at dinner in weeks."

"What about Jin?" Adi asked.

Cressida waved her potato-laden fork in the air. "Yeah, he's fine."

"'Fine' . . . what an honor,'" Jin murmured.

Amusement rolled off Cressida, and Lennor ducked her head as she laughed.

Astrea stabbed one of the potatoes with her fork. Garlic and parsley exploded on her tongue, rich and savory. As they ate, Jin updated his team on what they learned from his grandfather's journal, and Cressida shared that there was no news on the meteorite samples yet, though Mariya had confirmed all three samples felt off to her Stargazer magic. Zephyrine had no news from Helosia.

As their conversation shifted, Astrea couldn't help but notice the curiosity now flickering between Cressida and Lennor, almost like their emotions were twining together. Every time Cressida made a joke or sarcastic remark, Lennor giggled, which just made warm satisfaction roll off Cressida. Sitting next to the interaction was actually pleasant.

"So, Astrea," Zephyrine said, abruptly cutting off whatever Adi had been about to say. "Have you heard from—"

"No," Astrea said quickly. "No, nothing yet."

"Hm." Zephyrine's small nose wrinkled. "It's technically been longer than a day, hasn't it?"

"Technically," Astrea agreed. That worried her. She certainly didn't relish the thought of talking to Victor Nazarov ever again, but if there was a chance he had information, they needed to get it from him.

And the sooner they could get that information, the better.

"And no word from the grand duchess or the commander?" Zephyrine asked.

"None," Jin said. "I was going to go find him after this if he still hasn't shown up with news."

"What if Nazarov contacts me before then?" Astrea asked.

"Tell him you need more time," Zephyrine said.

"He's not going to like that." Astrea swallowed hard. The last time she'd dared to defy Nazarov, he'd burned her and stabbed her in the shoulder. Threatened to kill her. She needed a plan. "Where should I ask to meet him? I know the palace is off limits."

"Someplace public," Cressida said.

"Even if the Novarians aren't invited as a condition of this meeting," Zephyrine said, "I think it would be wise to choose someplace where they'll have easy access, in case something goes wrong."

"You don't think we could sneak some of them in?" Astrea asked.

Zephyrine shrugged one slender shoulder. "It's impossible to know which guards Nazarov would recognize. But if he didn't say Helosians are off limits, then we'll all go with you. Excluding Eliana, of course."

"Alright." Astrea had known Jin was going with her, but to have confirmation that his whole team would be there made her feel marginally better. "Thank you, General."

"Please, just call me Zephyrine." Her lips quirked up into a smile as she added, "Skies knows the rest of this bunch never bothered with such formalities. Neither should you."

"We never even served under you!" Lennor protested. "And you told us not to use your title."

"Pretty sure titles would get us kicked off the team," Adi quipped.

"So would calling her Zeph," Jin added.

"Such disrespect, kid."

Even Astrea had to smile at that. Jin hated when Zephyrine called him that, but now, he grinned.

"Let's just get this cleaned up so Az and I can go track down Lucian," Jin said. "I'll let you know what he says and when we're going to meet Nazarov."

As his team echoed their agreement, Astrea helped Cressida gather up some of the plates and glasses. They brought them back to the cart, piling the items carefully to give to one of the staff surely lurking outside.

"So," Cressida whispered, "Lennor's nice."

"You really want to talk about this now?" Astrea asked.

"Yes. Although that's all I really have to say."

Astrea peeked over her shoulder. Lennor punched Adi in the shoulder as they both laughed. "If you like her, just talk to her more. What have you got to lose?"

"I didn't say I like her."

"You like her enough. And she's curious about you," Astrea said. Maybe it was a complete invasion of privacy, but what good was it to be a Lightbringer if she couldn't use it to play wing woman? She'd done it for Cressida before. Besides, it was better than thinking about everything else. "See if she wants to spar with you tomorrow."

"Now there's an idea."

Cressida finished rearranging some of the dishes, then sauntered over to where Lennor and Adi were still joking around. Civan slipped out the door without so much as a goodbye, and Zephyrine followed not long after. Jin joined Astrea just as Cressida made the sparring suggestion to Lennor, whose small, heart-shaped face lit up with a brilliant smile.

"What's that about?" Jin asked as he slung his arm around Astrea's shoulders.

"Nothing."

"Hm." He tugged her closer, and she wrapped her arm around his waist. "Well, shall we go find the commander?"

Commander Lucian was in none of the expected spots in the chilly palace. Jin and Astrea checked the guard house, the throne room, and even asked several of the guards stationed around if they'd seen their commander. It wasn't until they asked a fifth guard that they got their answer.

"I saw him going to the grand duchess's private dining room not long ago, Your Imperial Highness," the young guard said to Jin. They looked younger than even Astrea and Jin, fresh-faced and wide-eyed as they spoke to *the* Helosian prince. "Would you like me to escort you?"

"That's alright, we know the way," Jin said. "Thank you."

The young guard sketched a quick bow, and Jin's shoulders barely tightened as he nodded at them. Then he turned and headed back the way they'd just came, Astrea right beside him.

"Do you think he went to find Ysabel?" Astrea asked as they turned down a different corridor, grateful Jin seemed to know the way. Everything looked the same in this part of the palace.

"Probably. Hopefully Ysabel doesn't mind us crashing her little dinner party."

"And if she does?"

"Then she'll just have to deal with it," Jin said, nodding to the pair of guards walking toward them.

Three more hallways, and finally, they were at the dining room doors Astrea recognized from weeks before. Not the night they'd dined with the entire council but the night they'd dined with just Ysabel and her heirs, Crown Prince Veiko and Princess Delfine. As they reached the doors, the one on the right opened. Out strolled the very man they were searching for, and behind him came Eliana and Nicos.

"Varojin," Lucian said, the word stiff and awkward. "You're here."

"Looking for you," Jin said.

"I was just going to escort your sister upstairs."

With Nicos right there? Astrea thought, offering the freckled Helosian a tight-lipped smile when he met her gaze.

"Astrea and I need to talk to you," Jin said.

Eliana glanced over her shoulder at the closed dining room door. "We should all talk, Commander."

"Very well. Let's go to my office."

All that just to walk somewhere else, Astrea thought ruefully as they began crisscrossing the palace hallways again. By the time they stopped, they were in a cozy part of the guard house. Warm lights shone from the ceiling, highlighting the smooth wood floors and thick runner lining the hallway.

Lucian unlocked and opened a door, revealing a spacious office inside. The commander's office was tidy, with few personal items and many maps of Talmaris and Novaria hanging on the walls. A sturdy desk sat opposite the door. There were two chairs in front of it, which Nicos and Jin insisted Eliana and Astrea sit in.

"So," Lucian said once he was settled behind his desk, "what did you want to speak about, Varojin?"

"You know why we're here," Jin said. "What did Ysabel say about taking Nazarov up on his offer?"

"She thinks you've lost your skies damned minds," Lucian said. "But she's agreed to stay out of your way if it's what you want to do."

"And you'll help us?" Jin asked.

"I will."

"I assume you'll be providing security," Eliana said. "I know my brother's team is strong, but I don't feel comfortable letting them go without backup."

"We already talked about—" Darkness surged around Astrea, disorienting and all-consuming. It sounded like she was underwater, but she swore she heard Eliana calling both her and Jin's names.

Sunreaper, Nazarov purred. Astrea gripped the edge of her chair as she prepared for a vision, but nothing replaced that impenetrable shadow. *And my favorite little Lightbringer. Have you thought about my proposal?*

Yes— she started, but he cut her off.

No Novarians, remember? Nazarov asked.

No Novarians, Jin agreed, voice strained. *Where did you want to meet? It has to be someplace public.*

Nazarov clicked his tongue, then said, *Scared of what I'll do if I'm left alone with Miss Sovna again?*

Shut up, Nazarov.

We could meet at one of the parks in the city, Astrea said despite the way her pulse jumped. *If you're near Talmaris.*

Not a park, Nazarov replied. A vision took hold. Talmaris, based on the sweeping, antique architecture and skyline in the background. In front of them, a glittering building rose up into the twilight. A crowd dressed in dark, expensive clothing filtered inside several sets of doors. *Here.*

Where is that? Jin asked.

Club Twilight, downtown Talmaris, Nazarov said. *Three nights from now. We'll talk. No Novarians, or the deal's off.*

Before Astrea or Jin could say anything, the image and darkness fell away. Lucian's warm office replaced it, as did the commander's concerned face and Eliana and Nicos's wildly jumping emotions.

"Was that him?" Eliana asked.

"Yes." Jin blew out a harsh breath as he glanced at Astrea. She blinked past the tears forming at her lash line, though whether it was from the sound of Nazarov's voice or the pain lingering in her sternum, she wasn't sure. "Meeting's all set."

"Where?" Lucian asked.

"Club Twilight, three nights from now," Astrea said.

"Club Twilight?" Lucian echoed.

"You know the place?" Nicos asked.

"Yes." Lucian unlocked a drawer on his desk and pulled out a notepad. "I'll start drawing up plans immediately."

"I can help," Nicos offered.

"I'd appreciate it. First thing in the morning, we can start going over everything," Lucian said. He looked to Astrea and Jin next. "Anything else?"

Jin shook his head. "He just reiterated that no Novarians are allowed. So those plans better not include any of you in the club with us."

"They won't," Lucian said. "We'll do what we must to get this information."

Darkness pulsed around her. The shadows stretched and elongated as they reached for her.

"They will not keep you safe, little Lightbringer."

She ran. She ran and ran and ran through endless darkness.

"No one can run from the Paragon." Red eyes flashed in front of her as a knife plunged into her sternum. Hot blood gushed down her chest. "Not even the sun and moon."

Astrea woke with a start, chest heaving as she pulled at the buttons keeping her shirt closed. Her fingers brushed her bare skin, finding nothing there. No knives. No blood. Nothing.

Next to her, Jin stirred. His eyebrows furrowed as his lips formed a pout. But he settled again, his breaths slow and even.

Astrea pushed back the blankets and crept out of bed. Her bare feet hardly made a noise on the plush rug or even on the tiles in the bathroom. She closed the bathroom door, leaving it open just enough that the soft lamplight filtered in through the crack.

"Breathe," she whispered as she padded toward the sink. "Breathe."

She couldn't breathe.

Since she'd heard Nazarov's voice earlier that night, she hadn't been able to breathe at all. Astrea just wanted it to stop. Just one night. She didn't remember her dreams every night, but she always woke up disoriented, exhausted, on edge.

Just one night. Was that so much to ask?

Leaning against the counter, Astrea closed her eyes, trying to ignore the overbearing number of people just on the other side of the wall. She didn't dare pull her magic in toward herself too closely.

What would Saros think if he knew this was going on? What would Sarsali and Balthazar have to say? Did they have any idea what she and Cressida had gotten themselves into? Surely not, and maybe that was for the best. Balthazar would be worried sick. He'd always been the Nikaphoros parent most worried about them. And Saros, well . . .

She splashed cool water on her face, then dried her skin with a washcloth. There was no use thinking about her family. All it did was make her heart hurt even more than it already did.

Taking one more deep breath, Astrea shook out her arms and crept back to the bathroom door. Jin hadn't moved in the few minutes she'd been out of bed. She slid back in next to him as gently as she could. As she burrowed down into the blankets, he scooted closer and draped one arm over her waist.

"You're doing that a lot, too," he whispered, voice heavy with sleep.

"What?"

"Getting up at night. Not just losing focus during the day."

"I'm sorry I woke you," she whispered. "Go back to sleep."

Jin pressed a kiss to her shoulder. Astrea grew dizzy as his worry drifted toward her, cold on her blazing hot cheeks. She rolled onto her side away from him, but when he tugged her back against his chest, she relaxed as much as she could.

Safe. She knew she was safe, at least for the moment. So why did it seem so hard to believe?

CHAPTER 15

Though decorated with many of the comforts Astrea had come to know of Grand Duchess Ysabel's palace, the war room was different. Maps of the continent lined the walls, and the long rectangular table could seat twenty. With no windows, several Novarian banners hanging from the ceiling, and even a suit of old armor on display in the corner, the atmosphere was more somber than the rest of the palace.

Thankfully, Jin hadn't tried to bring up Astrea's midnight trip to the bathroom at all. He had, however, held her close as soon as he'd woken up. Longer than he usually did. Astrea was fairly certain he'd thought her asleep, and she hadn't exactly let on that she was awake. She'd just tried to enjoy feeling close to him until the Novarians had eventually come knocking.

And now here they were, all the Helosians seated in the war room with Lucian and Marko. Coffee cups and floor plans for the nightclub were spread out across the long table.

"This place is bigger than I thought it would be," Eliana murmured as she examined some of the papers. "I mean, nothing in Kalama was quite this large, and Kalamians do love to gamble."

"The owners of Club Twilight only purchased the building a few years ago," Lucian said. "It was originally home to multiple shops and offices, but they redid the interior to make it one *large* club."

"I don't really care when they bought it," Jin said. "I care about the size. Four floors and able to accommodate, what, close to six hundred?"

"Give or take," Lucian said.

"How are seven of us supposed to patrol that size space?" Jin folded his arms over his chest. "I assume you can keep a fairly tight perimeter on the outside, Commander?"

"It depends on how much we want to risk upsetting Nazarov," Lucian said. "We can keep it as close as you'd like, but then we risk him spotting us."

"He'll see you anyway," Zephyrine said. "There's no way he's coming alone. And he'd be a fool to arrive before we did if he's serious about his conditions. He'll be watching from the outside."

Astrea sipped her coffee and stared at the floor plans. The drawings and labels were clear: the atrium on the first floor; markings for stairs, elevators, bars, and stages on the four floors; various sized rooms, some even indicating they were for private tables only. Jin was right. It was too much space.

"I might be able to feel the whole place," Astrea said, "but it's going to be a lot."

Lucian shook his head. "You won't be able to make sense of any of it. Don't push yourself when you don't have to."

Maybe he had a point. Trying to sift through hundreds of individual emotions and energies would overwhelm any mage.

"How do we know this isn't just a trap?" Nicos asked. "Who are the owners? Could they be connected to the Paragon?"

"The scouts I sent to the club last night searched the place top to bottom and found no sign of any void mages," Lucian said. "Nothing they could sense, nor anything else obviously connected to the Paragon. We're running down some leads on the club's owners."

"Because that worked so well for us last time," Nicos muttered.

It was a fair concern, Astrea supposed, but she still didn't see any other option.

Lucian didn't address Nicos's comment either. Instead, he said, "I'll station Lightbringers as close to the building as possible while you're inside. If Nazarov brings anyone, Astrea, who would it be?"

She kept her gaze trained on the plans. Curiosity, anxiety, regret—it all washed over her, an uncomfortable mix that made her skin itch. "A man named Tovan and a woman named Solana." Just saying their names made Astrea's breath catch in her chest. "Tovan isn't a void mage, but Solana is."

"Anyone else?" Marko asked.

"I'm not sure. But I know they were on Nazarov's side in whatever issue he has with The One. I saw them help him several times."

Help Nazarov torture her, for one. Help him after he stabbed The One, for another. And Astrea was fairly certain Solana was the mage who grabbed Astrea from the palace while Nazarov fought with Jin. But she wasn't going to get into specifics if she didn't have to.

"We'll assume he comes with more backup than that," Lucian said. "The grand duchess has given us access to whatever resources we need to pull this off."

"But no grand duchess herself," Eliana said dryly.

What made Ysabel so disinterested in—or distrustful of—the situation? Astrea couldn't understand it. Yes, it was a risk, but they couldn't keep playing it safe or waiting.

"No, but we'll handle it just fine," Lucian said. "I've got copies of the floor plans for your team, Varojin, so you can study them on your own time. I assume you've done something like this before?"

"Survived all kinds of missions," Jin said as he glanced at his team. "This one won't be any different. We know how to get an asset out of danger."

"Don't forget *you* are one of those assets," Eliana said. "They're not just interested in Az."

"I know. Believe me, I know." Jin's jaw tightened, then relaxed, before he turned toward Lucian. "Can you send those plans up to my room?"

Lucian nodded, then nodded again when Eliana asked for a set to be sent to her room as well.

"Are we done here?" Astrea asked. "I thought Adi and I might go train . . . if the grand duchess will still allow us to use the gardens."

"You may," Lucian said. "I think we're done for now, unless anyone else has any concerns." Around the table, everyone shook their heads. "Then I'll talk to you all soon."

Wind slapped Astrea's face, whipping her braid around and stinging her skin. She pulled on the energy pooling inside her to summon her shield of sparkling starlight. Lennor's wind no longer hit her body, now pummeling her shield instead. Astrea dug her heels into the grass, bracing herself.

"Hold it, Az!" Jin called from her right.

Astrea's arms shook with the effort of holding Lennor's wind at bay, and when Civan's water whips snapped out, Astrea barely pivoted in time to block them. Cressida hooted from the sidelines, and Lennor, distracted, let her wind falter.

Thank you, Astrea thought at her best friend. With Lennor distracted, Astrea let her shield drop. She pivoted out of reach of Civan's water. It didn't stop him. A long tendril snapped out, the cold water circling around Astrea's wrist. She dug her heels into the ground again, resisting the water as it tried pulling her forward.

Lavender surprise flickered around Lennor. It doubled when Astrea used her free hand to aim a compact ball of light at her. Lennor moved half a heartbeat too late. The light caught the edge of her arm, burning through her shirt. Ghost pain hit Astrea. She gritted her teeth.

Instinct told her to run to Lennor and heal her. But when Adi shouted something about sticking it out, Astrea pushed the need to heal away. The rules Adi and Jin had set for this exercise dictated that when one of the twins was hit by her magic, they had to sit out for the rest of the battle. It was just her and Civan now.

And his water was still wrapped around her wrist.

Astrea pulled on her light again. As soon as its heat neared the water, Civan's whip began to evaporate. She freed herself, but her victory was short-lived. More water wrapped around her ankles, then both wrists, as it flowed from the nearby lake into Civan's control.

She was done for.

As Civan's water dragged her to the ground, Astrea barely managed to turn and fall on her side instead of her face. Her breath left her chest in a whoosh, and she groaned as she rolled onto her back.

She'd never actually worked with Lennor or Civan before. In the weeks she'd been training with Lucian, Jin, and Adi, they'd never suggested she spar with the twins. She'd never worked with Marko, either.

Astrea pushed herself up as Cressida jogged over to her. She stuck her hand out, and Astrea grabbed it, pulling herself off the ground.

"That was pretty good!" Cressida exclaimed as Astrea brushed grass off the back of her pants. "It was a whole lot more than you could do a month ago."

"Knocked me flat on my ass a number of times before we came back to Talmaris," Adi said as he and Jin joined them.

"So I heard," Cressida teased.

A wry smile pulled at the corner of Astrea's mouth as she headed Lennor's way. "How about I heal Lennor first?"

"Oh, that's alright." Lennor inspected the hole in her shirt sleeve, wincing as she poked at her reddened skin. "It looks almost like a sunburn."

"Never been hit by a Lightbringer before?" Cressida asked.

A deep blush colored Lennor's tan cheeks. "Well—I mean, no . . ."

"It's not like I've ever hit you with it either, Cress," Astrea said as she nudged Lennor's hand to the side. "Please, let me," she said when Lennor hesitated. "It's good practice."

Only then did Lennor agree. Astrea pulled on her light, gentle and low this time. Her hand glowed as she laid it on top of Lennor's skin. Mirror healing and pain battled on Astrea's own arm, then dropped off into a low ache.

Lennor smiled, her shoulders sagging. "Thanks."

"Have you ever sparred with a Metalli?" Cressida asked. "I don't want to take you by surprise when we get out there."

"Some, back at Fort Ironwing." Lennor tucked a few loose hairs behind her ears. When she trained, she usually tied her hair back into two braids, and some of the shorter pieces always sprang free. Astrea had seen her do the same thing many times over the last month. "But certainly not as much as I would've liked. Has Jin ever told you about the Metalli sharpshooter on our first mission in Corsyca?"

"No," Cressida said.

Astrea knew all about it. He'd written her a letter about it, and when they'd first arrived in Talmaris, he'd explained where the scar on his left shoulder came from. It had been Lennor and Civan's first mission during the war, and a Metalli sharpshooter had shot Jin in the shoulder. Civan had been grazed by another bullet, but he, Lennor, and Adi had managed to take the sharpshooter out.

"It's a very short story, Cress," Jin said as he joined them. "We were in Corsyca, and I got shot."

"You got *shot*?" Cressida asked, lavender surprise spiking high above her head.

"Twice on that mission, but that's hardly the worst thing I've seen," he replied. "I'm fine."

Mouth hanging half-open, Cressida looked from Jin to Astrea, then Lennor. "He got shot *twice*, and he's *fine*?"

Lennor grinned. "He's right. It's hardly the worst thing."

After muttering a quick curse, Cressida fixed her attention back on Lennor. "Well, I'm no sharpshooter, and I promise not to shoot you if you want to run a few drills."

Lennor's grin grew. "I'd love to . . . if Astrea's on standby, just in case."

Jin waved them off as Astrea promised to hang around, and the two women headed for where Civan and Adi were in deep discussion. Curiosity and amusement bounced between Lennor and Cressida, tangling together as they walked.

"You good?" Jin asked. "You hit the ground pretty hard."

"I've gotten very used to falling down during training."

Chuckling, Jin slung his arm around Astrea's shoulders and pulled her into his side. "I still take my fair share of falls when I'm up against those three."

"Trust me, I know."

"You *know*, do you?" he asked. It was the first time in the last couple of days she'd heard that tone, the teasing.

"I watched you enough at the base. I can recall at least a dozen—"

Giving her shoulders a little shake, he said, "Alright, alright. I mean, I said it was my fair share, didn't I?"

"Are you going to flirt with Az all day, or are you coming out here, Captain?" Adi yelled.

"Shut up!" Jin called back before peering down at Astrea. "What do you think? Should I go kick his ass?"

"I'd like to see you try," Astrea quipped.

Sweet amusement and approval coated her tongue just before Jin dropped his arm from her shoulders. He jogged toward where Adi stood waiting, arms crossed over his chest.

As Jin ran, Astrea shouted, "I'll be on standby when you need me!"

He turned over his shoulder and saluted her, then yelped as he dodged a chunk of earth Adi sent his way. Astrea dropped into the grass and let the sun hit her face as she watched. She'd tap back in for the next round, but for now, she'd let the others battle it out.

CHAPTER 16

The soft sofa under Astrea begged her to sleep, but she couldn't. Not just because she felt as awful as she did every night, but because Jin and Eliana were talking through theories about his maternal family.

He'd scrounged up a few more documents from the library's basement after their training session that morning, but that seemed to be the end of the line, at least until he approached Ysabel. Now, they were in Eliana's sitting room, and the two siblings were all energy despite the late hour.

"I know nothing we've found definitively ties my family to that house, but I think it's safe to assume the Talmaran house my grandfather mentioned in some of his letters has to be the same one the Paragon's been using," Jin said.

Astrea nodded sleepily as she leaned back into the sofa. The thought of resting her head on Jin's shoulder was tempting, but she left a few inches of space between their bodies.

"I think there are really just two explanations for why Ysabel is hiding this," he continued.

Stifling a yawn, Astrea asked, "And those are?"

"Either she's completely unaware of *where* the house was and what her people found in it, and she's an incompetent ruler—"

"I highly doubt that," Eliana said, cutting Jin off. She padded from her spot in front of the fireplace to where a handful of her dresses were piled up on one of the armchairs. "Ysabel likes to be involved from what I've gathered in the time we've been here."

"Alright, second theory, then," Jin said as Eliana began sifting through the clothes. "Ysabel already told me that my grandfather secretly married my grandmother, the grand duke's youngest daughter." As Eliana dropped one of the gowns and huffed, Jin sighed. "What are you doing, Ellie?"

"Trying to clean up before Nicos returns. I can multitask."

Jin shook his head. "Anyway, both of my grandparents were ostracized after that, and it brought a lot of shame on the family. If this Paragon connection is new to Ysabel, maybe she's . . . embarrassed."

"Embarrassed?" Astrea asked. "Shouldn't she be concerned?"

"Concerned, sure," Eliana said, "but these families are also quite concerned about appearances. Just think of all the Helosian nobles I've told you about, Az, and the gossip they try to hide from."

Plenty of gossip traveled around the Helosian court, but an apparent Paragon connection was hardly *gossip*.

"She's probably embarrassed she didn't know," Jin said. "Embarrassed for her father, too."

"I thought he was long dead," Astrea said.

"He is, but that must still feel bad," he replied. "And she's probably either trying to figure it out for herself or trying to sweep it under the rug to avoid more issues."

"If I learned anything from Saros's tendency to avoid things," Astrea mumbled, "it's that avoiding things doesn't actually prevent those issues from coming up."

"You just need to talk to her," Eliana said.

"*We* need to talk to her, Ellie. She's your family too, in a way."

"Yes, well . . . When do you want to confront her? That ought to be quite the conversation."

"Tomorrow. I'd like to get this sorted out as soon as possible. I'll bring all the documents so she knows what we've found."

Eliana nodded and stopped fiddling with the dresses. She'd barely done anything to tidy them up. "How about at breakfast? She invited me anyway."

"Breakfast it is."

The door opened with a quiet creak. Nicos strolled in, a bundle of long, rolled papers under his arm. He glanced between the three of them. "What's going on?" As his attention shifted back to Eliana, he sighed. "You still haven't cleaned up?"

"We were busy talking about Jin's maternal family," Eliana said.

"What happened to multitasking, Ellie?" Jin teased.

"Oh, hush." She smiled up at Nicos. "You spoke with the commander?"

He nodded. "I did."

"Good."

"About what?" Jin asked.

"Just ensuring you're going to have as much extra security as promised," Nicos said.

"You think she wouldn't give us security?" Jin's question was more directed at Eliana than Nicos.

Eliana shrugged. "I just wanted to be sure."

Astrea rubbed her eyes and tried stifling another yawn. It wasn't *that* late. She usually had a bit more energy than this.

"Sleepy?" Jin asked.

"No, you're just boring."

"Ouch." Chuckling, he patted her thigh a few times. His hand lingered there, making sparks dance through her belly. "Alright. Ellie, finish cleaning your room. Az, you're going to bed."

"Who made you the boss?" Eliana asked.

Jin stood, then offered his hand to Astrea and helped her to her feet. "I'm fairly certain that being your older brother makes me the boss."

"Well then who made you the boss of Az?"

"Maybe she likes it, El," Nicos said. His aura immediately flared with magenta embarrassment. "Skies, sorry Az, I didn't mean—"

Eliana's cackle cut him off. Even Astrea couldn't help but laugh. She'd never heard Nicos make such a comment before, and the fact that his whole face was as red as a tomato only made it funnier.

"We'll just . . . get out of your hair," Jin mumbled. "Goodnight."

Even when they got into the hallway and shut Eliana's door, amusement and embarrassment tangled together and reached for Astrea. She couldn't help but be a little satisfied at Jin's obvious shyness now, too. It was cute.

It didn't disappear even when they were alone in their room and getting ready for bed. Astrea washed up first, moving through her routine quickly. Jin went in next, and the whole time he was in the bathroom, a hint of embarrassment crept through the walls.

"Nicos's comment bothered you that much?" Astrea asked as he walked back into the bedroom.

Jin's ears turned red. "I'm not bothered."

"I beg to differ."

"I'm not *bothered*. Just . . ."

"Just what?"

"Just . . ." He rubbed the back of his neck. "I don't want you to feel like I'm trying to order you around."

Astrea headed for the wardrobe and began unbuttoning her blouse. "To be fair, you can get a *bit* bossy."

Worry whispered over her skin. "I do?"

"Yes."

"Sorry, I don't want to—"

"But to be even fairer," she continued, "I don't mind." Astrea slipped the garment off her shoulders, then hung it up in the wardrobe and began unzipping her skirt.

"You yelled at me in Sezia for telling you what to do."

"That was different. You weren't being nice about it."

"Oh, so you only like when I'm 'nice' bossy?"

"Exactly."

In actuality, Astrea didn't mind Jin taking the lead in a lot of scenarios . . . at least, she didn't mind him taking the lead in the situations they found themselves in lately. He certainly had more experience leading missions than she did. She'd defer to his judgment on those issues any day, and it wasn't like he was rigid when he was taking charge. She'd seen enough of his interactions with his team at the old base to know that was true.

"And being bossy in *this* room isn't exactly a bad thing," she added for good measure. Teasing him was fun, and the gentle warmth spreading over her skin suggested Jin liked it, too.

"What?"

"You heard me."

Astrea slipped her skirt off, then returned it to its spot in the wardrobe. She was about to unhook her brassiere when warm fingers brushed hers.

"Let me." Jin's voice was low. Tart lust and that steady heat wrapped around Astrea, both of them almost lazy as they joined the fatigue rolling off Jin in waves.

"What happened to sleep?" she asked as he pushed the straps off her shoulders.

"How do you know I'm thinking about more than sleep?"

"Hm, I wonder . . ."

His chuckle rumbled pleasantly in her bones. Jin finished unhooking the back of the garment, then pushed it the rest of the way off. He wrapped his arms around her shoulders and held her loosely against his body. After pressing a kiss to the back of her head, he asked, "Do *you* want to sleep?"

Astrea turned in his arms, her bare breasts brushing against his silk shirt. "I just said I like you taking charge in here, and now you're asking if I want to sleep?"

He laughed again, his hands roaming from her shoulders down to grab her ass. "A good boss still asks what other people want."

"Oh, lovely, lessons in management. Just what I wanted tonight."

Leaning down, Jin nipped at her neck. "Bed. Now."

"But what about my lesson?"

"I'll teach you anything you want if you get in that bed and take your bloomers off."

"What a deal," she teased as she slipped just out of his reach.

Astrea's body barely hit the bed when Jin started shucking his clothes off. Shirt, trousers, undergarments, all gone before Astrea could even take her bloomers off. She *was* tired, but Jin's lust burned around the room in shades of raspberry and pink, and she couldn't get enough. Her muscles were already taut with anticipation.

"What happened to bloomers off?" Jin chided as he strode toward the bed, body on full display.

"You've hardly given me any time."

"Then allow me to help." He hooked his thumbs into the waistband of her bloomers and pulled them down to her knees, then off fully, and chucked them onto the floor. Astrea sucked in a sharp breath as Jin kissed her belly, then left a trail of kisses up her sternum. His fingers drifted down between her legs. "That's better."

"Fuck," Astrea whispered, her head falling back as Jin stroked her in smooth, gentle motions. The pads of his fingers warmed with his magic, and Astrea swore again.

"Yeah?" he asked, warm pride rolling over Astrea's skin.

She pulled his face toward hers. As their lips met, Jin slid one finger into her entrance, then another. She moaned into his mouth, drawing out more of that pride. It blistered her skin in the best way. Astrea's hips bucked up.

Jin hummed, then pulled away. "Get on top," he murmured against her mouth. After one more kiss, he rolled onto his back.

Astrea pushed up on her arm, then steadied herself as she straddled Jin's lap. His thick erection pointed toward his abdomen, and Astrea was about to line it up with herself when Jin grabbed her hips.

"No." He tugged her toward him. "Up here." When she hesitated, he asked, "Too bossy?"

"What? No. I'm scared I'll fall," she admitted. "My legs hurt from earlier."

"Skies damned Adi," Jin murmured. "Hold the headboard. I won't let you fall." His heavy eyelids obscured most of his beautiful gold irises, but the raspberry vibrating around him was all the confirmation Astrea needed.

She moved up slowly, gripping the headboard but holding her hips high above Jin's face. He laughed and tugged them down. Astrea gasped as his tongue pressed into her, then again as he held her hips in place. She squirmed, but that only made him hold her tighter. Jin moaned, the vibrations traveling up into her belly. When his fingers penetrated her again, Astrea's head tilted back. The tension in her thighs built, and it had absolutely nothing to do with training earlier in the day.

Astrea ground against his face. She gripped the headboard tighter. Part of her thought to draw this out, to prolong the feeling as long as she could, but she had no control. Pleasure washed over her in quick, short waves, there for a few heartbeats and then gone. Jin kissed the inside of her thigh and released his tight hold.

"Good?" he asked.

Astrea nodded breathlessly as she rolled off to one side of the bed. "Do you want me to su—"

"No." Jin gripped her face and kissed her, the taste of her own sex heavy on his breath. "I want to be buried so deep inside you that I can't tell where I end and you begin, alright?"

"Yeah," she whispered, her insides burning.

As he climbed on top of her, Astrea spread her legs. He slid into her with a satisfied hum. "Fuck, Az. You're soaked."

"What did you expect?"

He laughed and leaned down, kissing her again. Astrea opened her mouth to his, just enough that he could bite her lower lip. Pleasure jolted through Astrea again and again, in perfect time with Jin's thrusts. His mouth wandered down to her throat, where he sucked on the delicate skin near the base of her neck.

"You're going to make me come again," Astrea whispered. She was overloaded in the best way, her whole body sensitive. "Too fast."

Jin sat up a little and pushed her legs back, then settled them over his shoulders. He thrust into her again. "Good." He pressed his thumb right into her clit and began rubbing small, smooth circles. But his hand pulled away, and he said, "Touch yourself."

"You're taking this bossy thing very seriously."

"I thought you liked it."

"I do."

Astrea's right hand slid down between their bodies, pressing into the spot Jin had just been touching. Approval and pride, lust and desire—they rained down on her like a Kalamian thunderstorm. She grabbed Jin's arm with her free hand, trying to focus on the way his muscles flexed under her touch. He hit the right spot over and over again. She couldn't think. She could barely make her own fingers keep moving.

"Come on, Az," Jin murmured. "Let go."

Her back arched. Her face warmed. And she was lost. Astrea's whole body trembled, and Jin followed her right over the edge.

Slowly, Jin lowered Astrea's legs, pulled out of her, and rolled onto his back. All the desire once swirling around the room disappeared, replaced by that soft, familiar warmth and fatigue.

"You alright?" she whispered as she snuggled closer to him.

He kissed the top of her head. "Very much so."

They lay in silence for a while, wrapped around each other. Astrea ran her fingers through Jin's curls, and he drew patterns on her back. But finally, Jin made both of them get up to clean up for a second time.

Astrea had just spit out her mouthwash when Jin asked, "How would you feel about taking a bath?"

"I never take baths."

"Why not?"

"I hate how quickly the water gets cold."

"I can keep it warm."

Astrea met his soft gaze in the mirror. "Why?"

"Why can I keep it warm?"

"No, why take a bath? I thought we were going to bed."

"It'll be good for your legs. And mine. I'm beat after training earlier, too."

Astrea wasn't so sure that was his real reason. But she still agreed, and once the tub was sufficiently full, she climbed in with Jin. She settled between his legs and leaned her back against his chest. The hot water *did* feel good on her sore muscles. So did Jin's arms wrapped around her shoulders.

The deeper she sank into the tub, though, and the longer they sat there, Astrea's mind began to wander. "Should we be doing this?"

"Doing what?" Jin asked.

"This . . ." She gestured to the water. "What if they come now?"

Jin was silent for a moment, but understanding brushed over her skin, delicate like butterfly wings. "The Paragon, you mean."

"Yes." Astrea sometimes worried about that while doing other things that left her, for the most part, vulnerable. Showers. Sleeping, of course. Sex. Here, in this bath.

"Well." Jin sighed. "I suppose I could fight them naked, though I've never had to do that before." Despite herself, Astrea laughed. He kissed the back of her head. "We can only be so vigilant. We still have to live."

"I know," she whispered.

Even as Jin held her closer, that familiar rope tightened around Astrea's heart. It squeezed and squeezed, making tears spring to her eyes. Why did her mind have to go there now? She'd just been having fun. She'd just felt so good, if only for a short while. She'd almost felt like her old self again.

Why couldn't her mind let her have this one night? Astrea sucked in a deep breath, then let it out slowly.

"Az?" Jin asked.

"I'm tired."

"Then let's go to bed."

As Jin left the bathroom to get them clothes, Astrea wiped at her lash line with her towel and got rid of the last of her tears. She didn't want to cry, especially not over the thing she'd already cried so much about. So when Jin returned, she forced herself to smile.

"Sorry to cut your bath short."

He chuckled as he tugged his undergarments on. "I'll live."

"You can get back in if you want."

"I'm exhausted, but I don't think I have to tell you that. Bed sounds good." He took the towels from her, then tilted his head toward the door. "Go lie down. I'll finish cleaning up in here."

Astrea forced another smile. "Here we go again with the orders." Even to her own ears, the joke was half-hearted.

Jin watched her, expression soft. "I'll be there in a moment."

Leaving him to clean up the bathroom, Astrea returned to bed. She climbed in and pulled the covers up high, then pushed her magic out wider for one last check. No voids as far as she could tell. She pulled her barrier back toward herself, not so close she couldn't breathe but close enough to ignore even the guards in the hallway just beyond their room.

The mattress dipped as Jin joined her in bed. The lamp in the corner cast a warm glow over the room. Astrea moved closer to him, and Jin draped his arm over her waist. And soon, he was asleep.

Astrea closed her eyes, begging the knot in her chest to loosen. Maybe she'd feel better in the morning. Maybe she'd finally begin to find some peace.

Chapter 17

Sweat beaded on Astrea's brow. Talmaris was by no means hot, but Adi had been putting her to work for the last two hours. Every muscle in Astrea's body screamed as she plopped into a shaded grassy area near the palace's enormous lake.

"Shit, I haven't worked like that in weeks," Cressida muttered as she collapsed next to Astrea.

"You'll thank me later." Adi had put in the work, too, but didn't look nearly as worn out. The man was in impeccable shape. "But you both did great today."

Though Astrea hadn't been training with her lightbringing for even two whole months yet, she took solace in Adi's words. She'd come a long way in that short time. As he'd told her several times, she didn't have to master everything right away; she just needed to know enough.

The grounds sloped away from the palace and down toward the lake, but Astrea could still make out its towers from her low angle. Behind that, a clear blue sky made the day seem almost cheerful. Songbirds chirped from their hideaways in the garden, and ducks splashed in the pond.

"You think Jin and Ellie are doing alright?" Cressida asked.

"I don't think Ysabel's been happy to see us, honestly," Astrea said. After Jin and Eliana had left to join Ysabel for breakfast, Astrea had filled

Cressida and Adi in on what the new theory was, as well as the siblings' plan. "I doubt she's going to appreciate Jin demanding answers, either."

"Then she shouldn't be keeping secrets," Adi replied matter-of-factly. "That's on her."

Grunting her agreement, Astrea slung her arm over her eyes. That kind of information was crucial when they still had so little knowledge about the Paragon. But it also just seemed wrong to keep that from Jin after he'd been in the dark about his mother for twenty-six years.

"Do either of you want to come with me to see Mariya today?" Cressida asked. "She was going to run some final tests on the meteorite samples overnight."

"I'll go," Astrea said. It beat sitting around with Marko all day. Besides, she'd been away from Cressida for a month. Spending time together would do Astrea's heart some good, even if it was ultimately about solving this conspiracy.

"I actually promised Lennor I'd work with her on a few things today," Adi said. "Good luck to you two, though."

"And good luck to you," Cressida replied. "Lennor kicked my ass yesterday."

"Bruised ego?" Adi teased as he helped Cressida, then Astrea, off the ground.

"No," Cressida said quickly. "Though I'm pretty sure I bruised my ass."

Astrea giggled. She'd spent most of the afternoon watching the others run drills—and sometimes joining them. Lennor and Cressida had gotten competitive, but only Astrea had been able to see the growing playfulness with her magic. It had been nice. A welcome distraction. Something good to feel, which Astrea rarely seemed to feel at all anymore. Not just from within herself but from everyone else, too.

"That's not a problem I can help you with," Adi quipped. "Maybe Az can."

"Seems fine to me," Astrea said as she and Cressida headed back toward the palace. Both women waved goodbye to Adi. "Do you actually need any—"

"Oh, I'm just teasing," Cressida said. "My ass is fine."

"Maybe we can ask Lennor and get her opinion on the whole thing."

"Don't you dare," Cressida warned, but her voice lacked any real edge.

They made their way past groups of Novarian soldiers in silence, then greeted the twins as both Lennor and Civan headed out into the gardens. When they finally got to their floor in their wing of the palace, Cressida tried to follow Astrea into her and Jin's room.

Despite Lucian's orders about not leaving them alone, Astrea just needed twenty minutes to herself. Twenty minutes to shower and not worry about someone else in the other room. She hadn't been truly alone in weeks.

"Cress, I know you're just sticking to orders, but can you give me some time?" Astrea asked when they were in the sitting room.

Hesitation whispered over Astrea's skin. "But—"

"I know, but skies, Cress, I haven't had any time to myself since we left Kalama. Please? Just while I clean up."

Cressida pressed her lips together. "You think you'll be alright?"

"I'll be fine. Besides, Marko's going to be outside the door in the next twenty seconds, and there are only a dozen other guards within earshot." In fact, Astrea didn't really consider it alone time at all, but she would take whatever she could get.

"Alright," Cressida said. "Half an hour, then I'm coming back whether you like it or not."

"I only need twenty minutes."

With that, Cressida slipped out the door. Astrea closed it behind her, then slumped against the smooth wood. They still had so much work to do, but she'd take her time while she could. She'd try to enjoy this reprieve, Paragon be damned.

As anticipated, both Marko and Cressida had been outside her door when she finished cleaning up. Not only had Astrea reveled in having quiet time to herself, but she'd put on her favorite lavender dress and brogues. Practical? Maybe not for wartime. But wearing her favorite things, the things that felt like her, had to help her mood, right?

As she and Cressida made their way to Mariya's observatory, Marko trailed a dozen feet behind them. Even these once-empty parts of the palace gardens were now crawling with soldiers.

"Have you learned anything at all since we got those samples?" Astrea asked. Gravel crunched underfoot, and in a nearby tree, two birds chirped afternoon songs. A few insects joined, making Astrea's skin crawl.

"Besides them feeling just like the other sample to Mariya?" Cressida shrugged. Like Astrea, she'd worn civilian clothing, a black and white striped blouse paired with a beautiful ruby red skirt. It was a welcome sight after so many weeks surrounded by soldiers who only wore black or midnight blue. "No. They still feel the same to me. I don't think they have an effect on Metalli."

"Is that a good thing?" Astrea asked.

"I mean, on the one hand, it'd be nice if they felt different, just so we had information," Cressida said, "but I suppose them feeling normal is also information. Maybe it's a good thing. It means other Metalli won't have any kind of advantage with that material. No sharpshooters or anything, like from Jin's story."

"Yeah."

"Did you know about that?"

"About him getting shot?" When Cressida nodded, Astrea said, "Yes. And stabbed. Multiple times."

Orange anxiety undulated around Cressida. "Scary."

"Yeah."

Astrea and Jin had talked more about his time at war in the weeks they'd been at that old base. Some were stories she already knew, and some she actually heard from Adi or the twins. Jin had also shared more about his life and the months of peacetime. He'd been a fireweaving teacher for a while. He'd taken bullets and been stabbed by more than one Delian. He'd nearly lost his life, and he'd had other close calls. But he'd also met Adi, Zephyrine, Lennor, and Civan, four people who meant a lot to him.

"Scary to think that's what's waiting for us back home," Cressida said. "Or right around the corner, if the Paragon really are that keen on getting you and Jin. To be willing to go to war with Novaria over just two people …"

Astrea swallowed hard. Of course it was scary. Terrifying. War was a far cry from what she'd ever imagined she'd be getting herself into. But she'd examined the situation from every angle she could think of, and that seemed like the only possible outcome. Neither Nazarov nor The One would go down without a fight.

"We'll just have to get through it," Astrea said. "As a team."

They walked the rest of the way in silence, though that orange anxiety never disappeared from Cressida's aura. As the trees around them thickened and the shrubs and bushes became less manicured, Marko caught up to them. From there, it was just a couple more minutes' walk until the tower appeared amid the sea of green foliage.

Mariya's tower wasn't nearly as tall as the observatory back home, and its off-white bricks were clean and solid, unlike the salt-worn tower she'd lived in with Saros for fourteen years. Even still, it was familiar, with its nearby pond and quiet, unkempt gardens. Astrea hoped Saros was at home now, making coffee and getting ready for his day.

The soldiers stationed outside saluted Marko as the group entered the tower. The interior was nothing like the observatory back home. The bottom floor was wide open to a mezzanine on the second story, and that opened to a glass dome like the ones in the palace. Bookcases, a sitting area, and a credenza marked the entrance to the tower, and through an archway beyond was a wide desk and more bookcases.

Cressida led the way through the Stargazer's office. There was no old, giant telescope here, but Mariya's collection of books, decorations, spare papers, and a few too many coffee cups made it look just like Saros's office. Cressida stopped in front of a narrow, arched doorway. The next room had low lighting thanks to its lack of windows and relatively low ceiling. Several long tables stretched along two walls and were full of contraptions Astrea couldn't name. Near one such contraption stood Mariya, her back to the door.

"Ah!" she exclaimed as she turned. "There you are, Cressida. And you've brought guests."

"Thought I'd see what last night revealed."

"Come in, come in." Mariya motioned them in with her cane. "The experiments are right there." She used her free hand to gesture toward the adjacent tables.

"And?" Marko asked, the first time he'd spoken in nearly fifteen minutes.

"*And*, if you'll be patient, I'll explain, Marko." As Mariya moved past Cressida and Astrea to the right-side table, she smiled up at them. "With Cressida's help, I've been running some tests. Tests with light—including my light—and then also the—"

"Shall we just skip to the results?" Marko asked.

"None of my tests showed anything," Cressida said.

"Nothing?" Astrea asked. "But Emperor Aelius—"

"As far as we can tell, Miss Sovna," Mariya said, "there is nothing particularly . . . unique about this metal. Well, aside from what it feels like to my stargazing and your lightbringing, of course."

Folding her arms over her chest, Cressida said, "If I had some of the tools back at Lodestar, I might be able to give you more information."

"No one in the city would have them?" Marko asked.

"Not *those* tools," Cressida said. When he raised an eyebrow, she said, "Proprietary information. Sorry. And not something I can recreate easily. I'm good—great, really—but those machines aren't my area of expertise."

He rolled his eyes. "So what now?"

"I could just try working with it," Cressida said. "I could try actually making something. The sample is full of iron . . . I could make steel, then see what happens with it."

"What will you make?" Mariya asked.

"A dagger would be simple enough. Emperor Aelius wanted me to fuse the meteorite to existing weaponry but never let me actually smelt steel from it. He was being slow . . . cautious with it. He thought fusing it would make the weapons stronger, but—"

"But maybe that kind of heat will reveal its true strength." With a sage nod, Mariya said, "Yes, yes. Let's do that. It's our next best step."

"I'll still need some things. A lot of things, actually. If someone can get me what I need today, that would be great." Cressida turned to Astrea. "You want to stay and help?"

Astrea loved Cressida, and she admired her natural skill, not just with her magic but her innate ability to simply understand all kinds of things, like weapons, engines, and more. And though she wanted to spend time with Cressida, Astrea did not love being in her friend's workshop. She never had. It was loud, and ingredients she used for various builds often smelled terrible.

"I think I'll go back to the palace," Astrea said. "But you know where to find me if you need me."

"Suit yourself!" Cressida called over her shoulder as Astrea and Marko headed back out into Mariya's office.

As they stepped back into the warm afternoon sunshine, Astrea wasn't actually sure how she'd spend the rest of the day. But maybe she'd get lucky and convince Marko to give her some more space.

Astrea's hopes of convincing Marko for time alone were dashed not just by him but by the fact that Jin, Eliana, and Zephyrine were gathered in the sitting room when she returned from the observatory.

"Sorry." She stopped in her tracks as soon as she saw them.

Jin waved her inside. "Marko, if you can give me a few minutes, I need to go speak with Lucian after this."

"I suppose I'll just wait out here then," Marko said as he closed the door.

"What's going on?" Astrea asked as she sat next to Jin on the sofa.

"We were just telling Zephyrine about our breakfast with Ysabel." Eliana reached for a teacup sitting on the coffee table, its delicate porcelain painted with blue flowers. "Ysabel knew."

"What?" The word stuck in Astrea's throat.

"She doesn't know much more than us," Jin corrected. "She started piecing it together a couple of weeks ago."

"But she was still keeping it from us," Astrea said.

"She was," Jin agreed. "And I really, really don't like that."

"Well, did she know anything else?" Astrea twisted the ends of her skirt around in her hands. "You said she knew more than us?"

Leaning back, Jin crossed his arms over his chest. "She recognized the address of the house a few weeks ago but wasn't sure why. As more information started coming in from Lucian's teams, she realized what it was. Ysabel had never been to the house herself and only remembered it because of some documents she'd seen when she had to deal with the Seviya estate many years ago after my grandfather died and my mother left for Kalama."

"Does she know if the Seviyas were actually connected to the Paragon?" Zephyrine asked. "I think that's the real question."

"That, we still can't say," Eliana said. "She doesn't know, either."

"Nor did she know what my mother's 'right' was as a Seviyan descendant," Jin said with a sigh. "Ysabel's theory is that my grandfather—Tanel—was just showboating and making a big deal out of the family name. Apparently he had a habit of doing that. The Seviyas were invited back to Talmaris when my mother was five years old, though they weren't allowed at court. Tanel kept the family mostly at their estate to the northeast, but whenever he was in the capital, he spent a lot of money and a lot of time trying to recover their social standing. Status was important to him."

"Maybe he shouldn't have seduced your grandmother, then," Eliana muttered.

"Do you believe Ysabel?" Astrea asked.

"I believe she doesn't know more than that," Jin said. "She seemed genuinely confused despite hiding it from us. She also didn't know how her team missed the letter at the house in the first place."

"Sometimes things get missed," Zephyrine said. "With as many people as were going in and out of that house, there easily could've been a miscommunication about what had and hadn't been checked."

"Maybe, but if Ysabel hid that from us, what else is she hiding?" Astrea asked.

"Hopefully nothing," Eliana said, so casually, as if it were truly just that simple.

"How can you three be so calm?" Astrea twisted the fabric of her dress again. Even if Ysabel was right and Tanel was just another overbearing, entitled aristocrat, she'd said she wanted to move forward together, especially as family. How was that being familial?

"She remembered how upset I was when she told me about my mother being her cousin," Jin said. "She wasn't sure how to tell me this without upsetting me further."

"So, she hid something to spare your feelings?" Astrea shook her head. This was not the time.

"Can't say I agree with it, nor do I like it, but yes. It was the wrong choice, and she knows I want to know everything about them going forward. She actually gave me some more journals and letters to go through, and she offered me access to my grandfather's estate." He glanced at Zephyrine, who lounged in her chair as if none of this were serious at all. "Do you think she's telling the truth, Zephyrine? You've spent more time with her recently than I have."

"I already told you I think she's telling the truth," Eliana muttered with a pointed look in Astrea's direction.

Zephyrine watched Jin carefully, then nodded. "I agree with your sister. For the most part, Ysabel's been helpful, even when she doesn't want to be involved in any of this. I think she made a poor decision because she was trying to spare your feelings. Doesn't make it right, but it also doesn't mean she's keeping all sorts of secrets. She knows what's at stake with the Paragon and your father. She wouldn't let something bad happen to her people just because of strange—and long-dead—extended family members."

Astrea tilted her head back against the soft cushions. Ysabel may not have been happy to see Jin and Astrea back from that old base, and she may not have liked their decision to take Nazarov up on his offer, but she was still letting them be here. She was giving them resources they needed. Ysabel was their ally, but she was also human, and humans sometimes made mistakes and poor judgment calls.

"Alright," Jin said. "I'm sure Marko's dying to get out of here. I'm going to go see where Lucian's at with plans for tomorrow night. Zephyrine?"

"I'll join you." The general stood and smoothed her white hair away from her face. "Where's the rest of the team?"

"Adi was working with Lennor and Civan last time I saw them," Astrea said. "Maybe an hour ago."

"They'll still be out there, then. We can fill them in later." Jin reached for Astrea's hand and squeezed it once. Astrea squeezed it back, missing the warmth of his skin as soon as he pulled away. "We'll be back soon."

And then they were gone, and it was just Astrea and Eliana left in the quiet room. There wasn't even a crackling fire to break up the silence.

"Where's Nicos?" Astrea asked.

"Already with Lucian, actually," Eliana said.

"But you aren't going with us tomorrow."

"No, but Nicos wanted to help. He hates not feeling useful."

Astrea knew that feeling, though she thought Nicos was plenty useful. Guarding the future empress . . . the hopeful future empress . . . was a big job, even if it probably felt boring sometimes.

"Where's Cress?" Eliana asked. When Astrea explained what Cressida and Mariya were going to work on, Eliana just nodded. "And what do you want to do the rest of the afternoon?"

"I'm not sure. Why, did you have something in mind?"

"Remember my plans for the reformed Helosian government I showed you and Cress before . . . everything? I was going to start going through some notes Zephyrine gave me now that she's done going through it all. Want to help?"

Politics and governing weren't exactly Astrea's area of expertise, but if it would help Eliana, it was worth diving into. "Let's get to it."

Chapter 18

Sitting in front of a vanity mirror and watching Cressida add soft curls to Astrea's hair seemed like the last possible thing she needed to be doing, but Club Twilight had a strict dress code. It wasn't unlike the clubs back in Kalama, but it just felt silly.

Astrea played with a makeup brush, twirling it around in her hands as Cressida finished another curl with the hot iron. They'd spent the morning in another training session with Adi, which he'd used to go over more basic self-defense with Astrea. In the afternoon, they'd reviewed the building's blueprints with Lucian, Jin, and Marko again. Everything was set. This was either going to go fine or be some kind of trap.

In the mirror, Astrea watched Cressida wrap another section of hair around the iron. Behind them, Eliana was opening garment bags one of Ysabel's staff had brought by a half hour before.

"Alright, I know this is going to sound absolutely ridiculous considering the situation," Eliana said as she peeked into one of the bags, "but I'm almost jealous. These are gorgeous."

Cressida's lips quirked up, and Astrea breathed a laugh. Looking the part was just one small piece of the mission.

"At least if we die tonight, we'll look good," Cressida quipped.

"Oh, don't say *that*." Eliana finished unzipping the bags with a huff. "Nobody's going to die."

Astrea squeezed the makeup brush's smooth handle. "Do you know anything about Nazarov, Ellie?" she managed to ask past the tightness in her throat. "From Kalama, I mean."

"His family's estate is small," Eliana said. "Far north of Kalama, but not too close to the Novarian border. I never really interacted with him much, to be honest. He was rarely around."

"Maybe that's why he's doing all this," Cressida said. "Hates having such a small . . . estate."

Astrea forced herself to smile as Cressida finished the last of her curls. It was just how Astrea had styled her hair for many such nights in the past. The last time she'd done her hair like this was before that disastrous meeting with Ysabel's council. The night the Paragon had taken her. She sucked in a shaky breath.

Nazarov was definitely not doing any of this because of his family's lesser influence in Kalama. He was doing this because he wanted to bring down not just the Helosian government, but every government. He was doing this because he was following some prophecy. Because he believed himself the leader of the void mages despite The One still being alive.

"Thanks, Cress," Astrea murmured as she started arranging her hair around her shoulders and shaking out the curls. They draped down her back in soft, shiny waves.

"Come see your dress before you do your makeup," Eliana called.

Standing, Astrea followed Cressida to where Eliana had laid the outfits out on her bed. One was a short emerald dress covered in hundreds of dazzling bronze beaded flowers that winked in the light of the room's chandelier. The other was also short but made of a deep purple fabric, and rather than flowers, the silver beads were arranged in some swirling pattern Astrea didn't pay much attention to. She just wanted to get the night over with.

"I'm going to get changed," Cressida announced as she scooped up the green dress and headed into the bathroom.

When Eliana held up t-strap heels, Astrea just muttered "Looks good" and went back to the vanity. Surprise whispered over her skin, followed by cool curiosity.

"Az?" Eliana asked.

Picking up a kohl pencil, Astrea got to work lining her lashes. The first few strokes were a bit messy, but it wasn't anything that couldn't be covered up. She didn't stop until Eliana crouched down next to her and set a hand on her arm.

"Az," Eliana repeated.

"What?"

"Let me do that. You're shaking."

Astrea passed the pencil to Eliana, then folded her hands in her lap. They *were* shaking. She'd barely noticed; she seemed to shake all the time lately.

"How much do you want to wear?" Eliana asked.

"Just enough."

Eliana returned to the task, instructing Astrea when to close her eyes and when to look up instead. When she was finally done and told Astrea to look in the mirror, Astrea almost didn't want to. Not because she didn't trust Eliana, but because this all suddenly felt like too much. What had she been thinking, agreeing to go talk to Nazarov?

Still, Eliana's handiwork spoke for itself. Aside from the dark eyeliner, the rest of Astrea's makeup was soft. A light dusting of eyeshadow shimmered on her eyelids, and the blush on her cheeks matched the hint of rosy lipstick. It was pretty.

Astrea dared to meet Eliana's gaze in the mirror. "Do you think this was a bad idea?"

"The makeup?"

"No, agreeing to meet Nazarov."

"I think you were right days ago. It's our only option at this point." Astrea nodded once.

"And I think it's brave," Eliana said quietly. She began packing away some of the makeup into a small bag. "Jin told me everything before Ysabel sent you away. I don't think I'd be brave enough to ever see that scumbag again."

"I think Nicos would kill him if our positions were reversed," Astrea whispered.

"I'll be surprised if Jin *doesn't* kill him tonight," Eliana replied just as Cressida emerged from the bathroom. "Cress might do it first, though."

"I'll do what?" Cressida called as she strutted over to them. She twirled in a circle once she reached the vanity, the bottom of her dress flaring out. "What do you think?"

"Kill Nazarov," Eliana replied coolly. "You look great."

"I will if I have to."

"Let's just hope it doesn't come to that," Astrea said.

But she knew Eliana was right, not just about Jin and Cressida but the whole team. Jin's team was highly trained, and they were prepared. If anyone was going to make sure this went smoothly, it was them. She just needed to make sure she pulled her own weight and held it together long enough to find out what Nazarov wanted to tell them.

Though it had only taken Astrea another half hour to get ready, and though there was plenty of time before they needed to leave, she couldn't shake the need to do *something* from her bones.

She gave in to that feeling. As she paced the length of her sitting room, her heels barely made any sound on the rug. She'd expected to finish getting ready, then head to their destination. Not be stuck waiting for Jin.

"Anxious?" Marko drawled from his spot near the door.

"What else would I be?"

Marko simply smiled at her. "Can I do anything?"

"You've never asked me that before."

"Mostly because it seems pointless to ask," he said. "What *is* there to do in a situation like"—he gestured to the room—"this? Not a skies damned thing."

Astrea couldn't agree more. She just had to keep moving. "Where's Jin?"

"He'd been speaking with the grand duchess last I knew. I believe Lucian was with him."

"And why aren't we there?"

"He asked me to keep you here."

Astrea frowned. Why would Jin ask that of Marko? This wasn't some attempt to keep her from going on the mission, was it? She thought she'd been doing better, that she'd proven she could handle it.

Outside the room, a knot of anxiety and trepidation crept closer. The door opened, and Astrea stopped her pacing as Jin slipped into the room.

"Marko, give us a moment?" he asked. "We'll be out in a few minutes."

Marko glanced at Astrea, then Jin, before he exited the room. But his steady wall didn't go far, just across the hall.

Jin offered Astrea a tight smile. His black suit was somber, if not a bit striking. Even his wingtip shoes were black. But he wore no waistcoat, and the top two buttons of his black dress shirt were undone, revealing a hint of his broad chest and gold chain. As casual as he could get away with, as always. She didn't blame him.

"What's going on?" she asked as he crossed the room and took her hand.

"Just come sit." He guided her to the tufted sofa. She sat on its edge, muscles tense. But he was relaxed. "You look nice."

"Thanks."

"And you look nervous."

"Yes, well." Astrea resisted the urge to pick at the beads sewn onto her dress. "You had Marko holding me in here for nearly half an hour."

Sweet amusement coated Astrea's tongue. "Is that what he told you?"

"Yes."

"I'm sorry if he spooked you." Jin took Astrea's hands again, his touch almost asking permission. She tried to relax. "Zephyrine and the twins are already on their way to the club."

"Alright." Why was he telling her that? It was part of the plan.

"And I thought it'd be nice to have a moment to check in before we have to go pretend like we actually want to be out there tonight."

"You don't want to go?" Astrea heard herself ask, even though she very much didn't like the idea of venturing outside the palace.

"Fuck no. But it's the mission."

"Right."

"And you?" he asked. "Do *you* want to go?"

Forcing herself to sit up straighter, Astrea said, "Yes." When he pinned her with a look that said he knew she was lying, she added, "I want answers." And she did. She just also didn't want Jin to think she wasn't fit for a mission. "Are Cress and Adi ready to go?"

"I assume so."

"Good." Astrea started to stand. "Then let's—"

"Slow down," he said, chuckling as he tugged on her hand. "Come here. I want to give you something."

She sat back down. "What?"

"I wanted to check in, yes, but I want to give you something, too."

"It's not another dagger or armor, is it?" Astrea asked, trying to force some playfulness into her voice. And deep down, she meant it. She was just so tired.

Jin laughed again as he reached into his jacket. Even with the anxiety circling them both, the sound made Astrea's heart flutter. "No, it's not a dagger, nor is it armor." He pulled out a small black velvet box. "It's a gift."

"A gift?"

"Eight graduations and two birthdays, right?"

Astrea tipped her head back. "Skies, not this again. You know I was just joking, right?"

"And you know I'm serious."

As the box opened with a small squeak, Astrea looked at Jin again. Inside was a delicate silver chain, and on the end hung an opal. Tiny sparkling stones dotted each ray of the starburst setting. It was small. Delicate. Perfect, really. It was exactly what she liked.

"What—" she started, then shook her head. "Why?"

"A strange question to ask when your partner's giving you a gift, isn't it?" Jin teased as more of that sugary amusement coated Astrea's tongue. "You kept playing with your other necklace all those weeks we were here," he said quietly. "And you kept reaching for it while we were at that base. I know it's not the same, but I thought maybe something different . . ."

"Where'd you even get it?" Astrea asked. Another silly question. But it wasn't like they could go shopping.

"I arranged it a couple days ago. Marko and Ellie helped, actually." Jin hesitated as he turned the box around to look at it. And when he peeked up at her, the orange in his aura doubled. "Sorry, is it . . . Should I not have?"

"No," Astrea said quickly. "No, skies, sorry." His shoulders relaxed. "I don't know what's wrong with me. I just wasn't expecting it, I guess."

"Bad unexpected?"

"No," she said again. Why was she being so awkward about it? And why was he so nervous? "I'm just not feeling like myself today. Sorry. I love it, really."

"You're sure?"

Astrea smiled. "I'm sure." She plucked the box from his hands, then ran her fingers over the stone. The rainbow shooting through it made her think of the ones that often spread over Kalama after summer thunderstorms. "Will you put it on for me?" After the incident with the eyeliner in Eliana's room, Astrea wasn't sure she trusted herself to properly clasp anything.

After handing the box back to Jin, he carefully removed the necklace. Turning so her back was to him, Astrea moved her hair over one shoulder. Jin laid the stone on her chest, his fingers barely whispering over her skin as he brought the chain around the back of her neck.

"There," he murmured as she turned around again. His attention lingered on her chest, right on the stone. It lay a few inches below her collarbone, right above the V-shaped neckline of her dress.

"So, that's what, seven birthdays now?" she asked, trying to get the teasing back in her voice.

"I thought you said you were just joking."

"And I thought you were completely serious."

He laughed, the suddenness of it completely disarming. Astrea smiled up at him, and for a moment, it was just them. No guards outside the door. No team waiting downstairs. No mission.

Astrea didn't know who moved first, but it was like some invisible force drew them together. The distance between them closed, and as their lips touched, electricity sparked in her belly. Jin pulled her in closer until there was no space left between their bodies at all. Sunshine settled on her skin, delicate and soft and wonderfully warm.

And then the door opened. "Skies," Marko muttered.

Astrea couldn't help it. She laughed, even as Jin pressed his forehead against hers.

"Yes?" Jin asked over his shoulder.

"Car's waiting." There was no malice in Marko's voice, no embarrassment. "We should get going . . . if you two are done."

Astrea slid her hand into Jin's, then they followed Marko out the door.

Chapter 19

Club Twilight towered against the dusky sky, its cream exterior washed out by the brilliant marquees and flashing lights drawing people toward not one but three sets of gilded double doors. Doormen in crisp suits ushered patrons inside.

The car Ysabel had loaned them for the night could only be described as extravagant. Its shiny white exterior, gold accents and trim, and smooth leather seats reminded Astrea of Eliana's car back in Kalama. This vehicle, though, had no roof, and it only sat two. As they pulled up behind other cars outside of Club Twilight, green curiosity spiked around several pedestrians. Jin put the car in park and climbed out.

An attendant rushed for Astrea's side of the vehicle, but Jin waved them off. He opened her door, then helped her out. It wasn't unlike that night at the dinner party in Kalama when she'd held onto his arm for most of the event. And she held onto him now, a lifeline. Jin tossed the keys to the attendant.

They were really doing this. They were really here.

Club Twilight sat on the corner of two main Talmaran streets, and Lucian was supposed to have teams in position on both roads. There was also a team on the roof. All in all, two dozen highly trained Novarians—half of them Lightbringers and one of them Marko—were just steps away from the club's front doors. It would have to be enough.

"How does it feel?" Jin asked.

"Like complete chaos." As far as Astrea's senses could stretch, she was met with every emotion she could name. They slid across her skin, settled in her bones, danced as a rainbow of colors in her line of sight. Chaos barely described it. "But if Nazarov is here, I can't feel him."

"He's probably not here yet," Jin said. The clock hanging above the club's doors said it was just after the seventh evening bell. "He wasn't exactly specific about when to meet."

Cars continued pulling up to the curb, including a flashy black car Cressida drove. Adi climbed out of the passenger side, and Cressida passed the keys to another waiting attendant when she joined them all on the sidewalk. Zephyrine, Lennor, and Civan had left the palace earlier and would already be waiting inside for them.

"Well, let's go see what this scum wants," Cressida said with an insincere smile.

Jin and Astrea led the way inside. The atrium was grand, far more elaborate than any of the clubs Astrea had visited with Eliana. Cressida whistled. The ceiling soared up three stories, revealing intricately carved trim and paintings of the night sky. Shiny black and white tile floors spread out as far as Astrea could see, down the hallway straight ahead and into two rooms on either side of the atrium.

Several hostesses in glitzy black dresses worked behind stands the other patrons filed past. Tough-looking bouncers loitered nearby, though Astrea couldn't help but be impressed by the crispness of their white shirts. Their group joined one line, and in a matter of moments, were at the front.

"Welcome to Club Twilight," said the hostess in Novarian. "Have you and your wife been here before?"

Wife? Astrea's cheeks burned almost pleasantly. Jin's muscle flexed under her hand. She just hoped that in the atrium's low light, neither Jin nor the hostess would notice how flustered she was.

"Plenty of times," Jin lied, flashing one of his too-smooth smiles. "My wife and I love it here."

Astrea's entire body may as well have been on fire.

"Welcome back." The hostess dropped a gold coin into Jin's palm. "It's good for three games of your choice, our gift to guests tonight. Enjoy yourselves."

"Thank you," Astrea squeaked as Jin tugged her toward the wide hallway beyond.

As soon as Adi and Cressida were through, they congregated in an alcove off the corridor. Dark tapestries covered the walls, broken up only by the occasional sconce. Three elevator doors sat on the opposite wall. A slow, smooth song flowed from somewhere deeper in the club, a mix of brass instruments, drums, and piano.

"Anything, Az?" Jin asked.

"No." There were no voids anywhere. Lucian had warned her not to push her magic out too far, but until Nazarov showed up, Astrea wasn't pulling her senses back. The energy pulsing around her made her the slightest bit dizzy. "I'll tell you when he's here."

"So, what, we just wait here until he shows up?" Cressida asked, her voice low as a steady flow of patrons strode past them.

"Definitely not here." Jin's attention shifted toward the crowds. Several people gave their small group strange expressions, a mix of curiosity and annoyance pushing into Astrea's chest. "It'll draw the bouncers' attention, and besides, we need to find the team. Did you get the same coin as us?"

The coin floated over Cressida's palm. While Jin and Astrea's was engraved with a rose, Adi and Cressida's was decorated with a mountain.

"I'm not saying get distracted," he said, "but let's at least try to blend in. Get a drink to hold, watch some of the tables."

"Aye, aye, Captain," Cressida said, earning a smirk from Adi.

They joined the flow of patrons heading deeper into the club. When they got to the end of the corridor, it was like walking from complete darkness into the sun. Crystal and silver chandeliers hung from the ceiling, casting warm light over the enormous space. More sconces were spaced evenly on the four walls, along with thick drapes. Table after table filled the room, each one home to different card and dice games. The crowd stretching out before Astrea was twice the size of that at the Whiskey Dream, if not larger, and this was just the first room on the first floor. Some of the clubgoers moved toward the wide archway leading to the next room.

Finding Nazarov and any other void mages in here would be like finding a needle in a haystack, even with Astrea's lightbringing. Filtering through the myriad emotions might just prove impossible.

"Bar first?" Jin asked. "Keep an eye out for Zephyrine."

They pushed their way through the crowds, heading for the bar at the back of the room. Astrea kept a death grip on Jin's hand. Even in his simple black suit, Jin drew the notice of several patrons. Did they know who he was? Or was he just an anomaly, one of the tallest people in the room? Either way, maybe the attention was a good thing. Maybe with the crowd's eyes on them, Nazarov wouldn't try anything. And skies knew how many people in there were mages, not to mention the bouncers making the rounds.

A spot at the long, wide bar cleared just as they approached, allowing the four of them to squeeze in. A dazzling array of bottles lined shelves stretching nearly all the way to the ceiling, and several bartenders rushed around. Adi raised his hand, grabbing one's attention. A well-endowed woman made her way toward them, and she flashed a sly smile at Adi.

"What'll it be, sweetheart?" she asked in Novarian.

"Whiskey on the rocks, double," Adi said.

"You got it. And for your friends?"

"Whiskey neat," Jin said.

"White wine," Cressida said, which Astrea ordered, too.

As the woman got started on their drinks, Cressida leaned back against the bar and surveyed the crowd. "I don't see Zephyrine anywhere. Would she have gone upstairs? Oh . . . wait. Is that her?"

Astrea followed Cressida's gaze to the only spot of white hair in the room. With the crowd, it was hard to tell for sure. But then Zephyrine emerged into the clear area near the bar, Lennor and Civan right behind her. They were all dressed to the nines.

Like Jin, Adi and Civan wore black suits. The only difference was in how they'd styled themselves. Where Jin had opted for no waistcoat and left his top two shirt buttons undone, Adi had gone for a waistcoat. Civan hadn't, but he was all buttoned up. Even his suit jacket was buttoned, fitted perfectly to his thin body.

Zephyrine was the picture of elegance in her deep blue dress trimmed with white beads. Lennor was in a light blue suit—the same shade as her eyes—with fashionable wide-legged trousers. Astrea had never seen the Tempest wear anything besides black, but color suited her.

"I see we're all here in one piece," Zephyrine said, lifting her hand to flag down a different bartender. "Anything yet?"

Astrea shook her head.

When the bartender returned with their drinks, Jin slid several Novarian bills toward her. "Stick together," Jin said once she disappeared again. "Always within line of sight, alright? Eyes on each other at all times."

As they headed back toward the tables, Astrea pushed back against everything threatening to drown her. One person's lust. Another's amusement, and yet another's frustration. Excitement, drunken glee, and giddy anticipation all swarmed her senses, and the occasional puff of blue lotus smoke did nothing to help.

Lennor and Civan broke off first, stopping near a table where people were betting on dice rolls and some contraption with a tiny, spinning ball. Jin and Astrea stopped at an adjacent one, pretending to watch as clubgoers threw colorful chips at a dealer. Zephyrine moved to the other side of the table, and Adi and Cressida stopped at the next one over.

They continued this routine for so long that Astrea lost track of time. Around and around the enormous room they went. Even when invited, Jin and Astrea always declined to join games. Adi played a few hands at one table, though Astrea could see he obviously wasn't paying attention to the game.

"Oh," Cressida said as they approached a table with two spots opening up. "Should we play a hand?"

"Captain?" Lennor asked. Where Lennor was often relaxed, her posture was now rigid. All business. Adi definitely didn't act that way around Jin.

"Go," he said. "Just don't lose focus." As Cressida and Lennor took their seats next to each other, Jin said, "Let's stick with them."

Astrea followed him over to the table. She didn't know the name of the game, nor did she pay attention as the dealer explained the rules. Instead, she scanned the crowd. A few tables down, Adi and Zephyrine were watching Civan play something. She tried to focus on Cressida and Lennor, on the way Lennor grinned at Cressida when she won a round, but the noise and crowd were starting to warp her senses.

"Jin," she whispered.

"Yeah?"

"I need to pull back. Lucian was right; it's too much."

Jin didn't take his eyes off the room as he said, "Don't hurt yourself, Az."

With great effort, Astrea pulled and pulled her magic back until finally, the pressure eased. The dizziness receded. She blew out a sharp breath and focused on the clock on the far wall. They'd already been inside for over an hour; she'd just have her barrier up for two minutes, then let it go again.

Two minutes was enough time for Lennor to win another round. She bumped Cressida's shoulder, then murmured something too low for Astrea to hear. As she loosened her tight grip on her magic, Lennor's pride swelled in Astrea's chest.

"Looks like someone's a lucky lady tonight!" the dealer exclaimed as he pushed a stack of chips toward Lennor.

Jin had just leaned down to say something to Astrea when cold surged violently against her skin. Astrea's entire body tensed. Her pulse doubled.

Not just cold. Two voids entered her awareness, though they were still some distance away.

"He's here," Astrea whispered to Jin. "There's another void mage with him."

"Just the one?" Tugged her closer to his body, Jin peered over her head.

"As far as I can tell." Astrea just hoped Lucian's teams knew Nazarov had finally arrived.

Two void mages. Just two void mages in a club full of hundreds of other people. Dozens of bouncers. Jin's team. They could do this.

Jin must've passed some silent message on to the rest of the team. Adi and Civan abandoned their game. Cressida folded her hand first, then Lennor folded hers, and they stood from their seats. Jin nudged Astrea toward the wide walkway snaking between the game tables.

"Can you tell where he is?" Jin whispered as he twined his fingers with hers.

"Just that he's headed toward us." Astrea frantically searched the crowds. Where was he? Was Solana the second void moving closer? She shivered.

"Adi," Jin said, some silent request passing between the two men.

He and Cressida closed in around Jin and Astrea. Lennor and Civan slinked off into the crowd, in opposite directions from where Zephyrine disappeared. Several people shoved past their foursome, annoyed but curious.

And then Lord Victor Nazarov emerged from the crowd. A lithe woman with sepia skin and dark, shiny hair pulled up in a slick ponytail walked on his right. A bulking man with sand-hued skin, light brown hair, and corded muscles flanked his left. And as the group stopped, the bulking man smiled at Astrea. No masks, no armor or strange Paragon uniforms. They were dressed perfectly in their fashionable black dress and suit, respectively. And yet Astrea knew exactly who they were.

Solana and Tovan.

Astrea swallowed hard. Hot rage burned her skin, though whether it was Jin's, Adi's, or Cressida's, Astrea wasn't sure. Perhaps all of theirs.

"Miss Sovna," Nazarov drawled as he approached them. "I thought the deal was that you didn't bring friends."

"You said no Novarians," Jin snapped. "And they're not Novarian."

"They might not be, though I swore you were, Your Imperial Highness. Or at least, part Novarian." Nazarov's copper eyes swept over their group, lingering on where Astrea and Jin still held onto each other. "I'll allow it, though. A loophole is a loophole."

"What the fuck do you want, Nazarov?" Jin asked. "Let's just get on with it. You've wasted enough of our time."

"So impatient, Sunreaper." Nazarov smirked and shoved his hands into his pockets. The pinstripes on his black suit were the only thing setting him apart from how The One had dressed. "First, introductions. We don't want to be rude." He motioned to the woman. "This is Solana." Then, as he motioned to the man, Nazarov said, "And Tovan. I believe Miss Sovna already knows them."

Astrea flinched as Tovan reached forward, offering his hand to Jin for a shake.

Jin didn't take it, though. His jaw tightened as he said, "I asked what you want, Nazarov."

"I'm here to talk to Miss Sovna."

"So talk." Astrea hoped her voice was as steady as she thought it was. "I'm right here."

Nazarov held her gaze. "Alone."

"That wasn't part of the deal," Jin said.

"Nor was bringing your entourage, and yet here we are." When Nazarov smiled, Astrea swore a hint of black flashed around him, just as it had at the Whiskey Dream that fateful night months prior. But it was gone before she could be sure. "Astrea and I talk alone, or the deal's off."

Astrea hated the words already forming on the tip of her tongue. "I'll talk to you," she said. "But we stay in this room."

"Bargaining, are we?" Nazarov nodded. "Fine."

"You have one minute," Jin said.

"Ah uh." Nazarov clicked his tongue. "It takes however long it takes, Sunreaper. Astrea and I will stay in this room, but you three"—he gestured to Astrea's friends—"stay *right* here. Tovan and Solana will make sure you hold up your end of the bargain. And believe me, you don't want to know what happens if you don't stick to it."

"Az . . ." Jin whispered, and she finally dared look up at him. Bright white panic pulsed rapidly around his body.

"Take a chance, Astrea," Nazarov said. "I made you this offer so very long ago in Kalama, and now look what's happened. Imagine what might happen if you decline again."

The same white panic was mirrored around Adi and Cressida.

This wasn't part of the plan Jin, Lucian, and the others had so carefully crafted. But they'd come this far. It was the closest they'd come to getting any kind of information. They needed something. *Complete the mission.*

Astrea hoped Jin, Cressida, and Adi could see the silent apology rolling off her as she pushed her shoulders back and turned toward Nazarov. "I'll go with you," she said, her voice barely audible above the cheers of a crowd surrounding one of the nearby game tables.

"Perfect." Stepping to one side, Nazarov gestured for Astrea to go first. "Shall we?"

CHAPTER 20

Astrea fought every instinct screaming at her to run as she walked away from her friends. Nazarov followed her, so close she could feel his breath tickling her neck.

"Keep going," he growled. "I'll tell you where to stop."

Astrea didn't know whether to focus on the panic building behind her or Nazarov's cold void. She didn't think she could focus if she wanted to. She kept walking until Nazarov touched the small of her back. Flinching, Astrea pulled away from him.

"Calm down. Go to your right."

She turned right, slipping past a crowd of drunken clubgoers who shouted about winnings and their next round of drinks. In the next room over, whatever band was playing picked up the tempo, switching to swing music perfect for dancing. People cheered.

"There, on your left," Nazarov said.

To Astrea's left was a mostly empty card table. A dealer sat behind it, shuffling a deck for the one patron waiting for the game to start.

"We never did get to play cards that night in Kalama," Nazarov said. "Have a few drinks. Play a few hands. Then we'll talk."

"Why are you doing this?" Astrea asked, rooted to her spot. "Just tell me whatever it is you want to tell me. Or is this just a trick to keep us distracted?"

"Not a trick," Nazarov said. "You want to take down the Helosian Emperor and The One. So do I. And I have information you'll find helpful as you strive for those goals."

"Then what's all this for?" Astrea asked again. "Just tell me."

"Not until you play cards with me."

Astrea's brows knitted together as she looked back toward where her friends were, lost among the crowd somewhere. Whispers of panic still reached her, but there wasn't anything she could do. There was no way they'd be able to see her over here.

"Fine," Astrea snapped. "One round, then you tell me."

"Two rounds."

Why did everything have to be a negotiation?

"Fine," Astrea said again.

Grabbing her wrist, Nazarov pulled her toward the card table. Astrea stifled a cry as she stumbled after him. It was too much like the way he'd grabbed her under that house, but she shoved the feeling deep, deep down. *Complete the mission.*

"Have a seat, Miss Sovna," Nazarov said as he dropped her arm. "Here, next to me on my left."

That would put her next to the other player. Astrea reached for the chair, but before she could, the other player stood and pulled it out. An unexpected face smiled at her.

"Hello, Astrea," Lord Theodore Kadis said in Helosian.

"What is this?" Astrea whispered, her gaze darting from Theo to Nazarov to the confused dealer. Her heart raced faster. "Theo?"

Theo Kadis, Helosian antiquities dealer and Paragon member. Here, in Talmaris, in this club, with Victor Nazarov.

"Oh, please, don't look so surprised," Theo said. "Just sit. Victor's not going to hurt you." He leaned around Astrea and glared at Nazarov. "You're scaring the girl."

"Sit down, Astrea," Nazarov ordered, and Theo sighed, an exasperated sound.

As Astrea sat, her pulse thundered so loud in her ears that she barely heard Nazarov offer the dealer enough money to cover all of their hands. The dealer set stacks of colorful chips in front of each of them.

What the fuck is Theo doing here? It was the only thought running through her head, over and over again. *Focus.*

Astrea tried to look at the table more closely to figure out what she was supposed to be doing. She'd just throw the whole hand, but she was sure Nazarov wouldn't consider it "playing a round" if she did that.

"What's the game?" she asked him.

"It's Stay the Course," he said.

Astrea knew this one, or at least the concept. The players and the dealer each began with three cards. Players aimed for a total close to twenty-five without exceeding it—which would lead to a loss—having to decide whether to draw more cards or hold. The dealer could only see two of their cards until the end of the round, at which point they had to have at least twenty in total, or they would keep drawing. Players had to beat both the dealer and other players to win.

What Astrea didn't understand was how people guessed whether or not they wanted to hold. Eliana was quite good at the game, as was Cressida, but Astrea had never bothered to learn the strategy, nor had she wanted to gamble. And now, she didn't care if she won. She just had to seem like she was *trying*. She had to convince Theo and Nazarov that she was going along with their demands.

"Bets?" the dealer asked.

Theo and Nazarov each threw in three of their chips, so Astrea copied them. The dealer began setting cards in front of them, and Astrea watched hers carefully. They added up to sixteen.

"Ladies first," Nazarov said in Novarian, then motioned at the dealer.

"Another card," Astrea told the man. The next card he set in front of her was a seven in the water suit. Twenty-three total. "I'll hold."

Theo and Nazarov both made a show of taking more cards from the dealer, and genuine amusement even flowed off Theo, but Astrea kept her eyes trained on her cards. On his third extra card, Nazarov busted. As he swore, a pulse of that black showed up again, almost blending in with his dark hair. Astrea was sure she hadn't imagined it.

"Well, you all lose," the dealer said as he dealt himself another card for a perfect twenty-five. He scooped up the chips they'd bet, then began reshuffling the deck. "Another?"

"What do you say, Astrea?" Nazarov asked.

"If you answer some of my questions, yes."

"We'll play again," Nazarov told the dealer in Novarian. All three of them threw chips into the center again as the dealer began handing out cards. "What do you want to know?" he asked Astrea in Helosian.

"What are you doing here, Theo?" she asked.

"Looking for you and Jin," he replied.

"Why?"

"Victor and I thought we might finally do things our way now that we're no longer working for The One."

That hardly answered her question. "Why did you try to kill your leader?" Astrea asked Nazarov instead.

"Because he's lost sight of the true path," he replied.

Ninette had used a similar phrase, though Astrea had thought she was talking about other people. Ninette had seemed to think The One did follow the true path, whatever it was.

"And you're on the true path?" she asked.

"Miss," the dealer cut in. "What would you like to do with your hand?"

Astrea stared down at her cards, trying to make sense of the suits and numbers. She had a ten of stars, five of stars, and five of fire. Twenty. "I'll stand," she told the dealer. He nodded.

Nazarov took another card, then stood at twenty-three. Theo went bust, as did the dealer. The dealer slid a handful of chips back toward Nazarov, then began dealing another round when they'd all placed their next set of bets. The game moved quickly, more than Astrea had anticipated when she'd agreed to play just two hands with Nazarov. But she needed time. She needed information. That was the whole reason she was here.

"*We* are on the true path," Nazarov finally answered. "The One has lost sight. His plan was never going to work."

"And what was that?" Astrea asked.

"He wanted you and Varojin to come to our side by any means necessary. When you spoiled his plans at the Whiskey Dream and again at the festival, The One was ready to try again, but he wanted to make sure his people did things right for once."

Astrea had already heard this from The One all those weeks ago in his office. Part of her almost told Nazarov to skip the story. But some other part of her told her to wait, to see how he might change the details. Maybe it would tell her something.

"When you and Jin showed up in my shop that day," Theo said, "I thought I might be able to educate you both and bring you into the fold in a more . . . natural way. When you fled Helosia, he was unhappy. But imagine our surprise when you ended up with Professor Shalysko."

"But he barely educated us at all," Astrea protested, just as she'd told The One. "The Paragon destroyed his office."

Nazarov shrugged. "If the professor seemed too helpful, I thought it would be suspicious. Besides, I didn't think you'd actually come to our side through simple information. The One had high hopes that quickly diminished after that little trip to the ruins, so he let me move forward with my own plans."

Astrea wasn't so sure that was true. Even if it was, how had Nazarov gotten The One to agree to attacking the palace? He hadn't seemed keen on taking things as far as Nazarov had, at least not as far as torture went. In fact, he'd told Nazarov to stay away from Astrea. She remembered that much.

"And you just let him make those plans even though you thought they'd fail?" she made herself ask.

Nazarov clicked his tongue. "Deceit and distraction aren't your forte."

"It's a simple question." Her heart pounded all the way up her throat. "You tried to kill him. Clearly you disagreed about a lot of things."

"And now the rest of the Paragon see how weak he was."

Did that mean the Paragon had abandoned The One? Were they on Nazarov's side now? Astrea was about to ask, but the dealer cut her off.

"Miss?" he prompted.

Despite Astrea's cards totaling to just fifteen, she said, "I'll hold."

"Shouldn't have done that, girl," a tall, skinny fellow with cool tan skin and brown hair said in Novarian from the empty side of the table. Astrea hadn't even noticed him sit down. "You had a chance to—"

"Can't you see I'm trying to have a conversation with my friends?" Nazarov barked at the man, his hand finding Astrea's. Anger and shame boiled under her skin, and Astrea slipped her hand away from his. "This is a private table. Get lost," he said to the newcomer. The man scoffed, but he stood and wandered away. Nazarov turned to Astrea, his smile predatory. "Don't worry, little Lightbringer. I won't tell Varojin about this."

Theo chuckled before asking the dealer for another card.

"Do the Paragon follow you now?" Astrea asked.

"They are returning to the true path."

Astrea forced her expression to remain neutral. She wanted to push for more answers about the Paragon's shifting loyalties, but would Nazarov be honest? That last answer hardly said anything. Would he have shown up with more followers if he had them? Maybe Lucian would have eyes on them outside.

"If you didn't think I'd come to your side, then why come to me with information now?" she asked. This seemed like a safer line of questioning.

"Because, as I've told you so many times, you are destined to help me. I thought I'd offer my help, too. But if I give you that information, you have to give me something in return."

"I'm pretty sure I've proven I have nothing to offer you," Astrea said as the dealer dealt himself another card and lost the round. Theo won, and he greedily took the chips the dealer passed his way.

"Just tell her what we want, Victor," Theo said. "You're dragging this out unnecessarily, just like you always do."

"I beg to differ," Nazarov replied, staring at Astrea. She didn't look at him. "That display in those tunnels was impressive, little Lightbringer. But that's not what we want, at least not right now. We want Mattina's journal."

"Why? Can you read it?"

"I can," Theo said. "We want to know what he was working on when he betrayed us."

"When he betrayed the two of you or the Paragon?" Astrea asked.

"Both," the men replied at the same time.

She didn't like the sound of that at all.

When the dealer offered her cards, Astrea shook her head. "And what will you give us if we give you the journal?"

"We'll give you—" Theo started, but Nazarov cut him off.

"That's something you and I will discuss alone, little Lightbringer." He glanced sidelong at the dealer as he switched to Novarian and said, "Cash us out. We're done here."

"Now, Victor—" Theo started again, and again, Nazarov cut him off.

"Go find Varojin, and keep a very close eye on him," Nazarov spat. "It's time Astrea and I have a real chat."

"Victor," Theo warned.

"Go," Nazarov snapped. "Now."

Theo pushed out of his seat, setting a cold hand on Astrea's shoulder as he passed. She shrank away from his touch, then back again as Nazarov grabbed her hand.

"Stop," Astrea said as she pulled away. "I agreed to hear you out. You don't have to touch me."

"Afraid I'll whisk you away? It'd be so *easy*, wouldn't it?" Nazarov smiled as he stood and motioned for her to do the same. "Come."

Standing on unsteady legs, Astrea smoothed the bodice of her dress and followed Nazarov away from their private table. Clubgoers barely paid them any mind, even when Nazarov reached for her and she pulled away again. Black—shadow, it almost looked like—flared around him for another heartbeat.

The Lightbringer trick Lucian had taught Astrea required access to someone's emotions, and she'd lamented that it wouldn't work on void mages. But Nazarov seemed to be . . . well, she wasn't sure what to call it. But that black appeared whenever he got angry. Had it shown up while the Paragon held her in that house? Had it shown up around The One? Astrea couldn't remember, and it disappeared so quickly, she wasn't sure if she'd be able to hold onto it. Besides, was attacking Nazarov in this club, while she was alone, a good idea?

No. No, it wasn't.

Astrea searched for any sign of Theo or her friends. But the club was only getting more crowded as the hour grew later, and her mind was turning to molasses as it had lately. Now was not the time for this. She could barely focus on anything besides breathing. *The mission,* Astrea reminded herself. *Focus on the mission.*

"What will you give me if we give you the journal?" she asked Nazarov.

"Now, now, Astrea," he said, "we haven't had our night of fun yet."

"I already played cards with you. That was the deal. You can't keep changing the terms."

"As far as I'm concerned, I can change the terms as many times as I want," he drawled. "My comrades and I are in control tonight, unless you plan on setting yourself off like that again. But I'd wager you won't do that in this club, just like I'd bet your princeling won't play Sunreaper in here." When Astrea said nothing, Nazarov smiled at her. "If you won't talk to me here, I know plenty of other places I can take you so we can chat. Maybe Tovan and Solana can even join us again. Get the band back together. That'd be fun, wouldn't it? Tovan was just telling me earlier that he missed you so very much."

No. No, Astrea did not want that. She didn't know what her light-bringing might do if she imploded like that again, not in this crowd. In this building. Nazarov was right. She wouldn't even try that.

So, with as strong a voice as she could muster, she asked, "What's this night of fun?"

"Let's have a drink."

As he suggested it, Astrea realized they'd circled all the way back to the bar at the far end of the room. And as Nazarov led her to an empty seat, Astrea realized she had a perfect view of her friends, right where she'd left them. Theo had found them, and red rage burned around Jin. His back was to her.

"One drink," Astrea said, still focused on her friends. Adi turned around, mint relief spiking high into his aura as he met Astrea's gaze. He tapped Jin's shoulder. "Just one."

"That's all I ask," Nazarov said. "Give me a chance."

Jin turned around, locking eyes with Astrea as mint relief and white panic joined the crimson rage still surrounding him. And when Nazarov grabbed Astrea's hand for what felt like the millionth time, Jin's rage and panic tripled, all-consuming.

Astrea yanked her arm away. "Touch me again and the deal's off." Her own rage coursed through her, overshadowing the fear pulsing deep in her bones. Nazarov could threaten her all he wanted, but she would not let him touch her again. Never again.

"Oh, but it's so much fun to see him angry," Nazarov cooed as he leaned against the bar and waved at Jin. "Such a temper that runs in that family. Skies. You'd think they'd have figured out how to get it under control. Has Eliana ever told you about the time Prince Kaius went off on—"

"Stop playing games." Astrea's voice trembled. "Just stop. Theo's right. You're just wasting time."

"Fine. Give me the journal, and I'll give you two things. First, I'll tell you where I think Theo's book is."

She stared at him. Theo's book? "Why would you do that? I thought it was important to you."

"It is, but I'd rather you have it than Emperor Aelius."

Astrea swallowed hard. "And you can't get it yourself?"

"No."

She'd have to consider that later. "And what's the second thing?"

"I'll answer one more question of yours."

Myriad questions jumped to the forefront of Astrea's mind all at once. What was in the book that Emperor Aelius shouldn't have it? What could Mattina have been researching that Theo and Nazarov would want his journal that badly? What about The One? Where was he? Where had all those Paragon at that house gone? Did they truly follow Nazarov now? Had their goals changed if Nazarov was formally in charge, or was he following the same creed of chaos, destruction, and balance?

"I can't make that decision without talking to my team." Astrea wanted to say yes—if only to finally figure out what Theo's book was all about—but she needed time to consider what all of this meant. If handing it over was even a good idea.

"I think it's a very fair trade."

"You would, since you're the one who proposed it." All she wanted was to get away from this man. With every passing second, his expression turned more predatory. "Let me talk to my team."

"Then let's go talk to them."

Astrea bolted past him. Nazarov grabbed her wrist and yanked her back into his body so hard she stumbled. Jin still watched them, and she kept her gaze locked on his.

"Now, now," Nazarov growled in her ear as he pressed against her, "remember what happened last time you tried to run from me? What happened last time you tried to cross me? Tell me, little Lightbringer, do you still have the scars to prove it? Does the princeling like them?"

Goose bumps covered her skin. Images of that house came back to Astrea, not from Nazarov's dreamwalking but her own memory. The hallway where he'd caught up to her. The One's office. The impossible darkness of those tunnels. Her breath turned shallow.

He squeezed her forearm. "Walk calmly or else we aren't going to talk to your friends." Releasing her, Nazarov backed up one step.

Forcing herself to walk slowly, Astrea made her way right to where Jin, Adi, and Cressida watched her. Zephyrine and the twins were nowhere in sight, likely still spread out among the crowd. They wouldn't have gone too far, though. Even Theo, Solana, and Tovan all watched as Astrea and Nazarov approached.

The distance between them closed, and the sounds of the chaotic club died as Astrea's ears filled with the drumming of her own heart. She was so close. What if Nazarov decided to snatch her now? Jumping away with her at the last second seemed like something he would do.

Astrea held her breath.

Just a few more paces . . .

And she reached them. Without hesitation, Astrea grabbed Jin's hand. Nazarov simply continued his casual stroll in their direction. Astrea swore she heard Tovan snicker, but blood roared in her ears, drowning out some of the noise of the club.

"Did you all have a nice time getting to know each other?" Nazarov asked. "Because Miss Sovna and I have had a lovely start to our nights."

"I've heard enough from Theo," Jin snapped. "So what do you want?"

"Mattina's journal. Astrea knows the conditions of the trade I'm offering. She can fill you in."

"When do you need an answer?" Astrea asked.

"Though I was already generous in giving you time to mull over this meeting, I'm in a good mood after our fun tonight. I'll give you until the end of tomorrow to consider."

"And how do we tell you if we agree to this trade or not?"

"Oh, don't worry, little Lightbringer. I know where to find you, though I'd think twice about declining the trade. If you do, Tovan and I might have to have another chat with you." Nazarov winked, and Astrea's blood chilled. Rage exploded across Jin's aura, crimson and hot and so strong it obscured whatever Adi and Cressida were feeling. "Enjoy the rest of your evening."

Nazarov skirted around their group and headed toward the atrium without a glance back over his shoulder. Solana, Tovan, and Theo all followed. Astrea eventually lost sight of them in the crowd, but the two void mages were easy to track. They continued their retreat until they were too far out of her range.

It was all Astrea could do to keep herself from sinking to the ground in warring relief and disbelief. Her tense muscles nearly gave out, but she managed to stay upright.

"Well?" Cressida asked when nobody spoke. "What did he offer?"

"He wants Mattina's journal," Astrea said, "and in return, he'll tell us where he thinks Theo's book is, and we get to ask him one question."

"Where he *thinks* it is?" Cressida asked. "What good is that?"

Jin stared in the direction Nazarov had gone. "Let's just get the fuck out of here. We can talk about it back at the palace."

Astrea didn't know how she managed to walk through the club and its crowd again. She didn't know how she managed to stand on the sidewalk and wait for an attendant to bring their car around. And she didn't know how she managed to climb into the car without completely falling over. But she did. And it was only when they were finally driving through the glowing streets of Talmaris that Astrea let herself close her eyes and pull her barrier in around herself.

Chapter 21

By the time Jin stopped the car at the steps leading up to the palace's entrance, Astrea couldn't feel her body anymore. Not from the chilly night air. No, it was that strange feeling of static taking over, like an out-of-tune radio.

When Jin turned the car off, Astrea barely noticed that the engine no longer made her seat rumble. It was only Jin opening her car door and Eliana yelling as she ran down the palace's steps that made Astrea take a breath.

"You're back!" Eliana's words finally broke through to Astrea's mind. "Skies, you're back!"

"Hey, Ellie." Astrea failed to brace as Eliana threw herself into her arms, and they both stumbled back into the opulent car. Behind them, three more engines roared and tires squealed. The team.

"Did he show?" Nicos asked. Orange anxiety lit up the darkness around him. When had he come outside?

"Oh, he showed," Jin said. Car doors opened and shut behind them. "Come on, let's go in."

Astrea tried to walk to the palace on her own. But her whole body began to tremble. When Jin touched her shoulder, she flinched.

"Hey," he murmured. "Wait."

She waited, watching as their friends started for the building. Jin slipped off his suit jacket, then draped it over her shoulders. Astrea didn't have the heart to tell him she wasn't cold. Instead, she pulled the jacket tight around herself, trying to focus on its soft lining rather than her thundering heart.

Lucian joined them just as they started up the stairs. He asked Astrea something, but she didn't know what. Jin answered. *Tovan and I might have to have another chat with you.* They passed through the towering front doors and into the warmly lit palace.

Lucian asked another question, and again, Jin answered. *Remember what happened last time you tried to run from me?*

They caught up to the rest of the team, and Cressida asked something next. Astrea tried to look at her and say something, but her vision wouldn't focus. *Remember what happened last time you tried to cross me?*

Tears welled in Astrea's eyes. *Not now. Not here.* She pulled at Jin's suit jacket again, adjusting it to sit properly on her shoulders.

"Nazarov wants the journal we found back in Helosia," she said to Lucian. They were still standing in a corridor. "He's willing to give us information. I don't know if he's being honest, and he didn't really give us a choice. He threatened to take me from the palace again."

Lucian hesitated. Astrea had never seen him hesitate, but his mouth opened, then shut, and his eyebrows furrowed. Those midnight blue eyes of his, usually so hard, softened. "Let's regroup first thing in the morning. I'll have Marko, Cari, and Vernie posted outside your room all night."

"Thank you, Commander," Jin said.

Was Astrea supposed to know those names, aside from Marko? She couldn't remember. Jin's hand found hers, and they started walking again. Someone fell in step behind them, and the farther they walked, the farther Astrea's friends' voices became.

Tell me, little Lightbringer, do you still have the scars to prove it? Does the princeling like them? Astrea grabbed Jin's hand, a tether when she was so close to floating away.

Astrea wrapped her blanket around herself as she sat in front of the fire, shivering. The palace wasn't even cold. The night air hadn't been all that chilly when they'd been out for the mission. And yet Astrea couldn't stop shaking.

After getting to their room, Astrea had managed to change into her pajamas and wash the makeup off her face. Jin had suggested she sit in front of the fire while he cleaned up for bed. And so, there Astrea sat.

Was this what Nazarov wanted? To make her feel so small? If so, it was working. She'd been able to ignore most of the pain inside her once they'd gotten to that base. She'd mostly been able to ignore it even at the palace, so long as she kept busy. But her chest ached. Her heart hurt. It never stopped hurting. And now that she was safely tucked away in her room again, it was as if someone had ripped a hole in her chest and set her on fire.

Behind her, a lamp clicked on. Jin. Muffled footsteps and the occasional creak of the floors betrayed his movement. The faucet in the bathroom turned on, and as Astrea forced herself to breathe, she focused on the sound of the water. The faucet turned off again. Socked feet appeared in her peripheral vision, then Jin plopped down next to her.

Astrea watched the flames as they danced in the small fireplace, warm and low. She was sure Jin was controlling them; they barely popped or crackled like a natural fire would. Shadows flickered in the hearth as the flames continued their subtle dance.

"Tonight was hard," Jin said, breaking the tense silence.

She swallowed thickly. "Yeah."

"I hated watching you walk off with him."

"I hated going."

She'd only gone because it had seemed like the right choice. And it had probably been the only choice. *I'd think twice about declining the trade. Tovan and I might have to have another chat with you.* If Nazarov was threatening to take Astrea away again, he probably would've come for her had they not agreed to meet him in the first place.

Having to see Nazarov and Theo again had been bad enough. Worse, though, was the way she'd simply been frozen since she'd left Club Twilight. She knew she wasn't at that house—still knew she wasn't there—but her mind took her back anyway. The jumps through the darkness. The pinch of every needle. Tovan and Solana. All of it.

And freezing was so embarrassing. To have managed through the entire mission, only to lose focus at the end, to have Lucian look at her with such pity . . .

She'd been hiding it all so well until today.

And she wasn't sure she could hide it anymore.

"How can you even stand to be around me, Jin?" Astrea whispered, her gaze trained on the fire. "I'm broken."

Surprise danced over her skin. "You aren't broken."

"Really? Because I'm scared, and I'm tired, and I need . . . I'm a grown woman who needs to sleep with the lights on." She motioned behind her head to where her lamp sat, the one Jin had placed there just for her. It was an achingly sweet gesture, and Astrea hated it. She hated that she needed it. "They broke me," she said, voice cracking. "I'm not meant for any of this. I can't do what you do."

"Az—"

"I can't believe I let him anywhere near me." Astrea choked as she tried and failed to swallow the first sob. She pulled the blanket tighter around herself, burrowing into it as she cried, "It hurts all the time. *I* hurt all the time. It doesn't stop. I should've just stayed under that house. I should've just let them kill me."

Heavy grief and regret battled in Astrea's chest as Jin pulled her into his arms. His embrace crushed her, holding her steady as the torrent of tears came.

Why did Jin have to be so kind and warm? What could she have done to deserve it when she was nothing? She'd struggled to find any answers. Playing detective was getting her nowhere. She wasn't even a mediocre detective; she was a terrible one. Training would only get her so far. She was still a liability. She couldn't even answer Lucian's simple questions without falling apart. What good was she?

Some tiny part of her knew that wasn't all true. She'd learned so much about lightbringing in a month. Had gotten stronger physically. Had become a stronger healer. Had convinced Lucian to go to the eastern ruins, which seemed to be getting them *something*. It all just felt so small when looking at everything else still left to be done, when looking at all the ways she was still a liability and all the ways she'd already failed.

Jin ran his hand over her hair, stopping when he reached the back of her neck. His thumb drew small, smooth circles on her skin. His heart thumped steadily under Astrea's ear, calm even as his sadness pressed into every part of her.

When he kissed the top of her head, Astrea loosened her iron grip on her blanket. Her pulse began to slow. Her breath came back to her. Jin slid his arms under the blanket and circled her waist.

"I'm sorry," she whispered, sniffling.

"Don't ever be sorry for this." Jin laid his head on top of hers. "Never."

"I'm so scared he's going to come back for me."

"I am, too."

"Every time he grabbed my arm tonight . . ." Fresh tears spilled down her cheeks. "He asked me if I remembered what happened the last time I tried to cross him. He said Tovan missed me."

It was only a matter of time, Astrea was sure, before she had to deal with them again. Victor Nazarov would not give up so easily. The Paragon would not give up so easily. And how simple would it be for them to jump into the palace in the middle of the night, snatch them both, and leave without a trace? Nazarov had promised as much, and she had no doubt he could do it if he really wanted to.

Jin took Astrea's face in his hands, brushing away her tears with his thumbs. She forced herself to look into his eyes. The whites of them were red and watery, but the gold was so brilliant. Even as blue sadness swirled around him, gentle warmth caressed her skin.

"I know you're scared," Jin said, "and I know you're tired. I am, too. But needing to sleep with the lights on? Being afraid? Those things don't mean you're broken, Az. You're still here. You're still holding on." His hands slid down to her shoulders, and he gave her the gentlest shake. "Look at all you've done despite them. You're still standing. You're still fighting. I think tonight was proof of that. You handled him. You did it. You completed our mission."

Her heart broke and repaired itself with each word, warring pain and relief. She wanted to believe him. She really wanted to.

"I know it doesn't feel like any of that is true," Jin continued, "but Az, I promise, there's no shame in doing whatever it is that helps."

She swallowed hard. "Even if it means sleeping with the lights on?"

"Even that."

"You don't think it's silly?"

"No, I don't, but it wouldn't matter even if I did. If it helps you, it doesn't matter what I think. It doesn't matter what anyone else thinks."

Of course he was right. Sleeping with a lamp on didn't hurt anyone. And it definitely helped her. How many times had she woken up in the middle of the night in recent weeks, and instead of finding that awful darkness, found warmth?

Jin brushed more of her tears away as he said, "For a long time after the Delian-Helosian War, I could only sleep during the day. That way, if I woke up from a nightmare like I usually did, it was easier to jump back into the real world and remind myself it was just a dream. The sun was my version of the lamp back then."

"Does it ever get easier?"

"Yes." Jin sighed, a tired, heavy sound. "With time. But it's never truly gone away for me. I'm not sure it ever does."

Astrea fingered the corner of her blanket and let her gaze fall down to where Jin had wrapped his arms around her waist again. "Do you ever think back to those tunnels?"

"All the time. And I know it's so much easier said than done, but fixating on the past doesn't help."

Astrea didn't *want* to fixate on the past. But her mind often took her back anyway. She wiped her eyes with the back of her hand. "I need to find a way forward," she whispered.

"You already are."

"I haven't, not really."

"You've come a long way in your training in the last month. Honestly, I'm surprised you've gotten back to it so quickly. It took me a long time to find my way back to . . . anything . . . after what happened to me on Ilesouria."

"Really?"

"Ask Zephyrine if you don't believe me," he said. "And besides, you got us to those ruins. You went back to that house. That's not nothing. The training alone is hard work."

Astrea leaned against Jin's chest, breathing in the crisp scent of soap still clinging to him. "Maybe you're right."

"Oh, I know I'm right." When she flicked his chest, he laughed and crushed her to him. Sweet amusement coated her tongue. "Damn, Sovna. Maybe you've been training a little too much. That hurt."

"Maybe you need to worry about me less and train more, then."

"Hm." Jin searched her face. "I don't think I'll ever stop worrying about you."

"Not even when this is all over?"

"Not even then. I care, Az." Warmth spread over her limbs as he added, "I care so much about you." The words were so gentle yet so strong, desperate almost.

She leaned forward, pressing her mouth to his. He kissed her back gently.

"I care about you, too," she whispered. The warmth doubled, turning pleasantly hot as it reached every part of her and settled in her chest. "Thank you."

"For what?" He pressed a soft kiss to her temple.

"For being there tonight. For being here now."

"Always, Az. I'm not going anywhere."

Astrea didn't know how long they sat there like that, her back to the fire and head on Jin's shoulder. Jin traced patterns on her back, loops and curves and shapes she couldn't figure out, almost like he was writing on her skin. Every time Nazarov's words came back, she replaced them with what Jin had told her. That she was fighting. That she was moving forward.

Because as much as they liked to jest about who was right, the truth in Jin's words rang deep in Astrea's bones. She knew they were true. She knew he was right. She just had to get her aching heart on board.

CHAPTER 22

Astrea woke shortly after the fifth bell, far earlier than she'd been up in days. Memories of Tovan and Ninette had plagued her dreams all night. And tired as she was, she wasn't keen on fighting against the darkness anymore.

Careful not to wake Jin, Astrea rolled out of bed and went to the bathroom. The tile floor was cold under her bare feet. Even the air prickled her skin. As she cleaned up, she tried not to look in the mirror too closely. But it was hard not to, just as it was difficult to ignore the dark half moons under her eyes. Her face was puffy.

Tovan and I might have to have another chat with you. Astrea's fingers drummed against the smooth stone counter. Skies damned Victor Nazarov. His words from the night before still ran circles in her mind, unyielding even with the new day.

Stop, Az. Just go back to bed. Fixating on it wasn't going to change it. Today was supposed to be about moving forward.

Astrea flipped the bathroom lights off, then crept back into the bedroom. Jin was right where she'd left him, lying on his side. He looked so peaceful when he was asleep. No worry lines in his forehead. No tight shoulders. She slipped back under the covers and settled down.

"Hey," Jin whispered as he tugged her closer.

So much for him being asleep. Still, Astrea curled against him, welcoming his heat. After dreaming of those tunnels all night, there was nothing she wanted more than to stay warm.

"You good?" he asked.

"I just need this . . . if it's alright."

Jin hummed. "Oh, it's more than alright."

The way he pressed into her made Astrea's pulse jump pleasantly. For a few moments, she seriously considered staying there in bed with him. But there was something else she wanted—needed—to do.

"Can we go to the lake?" she asked. "Before the others wake up."

"Why?"

"To train."

"Do you want me to get Adi?"

"No. I want to train with just you."

Surprise tickled the end of her nose. Jin pushed up on his elbow behind her, and Astrea peeked over her shoulder at him. "With just me?" he asked, almost hesitant.

"Yes. You always just direct me from the sideline." When he didn't look convinced, she added, "Please?"

"And you want to go now?"

"Yes."

Jin rubbed his hand over his face, then through his messy curls. "Alright. Sure. Let's go to the lake."

"Thank you."

He pressed a hard, wet kiss to her cheek. "Anything for you."

Even though it took some time getting dressed, and even though Jin had insisted on stopping to get thermoses of coffee and water from the kitchen, it was still dark when they arrived at their usual spot by the water. A smattering of stars still clung to the sky directly above their heads. Through the towering trees, Astrea could make out the faintest hint of color on the horizon.

"What do you want to work on?" Jin asked as he set their drinks down near the base of a nearby oak tree.

"I was hoping you had something in mind."

Jin chuckled. "You drag me out of bed before sunrise—before I've even had a chance to cuddle—and you don't even know what you want to work on?"

"I haven't exactly memorized drills yet."

Jin glanced behind her toward the palace, then at her again. "Alright. Give me a moment to think."

"Seems like something *you'd* have memorized," she teased.

"I do. I'm just trying to figure out what you need to work on."

"Everything."

"What do you feel is weakest?" he asked. "Not what Adi or Lucian says, but what *you* think."

Astrea felt like everything was weak besides her healing capabilities. But as she considered . . . "My movement." She swallowed hard, the next thought making her chest tighten. "Including getting away from someone or breaking their hold on me."

After Club Twilight the night before, it was only more obvious that she needed to get faster. Stronger. Nazarov would come for her, and if he didn't, The One would. She needed to know how to get away from them.

Teal understanding blossomed around Jin as he said, "Right." It was the voice he always used when he was directing his team in drills. "Movement and self-defense. We can work with that."

With the first few drills Jin directed her through, Astrea felt awkward and stiff. Her body had yet to warm up for the day, and Jin didn't go easy on her. In one such drill, she was supposed to summon her shield as she ran, then use her momentum to push Jin out of the way. Every time she did, he pushed back hard. She fell on her ass four times before she got past him once, and she fell plenty more before he was satisfied with her ability to perform the move.

"Question," Jin said as Astrea shook out her arms. "How do you feel about being tackled?"

"Excuse me?" Astrea's brows furrowed, but Jin didn't crack a smile. He crossed his arms over his chest.

"We can keep the idea of the last drill with your shield but change what I'm doing."

If Jin had a trick, she'd gladly fall a few more times to learn. "Alright, let's do it."

"Tell me if it hurts too much."

"I can handle it."

"I know, but training isn't about getting hurt. We'll push your limits and build up your tolerance. We don't have to break bones to do that."

That seemed fair, and Astrea really wasn't keen on breaking another bone. Lucian's intense training at the old base had already resulted in that once.

"Okay," Astrea said. "What do we do?"

"You'll stay there," Jin said. "Right before I make contact with you, summon your shield and shove back against me as hard as you can. If you can, twist to one side as you push. Throw me off balance."

As they set their positions, Astrea pushed her shoulders back. Behind Jin, pink and orange had crept up the sky, pushing away the darkness and giving way to dawn. From a couple dozen feet away, Jin flashed her a quick smile.

Then he sprinted at her full speed.

Bracing herself, Astrea pulled on the adrenaline and magic mixing in her veins. Skies, he was fast. And when he'd almost reached her, Astrea tried to summon her shield. She was a fraction of a heartbeat too slow. Jin slammed into her, one arm wrapping around her waist and the other coming to cradle the back of her head. All of her breath left her body. He twisted them before they slammed into the ground. Jin took the brunt of the impact with his shoulder, though he didn't fully cushion their fall.

"Fuck," Astrea grunted, her head lolling back when Jin finally let go.

"Too slow." Jin tightened his grip on her waist, pressing their bodies together tightly. Sweet amusement filled Astrea's mouth. "This isn't half bad, though."

She huffed. "You're impossible."

With a chuckle, Jin hauled her back to her feet. "Again."

It took five tries before Astrea finally summoned her shield in time, and it took another three tries after that before she finally shoved Jin away from her and made him lose his balance.

She ran to his side. Rolling onto his back, Jin groaned and laughed. Pain surged through Astrea's right shoulder.

"Let me see," she said, dropping to her knees in the soft grass.

"I just bumped it," he said when Astrea put her hands on his right shoulder. "It's fine."

"Let me check anyway."

When he agreed, Astrea pulled on her light, letting it seep into Jin's shoulder. He was right; he hadn't actually injured anything. She still pushed healing energy into him, both of them sighing as his pain stopped.

"Better?" she asked.

Instead of answering, Jin reached up and threaded his fingers into her hair at the base of her neck. He pulled her down, kissing her so fiercely that Astrea's head began to spin.

"I've never been kissed for knocking someone to the ground," she said, breathless, when he pulled away.

"That's what I want you to do, Az."

" . . . Kiss people during training?"

He laughed and pushed himself up so he was sitting. "No. *That*. What we've been doing all morning. If any of those monsters come back, use that shield. Push back against them as hard as you can."

"Right."

"You've done it to Adi, and you've done it to me, and we're far bigger than you," Jin said. "You can do it to them, too. You're strong enough." He tapped her thigh. "Keep generating power from your legs like that."

"Can we go again?" Astrea asked. Now that she'd figured out the timing, she wanted to keep practicing it. "Just a few more rounds."

"Sure," he said. "Then we'll go back. Don't want to be late for our meeting with Lucian."

Astrea had managed to knock Jin down four of the six more times they practiced that final move. Every time, Jin had been so happy. So proud. It was almost a little funny, to think he was so glad to go sprawling on the ground.

They'd just finished showering and getting dressed for the day when someone knocked on their door. Jin answered it, revealing Commander Lucian.

"May I come in?" he asked.

"Is something wrong?" Jin asked as he stepped aside to let the commander in. "I thought we were meeting at half past eight."

The clock sitting on the fireplace mantel said they still had a half hour before they were supposed to meet.

"Nothing's wrong. I wanted to check on you before we go downstairs." Glancing between Jin and Astrea, Lucian added, "Cari told me you were up before sunrise."

"Just fitting in some drills," Astrea said, rolling up the cuffs on her white linen shirt.

Lucian nodded, as if that explained everything he needed to know. Usually he pushed for more information than that. "And are you alright?" he asked. "Both of you. You seemed shaken up last night."

"We're alright," Jin said.

"We are," Astrea echoed when Lucian's brows knitted together.

He gave her a pointed look, and she knew why. She hadn't had her barrier up in days, not really. Surely Lucian could sense every complicated thing she felt. After her talk with Jin the night before, some parts of her felt better and others felt the same. Knowing he was there to support her and fight with her eased the ache in her bones, but it didn't stop the pain that constantly squeezed her heart.

"Really," Astrea insisted. "Not great but alright."

Pressing his lips together, Lucian nodded. "If you say so."

"Is that the only reason you came up here?" Jin asked.

"I wanted to ask you two what happened last night. Adi filled me in as best he could, but I assume there was much he didn't see since Astrea went off on her own."

"Uhm . . . well . . ." Astrea's fingers twitched. Where did she even begin?

"Their Highnesses were going to join us as well," Lucian said.

Wonderful. Astrea forced a smile. "Then let's not keep them waiting."

Eliana, Nicos, Zephyrine, and Marko were already waiting in the hall. As a group, they started through the palace. Where was Cressida? Adi? The twins? Astrea supposed not everyone needed to be there, but it felt wrong somehow.

As they made their way through corridors and past guard after guard, Astrea began to tense. Her heart fluttered unpleasantly. She was going to have to tell an entire room full of people . . . everything.

Lucian led them to the same war room they'd used a couple days before. Now, Ysabel sat at the head of the table, Veiko to her right, and one of the Novarian councillors—a bald, brown-skinned man whose name Astrea couldn't remember—sat on her left. Her friends filled in around the table.

Astrea eyed Prince Veiko. This was the first time she'd seen him since returning from the old base. He was dressed far more casually than his aunt and the councillor. As his purple eyes met Astrea's, he gave her a small smile.

"Well." Grand Duchess Ysabel sat up straighter as everyone settled in. "Commander Lucian has informed me that you made contact with Lord Victor Nazarov and his associates."

"We did," Jin said. "He's making demands and threats."

"Did we expect otherwise?" Prince Veiko asked, pushing a few strands of his chestnut hair off his forehead. "This is the man who stabbed his own leader, correct? The one who tortured Miss Sovna?"

Heavy discomfort and regret pulsed around the table. *Lucian is here*, she reminded herself as she pulled her barrier in. *There are other Lightbringers here.* She could give herself this reprieve for a few minutes.

"That's him," Astrea managed to say past the block in her throat.

"I wouldn't say we expected otherwise," Lucian said, "but the demand was perhaps not what we . . . anticipated."

What had they even anticipated? Astrea's mind had run her through more than a dozen possibilities before the meeting. Theo had been the real surprise of the night. So had the knowledge that he could translate the journal.

"The journal, right?" Ysabel asked. She gestured toward where it sat in the middle of the table. Astrea hadn't even noticed it; she hadn't seen it in weeks, since before she left for the old base. Tomas, Mariya, and Cressida had been examining it.

"He's given me until tonight to get him an answer, Your Highness," Astrea said. "In exchange for this journal, he'll tell us where he thinks the book is that Emperor Aelius wants, and he will answer one question we have."

"Where he *thinks* the book is? And he'll answer *our* question?" Ysabel scoffed. "I should think he owes us far more in return if we give him what he wants. We need guarantees. Something more than a single clue."

"He's not willing to negotiate. He . . . He warned me not to forget what happened when I last crossed him." Astrea forced the words out. "He promised he would take me away again."

"And likely Varojin as well," Lucian said. "I know Nazarov seems particularly fixated on you, Astrea, but we must consider that possibility."

Of course she was considering that. If Nazarov only took her, it would be another attempt to manipulate Jin. And if he got both of them? Well, skies knew what would happen then.

"Is there any other way to translate the notebook?" Ysabel asked.

"Theo knows how to read the language," Astrea said. When the grand duchess asked who that was, Astrea explained. Nobody liked the fact that he'd shown up again.

"The professor seemed to think we had to find a way to translate it," Jin said slowly. "I don't think he knew anyone who could help aside from the Paragon. And it's not like he could just take it to them with the way we were keeping him at the palace."

"There must be someone in the group besides Theo who can read the language," Eliana said.

"A linguist might be able to decode it with enough examples and translations," Astrea offered, though they'd briefly discussed the idea before. "Though that could take a long time." Her studies at university had barely touched on the topic, but that was a monumental task that required time and care. They certainly didn't have time.

"What if we make a counter offer?" Eliana asked. "If Theo Kadis is our chance at learning what's in that journal, then we can meet him and watch him work. Get the translation for ourselves, too, and see what information they offer us in return."

"What's to stop them from lying to us, though?" Nicos asked. "I don't trust them to keep their word."

"Sometimes we just have to go with the best intel we have," Jin said, his gaze flicking to Zephyrine. She nodded. "Sometimes that's the only option."

"I don't like it," Marko whispered, so low Astrea was sure only she had heard him.

She didn't either, but what choice did they have? Keep running around in a desperate attempt to find information . . . or take a chance and see what Nazarov and Theo had to offer.

"I agree with Eliana," Veiko said. "It is the right option. The only option, it seems."

The councillor, who had remained silent for the entire conversation, finally said, "Is this wise? We all want to know more about these renegades, but what if the notebook has information they need to do . . . whatever it is they want to do?"

"At least we'll know it, too," Jin said. "It gives us even a small chance at knowing what they want to do, which is better than what we have otherwise."

"What if we get the translation, then assassinate them?" the councillor asked.

Astrea stiffened.

"Councillor Tarsaya…" Zephyrine drummed her fingers on the table. "It's not that simple."

"Why not?" he asked. "Go in, watch them work, take the translation, and kill them. This Nazarov only seems to have a small group behind him, yes? Surely Commander Lucian and Prince Varojin can take them out."

"I'm not against taking Nazarov out, but what if they give us a false translation?" Jin asked. "Or they escape again and we anger them? We don't even know the full extent of void magic yet. We have no idea what else they might be capable of."

"So we just let Nazarov live after everything he's done?" the councillor asked.

Jin's jaw muscles flexed. "For now."

"I'm inclined to agree with Varojin," Lucian said. "Who knows what else Nazarov may be able to tell us about Emperor Aelius or The One. It's worth keeping him alive for the time being."

"I agree," Ysabel said. "Miss Sovna, propose our terms when Nazarov contacts you today. And do let me know as soon as he's made contact, yes?"

"Of course, Your Highness," Astrea said.

"Now, is there anything else?" Ysabel asked. "I have calls to make. The embassies are beginning to question why I've had the palace shut down for so long."

"They still don't know?" Jin asked.

"No, and I don't plan on telling them more than they need to know right now," Ysabel said. "So, anything else?"

When everyone around the table declined to continue the discussion, Ysabel excused herself. Veiko joined her, as did the councillor.

"Well," Eliana said when the meeting room doors closed again, "now what? Do you know when Nazarov is going to reach out?"

"The end of the day, I'd guess, based on what he said last night," Astrea said. "But he wasn't specific. He never is."

"Perhaps you should simply relax until he reaches out," Lucian said, his tone gentle just as it had been when he'd asked Astrea and Jin how they were feeling. It was almost jarring. "We were all up very late last night, and if we're going to be dealing with Nazarov and his cronies, we want to be at our best."

"I think that's a good idea." Jin's hand brushed Astrea's under the table. "I'm exhausted."

"I'll have breakfast sent to your rooms," Lucian said. "Now go on, get some rest. I'll check in with you later."

As Astrea got up from the table and followed Eliana back out into the hallway, Nicos and Jin right behind them, Astrea wrung her hands together. The overwhelming need to do *something* poked at her mind, but she pushed back against it. The commander was right. If they were going to start working with Nazarov—however temporarily—they'd need their wits about them.

CHAPTER 23

Waiting around for Victor Nazarov to dreamwalk was not Astrea's ideal way of spending a day. In fact, it was never how she wanted to spend time again. But there wasn't anything to do; Tomas didn't need help in the library. Eliana was busy working on revisions for her plans for a new Helosian government. And napping, then eating breakfast with Jin, Adi, and Marko, had only taken a short time.

So when Cressida had shown up at Jin and Astrea's door to ask for Jin's help with something, Astrea had tagged along. So had Adi and Marko, who were just as bored.

Being out in the fresh air and sunshine helped loosen Astrea's taut muscles. So did the amusement tangling in the air between Adi and Marko as they followed Cressida through the gardens toward Mariya's observatory.

"I'm sorry, but the fact that you say strawberry muffins are best makes me seriously question your judgment, Marko. It's unthinkable, and I don't care what your logic is." Adi gestured vaguely to the lush greenery. "It's just factually incorrect. Everyone *knows* blueberry are best."

"People are entitled to their opinions, Adi," Marko drawled.

"Well, I suppose everyone's also entitled to be wrong sometimes."

"And that would be you today."

"*I'm* wrong? You ate three of the worst muffins for breakfast!"

"You two are still going on about this?" Jin called to them. That just made sugary amusement coat Astrea's tongue, almost like a too-sweet cup of coffee. She imagined Adi and Marko would both have strong opinions about the correct way to prepare that, too.

"This is just like the apple debate again," Adi said. "And you still won't admit I'm right about that, too."

"This is the most I've ever heard Marko talk at once, and it's about *this*?" Cressida said over her shoulder, an uncomfortable mix of annoyance and curiosity prickling Astrea's skin. She shook her head, making her floral-print bandanna flutter. Cressida always tied her hair back like that when she was working on something at home. "Skies."

"What apple debate?" Astrea asked.

"A week into our stay at the base, Adi tried to convince me that pink apples are best," Marko said.

"Because they are. Green are too tart, and pink are just tart enough."

Marko sucked in a breath—surely preparing to respond—when Jin said, "Oh, good, the observatory. We're here."

Adi puffed his chest out. "Thank goodness."

"Why? Can't take any more of my impeccable logic?" Marko taunted.

Adi shot him a dazzling smile and said, "No, it's just that you bore me."

"I *bore* you?" Marko scoffed. "Sure."

It wasn't just peach amusement swirling between the two men. Curiosity, desire, and approval both stretched into their auras; even a faint hint of orange annoyance spiked in Marko's. Astrea suppressed her smile.

Though Mariya's observatory was usually surrounded by thick foliage, part of it had been cleared away to make a smooth area for Cressida to work. The packed dirt was hard under Astrea's brogues, almost disappointing compared to the soft grass that filled the rest of the gardens.

A small, makeshift forge had been erected, and tools Astrea recognized from Cressida's workshop back home had been laid out on a nearby wooden table. She couldn't name any of them, but she'd definitely seen them before.

"So, what did you need help with, Cress?" Jin asked.

"I need a little more heat than I thought. I'm working on something with Mariya," she said.

"What's all this?" Adi asked, bright green curiosity snapping around him as they stopped near the table. Several small bars of dark metal sat there, shining in the late morning sun that filtered in through the trees.

"I finally have everything I need to make that dagger we talked about, Az," Cressida said. "Don't touch anything."

"Oh." Astrea hadn't forgotten about it, exactly, but with everything else on her mind, she hadn't exactly remembered either. "Right."

Pulling a cloth out of the back pocket of her black pants, Cressida wiped her hands on it. "Remember what I told you about your father back in Kalama, Jin?" she asked. "That he was tying my hands when it came to my tests back home? This was one thing he wouldn't let me do since he didn't want to waste the ore."

"And now we have plenty of ore to spare," Jin said, "so you need me to supply the heat for the whole process."

A brilliant smile lit up Cressida's face. "Exactly, Auris. A *lot* of heat." She waved her hand in the air, and one of the small, dark bars of metal floated toward her. "We use this sample," she said as she held it up, "to make our own steel, and who knows. It's worth a try. It won't be exactly perfect considering . . . well, considering we're in a random garden instead of a real facility, but if this doesn't reveal anything, it'll help me and Mariya figure out what to try next."

Jin began rolling up the sleeves of his boxy blue button-up shirt. His tan forearms flexed as he fiddled with the fabric. "Alright. Tell me what to do."

As Cressida began explaining the process, Astrea glanced around the gardens. She wanted Cressida to succeed, of course, but Astrea just couldn't focus on the weapon smithing lesson. Instead, she listened to the rhythmic crunch of soldiers patrolling nearby. She watched as sunlight filtered through the thick canopy of leaves, dapples of shadow and light playing together on the ground.

When would she get another day to be outside like this? With Nazarov's threat hanging over her head, Astrea couldn't help but wonder if it was time to go back into hiding. At least once they got information about where that book might be. Perhaps she and Jin could go to another remote part of Novaria, or even to one of the other countries. Tornama might be a decent option, out in the mountains. Surely it would take Nazarov a while to track them down there.

"Okay, ready when you are, Auris!" Cressida shouted.

Astrea forced her attention back to her friends. Fire and heat shot from Jin's palm in a steady stream, aimed at the side of the small forge. The top of the forge, half-covered by a brick, began to glow red-orange.

"Hotter!" Cressida yelled.

"You're sure?" Jin called back.

"Yeah!"

Jin's stream of fire narrowed, glowing white hot as he concentrated all that power at the forge. Astrea hadn't seen many Fireweavers in action before, but that was . . . intense. Did all Fireweavers have that much strength, or was it tied to his being a so-called Sunreaper?

When Cressida yelled for Jin to cut it off, he did like it was nothing more than flipping off a light switch. Cressida's magic guided a crucible out of the forge and onto a waiting brick. The whole thing glowed with heat, making Astrea squint.

"Thanks," Cressida said to Jin.

"Was that it?" he asked, wiping at some of the sweat beading on his forehead.

"Yeah, unless you can make this thing cool faster."

"That's not exactly in my wheelhouse," he said.

"Figures." Cressida flashed him a quick smile, then said, "Well, I guess we wait."

"You can't do anything else with it right now?" Marko—who had long since joined Astrea in sitting on the ground—asked.

"Not if I want to do this the right way."

"And how long will it take?" Jin asked.

"Oh, a while." Cressida pulled her cloth out of her back pocket again, then wiped at her face and neck.

"How specific," Marko murmured.

"I'll be done with it before dinner," she said. "If you want to stay and watch me work, just don't distract me, okay?"

"I actually have a few things I want to talk to Tomas about," Jin said. "I'll leave you to it, Cress."

"Adi? Az?" Cressida asked.

Wind blew through Astrea's braided hair, pulling at the loose strands around her face. The warm breeze danced over her skin, gentle and grounding. "I'll stay for a bit. I need some fresh air."

"Then I'll go with you," Adi said to Jin.

"Come find us immediately if Nazarov contacts you," Jin said. "We won't be long."

As Jin and Adi headed for the palace again, Marko leaned back on his elbows, watching Adi and Jin walk away. His curiosity and longing whispered over Astrea's skin like the breeze, there one second and gone the next. She almost asked if he wanted to go with them; she'd be plenty safe with Cressida and the nearby soldiers. But Astrea didn't think he'd take her up on the offer.

"So, what do you have left to do?" Astrea asked Cressida instead.

The Metalli fiddled with a few tools on the long table, then said over her shoulder, "After letting it cool, I'll need to actually form the blade, then sharpen it. Plus it needs a real handle. Something to grip."

"You plan on using it?" Marko asked. Astrea followed his gaze, but Adi and Jin were gone from sight.

"I need to stress test it at the very least. See if it's as strong as Emperor Aelius thought it would be."

"Need help?" Astrea asked, though she was sure she wouldn't be able to actually do anything to help, nor would she stick around once Cressida really got to work.

Cressida grinned. "You can help me choose a color for the hilt."

"Purple," Astrea said immediately.

"Typical."

"Or green. Marko's partial to green."

"Is he now?" Cressida arched an eyebrow.

"Purple would look better," Marko said. Surprise flickered around Cressida, and Astrea suppressed a smile. "What? It would."

"Purple it is, if we have what we need to make it." Cressida looked at the crucible again and sighed. "Meteoric steel. Who would've thought?"

Soft grass. A warm breeze. The sound of Adi, Lennor, Civan, and Eliana sparring a dozen yards away. Astrea had almost been lulled to sleep if not for that last part. That, plus Jin and Nicos occasionally shouting encouragement or direction from right next to Astrea.

"Watch your left, Ellie!" Nicos called.

Astrea was stretched out on the ground, her limbs aching after the last hour she'd spent practicing with Adi and Jin. They'd been trying to run down the clock as they waited for Nazarov to reach back out to them, and despite the setting sun, there hadn't been even a whisper from the void mage.

"I'm fine on my own, thank you!" Eliana shouted. Electricity crackled, and Lennor laughed.

"Stubborn," Nicos muttered. Still, all Astrea could feel was the warm pride and affection rolling off him.

Cressida sat cross-legged next to her, the brand new meteorite dagger resting in her palms. She'd finished making it before dinner, as promised, and had even wrapped the hilt in a mix of lavender and sage green leather. Now, its dark metal blade caught the rays of sunset.

"I expected the color to be different," Astrea said.

"What, the hilt?" Cressida lifted the dagger and examined it. "I thought the colors went together nicely."

"No, the metal." Astrea rolled over and pushed up on one elbow.

"Oh." Lips pressing together, Cressida shook her head once. "Yeah, it's not exactly what I was expecting."

"You didn't change it?"

"No, I didn't."

Astrea didn't like the sound of that.

"Come on, Ellie!" Nicos called. "I know you can take more than that!"

"And how would you know, Nicos?" Cressida yelled back, causing hot embarrassment to burn Astrea's skin. She couldn't help but laugh.

"Would both of you be quiet?" Eliana's voice carried no malice. In fact, sugary amusement coated Astrea's entire mouth, almost nauseating.

The feeling didn't last. Someone may as well have punched Astrea in the stomach despite the fact that she'd tapped out two rounds before.

Someone grunted; it sounded like Adi. Another hit, this time to the shoulder. Pain erupted in the back of Astrea's skull. She pulled her barrier toward herself, trying to hold in her groan.

"Alright!" Jin called. "Alright, enough! Civ, you good? Hey . . . Civan?"

Pushing herself up, Astrea tried to breathe through the dizziness clouding her mind. Civan was doubled over, gripping the sides of his head. Lennor crouched in front of him.

"He hit his head," Lennor said hurriedly as Astrea made her way toward them. "I didn't think my wind was going to be so—" Deep blue regret pulsed around her as Jin knelt next to her brother. Adi joined him.

"Lie down," Jin said to Civan.

"No, leave him." Astrea dropped to her knees behind the Tempest. Why were people always hitting their skies damned heads? Gritting her teeth, Astrea said, "Civan, I need to touch you."

"Yeah, alright," he mumbled.

"Hold still." Astrea couldn't see any blood in his thick tangle of dark brown hair. She coaxed her magic forward and placed her glowing hands on top of Civan's head. Ghost pain echoed through her skull, but it wasn't like on Solstice Night. That seemed so long ago now, the night she'd saved Eliana's life and revealed her magic.

"Az?" Jin asked.

"Not the worst," she said. "Also not the best. Last time . . . I don't know if I—"

"I've got you if you do," Jin said, no clarification needed. She'd passed out last time she'd healed a head injury.

Ignoring the weight of everyone watching and the heavy regret still pushing against her, Astrea set her hands on Civan's tan skin. Her magic shot forward, warm and light. Gentle, even as it explored and settled on one spot. The mirror healing and pain began their dance in Astrea's body, and skies, did it hurt. Her vision blurred. Bile crept up her throat.

The pain lessened bit by bit. Maybe this would be fine. Maybe she'd gotten strong enough that she wouldn't faint.

Civan sighed.

As Astrea made one final push with her healing, something stabbed between her shoulders. Crying out, she lurched forward. Jin grabbed her. Panic surged nearby as darkness took over Astrea's vision. But Jin held on to her, a lifeline as the waves of darkness threatened to drag her under.

Hello, little Lightbringer, Victor Nazarov purred. *Am I interrupting?*

Yes, Astrea spat.

Too bad. Have you considered my offer?

Astrea's body hurt too much. Her mind ached. She couldn't think. Couldn't breathe. *Bring Commander Lucian and Jin into this conversation.*

Don't want to deal with me on your own? A chuckle reverberated through Astrea's mind.

It's difficult to focus when I just healed someone's concussion.

Another laugh echoed through her head, almost pushing against the spot where she'd healed Civan's injury. *How incredibly* noble *of you, little Lightbringer.* Nazarov sighed. *Fine.*

Shadows warped around her. Jin's arms around her waist tightened, holding her flush against his body. She focused on that warmth as some tiny corner of her mind tried to take her elsewhere.

What is this? Lucian's voice rang out in Astrea's head, unexpected as the shadows settled again.

The little Lightbringer insisted you and the princeling be part of this conversation, Novarian, Nazarov spat. *Apparently her head hurts too much to chat. You Lightbringers are just* so *selfless, aren't you?*

I suggest you get to the point, Lucian snapped.

Nazarov sighed. *I was just asking her if she'd considered my offer.*

We have conditions. The longer Astrea was stuck in this shadowy realm, the more wildly the pain in the back of her skull pulsed.

Conditions, Nazarov mused. She could almost imagine him circling the desk in The One's office, the way he had the first time he'd shown up in that house. *Of course you have conditions. Never like to keep things simple, do you, Miss Sovna?*

We won't give you the journal, Jin said. *But we're willing to have Theo meet us here to translate it. We want to know what it says. That's the only way we'll agree to this.*

Oh, princeling. Astrea could hear the smile in Nazarov's voice as he continued, *Theo will be doing no such thing.*

Giving us one clue to where you think Theo's other book is, one we must go find, is hardly a fair trade without knowing what's in the journal, Jin said.

Pain shot through Astrea's head. *It's the only way,* she told Nazarov when he still said nothing. And when he remained silent for another heartbeat, two, three, Astrea gritted out, *Nazarov.*

So impatient, he said. *Fine. Theo will meet you, but so will Tovan and Solana.*

Goose bumps prickled Astrea's entire body. Jin's arms around her waist shifted slowly, almost like he could barely move. She couldn't, either. Dreamwalking seemed to paralyze her. She'd thought it was fear, but maybe it wasn't.

I will not have a void mage at the palace— Lucian started, but Nazarov cut him off.

And we won't meet at the palace.

Then we aren't meeting.

We meet at a neutral location, Commander, or we don't meet at all, and I'll just come take what I want.

Lucian huffed. *You chose our last location, so we'll choose this time.*

No, Lightbringer, you will not. We will meet here. An image wavered in Astrea's mind. The Talmaran skyline peeked over the trees, and there, at the end of a row of shops, was one with a white brick exterior and dark shutters. A sign reading Antiquities hung above the door. *Ember Lane, Shop Number Twelve. Tomorrow at noon. The Souleater and Sunreaper must come alone.*

Not happening, Nazarov, Jin said. *We will bring whomever we want, and we will bring as many people as we want.*

There will be four of us, so there can be four of you. No more. See you tomorrow.

The vision of the building disappeared. Jin held Astrea tight even as they both slumped to one side. She still couldn't think. Still couldn't breathe. Someone may as well have been stabbing her skull over and over and over again. She kept her eyes squeezed shut, little good it did her against the pain. Fear and concern stormed around her like a tornado, and as desperately as Astrea wanted to pull her barrier back, she couldn't find its edge.

"Az?" Cressida asked. "Jin?"

"Get Lucian," Astrea choked out, her hands going to her head. "Something's wrong. Is Civan alright, I think—"

"I'm fine," the Tidebacker said, voice rough.

Relief swept over Astrea's skin. Jin finally let go of her, but only for a moment. He hoisted her up in his arms. "The dreamwalking?"

"It made the ghost pain worse after healing Civan," Astrea said as Jin began moving. More footsteps followed them. Pain flared through her body with every long stride Jin took.

"Come this way," Eliana said. "It's a shortcut to the infirmary. Nic, go find Lucian and tell him to hurry."

"I can go," Civan offered.

"No, let's get you checked out again, too," Eliana said. "Nic, go."

Eventually, the crunching grass turned to gentle patters on the smooth palace floors. Curiosity, concern, fear—it all pressed, pressed, pressed against Astrea. She reached for her barrier again, but with the pain, she still couldn't find it.

"Oh, what's happened?" a sweet, unfamiliar voice said. "Your Imperial Highnesses?"

"Hello, Ivy," Eliana said. "We've already sent for Commander Lucian, but . . . well, it's complicated."

"Set her down here," Ivy said, and Jin began walking again. "Yes, right here. Now, what's happened?"

"I healed Civan's concussion just before a void mage entered my mind, and the ghost pain is even worse now," Astrea said as Jin lowered her onto a bed. The thick, soft mattress cradled her, and Astrea willed her muscles to loosen.

As Jin explained that Astrea was a Lightbringer and how the void mages could enter their minds, she focused on not throwing up. Every time bile surged up her throat, she managed to swallow it. Barely.

"And which one of you is Civan?" Ivy asked. Fabric rustled, then she said, "Alright, you sit down, too. Astrea, I'm going to check on Civan while we wait for the commander. This may be best left to another Lightbringer."

"Okay," Astrea whispered.

More footsteps shuffled around her. Lennor murmured something to her brother, then added, "Don't make Jin order you." That earned her a grunt. A bed squeaked to Astrea's left. She didn't bother trying to listen to what Ivy said to Civan.

"What did Nazarov want?" Eliana asked.

"Ellie, now isn't the time—" Jin started, but Astrea cut him off.

"Just tell her."

With a sigh, Jin explained what Nazarov wanted and where they were to meet. Curiosity and irritation swirled together in the room. When Astrea wasn't sure if anyone was going to say anything, a gentle hand touched Astrea's shoulder.

"Your friend's head is fine," Ivy said. "Since the commander still isn't here, I'm going to check you out, alright?" When Astrea agreed, Ivy said, "Can you open your eyes?"

Only with great effort did Astrea manage to crack her eyes open. A friendly smile was the first thing Astrea noticed about Ivy. The plump woman had beautiful umber skin, coily black hair, and bright blue irises.

"Excellent!" Ivy said as she set a cool hand on Astrea's forehead. "Now, I'm just a Purifier, but let's see what we can find, shall we?"

Despite the ache building behind them, Astrea forced her eyes to stay open. Her gaze tracked first to Jin, who was right beside her, then Eliana and Cressida at the foot of her bed. Adi murmured something to Lennor, but Astrea couldn't see them beyond Ivy's frame. The Purifier clicked her tongue.

"What is it?" Jin asked.

"Well, Your Imperial Highness, I'm not exactly sure." Ivy pulled her hand away. "It's—oh! Commander!" Two sets of footsteps rushed through the room. Jin moved away so Lucian could be next to Astrea's head. "Good. I was just checking out Astrea and something feels off, but I can't tell you what. She said a void mage was in her mind?"

Lucian thanked Ivy, then said to Astrea, "This hasn't happened before with him, has it?"

"No," she said, "but I'd just finished healing Civan's head when Nazarov dreamwalked."

Pressing one hand to Astrea's forehead, Lucian slipped the other under the back of her neck. The glow of his lightbringing made Astrea close her eyes again. The pain pulsed bright and hot through her, echoing again and again as it bounced between her and Lucian. But finally, it lessened by a fraction. It lessened again, not gone but bearable enough that she could open her eyes without wanting to vomit. Lucian pulled his hands away.

"So?" Ivy asked.

"I'm . . . not sure," Lucian said. "How do you feel, Astrea?"

"A little better."

As Ivy helped Astrea sit up, Lucian said, "I've never felt something like that. Not so intensely."

"Well, dreamwalking isn't painless." Astrea rubbed her forehead and sucked in a deep breath. "Maybe they just . . . compounded?"

"Let's try not to test the theory," Lucian said.

Astrea nodded. Why void magic would influence lightbringing that way, she didn't know. But she wouldn't find out tonight. Besides, they had more immediate concerns.

"What's this shop Nazarov wants us to go to?" she asked Lucian.

"I'm not sure. I'm going to scout it out tonight." His shifted toward Jin. "Start thinking about who the fourth person will be who joins us tomorrow. I'll leave that decision up to you."

After Lucian and Ivy both performed more magical exams on Civan and Astrea, they got clearance to leave the infirmary.

"You're sure you're good?" Jin asked Astrea as the others shuffled toward the door.

"Fine," Astrea lied. She may have been cleared, but her head still ached, and Civan winced a few times as he moved about. "We should have a meeting." After all, they needed to sit down and discuss their options for the next day, and Astrea had a feeling it was going to take a while to come to a consensus.

Chapter 24

The buckles of Astrea's armor clinked as their group's car sped over one bump in the road, then another. She placed a hand over the metal, willing them to be quiet. Jin, seated next to her in the back row of the car, had his hand on her thigh, his thumb absently drawing an invisible line on her pants. Mattina's journal was tucked into the narrow space between their thighs.

"And you're sure this place is secure?" Zephyrine asked Lucian. They were in the front row of the car, with Lucian driving and Zephyrine next to him.

"It's just as that night at Club Twilight," Lucian said. "My Lightbringers are standing by, as close to the building as they can be. This man likes loopholes, and he only said we cannot bring more than four inside. Not that we cannot have people stationed outside."

"Hm." Zephyrine pursed her lips.

The decision to bring Zephyrine as their fourth was not one the team had agreed to easily. Adi and Cressida had both wanted to go. Neither Lennor nor Civan had spoken up, though Lennor's anxiety about the whole situation had been obvious. Nicos had insisted they try to bring the whole team, while Eliana and Jin had thought Zephyrine was the best option.

In the shop they were going to, Adi wouldn't have earth to move. Cressida might have access to metal, yes, but Zephyrine was a Tempest.

Her weapon was all around her. And as she'd revealed, she was powerful enough to suck the air right out of someone's lungs or hold them in place with her wind. And the stories Jin had told Astrea about their time together in the military suggested Zephyrine was even stronger than she was letting on.

Before they'd left the palace, Astrea had explained to Lucian those strange inky shadows that sometimes spiked around Nazarov. She'd just seen it a couple of times before, but he promised to watch for it, too.

After a half hour, the car rolled to a stop. This part of Talmaris was far from the palace. Astrea had no idea *where* they were, exactly, but the neighborhood's quaint shops, light foot traffic, and quiet atmosphere reminded her of the Scholar's District back home in Kalama.

Grabbing the journal, Jin exited the car first. Astrea climbed out behind him. Several pedestrians passing by gave them funny looks, their curiosity tickling the end of Astrea's nose. She tugged at her armor. Unlike Kalama, where soldiers walked around in various uniforms, Talmaran foot traffic was made up almost exclusively of civilians.

"Ready?" Jin asked as Astrea gave her arms a small shake.

"Not really." After her ordeal at the infirmary the evening before, Astrea hadn't been able to sleep. Her mind had kept her up most of the night with whispers of everything that could go wrong at this meeting.

They joined Lucian and Zephyrine near the edge of the street. Tall trees lined both sides of the one-way road, casting shade over the trolley and two black cars driving by. Once the vehicles passed, the four of them headed toward the white brick building Nazarov had shown them in the vision the night before.

They hadn't even crossed to the other side of the street when cold void enveloped Astrea. Someone's heady anticipation and another's anger and curiosity barreled into her. *Breathe.*

As Lucian opened the front door, a bell tingled, announcing their arrival.

The store looked like many Astrea had visited back in Kalama. Bookshelves lined one wall, housing neatly organized books in varying sizes and colors. A selection of antique furniture and decor, ranging from pottery to writing desks to ornately carved chairs, sat near the middle of the shop. In other cabinets and on other shelves were statuettes, coins, and old weaponry. There was even a long counter near the back of the store. Its glass front revealed jewelry inside. A golden cash register sat at one end, and at the other were the four Paragon. Nazarov, Theo, Tovan, and Solana all stood there expectantly.

Grinning, Nazarov stretched his arms out to either side. "So good to see you all. Welcome."

"Let's get started," Lucian said.

"Now, now, Commander," Nazarov drawled. "I don't believe you and I have been formally introduced, nor have you met my companions."

"I don't need to meet them. I know all about you."

"Do you really?" Nazarov's brows quirked up as his gaze flicked to Astrea. "You told him about me? I'm flattered."

"Don't be," Astrea muttered.

Theo rolled his eyes.

"And General Kanakos." When Nazarov smiled, it was that same predatory smile Astrea had become all too familiar with. "*This* is a surprise. Good to see you again." He turned to Jin. "I see you have the journal, Sunreaper. Let me have a look."

Jin stepped forward and set the journal on the glass counter. When Nazarov reached for it, Jin pulled it back. "You don't get to touch it."

"You'd better watch your tone, princeling."

"And you'd better count yourself lucky that I don't just kill you right where you stand," Jin snapped. "Theo."

Though Nazarov glared at Jin, he eventually stepped back. Theo shuffled toward the counter and pushed his glasses up his nose. Jin opened the journal to a random page.

"Well?" Nazarov asked.

"Give me a moment." Leaning down, Theo examined both the left and right pages of text. Irritation scraped against Astrea's skin, rough like sandpaper. Theo's curls bounced as he nodded. "This is Leopold's."

"Now what?" Jin asked as he pulled the journal back toward himself. "How long will it take you to translate it?"

"Oh . . ." Theo shrugged a narrow shoulder. "Most of the day, I suspect. I have space set aside upstairs to work." When Jin's eyebrows furrowed, Theo said, "This is my shop."

"Of course it is," Jin muttered. "Fine. Astrea and I will come upstairs with you while you work."

"Tovan, go with them," Nazarov said. "Solana, you and I can have a chat with the commander and the general. It would be rude to leave them all alone down here."

Solana's smile was anything but nice. Her button nose wrinkled. "Manners *are* important."

"I would love nothing more than that, Mister Nazarov," Lucian growled. "It seems there's much for us to catch up on."

Astrea slinked past Lucian and Zephyrine, then followed Jin and Theo to a winding staircase tucked in one corner. Theo started up first, and Tovan motioned to Astrea. Her skin crawled as he said, "Ladies first."

As Astrea slipped past the hulking man and started after Theo, Jin wedged his body between Tovan and the stairs. "I go next," Jin snapped, making Tovan chuckle.

Unlike the upstairs of Theo's shop back home in Kalama, this one was bright and open. The ceiling slanted gently at the edges of the room, and large, arched windows flooded the space with light and views of the trees. A rectangular table sat at the far end of the room, just four chairs tucked around it. Several paintings covered in drop cloths leaned against one wall, and a few boxes were stacked in another. It was tidy. Empty.

"Here we go," Theo said as he motioned Astrea and Jin toward the table. "Please, have a seat. Tovan, you stay over there."

He scoffed. "Victor wants me to watch them."

"And you can watch them from over there." Theo shooed Tovan back toward the stairs. "Give us some space."

Jin sat down on the far side of the table. His back was to the windows, giving him a clear view of Tovan. Astrea sat next to him as he placed the journal on the smooth, dark tabletop.

"I want a translation," Jin said. "One I can take with me."

"Oh, Jin, come now." Theo sat down with a sigh. "That will take forever."

"And we're keeping the journal. You can make two copies of the translation."

The night before, their team had discussed the possibility that Theo might lie to them. If they kept the original journal and demanded a translation as well, it might better their odds of getting the real translation. There was no way Theo would want to make two fake copies of an entire notebook he wouldn't even get to keep.

"I don't think Victor will agree to this."

"He has no choice." Jin crossed his arms. "You just need to know what Mattina was working on. You can make your own copy, too, and do whatever the fuck it is you want with it."

"Jin—"

"You owe me that much, Theo. After all these years. You owe me." Jin's voice tightened on the last few words. Astrea wanted to grab his hand and let him know he wasn't alone, here facing the man who betrayed him. But Tovan stared at them, a peculiar smile tugging at his lips. Astrea didn't dare move a muscle.

"Fine." As Theo stood, his chair legs scraped against the floor. "I need to go get some things from downstairs if I'm going to be doing this extra work." As Theo stopped near the top of the stairs, he whispered something to Tovan. Then he disappeared, his footsteps loud on the metal staircase.

One heartbeat passed, then two. Astrea's pulse thundered in her ears as Tovan stared her down, his amber eyes flashing in the sunlight streaming through the windows. He strode toward their table and pulled out Theo's chair. He turned it around, then straddled it and settled his arms on its back.

"So, Your Imperial Highness," Tovan drawled in heavily accented Helosian, "has the little Lightbringer told you about our time together?" Tovan leaned forward, lowering his voice as he said, "She's a pain in the ass if you ask me. Though . . ." His attention drifted back toward Astrea. "I suppose I can see why you came back for her. Pretty one, isn't she?"

Jin still said nothing. Astrea sucked in as deep of a breath as she could, but her lungs tightened painfully.

"But pretty doesn't make up for all the trouble she's caused." Tovan smirked. "If only The One and Victor would've let me have a little more time with you. I'm pretty sure I could get you to talk."

"Go fuck yourself." Despite her voice coming out as a mere whisper, Tovan's eyebrows shot up. Lavender surprise and rusty annoyance flashed in the air. "Stop talking unless you want me to force you to your knees again. You remember what happened last time, right?"

He stared her down, then chuckled so loud that Astrea flinched. "What, princeling, you like 'em mouthy or something?"

Jin leaned forward and murmured, "Even though I'd *love* to see Astrea put you in your place, I suggest you listen to her and shut the fuck up."

Just as Tovan began to reply, Theo's loud footsteps returned. Metal clanged with each step, and his brown-and-gray curls appeared at the top of the stairs. "Tovan," he said, sighing. "I told you to leave them alone. Get away from them."

Tovan's gaze flicked from Jin to Astrea and back again. "Keep that energy up next time we're together, little Lightbringer," he sneered, "and we'll see who ends up on their knees." He shoved off the chair, then shoulder checked Theo as he returned to his post by the stairs.

Theo straightened his blazer with one hand, a thick stack of papers and several pens tucked under his arm. With another heavy sigh, he resumed his position at the table. "Now, shall we begin?"

"Gladly," Jin said. "Work as fast as you can. You've already wasted enough of our time."

"I hardly think this is a waste of time, Jin." Theo spread out the papers and pens, even going so far as sliding the journal toward himself. Jin didn't stop him. "Though I admit I could have tried talking to you sooner."

"You think talking to me would've changed any of this?" Jin hissed.

"I suppose not. You've always been stubborn, just like Caliste." Theo shook his head. "She knew what was at stake, and yet she decided to walk away from all of this. Everything that's to come."

"What?" Jin whispered.

"What do you mean *what*?" Theo pushed his glasses up his nose, finally looking up from his papers as he said, "Caliste was Paragon. The Seviyas were Paragon."

A Tempest may as well have sucked all the air out of the room. They'd known this was possible, likely even. Had theorized it after finding that letter in that house. They just hadn't had any proof to support the idea. And to hear it said so simply . . .

Jin swallowed hard. "What do you mean my mother was Paragon?"

"I mean exactly that. Your mother was Paragon. And she wanted to leave that life behind once she had you."

"Is that how you met?"

"No, no. I was still your father's advisor at the time, and she and I became friends. She was the one who told me about the Paragon. She was the one who showed me the true path."

"Did my father know?"

"No, I don't believe he did. You know him, Jin. If Aelius had known the Paragon existed, he would've tried to track them down. Of course, he's probably trying to track them down *now*, after everything that's happened. None of it was supposed to unfold this way."

"Enough chitchat," Tovan snapped from the other side of the room. "Don't make Victor wait all day."

Theo gestured to the writing supplies and journal. "I need to get started on this. If you want to know more about Caliste's connection to the Paragon, learn more about her father."

Later. They would have to deal with that later.

"Now, would you like to help?" Theo asked.

"No," Jin said. "Do both copies. We'll wait."

And so, as Theo began the tedious process of translating Mattina's journal, Astrea settled into her chair as much as she could. They needed to get this over with, not just to understand what Mattina was after but what Jin's maternal family had to do with the Paragon.

Despite Jin making Theo do all the work of copying Mattina's notes down, both Jin and Astrea read over Theo's work as he did, looking for any discrepancies in the two copies. They found nothing other than a few misspelled words and increasingly sloppy handwriting as Theo worked for hours on end. That made Astrea marginally more confident the translation was correct.

By the time he was on the last page of the journal, three hours had passed. And in that time, Astrea had learned that Mattina had been researching meteorite and the theory that it had properties similar to void magic. What those powers were, Mattina hadn't specified, though he referenced "the book" and needing it to confirm his theories.

The missing book—*Novaria: Myths and Other Legends*—Astrea assumed. Which Theo had once claimed Mattina had borrowed from him, though Astrea wasn't convinced Theo had ever actually owned it. Both Nazarov and Theo had also said that Mattina "betrayed" them during the course of his research.

So if Mattina really had stolen the book and at least had it for some time before someone stole it from him, these notes didn't seem to be up-to-date. Just her luck.

But they already knew the meteorite tunnels somehow interrupted Lightbringers' sensory range. That reminded Astrea of how void mages felt to her magic, even if it wasn't quite the same.

What more might it do? Amplify that void fire? Could it increase the distance a void mage could jump? Strengthen them as they dreamwalked, maybe letting them access more minds? Could that be how Nazarov was now dreamwalking to the whole team at once?

Or maybe, since it blocked out Lightbringers' ability to sense them, the Paragon would use that to their advantage? Astrea imagined that if someone were to line their clothing with it—difficult as that might be—they could possibly move around with a lower chance of detection.

Speculating wouldn't help.

As for the rest of his research, it was . . . disorganized. Cross-references to other books, notes about battles from the Great Wars, and even ramblings about finding "other" sources of meteorite. None of it seemed particularly concrete—not that Astrea had been able to dissect every detail while checking for discrepancies in the translations. Still, she couldn't wait to get the information to Mariya and Tomas. Finally, some real leads.

"Well," Theo said, shuffling around the last of the papers, "there you have it, Varojin. The translation. We're done."

"There's nothing else?" Jin asked.

"No." Theo's fatigue pressed against Astrea's skin, heavy and unwelcome. Taking his glasses off, Theo pinched the bridge of his nose. "There's nothing else."

"Took you long enough." Tovan's voice made Astrea flinch. He'd been so quiet for the last couple of hours that she'd almost been able to ignore him. Almost. "Victor's going to want answers."

Astrea scooped up Mattina's journal and one stack of the translated pages, cradling them to her chest as she stood. Jin followed close behind her as they made their way to the winding staircase, his body so close she could feel the heat pulsing off him. When they passed Tovan, he snarled, but he didn't make another move.

The staircase seemed steeper going down than it had going up, and Astrea watched each step carefully as she descended. Lucian, Zephyrine, Solana, and Nazarov were almost exactly where they'd been before, though they'd pulled over some of the antique chairs to sit in. None of them appeared the least bit thrilled.

"And they're done," Nazarov said as he stood. "Well?"

"All translated." Theo brought his copy of the translation to Nazarov. "He was researching the meteorite as well. Nothing specific enough to be useful."

"Useful for what?" Lucian asked.

"None of your skies damned business, Commander," Nazarov snapped.

"We kept up our end of the bargain," Astrea said. "So where's the *Myths and Other Legends* book?"

Nazarov looked at Theo's empty arms, then to where Astrea still cradled the journal to her chest. "The deal was you'd give us the journal."

"And we got the translation," Theo said before Astrea could reply. "I told them they could keep the journal."

"Who the fuck gave you the authority to make that decision?" Nazarov's entire body tensed, and for a moment, Astrea feared he might do something to hurt Theo. Those strange shadows spiked around him for a split second. After sucking in a deep breath, Nazarov smoothed the front of his black shirt. "Fine. You can keep the journal."

"Where's the book, Nazarov?" Jin asked.

"We have reason to believe it's in Kalama."

Astrea almost laughed. Jin didn't manage to hold in his chuckle as he said, "I'm sorry, what?"

"Does Emperor Aelius have it?" Lucian asked.

Theo moved behind the counter, then pulled out a ledger and small notebook from some hidden shelf. He flipped both open and began searching them as he said, "We believe it's at the Great Library."

Astrea's heart stopped. "What?"

"Yes, little Lightbringer." Nazarov smiled. "It seems your old boss has gotten her hands on the text."

"But . . . how?" Astrea couldn't believe that Raela, of all people, would be involved in any of this. Not Raela, who loved helping library patrons and was often late for meetings. Raela, who had mentored Astrea for years and was working hard to keep the pages employed. She just didn't believe it.

"We don't know." Pulling out a pen, Theo began writing in the notebook. "But it's in Kalama."

"You really didn't kill Mattina or those people in Sezia?" Jin asked.

"No, Sunreaper," Nazarov said. "I thought I already made that clear. We don't know who killed them."

They'd thought it might've been a third group, but just how many void mage factions were there? Could it have been Caliban, Emperor Aelius's void mage guard? Had he gotten the book all that time ago? If they had just stayed in Kalama, might they have found a way to have stopped this already?

"And why can't you go back to Kalama?" Zephyrine asked. "You can jump locations. Surely it would be easy for you to go back in and steal what you need."

"Like the Novarians"—Nazarov pinned Lucian with a look—"Emperor Aelius has realized there are ways to detect those of us gifted with the power of the void. He's set up a network of Lightbringers."

"Smart," Zephyrine said.

"Obnoxious," Nazarov corrected, pinning Lucian with another glare. "To jump in and out of Kalama would be . . . difficult."

Which means he can't just jump into Ysabel's palace, either. Relief flooded through Astrea like a tsunami, so forceful she could've fallen over. Nazarov was full of empty threats. Well, mostly empty. Empty as long as she was at the palace.

"And you want us to retrieve this book from Kalama?" Lucian asked. "What, to bring back here and hand it over to you? Why on earth would you possibly want us to have more information?"

"Of course I want the book, but it's not the only way for me to get what I need. It's better that you have it if I cannot. It's better for everyone if Emperor Aelius does not have it."

Goose bumps prickled Astrea's skin. Just what information could that book hold if even Victor Nazarov, a self-proclaimed agent of chaos and destruction, didn't want the emperor to have access to it?

"What about The One?" Astrea asked. "Doesn't he want that book, too? And Mattina's journal?"

"Oh, he does," Tovan muttered, and Solana nodded.

"Would he be foolish enough to try to jump into the palace? Does he know the book is in Kalama?" Lucian asked.

"No, and I'm not sure," Nazarov said. "Though frankly, if he beat you to it, I'd be fine with that outcome as well. But, I believe part of the bargain was that you also get to ask me *one* question," he continued. "Seeing as you've already asked me, oh, at least a half dozen, I think we're done here. I've been more than generous with my time and knowledge."

"Should I show 'em out, boss?" Tovan asked.

"No, they know where the exit is. I'm sure we'll be seeing each other again very soon."

Jin nudged Astrea toward the door first. She wove around the antiques and shelves until she finally reached it. The brass handle was cool to her touch. She turned it quickly, then hurried down the steps to the sidewalk.

None of them said a word until they'd climbed into the car, locked the doors, and merged back into traffic to return to the palace.

"Well?" Jin asked. "Lucian? Zephyrine?"

"I've never wanted to punch someone's teeth out more than Victor Nazarov," Lucian muttered. "Something about him makes my skin crawl."

"Did you see anything in his aura?" Astrea asked.

"Twice." Lucian stopped at a red light behind several other cars. "It was so quick. I almost didn't notice it."

"And?" Astrea asked.

"And I couldn't do anything. I never saw it on Solana."

"Damn."

"And the rest?" Lucian prompted. "Kalama? This book? What do you all think?"

"He could certainly be lying," Jin said, "but something in my gut tells me he isn't."

"Mine too," Zephyrine said. "I wouldn't be surprised if Aelius knew how Lightbringers could help detect void mages. He'd bring some home from the front if he had to just to create that network. No doubt he's disturbed by Nazarov's ability to teleport just as much as we are."

"You think that's how he escaped prison?" Lucian asked.

"Had to be," Zephyrine said. "There's no other way to break out of a Helosian prison."

"So, now what?" Astrea asked.

"We return to the palace, and we fill in the others," Lucian said. "And from there, we have a choice to make."

As far as Astrea was concerned, it wasn't a choice at all. If that book was in Kalama, and if it would be that devastating for Emperor Aelius to get his hands on it, they needed to find it immediately. But there was nothing she could do about that while stuck in the back seat of a car. So, she settled in next to Jin and clutched Mattina's journal tightly. Soon. She'd get to make that decision soon.

CHAPTER 25

By the time they pulled up to the palace garage, it was all Astrea could do to not jump out of the car and run back to tell their friends what had happened. She forced herself to go slow, to shake out the buzz pulsing under her skin and just breathe.

"We should go talk to Ysabel," Jin said. "I'd really like to get started."

"Let's—" Lucian started, only for a young blond guard to start calling his name. "Now what?" he muttered as the guard sprinted the rest of the distance to the open garage bay.

"Commander Lucian!" the guard called. "The grand duchess needs you. She says Prince Varojin must come, too." He gave a half-hearted bow to Jin. "And the Helosian general. It's urgent."

"Did she say what it's about?" Lucian asked despite already moving toward the tunnel that connected to the palace.

"No," the young guard said. "Just to come to the throne room and use her entrance."

"Back to your post," Lucian barked at the guard. Then he eyed the rest of them over his shoulder. "Well? Let's go."

Zephyrine followed Lucian into the tunnel with only a confused look, while Jin nudged Astrea forward by the small of her back.

What could the grand duchess need them for so urgently? She'd been keen on avoiding their group, or at least avoiding Astrea. She hadn't seen Ysabel in days, so unlike the first time she'd stayed in Talmaris.

"Should I be going?" Astrea asked. "The guard—"

"There's nothing Ysabel can say to me that I won't just tell you anyway," Jin said. "Come with us."

They continued on at Lucian's breakneck pace, through the underground tunnel and back up into the palace. Guards and soldiers swarmed the area, clearing a path as soon as they realized Lucian and Jin were the ones making their way to the throne room. Astrea clutched Mattina's notebook and the translated pages to her chest. She practically had to jog to keep up with the commander.

He led them down a few more hallways, then stopped in front of a door flanked by two guards. Lucian turned to Jin and said, "Give me a moment. I'll get you when we're ready."

Jin pressed his lips together and didn't argue as Lucian slipped into the throne room beyond. Through the thick stone walls, Astrea could just make out several closed-off people and a hint of determination. Nothing out of the ordinary, and still . . .

"You're back!" Eliana called from down the hall. Nicos and Marko trailed her. "How was it?"

"We got what we needed," Jin said, then motioned at the now-closed door. "What's this about? Did Ysabel call you, too?"

"Yes." Eliana glanced at Nicos, then Marko. "I don't know why, though."

The door opened again. Lucian's face was unreadable, as it often was. "Princess," he said to Eliana before looking at Jin, Astrea, and Zephyrine. "Take your armor off."

"Why?" Jin asked.

"Trust me, Varojin."

Astrea passed the notebook to Nicos, then began loosening the buckles and ties on her body armor.

"The grand duchess has managed to keep the palace closed off for weeks," Lucian said quietly. "Began taking meetings at embassies and claimed renovations, illness, anything to keep people away."

"Who's here?" Jin asked.

"The Helosian diplomats have basically forced this," Lucian said. Goose bumps prickled Astrea's skin even as Eliana's hot anger rolled through the hallway. "It seems your father is no longer keen on letting you two putz around up here."

Jin tugged his armor over his head. "They said that?"

"No, but what else do you think it could be?" Lucian asked.

"Let's just see what they have to say," Zephyrine said.

Astrea wasn't so sure about that. What good could come from speaking to Helosian diplomats? And yet, what was the point in hiding?

With their body armor discarded and sitting on the hall floor, they followed Lucian through the door into the throne room. It was strange, seeing it from this angle. Grand Duchess Ysabel was the picture of a regal, composed ruler perched upon her throne. Crown Prince Veiko stood to her right. Two people dressed in dark suits waited a few feet away from the dais. Determination pulsed around one, though Astrea couldn't read the other.

"Your Imperial Highnesses," they said in unison as they bowed.

"Ambassadors," Eliana said, voice tight as she ran a hand over the front of her crimson dress. It was less formal than Ysabel's dark blue gown, cut just above Eliana's knees and made from a light, flowing fabric. "To what do we owe the pleasure?" She joined Ysabel near her throne, though Jin and Zephyrine stayed off to one side. So did Astrea.

"Your Imperial Highness," said one of the Helosians, a stout man with a thick black beard and hair to match. "It seems what your father feared was true. You've come to Novaria."

"And why should he fear that, Mister Ambassador?" Eliana asked. "He was planning to host a delegation in Kalama for the autumn equinox. My brother can tell you all about it."

"We know you did not come on behalf of Helosia, Princess Eliana," the man replied. His umber skin almost sparkled with the light sheen of sweat beading on his forehead.

"Oh, I didn't?" she asked. "What would you know of my reasons for coming here?"

Why push them? Astrea tried not to stare too hard at Eliana, but skies. Did she have to get an attitude now?

"Your father—"

"Doesn't know a damn thing about why I'm here," Eliana said. "Mister Ambassador, why are *you* here? It's my understanding that Grand Duchess Ysabel was given no choice but to let you in."

"We come with a message from Kalama, Your Imperial Highness," said the other ambassador, a woman with fair skin and curly auburn hair.

"And what might that be, Madam Ambassador?" Ysabel asked. "As Princess Eliana said, you gave me no choice, nor did you go through proper channels. I don't see why I am not allowed to host two young royals from the court I'm set to visit not too long from now."

Had Ysabel decided to still go to Kalama, then? Astrea couldn't imagine the summit was still set to go on with Eliana and Jin on the run, nor could she imagine the grand duchess planned to actually go when Emperor Aelius was trying to harness void magic for his wars.

"We do apologize, Your Highness," the auburn-haired woman said. "Emperor Aelius said the message had to be delivered posthaste. It's urgent."

"And if he knows where I am, why could he not just call?" Eliana asked. "Why intrude on the grand duchess's court and hospitality like this?"

Behind Astrea, Nicos sighed quietly.

"We mean no disrespect, Your Imperial Highnesses," the man said. "But orders are orders, and if you would be so kind, we would like to deliver the message."

Eliana nodded. "Very well."

The woman cleared her throat. "Emperor Aelius would like you to know, Princess Eliana and Prince Varojin, that he finds your vacation has gone on long enough."

Astrea almost laughed. Vacation?

"And," the woman continued, "he has extended an offer."

"What might that be?" Eliana asked.

"He says you may stay in Novaria if you wish, but if you do, Princess Eliana, you forfeit your rights to the Helosian throne and will not be welcomed back into the country."

Cold disbelief swept through the room. Astrea hadn't expected Emperor Aelius to just let Eliana do whatever she wanted, but to hear it now, after being gone for so long . . .

"And you, Prince Varojin, will forfeit not only your position in the Helosian army but your rights as a child of the emperor. You will be considered a deserter, and you will be stripped of your royal titles and status."

Astrea swore Jin perked up ever so slightly. In fact, she could've sworn a whisper of relief slipped past his wall, but it was gone too quickly for her to be certain.

"Similar offers extend to your friends," the Helosian man continued for his colleague. "If they decide to stay here in Novaria, they will be stripped of rank, title, assets, and jobs accordingly."

"And if we return to Helosia?" Eliana asked.

"Your father will reinstate your positions, Your Imperial Highness," the man said.

"And if I want to continue my vacation here in Novaria, my father will simply let me?" Eliana asked. "Being stripped of titles notwithstanding, of course."

"Yes." The woman reached into her blazer and pulled out a thin envelope sealed with golden wax. So much like the one Astrea had received that fateful day at the library. "His Imperial Majesty wishes for you and Prince Varojin to read this letter. But the short of it is that if you stay in Novaria, he says he will not interfere."

"Has he given me a deadline?" Eliana asked.

"One week." The woman approached the dais and set the letter on the edge. "Should you make your decision, you may reach out to our office."

"Thank you for your time, Ambassadors," Eliana said. "We'll be in touch."

At the grand duchess's direction, four Novarian guards escorted the ambassadors down the long aisle and out of the throne room. Once the double doors closed, thick silence settled over their group on the dais. Astrea wasn't sure anyone was going to speak. What was there to say?

But then Eliana sighed and said, "I suppose we have much to discuss."

Astrea clutched her body armor to her chest as she followed Eliana, Nicos, and the Novarian royals toward Ysabel's office. Jin walked beside Astrea, his shoulders and face tight. Zephyrine and Marko had excused themselves to update the rest of their friends on the situation.

The Helosian ambassadors' words ran circles in Astrea's mind, so much so that she hardly noticed the orange anxiety penetrating Eliana's aura and lighting up the palace halls. Stripped of rank, title, assets, everything. Not an unexpected threat, Astrea supposed, but why now? Why after they'd been gone for months?

As Ysabel swept into her office, Crown Prince Veiko followed her. Eliana, however, stayed across the hall from the office door, gripping the emperor's letter tightly in her hands.

"I'll be inside soon," she said to Lucian. "I need to read this."

"You wouldn't like to do so inside, Your Imperial Highness?" Lucian asked.

"No, Jin and I need to read this. Alone." Eliana's pointed look at both Nicos and Astrea told Astrea she wasn't welcome in the hallway, either.

"El—" Nicos started.

"Please," she whispered, voice tight. "We'll return in just a few minutes."

"You're sure?" he asked softly. Eliana nodded. Pressing his lips together, Nicos turned to Lucian and said, "She'll come inside in a few minutes, Commander."

"Jin?" Astrea asked.

He smiled—barely. "How about you go tell Ysabel and Veiko what we found out?"

"Alright." Astrea tried to smile back at him but failed. She squeezed his hand gently, then went into Ysabel's office.

As soon as they'd all stepped inside, Lucian closed the door. "Princess Eliana and Prince Varojin are going to take a few moments, Your Highness," he said to Ysabel. "That was certainly not what I expected to return to."

"Nor what I expected, but here we are." Gathering her skirt, Ysabel plopped down in the chair behind her desk. She rubbed her temples as she muttered, "I don't even know where to begin."

Nicos set Mattina's notebook and the translation on the grand duchess's desk. Nobody made a move to grab it.

"The store we went to was apparently owned by Lord Theodore Kadis from Helosia," Lucian said.

"And you didn't figure this out before?" Ysabel asked.

"It wasn't registered in his name. How was I to know?"

"Registered under an alias or to someone else?" asked Crown Prince Veiko. He'd settled against the wall near the door, arms crossed over his chest.

Astrea hadn't seen much of him since returning to Talmaris, nor had she interacted with him much before leaving the city. But now, his aura was open, yellow worry pulsing out from him steadily. Out in the hallway were two very tight—very desperate—walls blocking her out.

"Someone else, as far as I know," Lucian said.

"Perhaps sympathetic to the Paragon?" Veiko asked. "Could we bring them in for questioning?"

"If we can find them," Lucian said. "They may have fled with what Nazarov was planning. I doubt he's staying in the city."

Astrea huffed. "Does it matter who owns the shop?" she asked. Ysabel's eyes narrowed, but Veiko offered her an encouraging smile. "The fact of the matter is that Theo Kadis is here and allied with Nazarov." After explaining the connection she and Jin had to him—though she left out the part about Jin's mother—Astrea added, "He made two translated copies of the notebook. Jin and I checked both over ourselves for any discrepancies and found none."

"And?" Ysabel asked.

"A lot of it was about meteorites that Mattina had been researching, including how he thought they shared properties with void magic, Your Highness."

"Meteorites like what Miss Nikaphoros is studying with Mariya?"

"The very same," Astrea said. "He didn't seem to have anything definitive to go on, but I think it'll help Mariya and Tomas."

"Were you able to learn anything else?" Veiko asked. "Anything about this Nazarov fellow, Commander Lucian? What did you think of him?"

"He's exactly the kind of man you'd expect to be doing everything he's done," Lucian said. "He told us he believes the book the Paragon is after is in Kalama, in the possession of Emperor Aelius. He wants us to go get it and said he'd rather us have it than the emperor."

"Did he say what was in it?" Nicos asked. "It's not every day your enemy is willing to just hand over that kind of intel."

"He did not," Lucian said. "Just that it was preferable. The implication—"

"—is that the emperor shouldn't have it," Nicos finished. "Yeah, I get it, Commander."

Astrea adjusted her armor, still cradled in her arms, with one hand and rubbed her forehead with the other. "We'd already assumed the book held information about void magic," she said. "I think we should assume it's something about that or the meteorite. The emperor has both, so whatever the book says must . . . I don't know. Unlock something for him?"

The meteorite being able to block out a Lightbringer would give Emperor Aelius an advantage in war. What if the meteorite really could also amplify void magic somehow, and he gave that to his void mages?

"And unlock it for the Paragon," Veiko said. "And us, if we can get our hands on it."

The office door opened with a soft click. Eliana walked in first, the letter back in its envelope and clutched in one hand. Jin followed her, shutting the door behind them. Both of their expressions were neutral. Impossible to read.

"Well?" Ysabel asked when Eliana sat down in one of the chairs in front of her desk. "What did it say?"

"Just more of the same as the ambassadors said," Eliana replied evenly. "Reiterated the two options he's giving us."

Jin had joined Astrea where she stood, and his hand found the small of her back as Eliana spoke. His muscles tensed.

"Nothing else?" Ysabel asked.

"I think he wanted us to see it in his handwriting," Jin said. "As if he were speaking to us directly, not just through the ambassadors."

Ysabel nodded. "Alright, well, Miss Sovna and Commander Lucian have filled us in on what happened at the shop."

"Good. Then you know we need to go back to Kalama," Jin said.

"Going back to Kalama?" Ysabel asked, disbelief pulsing off her in strong, relentless waves. "You want to go back to Kalama, Varojin? After what those ambassadors just said?"

"Not to return to my father. To get the book."

"What?" Ysabel asked, voice low. "Do you hear yourself?" Her lavender gaze flicked to Eliana, then Lucian. Nicos, then Astrea, then Veiko. Her pale cheeks burned scarlet. "Well, does anyone have anything to say? To talk some sense into him?"

Nobody said anything.

"You cannot be serious, Varojin," Ysabel said. "You heard your father's ambassadors. He'll let you off the hook if you leave him alone."

"We can't just leave him alone," Jin said. "I don't care what he's offering. This isn't just about me or Eliana or our friends. This is bigger than us."

"Unbelievable," Ysabel muttered. Still, neither Lucian nor Veiko spoke.

"I don't see why you're so upset about this," Jin said. "I'm not asking you to send your people. I'm volunteering my team to go. We'll get in, get the book, and get out. We won't be gone for more than a week."

"You don't understand why I'm upset?" Ysabel leaned forward, elbows resting on her desk. "Varojin, if you get caught, not only could this fall back on me, but your father will—"

"Father might throw all of you in prison," Eliana finally cut in. "You might very well be walking into a trap set by Nazarov or by Father. Walking toward your own death."

Astrea swallowed hard. Would Emperor Aelius really execute his own son over this? Imprison him, sure. But kill Jin? Would he really do that?

"We won't get caught," Jin said.

As if it were that simple.

Ysabel clicked her tongue. "You cannot guarantee that. You would risk your life over the possibility that Victor Nazarov was being truthful?"

"I know it's not a guarantee," Jin said. "Nothing is. But my gut is telling me to follow this lead, and my gut is almost always right. If there's even a small chance we can prevent my father from getting whatever it is he's after with that book, then we have to take it."

Ysabel sighed, a heavy, irritated sound, as she pinched the bridge of her thin nose and leaned back in her chair. Veiko crossed his arms, making his deep violet shirt wrinkle. Perhaps the greatest surprise out of the whole situation was that Lucian kept his mouth shut.

"Aunt Ysabel, Varojin must go," Veiko said. "We cannot send our own team. The emperor would interpret that as a true act of war."

"Varojin *is* one of ours," Ysabel muttered.

"But we think Aelius is unaware of that fact."

"I'm going whether you agree with me or not," Jin said. "If you won't help us, we'll find our own way back to Kalama."

And how would they do that? Steal an airship? Astrea doubted they could just fly back to Kalama. That would make them easy targets. Take the train? A convoy of cars across the continent?

"I need to talk to you, my sister, and Veiko," Jin said when the room remained quiet. "Alone."

For a moment, Astrea thought Ysabel might actually refuse Jin. Fine lines formed around her mouth as she pressed her lips together. But the grand duchess finally sighed and said, "Very well."

Gray confusion danced around Eliana and Nicos, but neither of them moved. Jin took Astrea's free hand in his.

"Will you tell Lucian and the others about my mother?" Jin asked, his voice hardly above a whisper.

"Sure, if you want me to." Astrea squeezed his hand. "Are you alright?"

The corners of Jin's lips quirked up in a tired smile. "Not great. We'll talk when I get back." Astrea squeezed Jin's hand again, and he returned the gesture before turning over his shoulder. "Lucian, can you escort Astrea upstairs? I'll join you when I'm finished."

"Of course, Your Highness."

As Astrea followed Lucian to the office door, she snuck one last peek at the others. Ysabel's mouth was set in a tight line, stony almost. Hopefully Jin would be able to break the news about the Seviyan connection to the Paragon without completely losing Ysabel's support.

CHAPTER 26

As Astrea stared out at Jin's team, she pulled her barrier in toward herself. Not so close that she couldn't feel anything, but not so far that her exhausted mind felt burdened, either. She'd kept her magic as open as possible while at Theo's Talmaran shop, on edge while she waited for one of the void mages to make a move. But they hadn't. And with so many other Lightbringers around and Nazarov nowhere in sight, Astrea finally let herself relax a fraction.

They were in Zephyrine's room, which, like the rest of the guest rooms, had a sitting room and attached bedroom. The setup was nearly the same, with a long sofa, two plush armchairs with ornately carved backs and legs, and a low coffee table. A fireplace sat on the far wall. The blue and gray color scheme complimented Zephyrine's soft gray eyes.

"Where are Jin and Eliana?" Zephyrine asked from where she lounged in one of the armchairs. The general had gathered everyone there to catch them up on what had happened at both the shop and in the throne room.

"Speaking with Ysabel," Astrea said. "Jin's asked me to tell you something."

"And?" Zephyrine asked.

Astrea fidgeted with the cuffs of her sleeves. Her back was to the fireplace, and Adi stood opposite her, his back to the door. Even with her senses pulled in as much as she dared, the anxiety pulsing around him made her own heartbeat quicken.

"I, well . . ." Where did she even begin? "While Jin and I were upstairs with Theo, he . . . told us something. Theo knew Jin's mother, as I think you already knew?" When the others nodded or murmured their agreement, she continued, "When we went back to the house where the Paragon took me, Jin and I found a letter in The One's desk marked with his mother's family name. The letter didn't confirm anything one way or another, so we started trying to look into the Seviya family."

Lucian and Marko were the only two in the room who didn't actually know about that, Astrea was sure. Jin seemed to tell his team everything.

"You found a letter from the Seviya family at the house?" Lucian asked.

"Jin wanted to try to figure out what it was on his own," Astrea said. "He's talked to Ysabel about it some, and we found some of Lord Tanel's old journals, but they didn't reveal anything definitive."

"Ysabel knew already?" Lucian asked, crossing his arms across his chest as he came to stand near Adi. Marko joined them.

"Not that the Seviya family were Paragon." Astrea picked at invisible lint on her sleeve, trying to ignore Lucian's simmering annoyance. "That's what Theo told us today. Jin's mother was Paragon. The Seviyas were Paragon."

"What do you mean his mother was Paragon?" Adi asked.

"I mean exactly that, Adi." What else could she possibly mean? "Caliste Seviya was a member of the Paragon."

Cressida peered up at Astrea from her spot next to Lennor on the sofa. "And Theo . . ."

"Apparently Caliste was the one who recruited Theo. At least, that's according to him."

"I don't like that," Civan said quietly. "I really don't like that. Paragon in the Helosian government?"

"Theo has not been an imperial advisor for over two decades," Zephyrine said. "Though I'm surprised he would give up that position considering his goals."

"He gave the position up?" Lucian asked.

"It was never quite clear what happened, actually." Zephyrine pursed her lips. "He's a few years older than I am, and neither of my parents had been invited to the council. I was not yet part of those social circles. Rumor had it that he had a falling out with Aelius. I think Jin was around . . . oh, maybe three years old when that happened. Eliana was still a baby."

"What was the falling out?" Astrea asked.

"I'm not sure, but that was when Caliste left the palace. My family *was* living in Kalama at the time, and we all heard those rumors. She'd been living with the Auris family until then."

"That doesn't sound like a coincidence," Marko said. "Theo, secretly Paragon and advisor to the emperor, has a fight with him, and then the Paragon mistress also leaves?"

"Does it matter what happened?" Adi asked. "Does Emperor Aelius know about Caliste? And Theo?"

"Theo said he doubted the emperor knew about Caliste's Paragon connections," Astrea said, "but he assumes the emperor knows about the Paragon now."

"A reasonable assumption," Cressida said.

"What do you think, Zephyrine?" Adi asked. "Do you think Nazarov's telling the truth about the book being in Kalama?"

"I do, unfortunately."

"As do I," Lucian said.

"I know the emperor's basically told us to stay out of his way, but we have to go back to Kalama," Astrea said. "And I don't just want to get the book while we're there."

Cressida's eyebrows furrowed, relaxing as teal understanding flared around her. The idea had come to Astrea on the car ride back to the palace, and she hadn't wanted to say anything out of fear the rest of the group wouldn't entertain her. But she had to suggest it. She had to fight for it despite what Emperor Aelius was threatening. *Because* of what he was threatening.

"I want to get our families out," Astrea said as the room remained quiet. "My uncle and Cressida's parents. Whatever the emperor is planning, I don't want them stuck in Kalama. I don't care what it takes."

"I want to get my sister, too," Adi said quickly. "I know you said she's out of the city, Zephyrine, but I want to bring her here. I can't let her stay in Helosia."

Astrea wasn't sure what she expected from the retired Helosian general. Disagreement? Outrage? Indifference? But none of that flitted across Zephyrine's aura. Instead, she smiled as she said, "Well, it sounds like we're going to need a plan."

The clock on Astrea's bedside table indicated it was the sixth evening bell. It was dinner time, and Jin still wasn't back from his chat with Ysabel. What could they still be discussing? Or had they gone to look for information about the Seviya family?

Astrea paced around their bedroom, her fingers twisting the end of her skirt around and around again. Zephyrine and the others had agreed to wait for Jin, Eliana, and Nicos to return before they came up with a plan for extracting the families from Kalama. Those three would especially have information they might need about the palace and how to get Saros out. Even Zephyrine, with her connections to the council, didn't spend *that* much time there. Not like Eliana and Nicos did.

But they needed to move quickly. They'd already wasted days playing Nazarov's little games. There was no telling how far Emperor Aelius had gotten in his own research.

"Az?" Cressida asked. She pushed up on her elbows and stared up at Astrea from where she'd long since lain on the floor. Adi and Marko were out in the sitting room, their quiet murmurs barely filtering through the cracked door. "You need to sit down or something?"

"Sorry." Astrea forced herself to stop pacing and dropped onto the floor next to her best friend. Pacing would do nothing except wear a hole in the rug. "Where are they?"

"Maybe Ysabel didn't take the news as well as we'd hoped." Cressida scrubbed her hands across her face and groaned. "Skies, I'm hungry."

"That's what you're thinking about right now?"

"I can't focus if I'm hungry."

"I wish I'd brought Mattina's journal back up here with me," Astrea muttered. It had still been sitting on the grand duchess's desk when Jin had asked for privacy.

"Could you really focus on it even if you had it?" Cressida asked. "They're probably taking so long because they're going through the whole thing letter by letter."

"I guess you're right."

"The grand duchess doesn't seem like the type to let something like this go."

"Yeah." Astrea flopped down on her back. "Do you think anyone else has been researching these meteorites?" she asked. She'd caught the group up on the contents of Mattina's journal before they split up for the afternoon, and Cressida had been just as eager to get her hands on it as Astrea.

"Like who?"

"Like . . . I don't know. The Delians? The Zaikudi? Skies, even the Tornamians. If any other Stargazers have found similar ones, surely they're being studied."

"I suppose they could be," Cressida said. "Though for what it's worth, Emperor Aelius seemed to think he was the only one with such an object."

"I don't know if that makes me feel better or worse."

Cressida laughed, but it sounded tired. "Me either."

Even before Adi knocked on the door, the energy in the hallway and sitting room changed. Astrea couldn't bring herself to move despite knowing it had to be Eliana and Jin.

As he poked his head into the room, Adi's thick eyebrows scrunched together. "What are you two doing?"

"Like you've never just been compelled to lie on the floor after a rough day?" Cressida asked.

"Not particularly," Adi replied. "Ellie and Jin are back."

Astrea pushed herself up first, then helped Cressida stand. With one last deep breath, she led the way into the sitting room. Eliana had already dropped onto the sofa, Nicos next to her. The journal was on the coffee table. And Jin. He watched Astrea closely, and she couldn't tell if he looked relieved or like he might cry.

"What did Ysabel say?" Astrea asked.

"Ysabel didn't have anything useful to add," Jin said. "She was shocked. I mean, truly shocked. She's going to send someone to my grandfather's old estate to look for more information. Ysabel's never really gone through the family's documents beyond estate details and finances after my mother died. She never thought to look for more."

"Who would?" Astrea asked. Without the suspicion that there was something more to the family, nothing would've prompted Ysabel to look for connections to void cults and secret organizations. "But that's good, right? Maybe we can figure out how much they were connected."

"Maybe. I guess that explains why they think I'm the sun in their prophecy, besides being a Sunreaper, or whatever they call me."

She hadn't even thought of that before, what with Tovan staring her down like a hungry predator, but . . .

Astrea stormed back into the bedroom. She yanked open the wardrobe, then pulled out the old Seviya letters and journals they'd found in the basement. Flipping through the pages, she let out a harsh breath.

"Az?" Eliana called. Curiosity drifted through the walls.

Astrea returned to the sitting room only to be met with confused looks from everyone. She strode toward Jin, where he was still rooted near the middle of the room. "There," she said, pointing at one of the open pages. "Your grandfather kept talking about your mother's true purpose."

"Me." Jin barely whispered the word, his eyes glued to the page. "What if that was her purpose? To make me? To create the sun they needed?"

Fiery hot rage and cold shame warred on Astrea's exposed skin, making her shudder. She laid a hand on Jin's forearm and pulled the old journal from his hands.

"And you . . ."

"And me." Astrea didn't even want to think about what that meant for her. But as Jin's realization washed over them both, her mind replayed The One's vision of Irvina in her mind, the one he'd shown her while she was trapped in those tunnels. *"Even Saros did not know the truth. Roxana had to be taken out."*

"Your mother?"

"No." No, Astrea didn't think her mother had been Paragon. How could she have been? She'd been a village healer, hadn't she? "I mean, maybe."

"Az, I'm—"

She snapped the journal shut. Was that what had happened? Their mothers had gotten mixed up with the wrong people and the wrong ideas, then tried to fulfill the Paragon's prophecy in their own ways? Astrea didn't want to think poorly of her mother, but she didn't know what else to think without more information.

"I'm confused," Adi said slowly.

"The Paragon think Jin and I are the sun and moon in their prophecy," Astrea said. "Jin's grandfather kept talking about Caliste's true purpose, and when the Paragon had me, The One indicated he knew my mother and Saros. What if the Paragon were trying to force the prophecy to come true, just as they are by kidnapping me and Jin? What if they thought that by birthing us, we would . . . I don't know. Somehow become whatever it was they wanted."

Adi pressed his lips together. Nicos and Marko stared at their shoes. But Eliana and Cressida both looked at each other, then Astrea.

"Az . . ." Cressida began.

"Maybe it wasn't my mother who was Paragon," Astrea said. Surely that was what both her friends were thinking. "Maybe it was my father."

"You don't know?" Marko asked.

"No, I don't know who my father is. My mother never told me nor my uncle."

"Could it have been The One?" Marko asked as worry rippled through the room. "You did say he indicated he knew your mother and uncle."

"Or if not him, maybe he knew your father," Nicos said.

"He gave no indication other than the dreamwalking," Astrea said, though even to her, it sounded lame. There was no way The One could really be her father, right? She didn't want to think about that too closely. "I don't know."

"I don't think we rule anything out at this point," Jin said.

Astrea nodded. No, there was no point in ruling anything out without definitive answers. Would The One tell her if he dreamwalked to her again? Should she dare ask him? Did she want to know?

"Well . . ." Adi cleared his throat. "Did the grand duchess say anything else? Are we going to Kalama?"

"No, she hasn't made a decision," Eliana said.

"She wants to tread carefully, as she put it," Nicos added. "I can see her view, at least with the ambassadors showing up."

"Veiko's going to talk to her tonight," Jin said. "He assured me in private that he'd get his aunt on board one way or another."

Astrea didn't know if that instilled any confidence in her. Crown Prince Veiko had also promised to help Eliana sway the Novarian council's favor but had been quiet when push came to shove that night of the dinner. Still, if he wanted to help now . . .

"So . . ." Cressida huffed. "We're just stuck here until she makes a decision?"

"I don't plan on letting it drag out," Jin said. "If she hasn't made a decision by the end of the day tomorrow, we're going back regardless." He glanced at Marko, then said, "I hope that doesn't offend you."

Marko smiled. "I'm hard to offend, Varojin."

"That's all well and good," Cressida said, "but how are we actually going to pull that off?"

"We'll find a way," Jin said. "I promise. We'll find one."

By the time Cressida, Eliana, and Nicos left, and by the time Marko agreed to leave Jin and Astrea alone for the night, all Astrea wanted to do was sleep. But as Jin closed the door between their bedroom and sitting room, Astrea didn't have time to think about getting in bed. Jin crossed the room in a few long strides, then pulled her into his arms and buried his face in the crook of her neck.

"Jin?" she asked.

"I'm sorry," he whispered.

"Why?" He'd been hard to read with their friends still around, but he was an open book for her now, heavy shame and regret pushing, pushing, pushing against her until she could barely breathe.

"Because." His breath shuddered out of him. "First my father makes some connection to the void and drags you into it, and now he's threatening to take everything away from you . . . I hate that you're involved with my family at all."

The fragile repairs Astrea had been making to her heart threatened to crack again as she clung to Jin and he clung to her. "I don't love what your father's doing, but I don't regret being involved with your family."

When he finally released her, Jin barely looked her in the eye. "I just wish it was different."

"I wish a lot of things were different," she admitted. Skies, there was so much Astrea wished had gone differently about her life. But she couldn't change anything. She couldn't change one single thing that had happened to her. "We'll figure it out though, right? Together?"

"Together," he whispered before he pulled her into another embrace.

Leaning into him, Astrea let her eyes close. She breathed in deeply, taking in the faint scent of eucalyptus that clung to Jin. Since returning to Talmaris, he'd secured more of that soap she loved so much. Her pulse slowed.

"How'd Lucian and Zephyrine take the news about my mother?" Jin asked as he pulled away from her a second time. He started for the wardrobe, unbuttoning his shirt as he walked.

"I don't think Lucian was thrilled that we kept it from him," Astrea said, "but honestly, I don't know that any of them were really that surprised."

"I wish I could say I was surprised." He ran a hand through his curls, then shucked off his shirt and opened the wardrobe. "That's good anyway, I guess. Lucian could've reacted poorly."

"Yes, I suppose he could have." Astrea fiddled with the end of her braid. "And we . . . *I* had an idea, while you and Ellie were downstairs." She didn't know if Jin would go for this, but every fiber of her being hoped he did. When he turned around, his eyebrows pulled together, she said, "I want to get Saros out of Kalama. And Sarsali and Balthazar. And Adi wants to get Noemi out of Helosia."

Jin stared down at her, his expression unreadable. "You want to turn this into a rescue mission?"

"They can't stay there, Jin. And Saros was going to try to find answers about what your father's been up to. And . . . and he might know more about my parents, right?"

She'd expected him to argue the inefficiency of it. The impracticality of extracting not just one but four civilians from a heavily fortified city where their whole team was probably wanted for treason. She'd expected Jin to explain it wasn't reasonable.

But he didn't do that. He tossed his shirt on the floor, then closed the distance between them. He cupped her face in his warm hands. And he kissed her. He kissed her so fiercely that Astrea thought she might fall backward, but one of his arms snaked around her waist and held her close.

"Of course we'll get them," Jin said when he pulled away, breathless. "We'll bring them back here with us."

"And if Saros doesn't want to come?" The fear had been nagging at Astrea since she'd first thought of the idea hours before in the car. He'd chosen to stay behind last time. What if he chose to do that again?

"I'll throw him over my shoulder and carry him all the way back to Novaria if I have to. We're getting your family. All three of them. For you and for Cress. I promise."

She kissed him this time, even more fiercely than he'd kissed her. He laughed against her mouth, minty relief coating her tongue.

"What's that for?" he asked as he pulled away.

"I thought you'd fight me on it."

"I took you from your family once, Az. I'm not going to let that happen again."

Chapter 27

Though Crown Prince Veiko had promised Jin he'd convince Grand Duchess Ysabel to support their cause overnight, it was already mid-morning and they'd heard nothing. Commander Lucian hadn't been by yet, either.

Astrea sat cross-legged on the ground near the lake, watching as Lennor, Cressida, Adi, Civan, and Jin sparred in some complicated dance. Though she'd trained with them for the last hour, Astrea simply didn't have any more to give at the moment. She was so tired all the time, beyond exhausted. Sunlight, fresh air, and exercise often helped when she felt like this, but ever since coming back from that house and those tunnels, Astrea just hadn't been able to shake the fatigue.

She'd tap back into the drills shortly. Even Cressida, talented as she was, was having difficulty keeping up with what Adi had suggested. Astrea doubted her leaden legs or heavy mind would do her any good should she join.

Marko sat next to Astrea in the soft grass. He stretched his legs out before him and leaned back on his elbows as he watched the rest of the group.

"You don't want to join them?" Astrea asked him.

"I can see just fine from here."

"I don't need you to sit by me if that's why you're still here."

"Ouch." The word was monotone, but the corners of Marko's thin lips tugged up. "I know you're fine to sit here alone. I'm just a bit lazy."

"I doubt you're lazy considering what I know of your career, Marko."

The breeze danced through his blond hair as he shrugged one shoulder. "One can be driven in some ways and lazy in others."

"I suppose." Astrea hugged her knees to her chest as she watched the rest of the group. Civan yanked his sister to the ground with one of his water whips, then sent Adi sprawling. Cressida managed to maneuver away, only to stumble as she avoided Jin's flames. "What was your career, anyway?"

"Back to the personal interrogations?"

"A good way to pass the time, isn't it?"

Marko chuckled. "I started off in the Novarian military, then was recruited by the palace. There's not much to it."

"What did you do in the military?"

"If you're going to ask me so many questions," Marko said, his gray eyes flicking to her for just a moment, "I think it's only fair I get to ask you some in return."

"What do you want to know?"

"What's got you so eager to go back to Kalama?" he asked. When Astrea began to protest, he added, "I'm not going to stop you, but really, could you not let Varojin and his team handle it?"

Astrea's cheeks burned. Of course she could *let* Jin and his team handle it. "It's not like the grand duchess is going to send Lucian with them," Astrea said. "They need me to watch for any void mages. You don't think I can handle it?"

"I never said that." Marko's gaze tracked Adi as he finally rolled over and pushed himself to his knees. "I merely asked a question."

"And you're avoiding mine."

"Do you really want me to answer?"

Astrea swallowed hard. "Yes."

"I think you can handle it," he said. "But I don't know if you should. I've seen many soldiers push themselves far beyond their limits, Astrea. Soldiers who haven't given themselves time to recover."

"Are you . . . worried about me?" Astrea asked, unsure whether she was flattered or annoyed or even amused.

Marko half smiled. "I've grown rather fond of you and your friends. Is it unreasonable to want to check in?"

"I'll be fine."

"Alright." Marko nodded. "Good."

The others continued through three more rounds of drills, including stopping halfway through the second because Cressida bruised her elbow. It wasn't anything Astrea couldn't fix, though. Jin had just yelled out instructions for a fourth drill when Eliana, Nicos, and Crown Prince Veiko crested the hill leading back to the main gardens and palace.

Astrea perked up. Eliana had declined the invitation to join them for practice without any real reason; had she gone to meet with Ysabel?

Jin called out orders for the drill to cease as the trio walked closer. Everyone rejoined Astrea and Marko where they sat near the edge of the lake and began picking up flasks of water and towels. Cressida drank greedily while Jin and Adi both wiped sweat from their arms and foreheads.

"Varojin," Veiko said as he, Eliana, and Nicos approached. "I'm glad to see you."

"You have news?" Jin asked.

"Indeed I do." He smiled down at Eliana. "Your sister came to me with an idea this morning, and I think it's the best way to convince my aunt to continue working together."

"You weren't able to convince her last night?" Jin asked.

"Unfortunately, no. She's worried about how this will fall back on Novaria. She doesn't want to admit there's risk no matter what. We assumed that risk the moment we let you and Eliana into the palace." Sighing, Veiko added, "Although it was obviously the right choice. This is far bigger than what she could've imagined."

"I was looking at the calendar this morning and realized we aren't that far from the autumn equinox," Eliana said.

"The date we were supposed to host the Novarian delegation," Jin murmured. He slung his towel over his shoulder. "You want us to wait that long to go to Kalama?"

"No," Eliana said. "I was thinking we invite Father north. Tell him Ysabel and Veiko still want to speak to him in person, just at an earlier date since circumstances have changed. And I'll tell him that I'll also speak to him."

"And you want to do this because . . . ?" Jin asked.

"Your sister believes that if we time this correctly," Veiko said, "we can draw him away from Kalama—far away from it—while you take your team and steal the book."

For a few heartbeats, the only sounds were the lapping of water against the shore and morning songbirds fluttering through the treetops. Finally, though, Jin said, "You want to trick him."

"Is it a trick, though?" Veiko asked. "Or simply a conversation we promised to have with him anyway? A conversation that happens to have the added benefit of creating a bigger opening for you."

"We promise him nothing but the meeting," Eliana said. "Just the invitation to talk to me will surely draw him out. He might think it's an opportunity to convince me to come home."

"And what happens when I'm not there to meet him, too?" Jin asked. "Don't you think he'll find that suspicious?"

"Oh, please." Eliana scoffed. "Jin, we both know you're Father's least favorite. If we tell him you want nothing to do with him, that you're not interested in talking to him, you think he'll still push for your presence?"

Jin's shoulders hunched up near his ears. With a sigh, he lowered them again. "I think he'll ask a load of questions, but maybe he'll be too distracted by you, Ysabel, and Veiko to push it much harder than that."

"You agree to the plan, then?" Veiko asked.

"If it gets Ysabel on board, and if it gets my father out of Kalama, then it's worth trying," Jin said.

As Veiko smiled, Astrea couldn't help but smile a bit, too. It wasn't a half-bad plan. She just hoped the grand duchess would agree.

Although Astrea had been eager to head straight for Ysabel's office, showing up covered in sweat and dirt hadn't seemed prudent. Ysabel was already hesitant; she might take that kind of interruption as disrespectful.

Instead, Astrea had showered off with Jin, then gotten changed into the black pleated skirt and plum blouse Ysabel had gifted Astrea upon their arrival in Talmaris. Jin, too, had worn one of his Novarian-provided outfits, just black slacks and a forest green shirt. Ysabel had agreed to meet them in her office, and they were on their way there with Eliana, Nicos, and Commander Lucian.

"Crown Prince Veiko spoke to me not long ago," Lucian said, his voice low as they passed several guards heading in the opposite direction. "For what it's worth, Your Imperial Highnesses, I support the plan. I'll be telling the grand duchess as much."

Astrea hadn't expected Lucian to disagree, but hearing that he was on their side was still reassuring.

They entered Ysabel's office with little fanfare. Prince Veiko was already there, a confident smile lighting up his face.

"Eliana, Varojin," Ysabel said. She didn't stand from her seat. "Commander."

"Thank you for agreeing to talk again today," Eliana said. "I had an idea that I think you're going to appreciate. It will help Jin go to Kalama to do what he needs to do, and it will also give you and me the opportunity to gather information."

One of Ysabel's narrow eyebrows arched. "Oh?" She motioned to the two chairs in front of her desk. "Let's hear it."

Eliana gathered her crimson skirt, then sat down with practiced grace. "Well . . ."

As Eliana began explaining the plan, Ysabel's already hard-to-read features turned stony. *Not good.* Astrea wasn't exactly sure why she'd been invited to this meeting, but it hadn't seemed appropriate to ask, and now certainly wasn't the time to interject herself into the discussion. Eliana, notably, left out the plans to pull their families out of the capital.

"Not only do you want to go back to Kalama," Ysabel said once Eliana had finished, "but now you want to place not just yourself but me in your father's path?"

"Consider it," Eliana said. "You *know* my father can't have that book, Ysabel. If you and I invite him north for a conversation, that creates an opening for Jin and his team. It's one less obstacle standing in the way of the book, and it's one more opportunity for us to actually try to get information from my father."

"And what if your brother fails?" Ysabel asked. "I mean no offense, Varojin, but if you get caught and your father connects the timing of everything—which I'm sure he will—then what? I've already opened my country up to possible conflict with the Helosian Empire. Trying to distract Emperor Aelius while you all break into his capital city seems like a very bad idea."

"We'll be in his path regardless, Aunt Ysabel," Veiko said. "I know he's given Eliana and Varojin the choice to stay in Novaria undisturbed, but let's be realistic. It's not like any of us in this room are actually going to stay out of whatever it is he's doing. This is an opportunity. Maybe one that speeds up our confrontation with Helosia, but that's a chance I'm willing to take if it means we get that book away from him and learn whatever we can about his plans."

"And the Paragon's plans," Jin said. "It's killing . . . well, several birds with one stone, really."

Ysabel huffed, her midnight blue blouse wrinkling as she crossed her arms over her chest.

"Your Highness," Lucian said quietly, "if I may?"

"You don't have to ask permission, Lucian," she said. "You know that."

"Then I must tell you that I agree with Princess Eliana," he said. Ysabel frowned. "Prince Veiko is right. This will likely shorten the timeline for our inevitable confrontation with the Helosians, but at least it gives us a shot at knowing what it is we'll be up against. Aren't you tired of being in the dark?"

"We aren't *in* the dark," Ysabel said, though it was almost like she didn't believe it. "Mariya's reviewing the translation with Miss Nikaphoros—"

"And that will get us a dead man's theories," Jin said. "Important, yes, but it doesn't give us the full picture."

Ysabel tilted her head to one side. "What do you think, Miss Sovna?"

"Me?" Astrea asked.

"Yes."

Why would Ysabel ask Astrea's opinion? It wasn't like she was well-versed in diplomacy or much of anything, really. Still, Astrea pushed her shoulders back. "I can't speak much on the emperor's reaction or plans." To that, Ysabel nodded once. "But I think I can speak to the Paragon. Victor Nazarov said Emperor Aelius cannot have the book. And I know Nazarov is our enemy, but Helosia is our common enemy. If he truly thinks that about the book, then I'm inclined to believe him."

"Even after he tortured you?" Ysabel asks. "You believe him?"

"I don't see the two as mutually exclusive, Your Highness. He can be a bad person and still see the bigger threat."

"Indeed," Ysabel murmured. She steepled her fingers in front of her mouth, her gaze unfocused as she stared out across her office. But finally, she looked up toward her nephew. "Let's hope you're right, Veiko." Turning to the rest of them, she sighed. "Let's hope you're all correct. Commander, begin making preparations. I want Marko on the team. I'll reach out to the Helosian embassy and see if Emperor Aelius is willing to hear us out."

<h1 style="text-align:center">CHAPTER 28</h1>

Planning a heist and three civilian extractions was more complicated than Astrea had imagined. She'd known it wouldn't be *simple*, but there was a reason Jin and his team had the jobs they did in the Helosian army. There was a reason they were in charge now despite being in Lucian's office.

Zephyrine, Civan, and Marko had gone to oversee preparations at Lucian's request. Jin, Eliana, Cressida, Adi, Lennor, and Nicos were all there, as was the commander. Ysabel had, noticeably, made herself scarce. Though she'd agreed to the plan, she certainly hadn't been enthusiastic about it.

"Let's start with this." Jin pointed at a rough sketch of the Helosian palace compound, one Eliana and Nicos had made for him. "This is going to be the most complicated part of the mission. Getting to Saros and getting him out, sight unseen."

"Is it even going to be possible?" Lucian's midnight blue eyes flicked up to Astrea, his mouth set in a thin line. "I understand your desire to get your family out of the city, but if it's not possible, we need to consider—"

"It's possible." Jin tapped on the sketch again, this time pointing at the observatory on the eastern side of the compound. "His tower is far enough away from the majority of guards."

"Hardly any go over there anyway," Astrea said.

"It certainly never was Commander Dagon's priority before," Nicos said. Lucian shot him a questioning look. "That's your Helosian counterpart."

"Wouldn't it be a priority now?" Lennor asked. "What with everything that's happened, do you think your father would still leave Saros mostly unguarded?"

"And *that's* the question." Jin straightened and crossed his arms over his chest. "I don't want to be in Kalama longer than we must be, but it's worth considering giving ourselves an extra day in the city to figure out guard rotations."

"Reconnaissance?" Adi asked. "Where could we stay without you getting recognized, though?"

"Or any of you," Nicos said. "The guards will be on the lookout for at least the three of you." He nodded at Jin, Adi, and Astrea. "Probably Cress and Zephyrine, too. Maybe not you"—he gestured to Lennor—"or your brother."

"Oh, he's definitely looking for Jin," Eliana said. "And if he isn't, Kaius will be sniffing around. He might join Father for the meeting, but I doubt they'd both leave the palace unless they have to."

"Would Saros leave with Civan and I?" Lennor asked. "If we can get into the palace . . ."

"I don't think he would," Astrea said.

"No way," Cressida agreed. "No offense to you and Civan. It's just that he wouldn't even leave with Az last time."

"Right . . ." Lennor half laughed. "I suppose I wouldn't go off with two strange mages breaking into the palace, either. Doesn't exactly suggest good intentions."

Bright peach amusement flared around Cressida, there one heartbeat and gone the next.

Jin stared down at the map of the palace, then at the map of Kalama Lucian had laid out next to it. The commander had already marked the Great Library's position, and Cressida had marked her parents' home. There was still the problem of getting to Noemi, too, who wasn't *in* Kalama. She was just north of the city, in a suburb where one of Jin and Adi's old teammates' family members lived.

"Well." Jin scratched at his beard. He'd trimmed it the night before, and the dark hairs were barely longer than stubble. "I don't like what I'm going to suggest, but I think it's the only way we can make this work."

"And that is?" Lucian asked.

"When we get to Kalama, we have to split up."

"Jin . . ." Adi hesitated, and orange anxiety pulsed around both him and Lennor.

Of course Jin didn't like to suggest it. That was one of his team's rules. They didn't split up if they could help it.

"Just hear me out." When nobody protested, Jin continued, "We split into pairs. Len and Civan will go to Noemi; she's met them before, right Adi?"

"Yeah, once."

"Good enough. Then Zephyrine and Marko will go to the Nikaphoroses. Your parents would trust Zephyrine, right, Cress?"

"They would," she said. "But what about me? Shouldn't I go to them?"

"You . . ." Jin nodded once to himself. "You and Az will go to the library and get that book. Adi and I will go to the palace and get Saros."

"Is that wise?" Eliana asked. "You'll be one of the first people the guards recognize."

"And sending Astrea in to get him isn't an option?" Lucian asked. "I know he wouldn't leave with you last time, but—"

"I'm not going to give Saros the choice to stay," Jin said. "And I don't think Az can carry him out if she has to."

Cressida snorted. "No, but I'd like to see her try. I'd like to see *you* try, Jin. You know how stubborn that man is." She offered Astrea an apologetic smile. "Sorry."

"Don't apologize," Astrea said. "He's the most stubborn person I know."

"Besides, Az knows books better than I do." Gesturing toward where the library was marked on the map, Jin said, "And if Raela's there, well, she knows you. So do the pages. You and Cress both. Better than her seeing the runaway prince trying to steal from her."

Astrea didn't know about that one. But Raela . . . Raela had always trusted Astrea. If they were unfortunate enough to run into the librarian, maybe Astrea *would* be able to talk to her and at least convince her not to call the police or the palace guards.

"And how are you going to get into Kalama?" Eliana asked. "None of the rest will matter if you can't get into the city."

"Or the country," Nicos said. "Public airships and trains are heavily monitored."

Lucian cleared his throat. "The most discreet way will be to fly to Tornama, then make your way to Kalama from there. Marko and I have some contacts in Thasia. If we can't get you there on a boat, we can get you there by car."

"Jin hates boats," Eliana murmured.

"I just get a little seasick," he said. "A boat would be the fastest. And probably the easiest way to get everyone else out. We'll likely need to make our way back to Tornama to come back up north."

"When can we leave?" Adi asked.

"The sooner the better," Jin said. "Tomorrow?"

"We should have everything ready to go before first light," Lucian said.

"Can you really have everything we need to leave in, what, six hours?" Cressida asked. It was already getting late, approaching the tenth evening bell. "Maybe seven?"

"We used to go out with as little notice as forty-five minutes," Lennor said. "*We* can be ready."

"We'll have everything you need, Cressida," Lucian said. "I promise. Now go pack and get some rest. I'll oversee final preparations."

By the time Astrea and Jin got back to their room, all Astrea wanted to do was sleep. But she had to pack. They'd been making sure everyone else had their things in order. Not just their armor but street clothes in case they needed them in Tornama or Helosia. And now it was Astrea's turn.

While Jin lit the fireplace, she hurried into the bedroom. Grabbing both their packs out of the wardrobe, she threw them on the bed. If they could pack now, they could still sleep for a few hours before they had to get on yet another airship.

"Az?" Jin asked as he strolled into the room.

"Let's get started." She moved between the wardrobe and bed, bringing her clean training clothes and undergarments. "Do you think this is too much?"

"Why are you in such a rush?"

"Because I want to shower and go to bed. Skies knows the airship isn't going to have good beds or good showers."

Amusement coated her tongue, sweet and light. "No, it won't, but you don't have to rush around like a wild woman."

"Come on, just get to work. We can both be done in a few minutes."

"Alright, alright."

Jin joined her in sorting through training clothes, undergarments, and choosing a couple of their old casual Kalamian outfits. Astrea went to put a few extra things away in the wardrobe, and when she turned, she found Jin gingerly folding up her clothes. Orange anxiety and tangerine fear twirled around him, bright even in the low light of the two lamps Astrea had turned on.

"You're worried."

A tight laugh escaped Jin before he said, "Yes, well, preparations for missions usually go much differently than this."

"Your other missions didn't feel like this?" She pulled her armor out of her pack, figuring that sticking her civilian clothes at the bottom would make the most sense. Easy access to her gear was best, right?

"That's the problem. It feels exactly like them."

"What?" Astrea's hand paused just inches from the pile of clothes she was about to grab.

"It's exactly how they always started. Barely any time to pack, a short briefing, and then off we'd go." He finally looked at her. "I don't want this life for you, Az. I never have."

Astrea swallowed hard as she held Jin's gaze. His expression was both soft and pained, like he didn't know how to feel or what to say. Her chest tightened. This wasn't going to turn into another fight, was it? Like the one they'd had before she'd been taken by the Paragon? She thought they'd sorted all of that out.

"I have to go, Jin," she whispered. "I have to."

"I know." He smiled weakly. "I'm not asking you to stay. I'm trying very hard to get my heart on board with what my head knows."

"And what's that?"

"That you're going to be safe with us and with Cress when we're in Kalama. That you're going to get the book."

"I will," she promised.

As Jin blew out a harsh breath, Astrea reached for his hand. "I see it all the time when I'm asleep. Them jumping you away that night, and the night we found you down there . . ." He closed his eyes. "The way you screamed . . . I'm never going to forget that sound for as long as I live."

"Jin . . ." Astrea's words caught in her throat. She understood; her mind was always taking her back to that dark place. "Why didn't you tell me sooner?"

"You're in enough pain, Az."

"That doesn't mean you had to keep all that from me."

"No, but I just . . ." He sighed. "My head knows this will work out, but my heart's convinced that it's going to happen again. That they're going to get you, and I'll fail you again like I failed you that night."

"You didn't fail me."

"It feels like I did. I hate the thought of you being out there." He twined his fingers with hers. "It's hard knowing that's one thing I can't protect you from. Can't protect any of us from, really."

Just the thought of going out there, away from this network of Lightbringers that would deter both The One and Nazarov, was enough to make Astrea's skin crawl. But this was their chance. The one lead they had. Fear had stopped her in her tracks so many times in her life. She couldn't let it stop her now. Even when every fiber of her being screamed at her to stop, she couldn't. She had to do this for Saros. For Sarsali and Balthazar. She had to do this for herself.

"It's not your job to protect us."

"Well, that was my job for eight years. Protect my team and protect Helosia from the worst threats. It's hard not to see it that way still. But I know. I know I can't protect everyone."

Deep blue regret pulsed around him, cool and sharp as it lashed out at Astrea's skin. Who was he thinking of now? Lando and the day he'd died? Astrea herself and that night with the Paragon? All his years in the army?

"These last few months have been so difficult," Astrea said. "Change isn't easy. None of this is easy."

Warmth seeped into Astrea's bones as Jin stared down at her. The sensation and his gaze were both so gentle, the same way he always looked at her first thing in the morning and every night before they went to bed. It reminded Astrea of Kalama. The soft warmth of the morning sun on her skin and the beautiful colors that would paint the sky over Tinale Bay at sunset. Those same colors danced around him now, pink and lavender, gold and purple so dark it almost looked like the midnight sky.

He brushed her cheek with the back of his left hand, the right one gripping her waist and tugging her into him. Their torsos and hips were flush against each other, and Astrea pressed into him as much as she could.

She didn't know who moved first, but their lips met. Jin tasted faintly of the coffee he'd been drinking in Lucian's office. Astrea didn't mind. Her hands slid into his hair, fingers twining with his curls as she tried to bring him closer.

"Az," he panted as he barely pulled away. She kissed the side of his neck, tart lust exploding on her tongue as he groaned, "Shit."

Still tangled together, they backed toward the bed. When Astrea's knees hit the mattress, she fell backward and took Jin with her. Their still-folded clothes took up half the mattress. Jin sighed.

"Fucking packing," he muttered as he began dropping the neat piles onto the floor. "I believe that was your idea."

"I didn't know this was going to happen," she protested.

Those colors still pulsed around him. Sweet amusement and approval overwhelmed her senses.

"Get undressed."

Astrea had barely slipped off her skirt and blouse when Jin pulled her onto his lap. His lips met her skin, tracing a path up her sternum to her throat and finally, her mouth. Tart lust raced through her, pleasantly sour and sweet and making Astrea shudder.

Jin tugged down the straps of her brassiere. Reaching behind her back, Astrea fumbled with the clasp for just a moment before it sprang free. He slid the garment all the way off her, tossing it off the side of the bed as he planted kisses on the tops of her breasts.

His erection pressed into her, hard and thick even through his trousers. She ground against him, eliciting a low rumble from his chest.

"Let me show you how I feel, Az," he rasped. "Please."

"I can already see." She choked on the last word as Jin gripped her thigh, his thumb dangerously close to her silky bloomers.

"What do you see?" he asked as he flipped them both over.

Jin's nimble fingers made quick work of the buttons on his shirt, then the ones on his pants. He hovered over her, silhouetted by the soft light coming from the floor lamp in the corner. She swallowed hard, staring as she took in his nearly naked form.

His body wasn't why she was staring, though. The same colors from before blazed around him, bright and unwavering like the sun. Marigold. Raspberry. Peach. Deep purple. Tangerine. Teal. Mint. Gold.

Pink. The softest, gentlest pink. It was so faint compared to the other colors, and somehow, it was the brightest color of them all.

"What do you see?" he repeated.

"Everything."

Everything. She could feel it all. See it all. Taste it all. The relief, the lust, the approval. It was all for her. A kaleidoscope of sensation and color, both overwhelming and not nearly enough. She wanted more. Needed more.

"Eyes on me, Az."

She hadn't realized she'd looked away, her eyes chasing the colors as they danced in the air. Astrea followed Jin's command, forcing her gaze back to his. Those eyes. Skies, those golden irises, obscured by his widening pupils. All she could see reflected in them was that sheen of pink. A familiar warmth settled in her bones, pleasant and calming.

"Tell me what you see," Jin said. "Please. Tell me."

"Gold."

"And what's that?"

"Joy."

He smiled. "What else?"

"Raspberry lust. Purple reverence. Tangerine fear. Peach amusement. Teal understanding. Mint relief. Marigold excitement."

"All that?"

"Yes."

"It sounds beautiful."

"It is." It was the most beautiful thing Astrea had ever seen.

"What else?"

"That's it," she lied.

"That's it," he mused.

Lowering himself, Jin kissed Astrea's mouth, her cheek, her jaw. He made his way down her throat and chest, his hands joining the exploration of every dip and curve of her body. And when he reached the top of her bloomers, Jin pulled them down to her knees, then farther still, and tossed them away. His hands traced the insides of her thighs, making Astrea shudder.

"Is this alright?"

As soon as her affirmation left her mouth, Jin pulled her legs apart, his fingers finding their way to her center. Raspberry flared brighter, pulsing around him as the other colors stayed steady. And when Jin went down on her, she was sure her own colors would be a mirror to his. She writhed against his mouth, letting her eyes fall closed as she grabbed his hair with one hand and the sheets with the other.

Something between a whimper and a moan escaped Astrea's throat. Jin pulled away, placing gentle kisses on her thighs. "Do you want me to stop?"

"Come here."

Jin shifted, settling between her legs and lowering his face toward hers. "Yes?"

Astrea kissed him. She kissed him so urgently she made her own head spin, and Jin kissed her back with such fierceness her heart ached. As the tip of his erection brushed against her again and again, Astrea reached between them, fumbling to line them up. Breaking the kiss, Jin pushed her hand away and guided his hips to meet hers. He pushed into her, and they both gasped at the same time.

"Fuck, Az," Jin moaned against her throat. He nipped at her skin, then chased it with a kiss. "Fuck, how is it possible for every part of you to feel so right?"

"I don't know." Her fingers tangled in his hair, holding him close. "I don't know."

And she didn't. But every part of Jin felt right too. This moment. Every moment since he'd come home months ago. Even as everything around them fell apart, Jin was one of the few things that felt right to Astrea. Being with him, not just now, but all the time. Waking up and falling asleep together. The missions. Training. Meals. Their whispered conversations and shared stories late into the night. Just holding his hand. All of it. Being with him felt right.

Jin's fingers brushing her clit jolted Astrea back to her body. She ground against him, head swimming as his emotions doubled right before her eyes. The lust, the fear, the worry, the respect. Everything. Astrea let out a breathy moan, fighting her eyelids as they threatened to close. She wanted to see him. Needed to see him.

But as she began to unravel, she lost that battle. Astrea's eyes fluttered shut, her body tightening and trembling.

"Fuck." His thrusts slowed, pulling all the way out before pushing back in. "Fuck, you feel so good."

"Shut up and kiss me."

A laugh rumbled in Jin's chest, traveling all the way down to where their bodies were still connected. Jin braced his arms on either side of her head, pinning her underneath him. Every time their lips met in between gasps for air, heat roamed Astrea's skin. Stars danced behind her eyelids, and pleasure—hers, his, both—shot through her. She breathed Jin in, the only air left in the room.

As the world fell out from under her for a second time, Jin followed her over the edge. His arms, still bracketing her head, began to shake. Warm bliss settled in her chest.

Jin rolled to one side, then pulled Astrea into him. He sighed, and when Astrea peeked up at him, all she saw were those same colors, just as bright as before.

Pink.

Love.

Jin *loved* her.

Of course he did, she realized. He didn't have to say it. She saw it every day, in all his actions, in every moment. All those soft, secret smiles he saved just for her. Bringing her breakfast in bed at the base. Making sure she ate. Breaking her out of her fixations when they became too much. Pushing her in training and making sure she could protect herself. Keeping the lights on for her while she slept. Holding her while she cried. Making her coffee the way she liked it.

And she loved him, too. Of course she did.

Jin was kind. Gentle. He was supportive. Protective, not just of her but everyone he loved. He was loyal, honest. Good. He tried to help her grow, though he never tried to change who she was. He understood her. Stood by her.

Yes, he made her stomach flutter and flip with the things he said, but her heart. Oh, her heart softened around him, like it knew it was safe with him.

Jin was her safe place.

He always had been.

She craved that peace. She craved him, everything about him.

That soft, gentle warmth pulsed out around him, brushing every part of Astrea's body as they lay together. It was so achingly soft. She'd never felt something so gentle from someone before, not like this. And she'd been feeling it for weeks, before she even got taken by the Paragon. Back when they were still in the guest house.

She didn't know whether to laugh or cry as her chest squeezed painfully.

"Hey." Jin swiped at the rogue tears streaming down her cheeks. "Hey, what's wrong? Did I hurt you? Shit, I'm sorry."

Tears clouded her vision. "No, you didn't, I just—"

"You're scared about the mission?"

How did she tell him? How did she say that word, tell him that she could see it and feel it around him?

"I lied," she croaked.

His eyebrows knitted together, gray confusion taking over his aura. "What?"

"You asked me if I saw anything else. I lied. I do." Jin's thumb brushed away more of her tears as she whispered, "I see pink."

Tangerine fear bubbled up around him. "What's pink?"

Astrea forced herself to look him in the eye as she said, "Love."

"I wasn't going to tell you until you were ready. I had a plan."

"How do you know I'm not ready?"

"You're crying." He brushed more tears from her cheek, tensing as Astrea laid a hand on his forearm. "You've—we've—been through so much lately, and—"

"Haven't you ever heard of happy tears?"

His eyebrows furrowed. "You're happy?"

"Of course I'm happy." Leaning up, Astrea pressed a soft kiss to his mouth. She pulled away just far enough to whisper, "I love you."

"Az . . ." Jin's hands slid to her face, and he pulled her into a deep, slow kiss. It burned through her, making her body tighten in the best way. "I love you so much. I'm pretty sure I've always loved you. You mean everything to me, Az. *Everything*." He kissed her again, gentler this time. "I never imagined I'd be lucky enough—worthy—of being with you. But here we are. I'm the luckiest fucking man in the entire world."

"Of course you're worthy," she whispered. Of course he was worthy of love. Of her. That he could even think otherwise was unfathomable to her, and it broke her heart a little. "How could you ever think you're not?"

"I want to give you the whole world, Az"—he sighed, deep blue regret mixing into his aura—"and all I can do is drag you back to Helosia. You deserve so much more than all this."

"I deserve to do what I want." She traced the edges of his beard with her fingertips, lowering her voice as she said, "And I want to be with you. Here. On missions. All the time. I want you, all of you, always. And I want to finish all of this. Together."

"Together," he whispered, a promise she knew he wouldn't break. "I'm jealous that you can see so much when you look at me, you know."

She smiled. "I can feel it, too."

"And what does it feel like?"

"Soft and warm. Gentle, like sunshine on a spring day."

"I know that feeling very well." Jin pressed his forehead to hers, both still slightly damp with perspiration. Astrea usually hated that feeling, but right now, she didn't mind. "Say it again. Please."

"I love you, Varojin Auris."

His eyes fluttered closed, that warmth pulsing steadily in her bones as he whispered, "And I love you, Astrea Sovna. I always will."

Chapter 29

As much as Astrea had wanted to stay up all night, listening to Jin proclaim his love and receiving all that love physically, they'd mostly gotten back on track with packing. Mostly. What should've taken them a half hour took almost thrice that long when they ended up tangled up in bed two more times.

After sleeping for just a couple hours, she and Jin had taken a shower, then loaded into one of several cars to head to Talmaris's airfield. As soon as they'd stepped foot in Zephyrine's airship, she'd handed Astrea a thermos of coffee. Astrea sipped on her drink and stared out the windows. Dawn hadn't broken yet. It was barely the fifth morning bell.

"We've already loaded maps onto the airship," Lucian explained. He'd been droning on about supplies for the last five minutes. "Marko knows who you're supposed to meet in Tornama. They'll keep the airship safe and help you secure your next mode of transportation."

Anxiety pulsed in the cabin, potent and unignorable. Astrea was sure her own worries were easy for Lucian to spot, too. They were supposed to fly to another country, trust this contact Marko and Lucian had, and then sneak into Helosia. Of course nobody felt great about this.

"Is there anything else we can do this morning?" Eliana asked. She sat on one of the sofas in the middle of the cabin, wringing her hands together in her lap. "Anything else you need?"

"It's all covered," Jin said. "But if we need anything else, we'll get it on the way. You just focus on your mission, alright, Ellie?"

Eliana nodded. "Should we wait for Ysabel? Is she coming to see you off?"

"Her Highness is not," Lucian said, "but Prince Veiko—"

A new, steady wall penetrated Astrea's emotional awareness. Lucian froze, too. That must've been Veiko. But Veiko? Why was Veiko coming instead of Ysabel?

The Novarian crown prince walked through the open airship door. He looked every bit as tired as Astrea felt. Dark circles tinged his warm pink skin, though his chestnut hair was neatly styled. Unlike Ysabel, who always seemed to dress up, Veiko wore simple black trousers, a dark green sweater, and boots. If Astrea didn't know he was royalty, she could've mistaken him for any other man on the street.

"Sorry for the delay," he said. "I just wanted to make sure you all get sent off with everything you need."

"Commander Lucian has given us everything and more," Jin said. "And it's much appreciated."

"I'd expect nothing less from the commander, but I know my aunt hasn't exactly been . . . hospitable . . . since you've been back, Varojin. Please know, though, that your friends' families are welcome here."

Relief and surprise flickered through the cabin.

"I should hope so," Jin said. "I didn't realize Ysabel was concerned about us bringing them back. I actually didn't even realize she knew we planned on that."

Veiko shoved his hands into his pockets. "She's just worried about the situation getting out of control."

"It's already out of control," Marko murmured from his spot next to Astrea.

That was certainly how it felt. Bringing a few civilians to Talmaris hardly seemed like letting the situation get out of control.

"But I've spoken to her, and it's going to be fine. We'll see you when you return. Marko." Prince Veiko turned to the Tempest and tossed him a small black bag. Marko caught it with ease. "Do whatever it is you need to do to ensure this is a success, alright? That's an order."

"Yes, Your Highness."

With a few more murmured goodbyes and well wishes, Veiko left the airship.

"And we should let you get going," Lucian said, then turned to Eliana. "Your Imperial Highness?"

Blue sadness wavered around Eliana, so thick it nearly obscured her maroon sweater. "I'll join you outside in a few moments, Commander."

"Of course, but let's not keep them."

Eliana pulled Jin away from the group and began speaking with him in hushed tones. Though that sadness and anxiety consumed her, Jin's heavy wall was up. Lucian shook hands with Zephyrine first, then motioned for Astrea to follow him a few feet away from where Cressida and Marko stood.

"Remember everything you've been working on, and you'll do great." Lucian extended his hand to her. Astrea took it, surprised by his gentle touch. "Be careful," he said as he pulled away, "and good luck."

A few quick goodbyes to the rest of the team, and then he was gone, heading out the door and back into the morning darkness. An uncomfortable weight settled in Astrea's chest. It was strange, not having him go with them.

Bringing her thermos back to her mouth, Astrea took a long drink. It was up to her now. The only Lightbringer on the team. She would have to stay sharp. Focused. And running on just a couple hours of sleep would do them no good.

As she joined Cressida again, Nicos approached them both. "I'm sorry I can't go with you all," he said. "I wish I could be more help."

"Keeping watch over her is more than enough," Cressida said, jerking her thumb over her shoulder toward where Eliana and Jin were now hugging. Orange anxiety pulsed brightly around both siblings. "She'll need you if the emperor really does show up. It's best that you're here."

"Well, still." He rubbed the back of his neck. "Is it awkward if I give you both hugs?"

Astrea had never actually hugged Nicos before. She didn't know if she'd ever even touched him. But when he opened his arms and pulled both Astrea and Cressida into an embrace, Astrea relaxed. It almost felt . . . normal.

When he released them, Cressida nudged him in the ribs. "Maybe a little awkward."

He laughed, his cheeks blushing crimson underneath his freckles and beard. "Be careful, alright? We'll see you soon."

Almost like they'd coordinated it, he and Eliana switched places. Astrea didn't even give Eliana a chance to speak. She pulled her into a tight hug, and Cressida piled on from the other side. Leaving Eliana behind every time they had to go somewhere away from Talmaris felt horrible. But Eliana was safe here. She was safe, and Helosia needed her to be safe.

"Please be careful," Eliana whispered without pulling away. "Do not underestimate Kaius or my father's guards if you run into them."

"We won't," Astrea promised.

"And please learn anything you can about what's been going on at home. Even just rumors. I need to know. Skies knows my father won't tell me the truth when I see him."

"We will," Cressida assured her. "My parents will be able to tell you a lot when they get here, too."

"Alright." Eliana squeezed them both tighter. Fear, relief, pride, and regret pressed painfully into Astrea's skin. "Alright. I'll leave you both to it. Be careful."

Eliana and Nicos met again in the middle of the cabin, and Eliana called out final goodbyes over her shoulder as she headed for the airship door. Outside the windows, Astrea could still see and feel their worry. Cressida crossed to the door and pulled it shut, then began twisting the large, spoked wheel that sealed the cabin.

Adi and Marko took their seats at the front of the ship and got to work. The engines roared to life.

This was it.

They were going back to Kalama.

Astrea stayed standing, watching through the windows as the guards outside rolled the ramp away from the side of the ship. Cressida joined her, wrapping one arm around Astrea's shoulders. She slid her arm around Cressida's waist. And a heartbeat later, Jin's arm circled both of their shoulders, his familiar warmth seeping under Astrea's skin.

And together, they watched Talmaris shrink in the distance as their ship headed into the early morning sky.

Flying to the Tornamian capital of Thasia, all the way in the southeastern part of the continent, was going to take nearly two days. On a normal flight, they could cut straight across Helosia and get there faster, but they needed to avoid Helosian air space at all costs. So they had to cross all of Novaria first, then fly south. They wouldn't arrive at their destination until dinner time the following day.

After takeoff, Astrea had taken a nap with Cressida; Jin had stayed up to talk with Zephyrine and the twins. She'd woken up just a few minutes earlier and found not only an empty bed but a fresh thermos of coffee on the small steel table next to the bed.

Astrea didn't know what to do with herself. She'd left Mattina's translated journal at the palace. She had no use for it on this mission, and besides, Mariya and Tomas might actually be able to find some connection in it. And Astrea hadn't brought anything else to read. She couldn't train. There wasn't even anything to unpack thanks to their neatly organized knapsacks.

Maybe Cressida would need help preparing lunch? Or maybe Astrea could help Jin look at the map of Kalama and plot some kind of route through the city. She knew lots of ways to get to the Great Library.

After fixing her hair into a neat braid, Astrea grabbed the coffee and headed into the hallway. Two people were asleep upstairs, or so she guessed based on the steady, peaceful energy radiating from down the corridor. Downstairs, though, was a different story. Cressida's laugh echoed up the stairs.

Astrea headed down. Cressida, Lennor, and Civan were seated around the low table in the middle of the cabin, and Cressida and Lennor were both surrounded by a tangle of peach amusement. As Astrea got closer, she spotted the playing cards in their hands and on the table. Up in the cockpit, only Marko's blond hair was visible.

"Oh, hey Az," Cressida said. "Want to join us?"

The thought of playing cards immediately sent chills up Astrea's spine, a reminder of Club Twilight. She plopped down next to Civan. "I'll just watch for now. Where are Adi and Jin?"

"Adi went to sleep for a bit, and Jin . . . I think he went into the kitchen?" A sheen of magenta pulsed around Cressida. Why was she embarrassed? "I haven't really been paying that close attention."

"I see."

Lennor peeked at her cards, then held them close to her chest and grinned. "It's a good thing we aren't playing for money because both of you would be broke."

"I have very deep pockets, Len," Cressida said.

"Maybe you do, but Civan doesn't."

Civan just shrugged.

The colors in Lennor's aura shifted, from that peach amusement to yellow worry. Worry about Civan's lack of response . . . or worry about her hand?

"Sorry, what game are you playing?" Astrea asked.

"Forfeit," Lennor said. "Why? I thought you were just going to watch."

"Just trying to catch up." Astrea faked a yawn. "Still sleepy."

Forfeit. It was a game Eliana liked to play, one about deceit and trying to get your opponents to fold their hands. That much Astrea knew.

Glancing at Lennor—who smiled brilliantly despite that yellow worry still surrounding her—Cressida set her cards down on the table. "I'll forfeit."

"Civ?" Lennor asked sweetly.

"I'm holding," he said.

Lennor set her cards on the table face-up. "Four of a kind. Beat that."

Civan set his down. "Straight flush."

"Damn!" Flopping back against the sofa, Lennor exclaimed, "How can I still not read you after twenty-three years? Aren't we supposed to have some twin thing to tell me that you have a better hand?"

"Why would we have that?" Civan asked.

The kitchen door swung open. "You seem to in a fight," Jin called. "I picked up on it with you two the day I saw you at Ironwing. So did Adi."

Civan grunted. "Or was that just because we've trained together our whole lives?"

Jin shrugged. "Does it matter?"

Civan grunted again, then picked up all the cards and began reshuffling the deck. As he did, Jin sat down on Astrea's other side and set a bowl of grapes on the table.

"Don't feel bad, Len." Cressida put her hand on Lennor's shoulder. "We're just lucky Az isn't playing."

"Why, are you good?" Lennor asked.

"Oh, no, I don't really know the rules."

"Because she could read you," Civan said.

"Oh, damn, I didn't even consider that. I've never played cards with a Lightbringer before." Lennor glanced at the thermos in Astrea's hands, her eyebrows furrowing. "Could you read me during that round?"

Astrea smiled. "I could see you were worried."

"Then I guess I should be glad you're sitting out." Lennor smiled again. She smiled a lot, actually, just like Adi. "Should we play something else? Is there a game you know better?"

"No, no, that's alright. I'm content watching."

"Maybe we should play something with teams," Lennor said. "I can teach you how to play something."

"If anyone's going to be on Az's team, it's me," Cressida replied. "Best friend gets first choice."

"Wow," Jin murmured, his arm sliding around Astrea's shoulders, "don't partners trump best friends, Cress?"

"Not a chance, Auris."

"It seems like you three just want Astrea to help you win," Civan said dryly. He continued shuffling the deck, mixing the cards up again and again.

At that, Jin chuckled. Lennor laughed, too, and said, "Well, yeah, Civ. Of course."

"That doesn't seem fair to her."

"Oh, no, that's alright," Astrea said when she realized Civan was being entirely serious. "I don't really mind."

"We're just teasing," Lennor added.

After another moment, Civan nodded. He'd finally stopped shuffling. "Alright. Should we play another round, then?"

Chapter 30

The rest of the flight south through Tornama was uneventful. Painfully so. Marko, Adi, and Zephyrine alternated on pilot duty and sleep schedules. Astrea and Jin spent a lot of time napping, as did Cressida. And there'd been many more rounds of cards played, though Astrea had still only watched.

Now that they were just an hour from their destination, Astrea's whole body hummed with energy. The sun was beginning to set outside the cabin windows, casting everything in golden light. Even the thick forest far below looked like it was drenched in gold.

"We'll land just outside of Thasia," Marko said. While Zephyrine and Adi piloted the ship, the Novarian was reviewing plans with the rest of them. "My contact will meet us at the airfield. She'll take us to a secure location in the city for the night."

"Are you ever going to tell us who she is?" Jin asked. "I trust you, Marko, but damn. We're going to meet her anyway. Why the secrecy?"

Marko glanced around the sitting area, then smoothed back his bun. "She is Commander Lucian's former wife."

"I'm sorry." Jin's eyebrows rose. "Lucian was married? I knew he'd been engaged, but he actually got married?"

"Indeed, he was. It ended a long time ago."

"Just how many women has he disappointed over the years?" Jin asked.

Marko shrugged. "Plenty."

"And she's just going to help us?" Cressida asked.

"She was formerly involved with joint Tornamian and Novarian military efforts," Marko said, "but has since moved on to other ventures."

"Cryptic," Jin murmured. "Is it a good or bad thing the commander isn't here?"

"Neither." Marko pointed at the map again. "As I was saying, she will meet us at the airfield and bring us into Thasia to a secure location. From there, we'll figure out exactly which way we'll get into Helosia. By sea would be fastest, though, of course, we need to wait for final confirmation of the emperor's travel dates from Lucian. Hopefully Rami can secure us passage."

"And Rami's the former wife?" Jin asked, and Marko nodded.

Rami. Astrea almost couldn't believe Lucian had been married at one point. Hopefully Rami would be able to get them to Kalama quickly. And she hoped Emperor Aelius would begin his trek north shortly, too. The morning they'd left, he hadn't yet agreed to a meeting, but at least they'd be ready to head for Kalama whenever the coast was clear.

"We should be ready to disembark as soon as we land," Marko said. "Don't want to stick around longer than we need to. Have any of you been to Thasia before?"

"Once, passing through to go visit my great-aunt when I was a child," Cressida said. "Not in . . . almost twenty years."

"The rest of you?" Marko asked. They all shook their heads. "Well, doesn't matter either way. But just . . . try not to draw attention to us."

"What do you think we're going to do?" Lennor asked.

"Let's just get ready to go," Marko said. "Dress for the weather. It's bound to be warm."

"As if I haven't lived in Kalama most of my life," Astrea muttered. Thasia's climate wasn't much different from Kalama; Astrea knew that much from geography lessons as a child.

"And leave nothing behind!" Marko called as Astrea and the others headed upstairs to their rooms.

"As if *I* haven't been deploying on missions for eight years," Jin said.

As they reached the second level, Astrea glanced over her shoulder. Civan was still near the bottom of the stairs, hesitating. But he finally started up. He'd hung back at the meeting with Marko, too.

Astrea had deduced that Civan, like herself, preferred the quiet and not being around too many people. But he hadn't avoided them like this before. Overstimulated, maybe?

"You all know the drill," Jin said. "Meet downstairs before landing."

"And wear something bright if you have it," Cressida said. "Something *not* black. You'll blend in better. Thasians love color."

Hesitation swept over Astrea's skin, rough like tree bark. "I don't have anything that bright," Lennor said.

"Nor do I," Civan echoed.

"Come with me, Len." Cressida waved the short Tempest into her room.

"Civan, I'll get you something of Adi's," Jin said.

As Jin led Civan toward Adi's room and Cressida led Lennor to her room, Astrea pushed her own door open and slipped inside. She'd already chosen her favorite lavender dress for the day, so she went into the bathroom to check her appearance. Her hair was a bit frizzy and mussed, so she braided it in one long plait. After her ordeal with the Paragon, the usual light pink undertones of her skin had seeped away, but they'd returned in the last couple of weeks. *Good enough.*

Astrea double-checked that all her belongings were in her pack, then grabbed Jin's knapsack. It was larger than hers, and heavier too. The bedroom door opened on nearly silent hinges, then shut again.

"All set?" she asked Jin as he circled the bed and dropped a third bag onto the mattress.

"Got Adi's things, and got Civan something to wear. Should be ready." Jin unbuttoned his black shirt and shucked it off. The muscles on his tan, broad chest and abdomen flexed with the movement. Jin's gaze flicked up from where he was digging around in his pack. He smiled. "What are you looking at?"

"Nothing."

"Liar." Jin produced the shirt, its midnight blue hue not much better than the black. But it would have to do. He pulled it on, then made quick work of the buttons and repacked his original shirt. "I'll take this stuff downstairs."

"I'll check on everyone else."

As Jin picked up the three packs and headed out the door, Astrea wandered across the hall to Cressida's closed door. Inside, muffled laughter echoed through the room, and amusement and desire wrapped around Astrea like a hug. When Astrea knocked on the door, Cressida called, "Yeah?"

"It's me. You two ready?"

"Just about!" Cressida called back.

The door opened. Astrea took half a step back as Lennor's petite frame filled up the doorway. The light blue shirt was boxy on her, but tucked into her black trousers, Lennor could pull it off. She slung her bag over her shoulder, then smiled. "See you down there."

Cressida strode toward the door, shaking out her violet blouse and cream linen trousers. She carried her knapsack by its straps, nearly dragging it on the floor.

"Jin's got everything set downstairs," Astrea said. "Let me just fetch Civan."

As Cressida headed for the stairs, Astrea walked down the corridor toward Civan's heavy wall. A few feet down, a door swung open. Civan had changed into a forest green shirt—not the brightest but better than his fatigues.

"Just wanted to make sure you have what you need," Astrea said when his eyebrows furrowed.

"Well . . ." He ran a hand over the back of his neck and took a step closer.

"What's wrong?"

"Honestly, my head's been hurting."

"Since when?" she asked. His fall had only been a few days before, but she hadn't felt any ghost pain while on the ship. Until now, at least. The closer he got, the stronger the ache grew in Astrea's head.

"Since this morning. I just don't like going out on a mission not being in top shape."

The ghost pain Astrea felt was mild, more of a nuisance than anything. Was *that* why he'd been avoiding her all morning? "Then let me help. I don't like the sound of that, either."

"I shouldn't have said anything," he said as he stared down at his boots.

"Why not?"

He shrugged his narrow shoulders. Like Lennor's borrowed shirt, Civan's was a bit too boxy on his slim frame. "I don't like asking. It's not like it's going to leave you in top shape."

"Civan, I'm a Lightbringer. I don't know what Jin's told you about me, but I didn't get to use my magic to heal anyone other than Cress, her parents, and myself for fourteen years. I don't mind a brief headache if it means you'll be able to do *your* job well."

"I—"

"*My* job is to heal people on the team." Nobody had actually discussed that with Astrea, but they didn't need to. "I know it probably seems silly to think of me as part of your team after what you, Jin, Adi, and Lennor have been through, but . . ."

"No, I understand," Civan said quickly. "I . . . don't like asking them for help."

"Well, I certainly know that feeling. But please, ask if you need something. I want to help." When he nodded, Astrea added, "And besides, we're not going out on the mission tonight. We can both sleep off any side effects."

Glancing up at her through his dark eyelashes, Civan said, "Alright."

"I need to touch your head," Astrea said, and Civan nodded again. He wasn't much taller than Cressida, so Astrea just reached up and gently placed both hands on the sides of his head. His hair was silky soft under her touch. The soft glow of her light warmed the hallway. Ghost pain flared stronger behind her eyes, but it was bearable. She pulled her hands away. "How's that?"

"Better. Thank you."

"You're welcome."

Jin's voice echoed up the stairs and through the corridor as he yelled, "Az? Civan?"

"Coming!" Astrea called.

Civan offered her a tight-lipped smile. "I guess we should go down."

"Yeah."

Everyone was waiting for them in the cabin except for Zephyrine and Adi, who were still flying the ship.

"All good?" Jin asked, looking between Astrea and Civan.

"Yes, I just needed Astrea's help," Civan said. "Headache."

Jin raised an eyebrow. "A headache?"

"All good now," Astrea said. Besides the slight pressure in her skull, she felt normal. Nothing like a few nights before.

"Alright . . . Just let me know if it gets worse, yeah, Civan?"

He ducked his head. "Yes, Captain."

Astrea wandered toward the windows on the far side of the cabin, and Jin followed her, his hand finding the small of her back. As they drew closer to the city, lights sparkled on the darkening horizon. Thasia, capital of the Republic of Tornama.

Like Novaria, the Tornamians tried to stay out of the battles fought between Helosia, Delia, and Zaikud in recent decades. Tornama had once been a small kingdom on the southeastern tip of the continent, made up of Tornamians and immigrants from the Taipoli Islands. But over the years—and during the Great Wars—they'd spread north, merging with a lot of the Novarian and Helosian populations around the Antare Mountains. And now, Tornama was a country in the middle of an economic boom, or that was what Eliana had told Astrea earlier in the year. It was part of why Emperor Aelius had Eliana working on a trade agreement with Tornama for so many months.

Closer to their ship was a dimly lit tract of land closed off by fences. An airfield, Astrea assumed, based on the hangars. The airship landed with a subtle thunk, then the engines shut off.

"It's pretty," Lennor said as she and Cressida joined them.

"Rami should be ready for us," Marko said. In the faint reflection in the windows, Astrea watched him rifle through his own knapsack. "Let's make this quick, shall we?"

Adi and Zephyrine finished whatever they were doing in the pilot's cabin, then joined the rest of them. Adi was already wearing a white shirt and black trousers, which Cressida deemed sufficient for the night. Zephyrine had paired a red blouse and tight black pants with knee-high black boots. She'd swept her white hair up into two braids that were now pinned to her head like a crown. She looked so chic for going to meet someone ready to help them break what Astrea assumed would be multiple laws.

As he unsealed the door, Marko called over his shoulder, "Follow me."

They marched into the darkness one by one, down a set of stairs that Marko had unlatched from the side of the ship. They weren't the most stable under Astrea's feet, and she held onto Jin's shoulder with one hand. When they were on solid ground, Astrea surveyed the airfield. Several other ships were out in the open space, though far away from theirs. One had lights on inside; the others were dark.

"Where's Rami?" Jin asked Marko.

"Around here somewhere."

Astrea pushed her senses out wider and wider. A few walls entered her awareness, though they were even farther away than the other ships. But there, headed toward them . . . curiosity, joy, anxiety. The green, gold, and orange lit up the night.

"Is that her?" Astrea asked, pointing into the darkness.

"Where?" Marko asked.

"Skies." Astrea barely whispered the word. "Right there, near that hangar." The colors outlined the shape of a person, though at this distance, they were little more than a dark blob.

Marko led them across the dark airfield, their steps mostly quiet on the paved ground. Astrea stuck close to Jin and Cressida, her senses still open wide for any changes or threats. But the night was calm. Those walls remained far off, and the one presence they drew closer to was obviously someone Marko knew based on the way he jogged toward her.

"Rami," he said, voice low as they all caught up to him.

The woman whose aura still burst with curiosity, joy, and anxiety wasn't much taller than Astrea, though her shoulders were broader and physique thinner. Her smooth, dark hair shone from the light of a nearby lamp attached to the side of the metal hangar. She'd pulled the top layers of her hair back and let the rest hang loose around her shoulders. One section just behind her right ear was braided.

"Marko!" Rami said, her voice deeper than Astrea expected. Rami pulled Marko into an embrace, her warm brown skin a contrast to Marko's lighter sandy complexion. "You made it." Though she spoke in Helosian, Rami's accent was distinctly Thasian.

"That we did." Marko pulled away from Rami and pivoted to one side to motion to the rest of them. "This is . . . everyone. Everyone, this is Rami Voskara."

"Thank you for helping us, Miss Voskara," Jin said.

"The pleasure is mine. I'm happy to help some of Lucian's friends." Rami grinned at them, her narrow brown eyes crinkling at the edges. "Do you have your airship keys? I'll have one of the girls put it in a hangar until your return."

Keys jingled as Adi dug into his pocket. He tossed them to Rami, who tucked them into the pocket of her cropped green trousers. Her coordinating green shirt was embroidered with gold and silver thread, creating soft floral and vine patterns.

"Let me show you to your accommodations," Rami said. "Then we'll get you some dinner and talk plans. I'm going to need all the details."

Chapter 31

With its colorful buildings, wide expanses of public parks, and extensive trolley system, Thasia reminded Astrea of Kalama. The architecture, though, was different. Ornate archways, narrow columns, and intricate metalwork on gates and windows were the most obvious differences Astrea could spot as they zipped past half-lit buildings.

They'd been driving for nearly an hour and were finally nearing their destination, or at least that was what Rami claimed. Astrea couldn't wait to get out of the car. They'd managed to cram all eight of them—plus Rami—inside.

They continued west, turning down roads that grew progressively narrower. The sea came into view, sparkling as lights from piers winked in and out of sight behind buildings. After one more turn, Rami slowed the car, then pulled to the side of the street. Buildings stretched on either side of them, just three stories tall. Even in the moonlight, Astrea could see the once bright colors had been worn down by the salty air.

"Let's get inside, shall we?" Rami asked from the front seat. "Quickly, quickly."

Astrea's limbs ached with relief as she climbed out of the car and stretched. She breathed in the slightly humid seaside air, another instant reminder of Kalama. *Soon*, she promised herself. They would be back soon.

Rami led them to a building with fading green paint. A worn teak sign hung off the front of the building and read Hotel. A hotel? That was where Lucian's ex-wife was taking them?

They had to enter single file through the narrow, elaborately carved front door. A bell tingled as Rami called out, "Talin! We've got guests!"

A short, plump man with dark brown skin waltzed out from behind a faded red curtain hanging up behind the counter directly across from the front door. He pushed up the sleeves of his deep blue tunic, revealing tattooed forearms. His smile and gray eyes were bright.

"Welcome, welcome!" Talin called in a deep voice as everyone shuffled inside. Behind them, Rami locked the door. "These are your ex-husband's friends, Rami?"

"Indeed, they are," she said. "Let's be nice."

"I'm always nice," Talin said with a grin. He pulled a ledger out from under the counter. "The eight of you? I'm afraid we don't have eight rooms. And how long are you staying?"

"We need to talk plans." Rami slipped past Astrea and to the arched windows on one side of the door. She flipped around a sign that said No Occupancy, then pulled the curtains closed. As Rami moved to the window on the other side of the door to adjust those curtains, she said, "Let's feed them first."

"Of course. We should have some leftovers." Pulling back the curtain, Talin said, "Right this way."

Talin led them down a dark, narrow hallway. A few frames hung on the walls, all of them containing paintings of sunsets and oceans. The tiled floor was smooth and dark, too. Talin veered right through a wide archway and into a dining room. A round table able to seat eight sat in the middle of the room, which was otherwise decorated with one potted palm, a credenza, and a few framed maps of Tornama. A window on the far side overlooked the ocean.

"It's a bit small," Rami said as everyone squeezed inside. "But Talin and I already ate, so you all can sit."

"While we appreciate the hospitality," Marko said, "we need to talk, Rami. We don't know our exact schedule, but we'll need to move soon and quickly."

"Yes, Lucian mentioned something about that." Rami sighed as she gestured for them to sit down. "Sit. Talin and I will bring you the food, then we'll get to business."

They all dropped their knapsacks on the floor in one corner near the entry, then took seats at the table. Astrea wasn't even hungry, but when Talin passed out dishes of steamy, spicy chicken and rice, her mouth watered. It smelled almost just like Balthazar's. One of her favorites. When she took a bite, it wasn't quite as good as Balthazar's recipe, but it was still incredible. So good, in fact, Astrea nearly groaned.

"So," Rami said, leaning on the wall near the windows and crossing her arms over her small bust, "Lucian wasn't exactly specific about what you all need, but seeing as I have a bunch of Helosians—and who I'm guessing is an Auris prince—in my hotel, I have a feeling it's not going to be easy."

"Sorry to drop in like this," Jin said, and Rami chuckled. "We need to get back to Kalama."

Talin, who'd just finished passing out glasses of water, whistled low. "Kalama? They've locked the city down."

"So, it's impossible?" Cressida asked. "We can't get in?"

"I didn't say impossible," Talin replied with a wink. "Just that they've locked it down. You'll need papers to get past the security checkpoints."

Astrea ate another bite of her dinner, savoring the taste but hating the way her stomach dropped at the news. But of course Emperor Aelius had increased security. Zephyrine fled. Jin and Eliana fled. The Paragon were doing skies knew what.

"Can you get them for us?" Marko asked.

"It won't be cheap," Talin said.

"That's fine." Marko gestured toward where their bags were sitting in a pile. "I've got cash."

"It won't be quick," Talin added.

"Well, it needs to be," Jin said. "We've got urgent business. The papers won't even solve our real issue."

"The fact that *you'll* be easily recognized?" Rami asked him.

"The fact that most of us will be," Zephyrine said. "We believe Marko, Lennor, and Civan will be able to get in without issue, but the rest of us are . . . well, the city guards will likely be on the lookout for us."

"That's not something I can solve." Rami sighed. "Lucian did not warn me about this."

"We don't expect you to solve it, Rami," Marko said. "We'll handle ourselves when we get to the city. We just need papers and transportation there and back."

"And *back*?" Rami asked.

"For an additional four civilians," Marko said.

Rami threw her hands above her head. "Now you're just making it difficult."

Marko shrugged. "Difficult isn't impossible."

Peach amusement and rusty annoyance flickered around Rami's dark hair. "I forgot how much I liked you, Marko." She nodded. "Alright. We will get you the papers. How urgent is urgent?"

"That's the final problem," Marko said. "We believe Emperor Aelius will depart the city within the next few days, so we need to time it with that."

At that, Talin actually laughed. It was a deep, booming laugh that echoed off the dining room walls and almost made Astrea want to join in. Jin's lips pressed together. "Your former spouse really owes you for this, Rami," Talin said.

"Indeed he does," she murmured. "But I know Lucian wouldn't send you to me if it were not important. We'll make it work. I assume he'll send a message to me when he knows the timeline?"

"That's the plan," Marko said.

Astrea's shoulders relaxed a fraction. Good. This was good. If Lucian and Marko trusted Rami and Talin, then Astrea trusted the pair. At least, she trusted them enough to get her and her friends to Kalama.

"Let's get you to bed, yes?" Rami suggested. "Finish up your dinner, then I'll show you upstairs. The limited rooms won't be an issue?"

"No issue," Marko said gruffly. "We'll be fine."

As everyone pushed away from the table, most of their dinners just half-eaten, they grabbed their knapsacks and followed Rami back through the narrow corridors. Instead of going back through the red curtain separating them from the front of the hotel, Rami turned left at the last moment and into an equally narrow stairwell. The green wallpaper was covered in patterns that looked almost like peacock feathers. At the top of the stairs, Rami motioned for them to go left.

"Rooms are down there. Already unlocked. There are just two bathrooms, I'm sorry to report," she said. "Talin and I sleep at the front of the hotel, just down this way." She gestured to her right. "Tell Talin if you need something. I'm going to go check on a few things and see if I can get these papers started tonight, plus I need to get that airship stored."

"Do you want—" Marko started, but she cut him off.

"I know you're good for it, Marko. Or Lucian is. Just pay me before you leave town." And with that, she squeezed past Civan, who loitered at the back of the group, and headed back downstairs.

Marko's mouth pressed into a thin line as he surveyed the rest of them. He sighed. "I suppose we should pick rooms." His attention flicked to Jin and Astrea. "I assume you two will share."

Astrea's face warmed as Jin confirmed it.

"I don't mind sharing," Cressida said.

"Nor do I," Lennor said quickly. "Civ, you're a light sleeper anyway. You should take your own room."

He stiffened. "I don't want to inconvenience—"

"You need some sleep, Civ," Jin said. "Bunk by yourself tonight. I doubt anyone here really cares. Zephyrine, how about you take your own room as well? Unless you're keen on sharing."

"If Marko and Adi don't mind, then I would appreciate it," Zephyrine said. "I've been told I'm not a delightful sleeping companion."

"Sure, we can bunk," Adi said, his amusement tickling Astrea's nose to the point that she sneezed.

One corner of Marko's mouth barely twitched up. Astrea glanced at Jin, whose smug expression told her everything.

"Well, get some sleep," Jin said. "We'll regroup first thing in the morning."

"What about guard rotations?" Lennor asked. "Should we—"

"This location is very secure." Marko gestured to the barren walls. "Rami needs such fortifications for her line of work. And Talin's a Lightbringer. He'll wake us up if needed."

They dispersed to their rooms. Jin led Astrea to one at the end of the hall, just across from Cressida's and next to Zephyrine's. Inside was cramped, with a bed barely big enough for two, one bedside table, and a narrow writing desk. There wasn't a wardrobe nor an overhead light, just a lamp. But the view. Astrea peeked past the purple curtains and was greeted by the moon reflecting off the ocean to the west.

"I can't believe Lucian's ex-wife is involved in . . . all this," Astrea said as she let the curtain drop. Jin had set his pack on the floor, and Astrea shrugged hers off. "What, is she some kind of smuggler?"

"Probably. This hotel is just some front for whatever it is she does."

"Never imagined Lucian would marry someone who went outside the law." Astrea set her bag on the bed. "Never imagined him getting married, to be honest."

"He didn't strike me as the type, either," Jin said. "Rami seems nice, though."

Astrea nodded. She wished there was time to ask Rami a thousand questions, especially ones about Lucian. Maybe then she'd finally have some real insight into why the commander was the way he was. "I'm going to get cleaned up."

"I'll go after you."

After grabbing her toothbrush from her pack, Astrea slipped into the hallway. Two open doors near the stairs seemed to be the two bathrooms. She'd just poked her head around one doorframe when Cressida swept out. As they nearly collided, Astrea grabbed Cressida's upper arms to rebalance both of them.

"You scared the shit out of me," Cressida said.

"Oh?" Astrea lowered her voice, then asked, "Where were you going in such a hurry?"

"Where do you think?" Cressida whispered. "Len practically volunteered to be my roommate. I have to get back to a beautiful woman who wants to share a bed with me."

"Well, I'm across the hall from you, so please, don't be too loud."

Cressida nudged Astrea's ribs. "Your request has been noted."

A door opened behind them, and Astrea whispered "Good luck" as Cressida slipped past her. Then, Astrea went into the bathroom and closed and locked the door. She made quick work of her routine, and when she opened the door again, she found Marko standing outside.

He offered her a tight-lipped smile, which she returned. Then she returned to her room. When she'd closed the door, Astrea turned around to find Jin searching for a place for the table lamp to go on the floor. But the room was so small there wasn't one.

"It's alright," she said. "I think I'll be fine tonight."

"You sure?" he asked. "We can make it work."

"If it gets bad, I'll just turn it on."

Jin watched her for a moment, then placed the lamp back on the bedside table and said, "Alright, let me go get ready for bed."

As Jin slipped into the hallway and closed the door behind him, Astrea dug through her pack and pulled out one of her black training shirts. After changing into it, she climbed into the bed with a frown. It was barely larger than her bed back home at the observatory. How were she and Jin both going to fit?

When he returned a few minutes later, Jin shed everything but his underwear, turned off the light, and climbed in next to her. The darkness made Astrea's throat squeeze. Jin wrapped his arms around her and pulled her close.

"Okay?" he asked. "Want me to turn—"

"No, Mother Hen. Don't turn it on."

"You're sure?"

"Skies, you're annoying."

He chuckled, then kissed the spot behind her ear. "And yet you love me anyway."

"Yeah, I guess I do." Despite the dark room and humid Thasian air, Astrea reveled in the sunshine gliding over her skin.

And as Jin whispered "I love you too, Az," she was sure she'd make it through the night.

Chapter 32

Waking up to a view of the ocean and an empty bed reminded Astrea of home. And while she loved the view, she didn't love waking up without Jin next to her.

She pushed up on her elbows. He must've cracked the curtains open before leaving. His knapsack was all tidied up, and his boots were gone. Talking to Adi, maybe? Astrea scrubbed at her face, then fell back into the pillows.

Up. She needed to get up. Rami might have news. Talin might have breakfast.

Astrea climbed out of bed, changed into a green linen dress, and slipped on her flat shoes. After braiding her hair, Astrea opened the bedroom door only to find Cressida poised to knock.

"Oh—" Astrea started, but Cressida pushed her back into the room and closed the door again. Orange anxiety flared bright against the wood-paneled walls. "Cress?"

"Shhh!"

"Cress," Astrea whispered, her pulse jumping. "What's wrong?" Her magic sensed nothing out of place. There were familiar walls and emotions—nothing unexpected.

"It's Len."

Astrea relaxed. "What about her?"

"She's still asleep."

"Alright . . . and?"

"She's still asleep in the bed we shared last night."

"I still don't understand what the problem is."

"The problem is that I have a very pretty girl in my bed, and it's a very small bed, and we spooned all night."

"Again, what's the—"

"I think I might like her."

"And you . . ." Astrea's eyebrows furrowed. "You don't want to like her?"

"No! No. I just . . . I don't know. She makes me nervous, Az."

"Yes, I'm very well aware of *that*. You haven't been able to hide it."

"Nervous in a way I haven't felt in a very long time." Cressida set her hands on Astrea's shoulders. "What do I do? Tell me what to do."

"Why are you asking me of all people?" Astrea asked with a laugh. "That's not my area of expertise." Before Jin, she'd had just two short-lived romantic relationships. And with Jin . . . well, things were going spectacularly, but it still wasn't like Astrea was an expert.

"Jin's been in love with you for months," Cressida said. "How'd you do it?"

Astrea hadn't seen pink around him until recently, but love was many things and shown in many ways. Sarsali and Balthazar loved each other deeply, yet Astrea didn't see pink floating around them all the time. Love was more than just one color, one feeling, one experience.

Astrea shrugged. "Be yourself?"

"Wow," Cressida muttered, dropping her hands to her sides, "helpful."

"I didn't *do* anything, Cress. We were just ourselves, and we were honest."

"Honest." Cressida pursed her lips. "Well, maybe this mission isn't the time for that."

"Maybe not, if you're not ready to tell her that you're interested."

"Don't need distractions," Cressida said. "When we get back to Novaria . . . I'll deal with it then. I'll figure out what to say . . . if I say anything."

"You won't say anything?"

"What exactly am I supposed to say? 'Oh, hey, I'm your commanding officer's old friend, and I know you just got out of one war zone and are basically entering another, and we only just got to know each other, but I think I might like you as more than a friend. Want to go out sometime once it's safe for us to hang around civilians so we can see if maybe this thing would work out?'"

"That's probably a little wordy."

"Smartass."

With a sigh, Astrea said, "I already told you I can *see* she's at least comfortable with you. You've been spending a good amount of time together since we got back from the base. So what's the problem?"

As Cressida began replying, a knock sounded on the door. Her eyes nearly bulged out of her head. Astrea squeezed past her to see who it was.

"Hey, Az," Adi said. "Is Jin awake?"

"I think he went downstairs already." She opened the door wider so Adi could see Cressida. "Do you need something?"

"No, no." Adi glanced down the hall, then back at Astrea. "I guess I'll go find Jin? Give you two some time to talk?"

"No, that's okay!" Cressida blurted. "We'll go with you!"

Adi's eyebrows rose, but he quietly led them down the corridor. Two more bedroom doors were still closed. The smell of frying bread and sugar wafted up the stairs and through the halls on the lower floor of the hotel. Astrea's stomach growled.

Back in the dining room, Jin, Zephyrine, and Marko were speaking with Rami. Civan and Lennor were nowhere to be found.

"Ah, the sleepyheads," Rami said as she motioned to a sky blue sideboard on the opposite side of the room. "There is coffee. Talin is making a favorite Jin requested . . . eggy bread?"

Astrea made a beeline for the coffee, Cressida hot on her heels and Adi right behind.

"How did you sleep?" Rami asked. "I hope everything was acceptable, especially for you, Varojin. I know it's no palace."

"Trust me, Rami, everything was great," Jin said. "Palaces are too big and drafty anyway."

Warm amusement flowed through the room. Astrea peeked over her shoulder as she spooned sugar into her coffee. Peach danced around Rami, but Astrea focused on the way Marko kept glancing at where Adi stood.

"Well, how about the rest of you?" Rami asked.

"I slept," Zephyrine said, and Cressida mumbled something about getting rest.

Marko craned his neck. "The beds might be a bit small."

"Don't pretend like you didn't like spooning, Marko," Adi called over his shoulder.

"You practically had me in a headlock all night."

"But did it hinder your sleep?" Adi asked. When Marko said nothing, Adi added, "See?"

Suppressing her smile, Astrea made her way back to the round table and took the seat next to Jin. His hand settled on her thigh, steady and warm. Just as he had been all night.

"Were you able to speak to your contact about the travel papers?" Marko asked Rami.

"They should have them done tonight," she replied. "We should be able to get you on a ship by dawn."

"But we haven't heard from Lucian yet?" Marko asked.

"No, but Magdi's not going to wait forever. Isn't there some place in Kalama you can stay until the emperor leaves the city?"

Zephyrine swallowed a mouthful of coffee, then said "I know a place. It won't be a problem."

Astrea almost asked where they could possibly be safe in Kalama, but Cressida dropped down next to the general and asked, "And how long is the boat trip from Thasia to Kalama?"

"With a mage crew, about a day," Rami said. "They might be able to push it and get you there by midnight if they leave before first light."

Astrea's breath caught in her chest. She could be reunited with Saros, Sarsali, and Balthazar so soon. So, so soon. But was it wise to leave before they knew Emperor Aelius's plans?

"Anything else we need to do before we leave?" Adi asked.

"I recommend you lay low," Rami said. "But if you need to make any final preparations, there's a market nearby. There've been no whispers of a Helosian prince or traitors. If you mind your own business, you'll be fine."

"Oh, can I go?" Cressida asked, her gaze flicking to Jin, then Marko. "I need oil for my hair. The humidity's going to kill it."

"How about we all go?" Jin said. "Just for an hour. Stretch our legs before we have to get on the boat."

"After breakfast!" Talin called as he walked into the room with a tray piled high with fried eggy bread smothered in jam and powdered sugar. "Don't want this to go to waste."

Salty ocean air warmed Astrea's skin as she followed Cressida, Adi, Lennor, and Marko down narrow street after narrow street near the hotel. Civan and Zephyrine had opted to stay behind, though Civan had tasked his sister with finding him a bar of chocolate for the trip.

Jin slipped his hand into Astrea's as they neared the next intersection. Drivers zipped past on motorcycles and bicycles. A few full-sized cars even squeezed through the narrow roadways. This part of Thasia reminded Astrea of the Warehouse District in southern Kalama with its short but tidy buildings, narrow thoroughfares, and lower and middle class pedestrians.

"Should be just at the next intersection," Marko said. "What, exactly, are we here for again?"

"Hair oil," Cressida said.

"And chocolate for Civan," Lennor added.

"That couldn't wait?"

"Civ really loves his chocolate."

Marko huffed.

"It won't even take us twenty minutes." Cressida hurried across the street at the next break in traffic, and they all followed. "Besides, it's not like we have anything better to do until tonight."

When Marko grunted, Adi slung his arm around his shoulders. "Oh, c'mon! Fresh air, a quick walk . . . It's good for you."

"Getting on with the mission is good for me." Marko made no attempt to move Adi's arm. "We need to be planning."

"Jin loves planning and he's not freaking out," Cressida said as they turned down a street lined with neat row houses decorated with overflowing flower boxes.

"Twenty minutes won't kill us, Marko," Jin said, then sneezed. "And we're already here."

Adi dropped his arm from Marko's shoulders. Ahead of them, the street opened up to a piazza not unlike those back home in Kalama. Tents and stalls lined the perimeter of the square, leaving space in the middle for the crowd to mingle and eat at café-style tables. Emotions crossing the full spectrum entered Astrea's awareness, like sound bursting to life unexpectedly from a radio.

"Anything?" Marko asked Astrea.

"No. Seems fine," she said.

He nodded. "Alright. Get whatever it is you need. Meet back here in ten minutes."

Cressida darted off in search of her oil. Though Marko wandered after her, his posture remained stiff.

Adi turned and raised an eyebrow at Jin. "You're letting him be awfully bossy."

"As if you don't like him being bossy," Jin quipped. Astrea didn't think she'd ever seen so much magenta burst in someone's aura before, especially not Adi's. "Marko's wound a bit tight, but he's not wrong. We should go back soon. If he wants to make sure that happens, far be it from me to stop him."

"And you think it's okay to leave tonight?" Astrea asked. "I didn't want to make it seem like I was undermining Zephyrine or Rami . . ."

"If Zephyrine has someplace in mind, then I'm willing to take the chance," Jin said. "Besides, if we're there early, we can enact our plans immediately. No chance we miss our window."

"And if he doesn't leave town?" she asked.

"Then we adjust the plan," Adi said.

Astrea wasn't so sure she was cut out for planning missions. But Jin, Adi, and Zephyrine were the experts. If they thought it'd work out, she'd believe them.

"I just need to find Civ his chocolate, then I'll be ready to go," Lennor said.

"I'll go with you," Astrea offered.

"Be careful," Jin said.

As if that needs to be said. Astrea and Lennor slipped through the crowd, Astrea's senses pushing out far beyond what was comfortable. The salty sea air, the strong scent of coffee and cinnamon, and even the clamor of shoppers almost felt like home, as did the way her mind begged for a break. She'd been sifting through such chaos for years in Kalama.

"Oh, there," Lennor said, pointing to a stall with a white awning.

Another customer was examining the goods, but they moved on as Lennor squeezed in to take a look. Pastries filled half of the stall while all sorts of candy filled the other.

"Does Civan always take chocolate on missions?" Astrea asked as Lennor picked up not one but two bars covered in foil.

"Well, this past spring and summer in . . ." As her voice trailed off, Astrea filled in the gap. *In Corsyca.* "He's learned that sometimes it's too hot to bring chocolate, but yeah, he tries to."

"He likes it that much?"

"It's . . ." Pursing her lips, Lennor passed a couple of coins to the vendor. "Civan doesn't like a lot of things. Certain foods, certain textures. He manages it pretty well, but sometimes, chocolate is the only thing he'll want to eat. So we try to make sure he has it."

"Really?" Astrea asked. Though the Nikaphoroses, Eliana, and Jin had known about Astrea's sensitivities and tried to accommodate them, Saros was the only other person Astrea had met who was so particular. "I'm like that about a lot of things, too."

"And is chocolate your favorite?"

"I like it, but no. I just . . . don't really eat if I'm feeling that way."

"Yeah, Civ gets like that sometimes too." She lifted up the two bars as they headed back into the crowd. "Even this doesn't always tempt him. It usually passes quickly though."

"That's good." Astrea scanned the market, then spotted Cressida stopped near a stall with a colorful green and blue awning. Marko hovered near her like a worried parent. "There they are."

"I'm going to go find Jin and Adi," Lennor said. "I think they went the other way."

As Lennor slinked into the crowd, Astrea headed over toward her best friend. As she joined them, Marko passed a couple of coins to the vendor, and Cressida thanked the woman in Tornamian.

"I told you it wouldn't take long, Marko," Cressida said in Helosian as she looped her arm through Astrea's. In her other hand, she held a small vial of oil. "They even have lavender scented, just like Ma makes."

"A little bit of home," Astrea murmured. Sarsali always had the best cosmetics, lotions, and shampoos, often infused with scents from flora and fauna grown in her garden.

"We should go find Jin—" Marko started, but Cressida waved her hand.

"He's just over there"—she pointed to where they stood at the edge of the crowd—"and we should look around. When was the last time you were in Thasia, Marko?"

"Well"—he huffed—"never."

"Exactly. You haven't even tried their coffee. If you love the Kalamian stuff, you're really going to love what they serve here."

"We had coffee with Talin and Rami this morning."

"And it was fine, but it's nothing like what you get at a market."

"I thought you'd only been here once when you were young to visit your great-aunt," Marko drawled as they joined Jin, Adi, and Lennor again.

"Yes, well, I believe what my parents say about the coffee in the markets. They talk about it at least once a month," Cressida retorted. "So let's try some, yeah? Az said it's safe. Right, Az?"

Astrea peeked over her shoulder at Marko. He narrowed his eyes. "It is," she said.

Marko huffed again. "Fine."

As they joined the others, Marko explained what Cressida wanted to do. And when they got to one of the carts selling coffees, Marko, Adi, Jin, and Lennor all got in line to buy them. Then Cressida tugged Astrea a dozen feet away to a stall selling jewelry.

"Don't think we're exactly here for a shopping trip, Cress," Astrea murmured. "I know I said it's safe, but . . ."

"I'm not here to shop. I just wanted to talk to you about Marko."

"Oh?" Astrea watched the others shuffle forward in line. Adi nudged Marko's shoulder and smiled brightly. "What about him?"

"What's your read on him? Should he really be taking the lead on all this?"

That was Cressida's question? Astrea frowned and looked back at her best friend, who was admiring a gold necklace.

In the time Astrea had spent with Marko, both in Talmaris and at the old base, he'd been nothing but kind. Aloof, maybe, but kind. Helpful. Understanding.

"I like Marko," she said. "Why?"

"Just feels strange, I suppose, to not be the ones really in charge. You know him better than I do."

"I don't think Marko sees himself as completely in charge. But he knows Rami. It makes sense for him to take the lead here."

Cressida shrugged one shoulder. "I guess."

"You don't trust him?" Astrea asked, voice low as she looked back at the rest of the group again. They were busy ordering.

"It's not that. He's obviously on our side. But he doesn't know our home like we do, and we—" Cressida paused, rough confusion scraping over Astrea's skin and pulling her attention back to the stall.

Cressida's hand hovered over a dull black stone on a silver chain. Gray confusion spiked high above her head as she reached for it.

"You like what you see?" asked the woman standing behind the stall. Her bright blue dress embroidered with flowers matched her blue eyes. Mixed metal bangles clanged together on her forearms as she tossed her silky black hair over her shoulders. "It's one of a kind."

"What kind of stone is it?" Cressida asked, that confusion now mingling with orange fear.

"Meteorite, if you can believe it." The women's bronze cheeks rounded as she smiled. It was a friendly, warm smile. Genuine.

That didn't stop Astrea's pulse from doubling.

A meteorite necklace in a Thasian market? She forced her senses out wider and wider, beyond the point of painful and beyond the edges of the market. She could almost envision her magic whisking past the Thasian shoppers, past the civilians clamoring for their morning coffee and buying everything from fruit to jewelry to hand-woven totes. But still, no void. Just the familiar chaos of the small market square.

"Wow," Cressida said. "Where'd you get something like that? I've never seen anything like it."

"One of my suppliers found it out near the Ring of Fire," the woman replied. She lowered her voice, then asked, "I heard you and your friend speaking Helosian. Have you ever been to the Ring of Fire?"

"Nope, never." Cressida shook her head. "How much for it? I'm always looking for unique jewelry."

"I could've guessed," the woman said, amused as she gestured to Cressida's ring-laden fingers. "For you . . . fifty Helosian lire. And I'm running a special today. Anyone who buys at least one piece from me receives a free gift."

That was a high price for a necklace that wasn't even made with a precious stone. Though, Astrea reasoned, it wasn't every day that one found jewelry made of meteorite. And they certainly couldn't just leave it here. She swallowed hard.

"You'll take Helosian currency?" Cressida asked.

"Why not? I can pay my supplier with it. He's always crossing the border."

Cressida pulled a handful of paper bills from the pocket of her wide-legged trousers. Astrea hadn't even realized Cressida had brought that much cash with her.

The stall owner accepted it with a smile, then asked, "Would you like me to box it up?"

"I'll just wear it now," Cressida said.

"Happy doing business with you, my friend." The woman lifted the necklace from its resting place, then gave it to Cressida. Then she reached into a box behind the counter and pulled out a flat, polished stone. Lavender, gray, and green shot through it. "And your gift. Come back soon."

Cressida fastened the necklace around her neck with lightning speed, then took the stone from the vendor. Her fingers played with the meteorite as they headed for where the rest of their friends were juggling six disposable coffee cups.

"Is it—" Astrea started.

"Wish Mariya were here," Cressida said. "I can't tell. Feels the same to me, just like the others."

"We should probably assume—"

"We definitely should." As soon as they were within a few feet of the others, Cressida said, "Well, this has been fun, but let's head back to the hotel, shall we?"

"Now you want to rush?" Marko muttered.

Cressida smiled an uneasy smile. "I need to show you what I got on my little shopping trip. I think you're going to be very interested."

As soon as they'd reached Rami's hotel, Cressida had filled in the team about the necklace she'd bought and the woman she'd bought it from. Then, they'd found Rami and Talin.

"You haven't heard *anything* about meteorite in Thasia?" Jin asked Rami as she leaned her head against the dining room wall.

"I didn't know I was supposed to be listening for such a thing," Rami muttered. "But no, I haven't. Lucian didn't mention any of this when he reached out."

"Well, it's not exactly like we want the world to know what my father's up to," Jin said. Rami grunted. "While we're gone, will you listen for any whispers of meteorite or void magic?"

"Of course I will. If it comes to Thasia, I'll be the first to find out."

"Thank you, Rami," Jin said as he watched Cressida, who had taken the necklace apart and was now toying with the meteorite. It floated above her hand, morphing from its irregular shape to a smooth ball, then back again. "At least we know you can still do that with it."

"I'll have Mariya look at it when we get back to Talmaris," Cressida said.

"Or Saros can check it once we're back on the airship," Astrea offered. He'd said the emperor's meteorite had felt strange to him. He would know if this piece was the same. Astrea was sure it was; that would be quite the coincidence if this meteorite just happened to be from the same region of Helosia at the same time the emperor was trying to do something with void magic.

Cressida nodded. "Or that."

"Meteorite aside, your ship is leaving the Thasian port near the fourth morning bell," Rami said. "Considering this development, I suggest you all stay put until it's time to go."

CHAPTER 33

By the time Rami's car pulled up to the Thasian docks, it was nearly four in the morning. The early morning breeze pulled at the strands of hair that had escaped Astrea's braid. Sunrise wouldn't come for a few hours yet.

Row after row of piers stretched into the bay. Most of the ships in the port were dark and lifeless. A few workers strolled down the docks, and one ship at the far pier had its lights on.

"Well," Rami said as she stepped out of the car and joined the rest of them, "this is where I wish you best of luck, Marko. Your ship's the one at the end"—she pointed—"there."

"Not making introductions?" he asked.

"No need. Magdi'll take care of you if you do as she asks." Rami flashed a smile at the rest of them. "We'll be here when you get back to Thasia. Take care of yourselves, yeah? I don't need Lucian making a trip down here just because you all got yourselves killed."

"We'll see you soon, Rami," Marko said with a chuckle. "Keep that airship ready."

"You've got it." And with that, Rami climbed back into her car and pulled away from the curb.

Adjusting his knapsack on his shoulders, Marko gestured toward the docks. "Let me take the lead here."

"Why?" Adi asked. "I don't think your natural charm's going to win us anything."

"I don't need charm," Marko said dryly. "I need His Highness to keep his mouth shut. You think this Magdi's going to want to smuggle him into Kalama?"

"No, and I don't blame her," Jin said. "Do what you must to ensure we get on that ship, Marko."

They started down the ramp to the docks, moving quietly and quickly. As they passed boat after boat, a few sailors came into Astrea's awareness, half sleepy and half curious as they poked their heads up to see who was passing by at that hour. But nobody questioned their group. Perhaps those sailors knew better than to question people heading for a ship at four in the morning.

The ship with its lights on at the final pier was smaller than the others in the port. While those were mostly large shipping vessels, Magdi's ship was just half that size, maybe a bit smaller. A smokestack jutted up into the night near the far end of the ship. The white, gray, and light blue hull were almost swallowed up by the night. The words *The Starseeker* were painted on its side in thick black letters. Just three new people entered Astrea's awareness, readable but calm.

"No void," Astrea said as they neared the ramp that led to the ship's deck.

"Oi!" a light, steady voice called from onboard. "What're you doing here?"

Astrea stiffened. Calm curiosity floated toward her on the breeze.

"Friends of Rami!" Marko replied.

Someone grunted a response, then said, "Alright, come on up."

"That easy?" Adi murmured, but Marko had already started up the ramp.

Here, right on the water and no longer blocked by the wide bodies of the other ships, the breeze kicked up. As she followed Marko, Astrea shivered and wrapped her arms around herself. It wasn't as chilly as Talmaris, but it certainly wasn't warm. The ship bobbed up and down lazily with the water, and already, Astrea felt unsteady. She'd never been on a boat before.

A tall, plump woman strode toward them, arms relaxed by her sides. Her straight brown hair skimmed the top of her shoulders, shining as it caught the light from the lamps flickering on the ship's pilothouse. Her lightly tanned cheeks marked by freckles betrayed how much time she likely spent in the sun, especially out on the ocean.

"And who do I have the pleasure of speaking with this morning?" she asked, crossing her arms over her ample chest. A dark, lace-trimmed shirt peeked out from under her long black jacket.

"Marko." The Tempest stuck his hand out toward the woman. "And you're Magdi, I assume?"

"Captain Magdi of *The Starseeker*, at your service." Magdi's brown eyes flicked over the group twice before she finally shook Marko's hand. "Eight in total. Good. As Rami promised. You got the papers?"

"We've got them," Marko confirmed. "Would you like to see them?"

"Nope. Bek's the one who got them for you. They've got connections to some of the best forgers in Thasia." Magdi surveyed their group again, her gaze settling on Jin where he stood in the back with Astrea and Zephyrine. "If Bek says the documents are good, then I trust their assessment."

"Then when would you like to set sail?" Marko asked.

"Let's get you all settled in below deck, then we'll get out of port."

Magdi motioned for them to follow her toward the deckhouse, the above-deck structure near the rear of the ship. They entered single file through a narrow door, stepping into the gray metallic interior. Another door sat against the opposite wall, but Magdi turned right and started down a set of metal stairs. The lights overhead barely illuminated the space as they descended below deck. They passed several closed doors, then turned left down a hallway. Four doors were open, revealing dark interiors.

"Places for you to bunk," Magdi said, shoving her hands into the pockets of her black trousers. Even her boots were black. "Nothing fancy though."

"This is fine, thank you," Marko said.

"When we're out on open water, you're free to come upstairs," Magdi said. "But when we get close to Kalama, I'll need you all down here. Don't want their coast guard seeing you."

"How far out are they patrolling?" Zephyrine asked.

"Far enough." Magdi shrugged one broad shoulder. "Bek, Nahta, and I have been running rum from the Taipoli Islands to Kalama for the last half year, but a couple months back, things started getting tighter. Security and all that."

A couple months, like when they fled Kalama. Astrea suppressed her frown.

"If you need something, just ask," Magdi said. "We're running a skeleton crew, but you can find one of us. Bek's the blond. Nahta's the brunette. Sleep tight." And with that, Magdi shouldered past them and strode back the direction they'd just come from.

"Surprised she didn't ask more questions," Cressida murmured.

"People like Magdi don't ask too many questions," Marko said. "It's bad for business. Now, I suggest you all get some sleep."

Astrea chose the room closest to her on the right and went inside. After flipping on the light switch, she was sorely disappointed. She hadn't expected much from a cabin on Magdi's rum running vessel, but skies. She was glad she was only on this ship for a day. The room was narrow and cramped, and the bed tucked in the corner was barely a double. The gray metal walls and floor reflected the dim overhead lights.

After tossing his knapsack on the floor, Jin slipped past Astrea and flopped onto the bed, his hands covering his face. "I hate boats."

"Why?"

"Seasick."

"Bad already?"

"It will be as soon as we set sail."

"Will healing help?" Astrea had never actually healed someone's seasickness before; it wasn't like she'd ever had the chance.

"Not really," Jin said. "I'll be fine. Being above deck will help. I'll go up after sunrise."

Even a few hours below deck seemed like torture to Astrea, especially with the way the ground swayed on what were surely calm waters. Flying wasn't bad, but ten minutes on the ship and her head was already beginning to feel funny.

Astrea set her pack down on the ground, turned off the light, then climbed into the bed with Jin. He scooted back so his back was nearly touching the wall. She settled in flush against his chest. It certainly wasn't comfortable; neither of them could really move, and the mattress was hard and thin.

"Jin?" she whispered. "Do you think we'll really be able to get Saros and the Nikaphoroses out of Kalama?"

The question had been weighing heavily on Astrea's mind for days. Finding that book was important. Getting it away from both Emperor Aelius and the Paragon was crucial. But reuniting with her family and taking them away from Helosia had to happen. It just had to.

His hold on her tightened. "We'll do everything we can to make sure it happens, Az. I promise."

Sleeping on a boat was worse than sleeping on an airship. By the time the sun rose and Jin suggested they go above deck, it had only been a couple of hours, but it felt like it had been forever. Astrea climbed the steps as quickly as she could, only to be greeted by sights of the gently rolling ocean and a pale morning sky.

Land was nowhere in sight.

Wonderful.

Astrea followed Jin out of the deckhouse and onto the open deck. Cressida was already there, the morning sun glinting off her dark, shiny curls. Marko stood next to her, and he chuckled at something she said. *At least that seems to be resolved.*

Jin led the way over to their friends, his steps surprisingly steady. He was a bit green, and when the ship tilted one way, he closed his eyes and took a deep breath.

"Don't like boats?" Marko called.

"Hate them," Jin replied.

The deck was mostly empty except for strange equipment. Astrea wouldn't dare touch that; she didn't know the first thing about ships. She did, however, step closer to the railing at the edge of the boat, bracing herself against it as she gazed out at the sea. The deep blue ocean water was opaque, capped by the occasional crest of white bubbles as *The Starseeker* plowed ahead toward Kalama. She hadn't realized ships could go so fast.

"Do you really think we'll be able to get to Kalama tonight?" Astrea asked none of them in particular. "Can we actually keep up this speed?"

"Oh, these smaller ships can definitely take the push," Cressida said. "Not the newest generation but still newer than I expected. We'll be fine."

"How can you even tell?" Astrea asked. "Did Magdi give you a tour?"

Cressida laughed. "No, but Lodestar helped design this generation about, oh, eight years ago. I studied the plans when Dad and I were looking at the plans for the new models."

"How convenient," Marko murmured.

"There's a lot of tech my father and I have had some hand in," Cressida replied with a demure shrug. "And I remember all of it."

"I knew I had a royal on my ship, but heir of Lodestar, too?"

That voice did not belong to any of their group. Astrea peeked over her shoulder to find Magdi strolling toward them. She wasn't wearing her coat, and now, two pistols with jewel-encrusted handles hung from the belt around her waist. One blond and one brunette walked beside her, both shorter and thinner than the captain.

"You—" Jin started, but Magdi waved a hand.

"Aurises are easily spotted." As she joined them, she glanced at Marko. "Rami didn't say I'd be trying to sneak the emperor's kid back into the city."

"Figured you didn't want to know too much," Marko retorted.

"Like I said, Aurises are easily spotted." Magdi tilted her round chin toward the water. "You aren't making this easy on yourselves. You really think you'll be able to get into Kalama unnoticed?"

"I've got to," Jin said. "We all do."

"And I assume the recent lockdowns are because the rumors are true, then."

"That my sister and I fled the country?" Jin nodded. "Yup."

"Wonderful," Magdi muttered. "Just what I needed to get myself wrapped up in." She fiddled with the handle of one of her pistols, then gestured to her blond companion. "This is Bek, my Fireweaver and a damn good one at that."

Bek was small in every way: narrow face, wispy blond hair, and a short, slim build. Their amber eyes sparkled in the sun as they waved.

"And this is Nahta, my Tidebacker and navigator." Magdi nodded to the brunette.

Nahta's straight nose, wavy hair, and warm tan complexion reminded Astrea of many people in Kalama. Her aquamarine eyes squinted against the sun as it continued rising in the sky.

Like Magdi, both Bek and Nahta were dressed in all black and carried pistols on their hips. If Astrea had run into them anywhere else in the world, she would've been intimidated. Well, she was intimidated even now, but knowing of their loose connection to Lucian and Marko made the three smugglers not quite so scary.

"Thank you for taking us to Kalama," Jin said. "I know it's not going to be easy for you given the circumstances, but it's important we get there and get back to Thasia in one piece."

Magdi chuckled. "I'd assume so considering you're running from the most powerful man on the continent."

"I've been trying to run from my father for a long time. Finally had a good enough reason to make it happen for real."

"Do I want to know?"

"Probably not."

Bek arched an eyebrow, but Nahta glanced over her shoulder at the deckhouse. "I need to keep an eye on things. Do you need me down here, Magdi?"

"Just make sure we get there on time."

"Can we do anything to help?" Cressida asked as Nahta walked off toward her station. "Need someone to look at your engine?"

"I've got it covered," Bek said.

"Just make yourselves comfortable and don't touch anything," Magdi said. "And don't go too close to the railing. Don't need to slow down the trip to rescue one of you if you go overboard."

As Magdi and Bek sauntered off again, Astrea turned to Jin. "Now what?" She hated feeling so useless.

"Let's just stay out of their way," Jin said. "We should be able to do that and still waste a few hours."

Wasting time on a ship in the middle of the ocean was hard. Like their flight to Thasia, the trek across the ocean consisted of a whole lot of nothing. Another nap, a brief lunch, and endless hours sitting around.

Astrea leaned back against one of the crates on Magdi's ship and stared out at the now-setting sun. It would still be several hours before they got close to Kalama, but at least most of the day had passed. Several more hours and Astrea would be that much closer to being reunited with her family.

She'd have to wake Jin soon. He and Adi had both gone back to sleep, though Astrea had no idea what Marko and Zephyrine were up to. She hadn't seen them in a couple of hours.

"Do you think Magdi would be upset if I used her crates for target practice?" Cressida asked.

"Huh?" Astrea forced her attention back to where Cressida sat cross-legged next to her. Across from both of them were Civan and Lennor. Civan snapped a square of chocolate from one of the bars Lennor had bought for him at the market.

"Like using this." Cressida waved her meteorite dagger in the air. "I need something to distract me."

"I'm bored too, but I don't think she'd appreciate that at all," Lennor said. "Aren't these crates full of expensive alcohol?"

"Maybe the alcohol could distract us."

"I don't think getting drunk on Magdi's rum is a good idea, either," Lennor said.

Cressida bumped her head against the crate. "I've never been so bored in my life. This is why I have so many projects at home. Is this how all your missions were in Corsyca?"

Civan shrugged. "Not usually so much travel."

"Some travel," his sister corrected. "Usually just on an airship for a few hours."

"Still sounds boring," Cressida said. "There's always something to keep my hands busy at home, and there's nothing here for me to—Oh!" She dug around in the pocket of her trousers, then pulled out the stone the vendor had gifted her in the Thasian market. "I do have something."

"You can't reshape that," Lennor said.

"I most definitely can."

"Alright, you can, but you shouldn't."

"Why not?"

"Well . . . because it's pretty. It even matches the hilt of your dagger."

As Cressida held the stone up, the fading sunlight winked across its green, purple, and white surface. It *was* strangely similar to the dagger.

"Will you keep the same color pattern if you reshape it?" Lennor asked.

"I probably can if I try." Cressida tilted the stone back and forth. "Why would the vendor give me this, anyway? Some free gift. What am I going to do with this?"

"It looks like a pocket stone," Civan said before shoving another piece of chocolate into his mouth.

"What's that?" Cressida asked.

"Our father's from the Zaikudi side of the Macadian Mountains," Lennor said. "His tribe had a tradition of exchanging stones with loved ones. You're supposed to pick a stone that reminds you of the recipient, and then they keep it in their pocket with them. It's supposed to keep you connected."

"Not that it actually does anything," Civan remarked dryly.

"It's a nice tradition," Lennor murmured. "I think it's nice, anyway."

"Is that where you grew up? In the Macadian Mountains?" Astrea asked.

"One of the valley towns on the Helosian side, but yeah," Lennor said. "It's pretty rural. Going down to Narizon for one of our first mage tour matches was the farthest we'd ever been from home."

"Is that where your parents still live?" Cressida asked. "Why didn't you ask Jin to get them out, too?"

Civan's shoulders scrunched up toward his ears. Lennor pursed her lips, then said, "Our dad moved back to Zaikud when we were seventeen . . . after our mom died in an accident. We stayed with our maternal grandmother until she passed when we were nineteen, and by then, we were trying to make it in the mage leagues."

"And then the draft . . ." Cressida trailed off. "Sorry."

"Not your fault." She sighed. "We haven't talked to our dad in a few years, but last I heard, he was doing fine back in Zaikud. At least he's not in Helosia now that this is all happening."

Warm ocean air rushed through Astrea's hair as the wind kicked up. It was the closest thing they could get to a win, or at least that was how Astrea thought of it. One less family to get sucked into Emperor Aelius and the Paragon's nonsense.

"Nikaphoros!" A mop of blond hair appeared around the corner. Bek called, "Your offer still stand for help with the engine?"

"Yeah, of course." Cressida slid the dagger into her boot and stood. "What's wrong with it?"

"Nothing wrong, but I could use the help while I assist Magdi with something." Shielding their eyes against the sun, Bek added, "And yeah, keep your hands off the rum. Magdi'll kill you if anything happens to it."

At that Civan grimaced, and Astrea ducked her head. Not that she'd actually thought to touch the rum, but still. Making the smuggler captain mad was the last thing Astrea wanted to do.

Cressida just flashed a smile over her shoulder at the rest of them. "Duty calls." But before she left, she tossed the pocket stone to Lennor. "Here."

Lennor peered down at the rock, then up at Cressida. "What? Really? Why?"

"I'll be too tempted to mess it up, and you're right. It's pretty." Though Cressida's words were calm, orange anxiety spiked high into her aura. "It'll have a better home with you." Then she disappeared around the corner with Bek, not even giving Lennor a chance to respond.

"Cool," Civan said, plucking the stone out of Lennor's open palm. "That was nice."

Warmth settled on Astrea's skin, something between the hot rush of embarrassment and the low burn of desire. Lennor's cheeks tinged pink. "Yeah," she murmured. "It was."

Astrea couldn't help but smile.

CHAPTER 34

The Starseeker made excellent time, as Magdi had promised, and they were closing in on Kalama fast. They weren't more than a half hour from port. And, as Magdi had worried, Helosia's coast guard was out in force, patrolling Tinale Bay and the waters closest to Helosia's borders. In the dark, Astrea could see little more than the occasional flash of their lights.

"Alright!" Magdi called as she marched across the deck. "You'd better head down in the next few minutes. The Helosians are going to radio us the closer we get to port. I don't want there to even be a chance that you get spotted, Varojin. But Marko, you're staying up here with me."

"Aye, aye, Captain," Marko drawled.

Rolling her eyes, Magdi said, "When we dock the ship, the rest of you will need to move quickly. While Bek and I speak to the customs agents, Nahta will show you the way."

"And when will you be back in Kalama to pick us up?" Marko asked.

"In four nights. I'm leaving first thing in the morning to bring a shipment to Thasia, then I'll come back."

Four nights. They had to stay in Kalama for four nights? Astrea resisted the urge to play with her braid, instead clasping her hands together tightly.

"Plenty of time to do what we need to do," Zephyrine said.

Astrea wasn't so sure. It somehow seemed both like too much time and not enough time at all. They had no idea if the emperor was still in town. Wouldn't staying longer mean more risk of getting caught?

"Alright, below deck, go," Magdi ordered.

Astrea followed everyone but Marko back down into the ship's hull. She'd gotten used to the occasional groan of metal and strange sounds the ship made as it moved through the sea. Now, a steady thump of anxiety pulsed around her as they prepared to disembark.

"Grab your gear," Zephyrine said. "Let's be ready when Nahta comes for us."

Astrea wasn't sure how long they stayed huddled near the exit, knapsacks strapped to their backs and breaths held. The ship slowed, or at least that was how it felt. The hum in Astrea's ears quieted. Something clunked outside the hull. And as she let her lightbringing push out wider and wider, someone new came into her awareness. Curiosity. Boredom.

"I think we docked," Astrea whispered. "Someone new is on the ship."

Zephyrine nodded. "Customs agent, I'm sure."

That new presence didn't seem to move or change for the longest time. Then the shouting started, audible but unintelligible. But it wasn't rage that burned Astrea's skin. No, whoever was up there was annoyed.

A bell clanged, muffled but distinct through the metal deck and walls of *The Starseeker*. Astrea cringed, then cringed again when a door slammed somewhere down the hall. Nahta appeared, her light brown hair pulled into a tight braid.

"That's our signal. Let's get you out of here," she said. "Follow me, and move fast."

Instead of going back up the way they'd come, Nahta led them past the rooms they'd slept in and to a different, much narrower staircase. Nahta ascended in quick, rushed steps, her boots clanging loudly on the metal stairs. Was it wise to be making so much noise?

As Nahta pushed open a hatch, fresh salty air tickled Astrea's cheeks. They climbed through the hatch one by one. Crates stacked high blocked most of Astrea's line of sight. Water gently lapped against the side of the unmoving boat. And three of those presences from earlier were moving away, farther and farther west. Onto the docks. Toward Kalama.

"Go right and go carefully," Nahta warned, voice low. "Bek's at the bottom of the ramp. Magdi will have customs distracted for just a few minutes."

"Thank you," Jin said to her. Nahta slipped around the boxes stacked to their left without another word. When she was gone, Jin said, "Tight on me and Adi. Careful and quick, got it?"

"Yes, Captain," Civan and Lennor said in unison.

As they moved past the crates and toward the front of the ship, Kalama came into view. The city was dark, lit up only by the glow of street lamps in the distance and the half-obscured moon high above. A few gas lamps flickered on the docks. To their right towered the palace, high up on its hill that overlooked the city and Tinale Bay. Astrea couldn't make out the observatory in the dark, but it was up there. Saros was up there.

Jin stopped. Astrea almost collided with him but managed to stop just in time. He stared at something on the pier next to the ship. All Astrea could make out were more stacks of crates blocking *The Starseeker's* ramp from direct sight of the docks. Bek leaned against the boxes. Farther down the pier, Magdi and Marko strolled toward the city.

Without a single command, Jin darted to the ship's ramp, and Astrea scrambled after him. Adi, Cressida, and the others followed. As soon as their feet hit the pier, Jin tugged Astrea toward the crates.

"The customs office and gate will be on your left," Bek said. "Avoid it at all costs. We docked closer to it than Magdi wanted to."

"Got it," Jin said. Bek nodded at Jin, then at Cressida, and stalked back up the ramp. "Az?" Jin asked.

Nothing unusual met Astrea's senses. No voids. Nothing to suggest anyone had seen them. Other than everyone grouped near *The Starseeker*, the area was empty. "I think we're good," she said.

He peeked around the corner of the crates, his emotions locked down tight. Astrea couldn't even tell what he was looking at or looking for. When Jin turned back to the group, he said, "There's no cover until we get to the end of the pier."

"I don't like it," Zephyrine murmured, "but what choice do we have?"

Jin huffed, then nodded. "Let's go."

As they moved down the pier, Astrea forced her gaze to stay on Jin's wide shoulders in front of her and not stray to the palace in the distance. Getting distracted would do no good. She focused on the calmness around them as they tried to stick to the shadows of the enormous shipping vessel towering to their left.

The closer they crept to the end of the pier, the more new people she could feel. They were distant but not terribly far away. Stationary, at least.

"What do you mean my license is out of date?" Magdi shouted from somewhere around the corner. No irritation or rage reached out to Astrea.

"Ma'am—"

"*Captain*," Magdi corrected. "I demand to speak to whoever's in charge of this pathetic port. I was here with this license just a week ago with no issue. Check your logs and you'll see."

"Captain," said that second voice. "I assure you—"

"Assure my ass," Magdi snapped. "You're telling me my sixty crates of premium Taipoli rum can't come into the city because *you* can't read a license?"

Irritation seared Astrea's skin, but it didn't seem to be Magdi's. *She's certainly a good actress.*

"Let me show your passenger to the checkpoint so he can be on his way, then we'll go to my office and sort this out," said the second voice.

"Fine," Magdi growled. "But if we don't get this sorted out tonight, it'll be *your* job I come after!"

"They're heading southwest," Astrea whispered as the rest of their group waited in the shadows of the shipping vessel.

Jin scanned the docks. Straight ahead was an earthen wall, separating them from the rest of the city. A few low buildings were spread out near the wall, but that was it. "Adi?" Jin asked.

"I could take us through, but the guards might feel it."

"Even if we do it this far from the checkpoint?"

"Still might."

"Seems like it's our best bet," Zephyrine replied.

"On my count," Jin said. "One, two"—Astrea's muscles tensed—"three."

They dashed across the open docks. Astrea risked a glance to their left, the direction Magdi and Marko had gone. *The Starseeker*'s captain ambled along with someone short, her arms gesticulating wildly in the air. Rusty annoyance flared around the shorter person. Marko was nowhere in sight. A few long shadows stretched out near the wall, but Astrea couldn't see who they belonged to past a thick brick building.

The wall looming before them had to be three stories tall, maybe four. Astrea hadn't actually been to the docks in all the years she'd lived in Kalama; she'd never had a reason to visit. She'd never traveled by boat, and she certainly had no business here.

As soon as they neared the wall, Adi clapped his hands together in front of him, then pulled them apart as if he were opening curtains.

The graying, salt-stained bricks of the wall twitched, then pulled apart to create a narrow doorway.

"Go," Adi hissed. "Quickly."

Lennor and Civan ducked through first. Zephyrine and Cressida followed. As Astrea stepped forward, confusion and worry prickled her skin. She hurried through the opening. Jin and Adi followed right behind her, and by the time Astrea peeked over her shoulder, the bricks had returned to their original state. That concern kept moving closer to where they'd just stepped through the wall.

"Need to move," she whispered. "Someone's coming."

Zephyrine motioned northeast, away from the port entrance.

Tan and white brick buildings rose up around them, many of them businesses and restaurants but some clearly residential, too. They didn't have the same wrought iron decorations or elaborate designs like some of the homes in Nobleman's Hill. They were quaint. And quiet. It all reminded Astrea of the ones she'd seen with Jin the day they'd visited that witness months ago. So long ago. Before they knew the shadow man was a void mage.

Zephyrine led them up one street, down another, then down another still. And by the time they circled back near the port's entrance, Marko was finally in view. Well, he was if Astrea peeked around the corner of the closed shop to her left. He stood just behind the gates blocking the entrance and exit to the port, waiting as the officer at the gate checked over his papers.

Astrea held her breath. The warm light from the flickering gas lamps hanging above the gates cast strange shadows over Marko's fair complexion and hair. The officer, dressed in a stiff red uniform, finally handed Marko's papers back to him. The gate opened. Marko strolled through.

Ducking back behind the building, Astrea waited. Marko's steady wall moved closer, and that guard stayed put. No shouts came. Nobody rushed to arrest Marko. And finally, he made it to their road. He turned down it, nearly running into Astrea in the process.

"Well?" Zephyrine asked.

"Wanted posters for Astrea and Cressida in the guard house," Marko said. "Didn't see any of the rest of you."

"Strange," Zephyrine murmured.

Strange, indeed. Just the thought of being on a Wanted poster made Astrea's skin crawl, like she'd done something terribly wrong. But she hadn't. That didn't make her feel better. How was she supposed to get to the library if there were Wanted posters out there?

"We'll deal with it in the morning," Jin said. "We need to move."

"Follow me," Zephyrine said. "I have the perfect place."

Chapter 35

Skulking through Kalama's dark streets seemed like the worst timing, at least to Astrea. They dodged guards and police officers, took every side street and alley possible, and even passed by a few pedestrians who looked up to no good themselves. As the city bells chimed and revealed it was already one in the morning, Astrea couldn't help but wonder if arriving in the middle of the day, dressed in street clothes and trying to blend into a crowd, would've been a better idea.

But finally, they were approaching territory Astrea was familiar with. The Market District, so unusually quiet. Even car traffic was minimal. They passed the street the White Lily was on.

After several more turns down dark alleys, though, Astrea was lost again. She never navigated Kalama this way; she stuck to main roads and pedestrian thoroughfares. Zephyrine stopped behind a building and knocked on its steel door in a strange pattern.

Astrea swallowed, her senses stretched out beyond comfort. One person was inside the building, a faint wisp of curiosity and relief brushing over Astrea's skin. Several people walked down the nearby main road, shouting as drunken glee pushed against Astrea's chest.

The door opened, but nobody stepped out. Zephyrine ushered everyone into the dark interior. Astrea's pulse thudded in her ears even with Cressida in front of her and Jin behind her. It was so dark. She grabbed

Cressida's hand and pushed herself forward as a hint of blue lotus smoke tickled her nose.

Cressida pulled Astrea through a set of dark velvet curtains, revealing the last place Astrea ever would've guessed.

The Whiskey Dream club sat empty, its low lights and dark interior both familiar and foreign. Months before, when she'd been there with Eliana and Cressida, all manner of Kalama's upper class had been there decorated in jewels and silky outfits and had been drunk off their asses. Not tonight. Just one man stood in front of them, his bulky build and warm pink skin familiar.

"Osin?" Cressida choked out just as Jin asked, "Zephyrine, what is this?"

Osin, the man Cressida had gone to speak with because he did business with her father. Osin, the man Jin had seemed interested in talking to that night so long ago. Even his pinstripe slacks and gray shirt seemed the same.

Osin smiled. "Zephyrine didn't tell you, eh?"

Where shock—then understanding—rippled around Cressida in waves of icy blue and teal, Jin's wall was as thick as ever. Wariness prickled Astrea's scalp and the back of her neck.

"No, I didn't," Zephyrine said as she stepped forward next to Osin and faced the group. "Osin is on our side. Has been for years."

"*Years*?" Cressida asked.

The owner of the Whiskey Dream supported Eliana's claim to the throne? Was that why Eliana had always proclaimed the spot to be her favorite? Just how much groundwork had she been laying in secret?

The twins, Adi, and Marko all shifted their weight from foot to foot. Right. Marko certainly had no idea who this man was. Astrea had no idea how much the twins or Adi knew, or if they'd ever even been to the Whiskey Dream.

"I must keep my connections and personal politics quiet for a reason," Osin said. "People talk when they're drinking and gambling. If they knew what I thought, they might stop being so open."

"I had no idea," Jin murmured.

"Then I'm playing my role well," Osin said with a wink. "Anyone want a drink?"

"Is that why you brought me here those times?" Jin asked Zephyrine.

She shrugged one slender shoulder. "Mostly because I needed to check in with Osin and also needed to keep you sane and out of the palace. It's one of the few places in Kalama where I know there are people I can trust."

"Right," Jin muttered, then scratched at his beard. "Well. This is good, I suppose."

"You suppose?" Osin chuckled. "I'm flattered. Let's get you all settled."

He led them to the elevator. The door opened with a pleasant chime, revealing a wide interior that could fit all nine of them. Its dark metal floors and walls gleamed in the low light overhead. Osin removed a key from his pocket, placed it in a keyhole in the wall near the door, and turned it. Then he pressed a button marked B, and the elevator started down.

When the elevator stopped and its doors opened again, a long, wide hallway stretched out before them. A few crates were stacked up along one side. Farther down, there were several closed doors nestled into the stone walls. Osin led them to one and unlocked it.

"Nothing fancy," he said, "but it should do. I assume you're staying for a while, Zephyrine?"

The storeroom he'd opened was wide but mostly barren. Shelves filled with bottles of alcohol lined one wall, and a couple of cots were pushed into one corner. The gray stone floors and walls were almost sad.

"Just a few days," Zephyrine said.

"Wanna tell me why you're here?" Osin asked, arms folding over his chest. "Not that I'm not happy to see you alive and well, but skies, the rumors going around right now . . ."

"Where to even begin?" Zephyrine murmured, mostly to herself. "Allow me to introduce the team." She introduced Osin to Marko and the twins, though it seemed he and Adi already knew each other. Then Zephyrine said, "We're here to pull out a few civilians and steal a book."

Osin laughed, low and deep. "You're what?"

"It's not funny, Osin. I'm being perfectly serious."

"And what's so important about this book and these people that you'd risk coming back here? How'd you even get into the city in the first place?"

As Zephyrine explained their trip to Kalama and how they'd entered through the port, Cressida stared at the ground, teal understanding, gray confusion, and even magenta embarrassment pulsing around her in faint waves. Jin was more relaxed, as was Adi. That was good at least, right?

"We need to get to the Great Library and the palace while we're here," Jin said once Zephyrine had finished her explanation.

Again, Osin laughed. "The palace? Good fucking luck, Jin."

"Why?"

"What your father's set up at the port is nothing compared to the way he's locked down Nobleman's Hill and the palace," Osin said. "It's been eating at business, actually."

"What's he been telling the city?" Jin asked. "Last we heard, he was trying to convince people that he sent Eliana and me away for our own safety."

"Indeed, that's his story."

"And people believe it?" Jin asked. "Has he said who made the threats?"

"People seem to believe it. It's hard not to when Kaius has also disappeared from the public eye. There have been whispers that it's the Zaikudi and Delians making threats, what with things as bad as they are in Corsyca."

"Does anyone think otherwise?" Marko asked. "Surely some people see through his lies, right?"

"I've heard talk of such concerns, yes," Osin said. "But with how much your father has increased security in the city, everything looks like he's preparing for some kind of defensive."

"Has this swayed any of the rebels to my father's side?" Jin asked.

"No, I don't think so. People who were skeptical or outright disapproving of him before feel the same, especially since word's gotten out that military paychecks aren't being issued. Haven't been for, oh . . ."

"About two months?" Jin asked. When Osin's eyebrows furrowed, Jin said, "My father was already planning that well before I left town."

Astrea scrubbed at her face. Kaius was out of the public eye, too? Had he actually left Kalama, or was he just keeping a low profile?

"What we really need to know is if Emperor Aelius has left town," Zephyrine said.

"Left?" Osin asked with a half laugh. "When was the last time he left Kalama?"

"He should be heading up to Novaria in the next couple of days if he hasn't already," Jin said. "I'd really like to wait for him to leave before we enact our plans."

Osin just shrugged. "Well, I'll keep my eyes and ears open."

"We also need to get Lennor and Civan out of Kalama and up to Athran soon," Zephyrine said. "Think you can help with that?"

"Sure can." Osin nodded as he glanced at the twins. "Won't be easy."

"That's alright," Lennor said. "We can handle it."

"Then I'll need to make a couple of calls." Osin gestured to the two cots tucked in the corner. "Staff or I will usually sleep here. Obviously they won't be coming down during your stay. I've got a few more cots in another room if you want to help me get them, Zephyrine."

"Happy to help," she said, flicking her long white braid over her shoulder as she followed Osin out of the storeroom.

Cressida whirled on Jin. "You really didn't know about this?"

"I didn't, Cress, I swear. I knew Osin and Zephyrine knew each other, but not . . . not because of this."

"Fuck me," Cressida muttered, her fingers digging into her hair. "I can't believe I didn't know. Do you think my parents knew about Osin's beliefs? Is that why my father does business with him?"

Would Balthazar and Sarsali Nikaphoros have worked with Osin knowing his sympathies for the so-called rebel cause? She'd never talked about it outright with them, but Astrea assumed they supported Eliana being named heir. Both Balthazar and Sarsali disagreed with many of the emperor's policies, whether it was about war or something less high stakes. And they both liked Eliana more than they liked Kaius.

But would they have been working with the rebels in some way without Cressida knowing? Astrea wasn't so sure about that. Balthazar and Sarsali were open with Cressida about basically everything now that she was an adult.

"You can ask them soon," Jin said. "Len, Civ, we'll need to get you out of Kalama as soon as possible if Osin can manage it. Any head start we can get you is worth it. Let's talk."

Jin, Adi, and the twins all dropped their knapsacks in an empty corner of the storeroom, then headed out into the hallway. The two pathetic cots in the corner and dark walls were a little too much like that cell the Paragon had kept Astrea in. Sure, the walls here were gray stone, not dark meteorite, but the small beds and barren interior still made her lungs tighten.

As Zephyrine and Osin brought in a few more cots—all folded in half—Marko and Cressida began setting them up. Astrea took the thin pillows and blankets Osin offered to her, then set about making up the beds. It didn't take long, but it kept her hands busy as she tried to wrap her mind around being back in Kalama.

Saros was just a few miles away. The Nikaphoroses were just a few miles away. And yet they still felt impossibly far.

"So, you really only saw posters for Az and me at the docks?" Cressida asked, breaking the tense silence that had settled over the storeroom. Osin and Zephyrine had gone to find Jin and the others.

"Only you two," Marko replied, grunting as he snapped one of the cot's legs into place. "Though if Emperor Aelius is playing hero and pretending he's sent his children off for their own safety, it certainly makes sense."

"Why set up posters for us at all though?" Astrea asked. "Could you see what they said?"

"No, I couldn't." Marko pushed himself to a stand and glared down at the bed. "I think I might rather sleep on the floor."

"The emperor probably figures that if he can find us, Az, he can get to Ellie and Jin in some way," Cressida said.

"Yeah, I guess." Astrea tossed a pillow to Marko, then one to Cressida.

She hadn't thought coming back to Kalama would be easy. She hadn't thought the mission would be simple. But Astrea wasn't sure how she and Cressida were going to get to the Great Library without being recognized by *someone*. Surely they couldn't avoid every guard and police officer, right?

We're just going to have to try, she told herself as she finished making the last cot. *We're just going to have to try.* Helosia's safety—the continent's safety—depended on it.

CHAPTER 36

Sleeping in the basement of a night club was about as pleasant as it sounded.

Astrea arched her back as she approached the circular bar near the middle of the empty club. Osin was working a small espresso machine behind the counter; its brass and copper parts winked in the dim club lights. With the windows at the front of the club blocked by heavy drapes, it was almost impossible to tell it was morning at all. But it was. And early.

"Here you are." Osin set a delicate crystal saucer and shot glass in front of Astrea.

Steam curled up from the hot liquid. Breathing in the sharp, sweet smell of espresso and sugar, Astrea sighed. "Can you make me another?" she asked Osin even though she'd barely sipped on the first.

He flashed her a grin. "Coming right up."

Cressida strode out of the washroom and headed for the bar, her half-full knapsack draped lazily over one shoulder. She'd pulled her hair up into two buns, one on each side of her head. Some of her curls poked out in every direction. Astrea always liked when Cressida wore her hair like that; it was both elegant and a bit whimsical, especially since she usually finished the look off with a silk scarf at the base of each bun.

There were no silk scarves that morning, though. Nothing elegant or whimsical about an abandoned night club. Deserted as it was, the

Whiskey Dream was almost unnerving. Creepy. Part of Astrea wished a band were on the empty stage just to bring some life back to the place.

"Espresso?" Osin asked Cressida as she plopped onto one of the stools next to Astrea.

"Double shot, please." Cressida reached for one of the flaky raspberry pastries set out on a nearby plate. "Shit, these are good."

"From the White Lily," Osin called over his shoulder. "And there are newspapers if you want them."

"The White Lily?" Astrea asked. She passed Cressida one of the three newspapers, then reached for a pastry for herself.

"Jin mentioned it's a favorite." Osin set Cressida's espresso in front of her. The crystal saucer and glass clinked almost cheerfully. "The owner's an old friend, so she opened up early for me. Well, more of an old fling." He winked.

"Carmella?" Astrea asked. "Is she a—"

"No, no." Osin laughed and leaned his elbows against the counter. "Carmella stays out of politics." He shook his head, then said, "And I don't know if Jin told you, but I managed to arrange what was necessary for your friends to get up to Athran. They're leaving in a bit."

Jin hadn't told Astrea that, mostly because she'd been asleep long before he returned to that store room in the basement. And when she'd gotten up, he'd still been asleep. Letting him rest for a few extra minutes had seemed like the right choice.

"Damn," Cressida murmured.

Astrea and Cressida ate their breakfast in silence while Osin started pulling more espresso shots. It was a good thing, too, because the rest of the team started filling in the bar. Zephyrine came up first, then Adi and Marko, then the twins. Finally, Jin joined them, though he didn't take a seat. He just accepted his espresso shot from Osin and downed it.

"Transport's going to be here any moment," Osin said, mostly to Zephyrine. His gaze flicked to the twins. "You two have your papers ready, just in case you need them?"

"All packed," Lennor said, patting the knapsack sitting on her lap. "It should be everything we need."

"I actually have something for you," Adi said. Orange anxiety vibrated around him as he pulled a letter out of his back pocket and slid it down the bar to Lennor. "For Noemi. Just in case you can't convince her to go with you."

"We'll convince her," Lennor said.

"Just in case," Adi repeated. Civan snatched the letter and tucked it in his bag.

"Three nights," Jin told the twins. "Get Noemi back here in three nights and get her to the docks. Find Magdi as soon as you can. If you get back to Kalama sooner, come here."

Lennor nodded. "You got it, Captain."

A car honked once outside, just a quick beep. Astrea flinched, but Osin perked up. "That'll be your ride," he said. "Shall we?"

Everyone stood and shuffled toward the back of the club as Osin explained they'd need to circle around to the front outside to catch their ride. Something about street clothes and early mornings and red flags. "It'll be the dark red car," Osin concluded. "Sergi will take good care of you both. He'll stay with you until you come back to the city."

"Give us a moment, Osin?" Jin asked.

Osin, Zephyrine, and Marko said their goodbyes to the twins and wished them luck. Astrea almost wondered if she should leave, too, but Jin caught her eye and shook his head. Cressida hovered near her.

"You two be careful," Jin said. "I mean it. Watch each other's backs, and do what you have to. Get yourselves and Noemi back here in one piece."

"You've got to stop worrying about us, Captain." Despite Lennor's smile, anxiety pushed against Astrea's chest, harsh and suffocating. "We'll see you in a few days."

Lennor exchanged hugs with both Jin and Adi, though Civan merely nodded at them. He didn't seem to like physical contact of any kind. Astrea understood that; she often didn't, either.

What surprised her, though, was when Lennor approached and pulled Astrea into a hug. She hugged the shorter woman back, giving her an awkward pat on the back. And Cressida was equally surprised; the emotion danced over Astrea's skin, almost tickling her, as Lennor hugged Cressida, too.

"Alright." Lennor pulled away and tugged at her blue shirt, the one she'd borrowed from Cressida in Thasia. "See you soon."

And with that, the twins slipped through the curtains blocking the back door and out of sight. Astrea blew out a harsh breath. This was just one part of their plan. *Three more parts to go.*

The rest of them recongregated at the bar, and as Cressida climbed back into one of the bar stools, she asked, "Now what?"

"Now we need to figure out logistics." Jin crossed his arms over his chest, making his black shirt pull at his thick arms. "Most importantly, we need to go figure out guard rotations and police beats, assuming you don't have that information, Osin."

"I hear a lot but not that," Osin said. "You'd be better off figuring it out for yourselves."

"Then we may as well get started," Jin said. "Zephyrine, Marko, Adi, you're with me."

"And us?" Astrea asked, gesturing to herself and Cressida.

"You two stay here."

"But—" Astrea started. Having a Lightbringer out there would be crucial. She could tell Jin how many people were around. If there were void mages around.

"For today, at least," Jin said. "Let us scout it out and figure out how obvious it is that you two aren't supposed to be in town."

Astrea couldn't really argue with that. With Wanted posters of them at the port's guard station, who knew how public those arrest warrants were? Even if her talents were useful, getting arrested would just ruin the plan. "Alright."

"We'll be back tonight," Jin said. "Can you keep the club closed down, Osin?"

"Really is too bad about that water leak that flooded the washrooms, isn't it?" Osin mused with a smile. "I'll spread the word that the Whiskey Dream needs a couple days to make repairs."

Though Astrea had thought the club off-putting before with its wide, empty space, it was even worse without Jin or any of the others there. All Astrea could do was sit at the bar and read over the paper as she tried to ignore the way the shadows overtook all four corners of the club.

She had one of the copies Osin had brought in earlier that morning, and Cressida had the other. They were going through section by section, combing through for anything noteworthy. Mentions of more murders. Anything to suggest the Paragon were still active in Kalama. Anything about the war or where Emperor Aelius had supposedly sent his children off to for their own safety.

Most of the paper was merely gossip or pieces that didn't matter. The latest gala some senator held in honor of the troops on the front lines. Shipping delays and product shortages due to the war. Accusations thrown at the Zaikudi and Delians because of the news that the imperial children had been sent away from Kalama for their own safety.

"Well, that was useless," Astrea muttered. The newspaper crinkled as she folded it up. It might not have been providing any clues about the emperor's true mission or the Paragon, but she would bring it back to Talmaris for Eliana. Maybe the names of politicians and nobles would mean more to Eliana and reveal some hidden nugget of information.

"I guess the real news doesn't get printed." Cressida folded up her copy too. "At least we killed some time."

The clock behind the bar said it was nearing the third afternoon bell. They may have successfully wasted the day, but it didn't make Astrea feel any better. Jin and the others still weren't back.

The elevator chimed. Its doors opened, revealing Osin whistling an out-of-tune song. He strolled across the empty club, examining the clipboard in his hands. With a satisfied smile, he checked several things off.

"Osin," Cressida said as he moved toward the bar, "can I ask you something?"

"Of course." Osin set the clipboard on the counter and fiddled with his sleeves, fixing them so they stayed rolled up above his elbows. "Ask away."

"Have you heard any whispers of meteorite in the city?"

Osin's thick eyebrows furrowed. "Meteorite?"

The chunk of meteorite hanging from Cressida's necklace separated from the chain and landed on the shiny counter with a clink. Then she pulled the dagger out and set it next to it. "Emperor Aelius is going after this meteorite in the Badlands, all to make weapons out of it. Thinks it has special properties."

"Yes, Zephyrine and Jin mentioned that last night, but I've not heard a thing, nor have I heard about this Paragon business they mentioned." Osin reached for the dagger, then hesitated. "May I?"

"Be my guest."

As he picked the weapon up, green curiosity sparked around Osin. He tilted the blade this way and that, watching as it caught the lights above the bar. "Interesting color."

"But you haven't heard *anything* about what the emperor's doing in the Badlands?" Astrea asked. "Not even a hint?"

With a shrug, Osin set the dagger back down. "No, but I wish I had. Makes me worried about all the troops in Corsyca. Zephyrine wasn't specific about the nature of the power, but I can only imagine. I'll certainly listen for such talk, though." Picking his clipboard back up, Osin added, "Do you ladies want to help me with a few things?"

Astrea hopped off her bar stool. "Sure." Anything would be better than sitting around and staring at the walls while waiting for the others to return.

What started as a simple agreement to help Osin turned into all kinds of tasks for Astrea and Cressida. While Astrea was given duties to dust and clean up around the club, Osin recruited Cressida to help him fix a furnace in the basement. Staying alone on the main floor of the club wasn't exactly following protocol—Astrea figured it was still a good idea to pair up in case the Paragon returned—but what was she going to do, argue with the man hiding them?

Per the list on the clipboard Osin had left for her, Astrea tidied up behind the bar first, drying glasses and straightening the alcohol bottles. She made sure all the game tables were in order, then swept the empty stage. And when Cressida and Osin still weren't back by the fifth bell, Astrea sighed. There was only one thing on the list Osin had given her that she hadn't done yet. Straightening up all the sofas and sitting areas.

Astrea had been hoping to put it off until Cressida joined her. She'd been avoiding that part of the club altogether. The night she'd been here months before, the night when she'd reunited with Jin, had also been her first run-in with Victor Nazarov. And it had been just feet away from where she now stood.

"It's just a sofa," Astrea whispered to herself as she stared at the spot where he'd first grabbed her arm. "Just get it over with."

Her whole body tensed as she straightened up every other sitting area except that one. And when that was done, Astrea scolded herself again. *It's just a sofa.* Skies, what was wrong with her?

As she reached for the first pillow, she tried to ignore the fact that she was standing in the very same spot Nazarov had been that night. The song that had been playing at that moment seemed to float toward her from the stage.

She reached for the second pillow. Blue lotus smoke seemed to cling to the air, heavy and unwelcome. She reached for the third.

"Astrea?"

Astrea flinched so hard she slammed her shin into the bottom of the sofa. "Fuck." She sucked in a sharp breath and peered over her shoulder. Familiar white hair popped against the club's dark finishes. "I didn't hear you come back."

Zephyrine's thin eyebrows drew together. "A Lightbringer shouldn't need to hear someone come back. Are you alright?"

"Fine." As she focused, Astrea realized nobody else had returned. "Where's Jin? Did something happen?"

"No, we staggered our returns in case anyone was following. They'll all be arriving shortly."

"Oh," Astrea said as she finished straightening the pillows.

"And Osin and Cressida?"

"Fixing the furnace."

"Ah." Zephyrine crossed her arms. "You're sure nothing's wrong? You look like you saw a ghost."

Astrea shrugged. She had, in a way.

"Is it Nazarov?"

"What?" Astrea asked. How could Zephyrine possibly know that? "How—"

"I've seen that same look on many faces."

"What look?"

"The haunted one."

Astrea touched her own cheek. Did she look *haunted*? Did everyone in the entire world know just how much she'd been struggling? "I just—" She swallowed and dropped her hand. "I don't know why I have to see him everywhere. Not just the dreamwalking, either. This was the place where he first spoke to me."

"The club?"

"Well, that, but literally here." Astrea gestured to the floor. "Jin cut in before he could . . . well, I thought Nazarov was just being strange that night, and now I can see . . ."

"You can see that night for what might have actually happened," Zephyrine finished for her.

"Yes."

"But it didn't happen."

"No, but my mind and body don't seem to understand that sometimes."

Zephyrine nodded. "I've felt that many times before. So has Jin."

"He told me about Ilesouria."

"Ilesouria, yes, but there were many other times."

"He's mentioned those, too." Astrea sighed, and before she could think better of it, she whispered, "I just don't want to be scared anymore. I don't want him to have that power over me. And even just standing here in the same spot as that night terrifies me."

"It's natural to be scared."

Astrea frowned. How could this woman, this *general* who had seen so much war and battle and bloodshed, think this was natural? How could being scared of a sofa be normal?

"In all my years in the military, I've learned a few things. Well, more than a few." Zephyrine chuckled. Astrea didn't. "And I think the most important lesson I've learned is that healing is not some light switch we can flip. It's a different journey for everyone, and being scared is often part of it. Some days will feel manageable while others feel impossible."

Astrea didn't expect to feel better with the snap of her fingers, but hadn't it been long enough? She'd escaped the Paragon more than a month ago. She'd been safe for weeks, hadn't she?

Some small part of her knew that wasn't true. She'd put herself in harm's way again to talk to Nazarov not once but twice in person. She'd suffered through his dreamwalking and thought he could access the palace whenever he wanted. She hadn't felt safe at all despite being back with her friends.

"I've been around enough suffering to see the many ways people heal . . . and the many ways they don't. It's never a short journey. Just keep taking it one day at a time."

Astrea shrugged. "I guess."

The metal door at the back of the building creaked, and anxiety grated across Astrea's skin. Jin and Adi both emerged through the curtain.

"Give yourself some grace," Zephyrine said quietly. "You're doing a fine job, Astrea. I know it probably doesn't feel like it, but you are." Before Astrea could respond, Zephyrine turned around and called, "About time you two showed up. And Marko?"

"Wasn't far behind," Adi said. "He'll be here in a moment."

Zephyrine joined Adi near the bar, where they both helped themselves to water. Jin, however, walked over to where Astrea still stood rooted to the spot by that sofa.

"Osin's got you doing chores?" Jin asked, gesturing to the clipboard Astrea had set on the low table nearby.

"Figured Cress and I should help him out since we're making him shut down his business for a few days."

"He'll be fine." Jin stepped closer to Astrea. On the other side of the club, that metal door opened and closed again, and Adi called out to Marko. The elevator chimed, signaling Osin and Cressida's return. "You good?"

Astrea sucked in a deep breath. "Honestly, it's a bit hard being back *here*," she said. "But I'm alright."

When Jin didn't say anything, Astrea thought he might push her on the issue. He simply squeezed her hand and said, "How about we tell you what we found, then have some dinner? I think I can convince Osin to go out and get us fried rice balls."

Astrea half smiled. "I'd like that."

CHAPTER 37

Buckles jingled and clinked as Astrea dug through her knapsack. The flexible leather of her armor was smooth under her fingers, but that wasn't what she needed. She needed to stay inconspicuous, and wandering Kalama's streets wearing armor was anything but normal. She reached into the very bottom of her bag and pulled out a plum shirt and black skirt.

On Jin, Marko, and Adi's first scouting excursion into the city, they'd found several more Wanted posters of Astrea and Cressida, plus a heavier than usual police presence. So, they'd spent the last two days puttering around the club, from finishing the various chores Osin assigned to just sitting and doing nothing at all. Jin, Marko, and Adi had gone out several more times to study guard rotations near the palace. And that morning, they'd gotten confirmation from one of Osin's people that Emperor Aelius had indeed left the city two nights before with no news of when he'd return.

The emperor had left. Magdi's ship would be back in just a matter of hours.

It was time to complete the mission and get back to Novaria.

"Need any help?" Cressida asked. She'd already gotten dressed in black wide-legged trousers and a dark green blouse.

"No, that's alright." What Astrea wanted was a few moments to gather herself. To focus before she had to guide Cressida through Kalama's dark streets and break into the library. "Go on up without me. I'll just be a few minutes."

Cressida fastened on her meteorite necklace and tucked her dagger into the back of her waistband, then left without another word. With a sigh, Astrea turned back to her knapsack and grabbed her change of clothes. A large part of her actually wanted to wear her armor, just to feel the familiar heavy leather that would give her some protection. She fingered the soft fabric of her blouse and sighed.

"Az?" Jin asked after knocking twice on the open door. "What're you doing down here?"

"Just needed a moment," she said.

Unlike her, Jin wore his black fatigues and body armor. The only pieces missing from his full set of gear were his hood, mask, and fingerless gloves. He stepped farther into the storeroom and closed the door behind him.

She might need to avoid notice, but Astrea had a feeling Jin would be able to do that even dressed for battle. She made quick work of changing, finishing off her outfit with her flat shoes, then adjusted the opal necklace Jin had given her. With her hair braided in one long plait, she could've been going to the library for work, not to steal something.

Jin smiled weakly. "Ready?"

Was she? Astrea wasn't so sure. A thousand things could go wrong tonight. A change in guard schedules. A change in police beats. Saros or the Nikaphoroses refusing to leave Kalama. Magdi's ship not making it to port. So many things.

Jin's hands cupped Astrea's cheeks, his warm skin bringing her back to her body. He leaned down and kissed her gently at first, then more slowly as Astrea pulled him in, desperate. She just wanted him close. As close as he could be.

Barely pulling his mouth away from hers, Jin whispered, "I love you, Az."

"I love you, too."

He kissed her again, and even when he broke the second kiss, he kept his face right near hers. "Promise me you'll do whatever you have to tonight," he said as he leaned his forehead against hers. "I don't care if you and Cress have to blow the library to bits to get out of there in one piece."

"I don't know about *that*," Astrea said wryly.

Jin chuckled, a warm, deep sound. That invisible sunshine he seemed to emanate settled over Astrea's skin. "I mean it, Az. Promise me that you'll do whatever you have to."

"I promise."

"Good." Jin kissed her forehead, then picked up her knapsack and handed it to her. "We need to leave."

As they headed out of the storeroom and to the elevator, Astrea slipped her hand into Jin's. She focused on his warm skin and that sunshine still heating her face as the elevator started up toward the club. And even when they stepped out and were greeted by their friends, Astrea didn't let go.

"Well . . ." Jin said as he surveyed their small group.

This was it. Their mission. Either they were going to get what they came for, or they were going to leave Kalama empty-handed.

"Zephyrine, Marko, have Balthazar and Sarsali get you through the dock wall," Jin said. "Az, Cress, we'll wait for you by the wall. But if you get there before us, go in with Zephyrine. Any final questions?"

Everyone remained stoic. Silent under the weight of what they were going to attempt.

"No questions," Zephyrine finally said.

Jin nodded. "Then let's go."

Being able to walk around Kalama, to feel the evening sea breeze and see the once-familiar lights of home, should've warmed Astrea's bones. Would've had it not been for the fact that she was trying to guide Cressida through Kalama's populated streets without drawing the attention of any civilians or police. There would be no dodging passersby; it was too early in the evening for the street to be *that* quiet. But Astrea could guide them away from the most volatile and negative emotions.

"Go left up here," Cressida said. "Shortcut."

Astrea sensed nothing awful coming from that direction, so she turned left. They were already halfway to the Scholar's District. Another twenty minutes, if they could take the most direct route, and they'd be near the library.

This street in the Market District was filled with cafés and small restaurants. Tables spilled out onto the sidewalks, and as Astrea and Cressida slipped past completely ignored, all Astrea's mind wanted to do was focus on the smell of the food. Skies, she'd missed Kalama.

At the next break in buildings, they turned right. This street was quieter, emptier.

"We *can* get into the library, right?" Cressida asked.

"Unless they suddenly have security and replaced everything with platinum, yes," Astrea said. She had no idea if that would've happened since she'd fled. Would Emperor Aelius have increased security at the library if he was housing this important book there? If he was smart he would. But he was also cheap when it came to the library. Hopefully he still was.

"Guess we'll find out."

"Yeah."

They said little else as they traipsed through Kalama's streets. They passed several more restaurants, but as they moved toward the edge of the Market District and into the Scholar's District, the groups of evening pedestrians began to thin out. Restaurants turned mostly to closed storefronts, hotels, and the occasional café.

Astrea had missed this part of Kalama so much. It was always so much quieter than the rest of the city. And in a city of millions, that was no small feat. She just hoped Jin, Adi, and the others were making it to their destinations as easily.

The towering trees and abundant public gardens soon gave way to a familiar sight: the Great Library. It towered over the piazza below, its white stone walls bright even in the growing darkness. It hadn't changed.

No cars were parked near its curb. No students sat on its wide, shallow steps. It was quiet, just like the rest of the district. Astrea adjusted her knapsack; hopefully anyone who saw them thought they were just university students.

They headed down the sidewalk toward the library, passing shops Astrea used to walk by every day on her way to work. If only she could go back in time and warn herself what was to come. Maybe she could've been better prepared for all this.

As they closed the distance between themselves and the library, Astrea's steps slowed. With her senses pushed out, she realized not everything was the same after all. Two presences were at the top of the steps, likely obscured by the shadows of the colonnade. *Shit.*

Astrea grabbed Cressida's arm and pulled her straight down a side street that would let them circle to the back of the library. She hadn't planned on using the front doors anyway, but still. "Guards, I think," she whispered as they moved down the next street. "Two people, anyway."

"Well, shit," Cressida muttered. "Are they Lightbringers?"

"I have no idea." And Astrea had no way to tell.

"What about around back?"

"Can't tell yet."

The library was a deep building, far deeper than most in the area. It had to be to house the collection and everything else. As they closed in on the back alley where they could enter, Astrea sensed no one. No guards. No curious pedestrians. No voids. She tugged Cressida down the alley.

The streetlamps and moon were obscured by the building rising high above them and the thick clouds moving in. Storm clouds by the looks of it. The last thing they needed.

Vines growing up the back of the library hid its small steel back door. It was locked, as it always was. As far as Astrea could tell, nobody was on the other side of the door, though. All Cressida had to do was place her hand flat on the surface. Her long fingers twitched once, then again, and the lock tumbled free.

"Alright," Cressida said, voice low, "I know this is good for us, but how can they have so little security back here? Seems like a major oversight."

"Well, you know him," Astrea said. "Never wanted to put money into the library."

Truthfully, she didn't know why the emperor hadn't invested in better locks for the library's back entrance. But he hadn't invested in a lot of things the library needed over the years she'd worked there. He'd even cut their staff down to a skeleton crew. A door hardly seemed high on his list of priorities when he didn't value the items or people inside.

"Yeah, I guess," Cressida whispered as they stepped inside.

She relocked the door, then Astrea summoned her light as they headed down the dark corridor. It was a part of the basement where rarely anyone went, almost useless. The hallway was narrow, and its ancient stone walls curved up into a low ceiling. It was left over from much older days, preserved for some connection to the past, Astrea supposed. Raela had always wanted to turn it into storage, but nothing would've fit there.

As they neared the door that would take them to the main section of the basement, Astrea slowed again. Still, there was nothing. No guards inside that she could sense. What, did the emperor think two people outside the front door would really deter any would-be thieves? *Or maybe nobody else even knows about the book.* After all, who would Emperor Aelius really tell?

But surely he knew the Paragon could jump locations. Nazarov had suggested the emperor had a network of Lightbringers ready to detect void mage trespassers. So were those guards Lightbringers? Astrea would never be able to tell. But the simple fact that the guards hadn't stormed inside gave her a little hope.

The coast was clear. Pushing into the main part of the basement, Astrea cast her light around the space. A few crates were stacked up against one wall, but otherwise, there was nothing of note.

"Where would Raela keep this book?" Cressida asked.

Where, indeed? Astrea stared down the wide space. One door led to the catalog. Another was just a storage closet with a few basics. But another was part of their actual collection storage, where they kept artifacts and other pieces not yet on display or out of rotation.

"How are we on time?" Astrea asked.

Cressida peeked at the narrow wristwatch on her left arm. Nestled in with her other bracelets, it was almost invisible. "Two and a half hours to get from here back to the docks."

It would take an hour at most to get from the library back down to that part of the city. But that left them with just an hour and a half to go through the library to find what they were looking for.

"Let's check down here first," Astrea said. "Raela often stores things down here." And if Raela had been instructed to keep things out of sight, the basement was a good place to consider. Only staff had keys to get down here.

Breaking into the storeroom was just as easy as breaking in through the back door. A small bump from Cressida's magic got them into the room with ease. Astrea flipped on the lights, and the bulbs overhead buzzed as they warmed up.

"It's called *Novaria: Myths and Other Legends*," Astrea said as they split off onto opposite sides of the room.

Long rows of dark shelves lined three of the four walls, and the middle of the wide room held space for crates and other objects. Several boxes had their lids pried off, and Astrea peeked inside. One held an ornate chandelier; was Raela going to redecorate? In Astrea's two years at the library, she'd never seen decor pass through their hands. The other two crates that were open had old statues Astrea had seen before. No books.

She worked as quickly as she could, scanning shelves for this book everyone wanted so badly. Nothing. There were dozens of other volumes, many of them in need of repair or ones that Raela had replaced with newer editions. But there was nothing that even sounded remotely close to the title Theo had given her months ago, nor was there anything that even seemed to hint at the Paragon.

"Anything?" she asked Cressida.

"Nope."

"Damn." Astrea ran a hand over her braided hair, smoothing back a few loose strands.

"Where else would Raela put it?"

"Probably her office." If Raela really had the book for the emperor, it wouldn't be placed out in the library with all the other tomes patrons could look through. Especially not if it held some secret about void magic. "How's time?"

"Need to leave soon," Cressida said as they moved toward the door and flipped off the lights. "Half hour and we need to be back outside."

"Shit." How had so much time passed already?

Cressida relocked the storeroom door once they were back in the hallway, then Astrea led her upstairs. Astrea's magic stretched wider and wider, passing through the thick stone walls. The lobby was empty, and under the crack in the door, it was just darkness. The only thing she could sense were those two people, still near the front entrance.

"Guards are still at the front door," she said to Cressida. "And if they're Lightbringers, they should've sensed us by now."

"Good enough for me." Cressida unlocked the door to the lobby and pushed it open gingerly. She took a tentative step out, and Astrea dismissed her light and followed.

The empty lobby stretched before them, forlorn and sad in the dark of the night. A faint trickle of light shone in through the library's front glass doors. Two shadows moved around, but Astrea couldn't tell exactly who they were.

As they crept farther into the lobby and headed for the wide stone staircase, a new presence entered Astrea's awareness. Heavy fatigue pressed against her. Who was that? Not one of the pages, Astrea was sure of that much. They never worked late alone.

"Raela might be here," Astrea whispered as she pulled Cressida underneath the stairs, well out of sight of anyone peeking through the front doors. "Someone's over near her office."

"Now what?"

Astrea ran a hand over her face. If it really was Raela, they might stand a chance. If it wasn't Raela . . . they'd just have to deal with that possibility. They'd come this far. They'd tried so hard to find answers. They couldn't just give up.

"We go see who it is, I guess."

A sliver of light lit up the hallway where Raela's office and the other staff offices were located. Raela's office door was ajar, though Astrea couldn't see in. Her heart pounded in her chest. It had always been a possibility that they would run into someone, but the whole point of going to the library after it closed was to avoid this. Astrea wasn't prepared to see her old boss again, especially not when she needed to steal from her.

A familiar voice echoed through the hallway, soft and light and carrying Raela's slight accent. It sounded like she was talking to herself, as she sometimes did. Astrea's entire body tensed.

"That's definitely Raela," Cressida whispered. "What do you want to do?"

Even if Astrea didn't want to confront Raela, she had to go in there. She couldn't abandon this quest. Not now.

"Let me talk to her," Astrea said over her shoulder.

"And if she won't give us the book?"

"Complete the mission . . . right?" The words were cold, foreign. That wasn't who Astrea was. But she had to see this through.

Cressida nodded even as orange anxiety spiked high around her. "Right."

Astrea went first, stepping as carefully and quietly as she could. Her shoes barely made a sound on the tiled floor. When she reached Raela's door, Astrea sucked in a deep breath. Other than Raela's fatigue, she seemed alright. Not upset. Not angry. That might change soon, though.

Pushing her shoulders back, Astrea nudged the door open. The desk lamps in Raela's office cast strange shadows along the floor and walls, but Raela was lit up like a beacon. She sat behind her desk, a ledger open in front of her and pen in hand. Gray confusion and orange fear tangled around her before the confusion completely overtook her aura.

"Astrea?" Raela pushed out of her chair and stood.

"Hi, Raela." Astrea flashed a half smile.

Cressida joined Astrea in the open doorway. "Hey, Raela."

"Cressida?" The confusion tripled, followed by minty cool relief. Raela dropped into her chair. "What—" She cleared her throat. "How did you get in here?"

"I'm sorry," Astrea said as she stepped farther into Raela's office. "I'm sorry for disappearing, Raela, and I'm sorry to show up like this. But I think you have something I need."

A startled laugh escaped Astrea's old boss. "You call out one day because you need to go research something with Prince Varojin, then never come back . . . until tonight? Where the skies have you been, Astrea? What happened? I know Prince Varojin was sent out of Kalama for his safety—"

"That's not true." The words left Astrea before she could reconsider. "It's not true, Raela. Jin and I and . . . and Cressida fled the country. Emperor Aelius's project is not what it seems."

Raela stared at Astrea, her blue eyes wide. More confusion spiked up around her head. "The project?"

"The research project, the gala . . ." Astrea huffed. "Do you have the *Novaria: Myths and Other Legends* book? Did Emperor Aelius give it to you?"

"Why?"

"It's complicated—" Cressida started, but Astrea cut her off.

"To make a long story short . . ." Where did Astrea begin? "There's a sixth type of magic, void magic. And there's a group of void mages after this book. Emperor Aelius wants that book and void magic for himself."

"Void magic?" Raela half laughed. "You disappear from Kalama, then show up months later claiming a sixth branch of magic exists? You expect me to believe that?" She lowered her voice and added, "There are Wanted posters of you all over the city."

"It exists, Raela," Cressida said. "I swear. We've fought them. Emperor Aelius has a void mage working for him."

"Who?"

"Caliban, his guard," Astrea said.

Raela's features tightened as she glanced down at her desk. "The man with the white hair?"

"That's him."

"I don't know what to think," Raela muttered.

How could Astrea convince Raela in the few minutes they had to spare? She had no proof to offer. She could show Raela the scars on her back, but those didn't mean void magic existed. Same with Cressida's dagger and necklace. Meteorite proved nothing.

"That's why we left Kalama like we did." Astrea didn't want to hurt Raela to get the book, but if they had to restrain her so they could find it ... "We went to Sezia to look for that book. Jin and the rest of us figured out something was wrong. Prince Kaius and Caliban attacked us on the airfield, but we escaped and went to Novaria to find more answers."

"And now you're back," Raela said tightly. She barely reached toward the right side of her desk. Her hand hovered there, hesitating.

"Please, Raela," Astrea whispered. "I know it's asking a lot. I know you could get in trouble if you lose the book. But we think the emperor is trying to use void magic for his military pursuits, and this other group ... they want to use the knowledge to take down Helosia and the other governments on the continent."

"And you think this book is key to stopping them?" Raela asked as she set her hands in her lap.

"We don't know for sure, but if we don't take that book, someone is going to do something bad with it. I know that much," Astrea said.

Glancing away, Raela's mouth pressed into a grim line. Could she really think about siding with the emperor on this? Astrea didn't know her specific politics, but Raela had never been a fan of the wars and often complained about the way the imperial government treated the library.

"It's going to be so much worse than just what's happening in Corsyca," Astrea tried. "Please, Raela. You have to believe me."

"I was so worried about you, Astrea, especially when the Wanted posters began showing up," Raela said. "That Caliban you mentioned came here several times to question me and the pages. And now here you are, with this story. I don't know what to make of it, but . . ." She shook her head. "But you've never been anything but honest with me. If you say you need this book, I believe you."

Astrea took a step toward forward. "Really?"

When Raela smiled, it was warm. Friendly. Soft. "Really." Then she reached for the right side of her desk again and opened the top drawer. She pulled out a book with a black cover and set it on top of the ledger.

"Thank you," Astrea said. "Skies, Raela, thank you. I promise, I'll get it to someone who can help."

"Emperor Aelius instructed me to keep this safe as it was an important part of Helosian and Novarian history," Raela said as she looked down at the book. "He didn't tell me much more than that."

"We think it highlights something about the Great Wars," Astrea said. "Something with void magic from that time. Have you read it?"

"No, I've been too busy with the million other things to do around here."

Astrea just started to ask what had been going on when the energy at the edge of her magical radius shifted. Someone new. Two new people, actually, moving closer. Close to the two guards.

"Someone's coming," she whispered.

"Who?" Cressida asked.

"I don't know. Not void mages, though."

"How can you tell?" Raela asked, her voice low. "I don't hear anyone."

"I'm a Lightbringer, Raela," Astrea said. "I can feel them. Who usually comes by this late?"

Teal understanding and gray confusion warred in Raela's aura before she finally said, "No one, usually. Guard changes mostly, though sometimes Emperor Aelius and Prince Kai—"

"We need to go," Cressida said.

"How'd you get in?" Raela asked as she passed Astrea the book.

The black cloth cover was smooth in Astrea's hand, but she didn't waste time inspecting the book other than to check the title and skim over the contents. It certainly seemed like Theo's book. She shoved it into the top of her knapsack, hastily reclasping the buckles as two of the four people outside the library moved closer.

"Basement," Cressida said.

"They're coming inside," Astrea whispered.

White panic pulsed around Raela as she circled her desk. "I'll go see who it is. I'll try to get them to leave." As she strode out of her office, her long violet skirt billowed around her legs.

Astrea and Cressida closed the door over enough that they could hide. Whoever it was out in the lobby, more panic pressed into Astrea. That couldn't be good.

"We need to see who it is."

"You really want to go out there, Sovna?" Cressida hissed.

"Well, we can't just stay here." She gestured to Cressida's watch. There were just the two ways out of the library: the front door and the basement door. If they didn't get out of here in the next few minutes, they'd risk running late and miss their boat out of the city. "We're almost out of time."

"Fine."

Astrea crept down the hallway from Raela's office back toward the lobby. Cressida stayed right behind her, her hand planted on Astrea's knapsack. They stopped when they got to the end of the hall, and Astrea strained to hear any conversation. Raela and two people were in the lobby.

"Well, Prince Kaius, I apologize, but I wasn't expecting you tonight," Raela said.

Whatever Kaius replied with, Astrea couldn't quite make out past the roar of blood in her ears. It sounded like he said something about how his presence should "always be expected."

"Perhaps you'd be interested in taking our meeting upstairs?" Raela asked. "Our second floor has much more comfortable furnishings than our meeting rooms—"

"Why are you so skittish?" Kaius asked. "Moreso than usual, Miss Zornovski. Something wrong?"

"Just had a bit too much coffee today, Your Imperial Highness."

That was a lie. Raela's panic pushed and pushed against Astrea's skin, painful and cold.

"Yes, well . . ."

Astrea peeked around the corner. She couldn't see anything, not from here. A few bookshelves in the wrong place completely blocked her line of sight.

"Prince Kaius, please—"

"He's coming," Astrea whispered.

She whirled, grabbing Cressida's wrist and dragging her toward one of the old staff offices she used to share with the pages. They scrambled into the dark room, shutting the door as silently as they could.

Kaius's energy stalked closer, a tangled mess of disinterest, annoyance, and curiosity. Raela's wasn't far behind, nor was the third person, who was unreadable. Astrea's eyes strained against the darkness as she pressed herself against the wall near the door. Cressida slinked beside her.

"I thought you said you were alone tonight," Kaius drawled, his voice slightly muffled by the thick door.

"I am, Your Imperial Highness." Raela let out an uneasy chuckle. "Aside from you and your guard, of course."

"Then why is your office looking a mess?" he asked.

"Oh . . ." Embarrassment sizzled on Astrea's skin. "My desk always looks like that, Prince Kaius."

"And the chair for your guests?" Kaius asked. "It looks like it's been moved."

"I was having a meeting with one of my employees a couple hours ago. I'm terrible at keeping my personal space tidy."

Kaius paused for one heartbeat, two. "See to it that you clean it up once we're done here."

"Of course, Your Imperial Highness," Raela said quickly. "Is there anything else you need from me tonight?"

Cressida reached for Astrea's hand.

"Yes," Kaius said. "My father asked me to revisit the book before he left town for some business. There are some things I need to double-check."

Shit. The knapsack on Astrea's back doubled in weight.

"I'd be happy to show you tomorrow, Your Imperial Highness," Raela said slowly. "I was about to leave for the night. I've been feeling very poorly for the last hour and really thought I should see a healer . . ."

"You don't look ill."

"It's my head," Raela lied. Astrea felt no such pain. "I've had chronic headaches since I was a little girl, dreadful ones that debilitate me for days if I don't get treatment, Your Imperial Highness. I'm sure it's a terrible inconvenience, but . . ."

The silence dragged on, unbearable. Astrea swallowed hard. Would Kaius actually buy it? He didn't seem to have an empathetic bone in his body. He never had, not even when they were all children.

"Fine," Kaius said. "I think the book should stay with me at the palace anyway. I don't know why my father's been keeping it here. Ridiculous, really." He sighed dramatically. "Grab your things and bring the book. I'll take you to the palace healer. Save yourself the cost. I know my father doesn't pay you that much."

"O-of course, Your Imperial Highness. I'll meet you outside in a few minutes."

"Make it quick."

Astrea covered her mouth with her hand to stop the strangled cry about to escape. Raela couldn't go with Kaius. She'd be in so much trouble for not having the book. For trying to trick Kaius and the emperor. It wasn't that Astrea hadn't known taking the book would put Raela at risk, but if the book really had just been stolen away in the middle of the night . . . when Raela wasn't around . . .

Kaius's energy retreated, moving farther and farther away until finally, he was outside. Astrea loosed a breath. Panic pulsed against her skin, her eyes, her head as she finally opened the door. Raela stood there, frozen in place.

"Raela?" Astrea whispered.

"Girls." Raela flashed a tight half smile. "Wait another three minutes, then go out the basement." She headed for her office and began gathering up papers and folders and shoving them into her leather bag.

"You could come with us," Cressida said as both she and Astrea followed. "Jin can get you out."

"Prince Kaius will shut this city down if I disappear," Raela said. "If what you girls told me is true, then you need time to get that book out of here. You can't do that if Kaius comes looking for me."

"But . . ." All protests died on the tip of Astrea's tongue. Raela was right. Kaius would tear Kalama apart brick by brick if Raela didn't get in the car with him.

"What's your plan?" Raela asked. "No details."

"We're leaving Kalama in . . . just over an hour," Cressida said as she peered down at her watch.

Raela nodded as she closed up her bag and circled the desk. "I can stall for that long. It'll take a while to get back to the palace, anyway."

Astrea threw her arms around Raela's neck, pulling her former boss into a tight hug. "Thank you," she whispered as guilt, grief, and gratitude mixed in her gut. "Thank you for everything. And I'm sorry for everything, too."

Raela returned her embrace as much as she could with Astrea's knapsack in the way. "Thank *you* for helping me run this place the last few years. Be safe, and tell Jin I said hello."

Astrea let out a choked laugh. In the few weeks Jin had been in Kalama, he'd made quite the impression on Raela. "I will. Please, take care of yourself."

"Alright." Raela patted Astrea's cheek and smiled. "I need to go. Leave a note for Serra from me, would you? Just in case I'm late tomorrow."

"Of course," Astrea said, though she knew the awful truth. Raela *would* be late. Astrea wasn't sure if Raela would ever be at the library again.

"Bye, girls." Raela slipped past them, down the hall and out of sight as she rounded the corner to the lobby. Panic, grief, and determination all rolled through the building, overwhelming Astrea.

A few tears slipped down Astrea's cheeks. Just like that, Raela was gone.

Gone, because she believed Astrea and wanted to help.

"Az?" Cressida whispered.

"Let me write that note," Astrea said past the lump in her throat.

She went to Raela's desk, rummaging through the chaos until she found blank paper and a pencil. She scrawled out a quick message, letting

Serra know where Raela had gone for her meeting. Would it help? Astrea had no idea. But someone in Kalama needed to know where Raela had gone.

Cressida left Raela's office first. Astrea flipped the lights off. They went back into the staff office, and Astrea placed the note where she knew Serra would see it.

"Let's go," Cressida said, her hand finding Astrea's as they headed for the lobby. "We need to get out of here."

They retraced their steps, darting past the front door and making it back to the basement with little issue. Astrea looked over her shoulder at the empty lobby one last time. Then she closed the door, summoned her light, and followed Cressida down the basement stairs.

Chapter 38

Kalama's streets had quieted even more in the time Astrea and Cressida had been in the library. Darker storm clouds had rolled in off Tinale Bay, and thunder rumbled overhead. Appropriate, Astrea thought, considering the fact that Raela was on her way to what was likely her own imprisonment. Astrea couldn't focus on that, though. She had a mission to complete.

"Let's try to make it back before the rain starts," Cressida said as they hurried down a side street in the Scholar's District.

"Do you know where we're going?" Astrea asked. She had only a slight clue about how to get to the docks from there.

"Yeah," Cressida said over her shoulder.

A few bars and restaurants they passed at the edge of the district were still open, though the once-full tables were mostly empty of customers. Several pedestrians they passed were obviously intoxicated, stumbling over their own feet and words as they laughed and drunken delight slid over Astrea's skin.

The bag on Astrea's back grew heavier with every step she took. Theo's book. She finally had Theo's book. After months of not knowing where it was, she finally had it, and all she'd had to trade for it was Raela.

A terrible trade. An unfair one.

She shoved the thought away. Hopefully the others were having this much success with their missions.

"This way," Cressida said, pulling Astrea down one of the wide main roads running through the Market District.

They headed east toward Tinale Bay. Overhead, thunder rumbled again. Even this late in the summer, storms were a common nightly occurrence. In fact, it was usually odd to have no hint of thunder in Kalama at this time of year.

Astrea clutched her knapsack straps as they started downhill. As they turned onto another street, this one lined with leafy trees and houses fenced off by wrought iron gates, something shifted in the air. Thunder rumbled again. But it wasn't the storm.

That familiar feeling prickled her skin. Turned her cold from the inside out.

"Void," Astrea said as she grabbed Cressida's arm.

"Where?"

"I don't—"

Shadows swirled up in the middle of the road in front of them. Astrea expected Victor Nazarov to appear, but instead, Solana materialized, Tovan in tow.

"Hello, little Lightbringer," he snarled from behind his mask. "You have something for us?"

She should've known. Had half expected this, really. Nazarov wouldn't just let them go get the book with no attempt to take it for himself. But she wouldn't let that happen. Not after Raela had sacrificed her own safety. Not after everything.

Metal screeched as it peeled off the side of a car parked a few dozen feet away. It flew through the air toward Cressida, splitting off into smaller pieces as it wrapped around her forearms and chest as armor. She attacked.

Iron from the nearby house fences pulled out of the ground, shooting toward Solana almost like a whip. It wrapped around the woman's leg just before she disappeared in a puff of smoke and shadow.

Tovan stalked toward Astrea. "Just give us the book, little Light-bringer, and Victor said we can let you go."

"Fuck you," Astrea snapped. They would not take the book.

"Take him," Cressida said. "Let me handle the void one."

Solana reappeared a few dozen feet down the road, and Cressida sprinted in her direction. *Be careful, Cress,* Astrea thought as she fixated on Tovan.

"Aw, just you and me?" he cooed. "Victor's going to be jealous."

He charged. His emotions flared as bright as the lightning that scorched the night sky. Sickening golden joy. The rush of anticipation whispering over Astrea's skin. She braced herself, lowering her center of gravity and tensing every muscle in her body.

As he neared, Astrea's light shield flared to life. It was as wide and tall as her, but Tovan didn't change trajectory. As he slammed into her, Astrea pushed back with all her strength. He stumbled back with a snarl.

"That's new," he hissed, rusty annoyance spiking high around him.

When he charged a second time, she shoved him back again. Tovan's footing faltered, and that annoyance spiked higher and higher.

Astrea circled him, but as she did, she backpedaled in the direction Cressida had gone. Getting separated would do them no good. They had to stick together. Behind her, that cold wrongness flared as more metal screeched.

"Running away again?" Tovan reached for the dagger at his waist and snapped, "I don't want to hurt you again, but I will. Victor's got a nice new setup in the mountains if you want to see it."

The knot that had stayed around Astrea's heart since leaving Raela squeezed tighter. She let Tovan get closer, then backpedaled again. Every time she moved away from him and every time she ignored his taunts, his irritation and rage grew. Red and rust swirled around him as blue lightning flashed in the sky.

He stepped closer, his anger flaring in time with Astrea's pulse. Behind her, Cressida grunted and ghost pain scraped against Astrea's upper arm.

"Well?" Tovan asked. "Come on, Lightbringer."

"No."

As Tovan lunged for her, dagger angled toward her, Astrea let her shield drop. She grabbed hold of all that anger and rage. It burned through her, red hot, and she welcomed it. Welcomed it as it mingled with her own fury. How dare this man. How dare he try to make her comply. How dare he threaten to take her away again.

Tovan's dagger sliced through her skirt, just above her knee. Astrea pulled on that pain. She pulled on her rage, and she pulled on Tovan's disgusting mix of satisfaction and joy and irritation. She pulled and pulled until she couldn't pull anymore, and then she shoved back against Tovan.

He roared as ghost pain lanced Astrea's heart. He roared so loud even the next crash of thunder couldn't drown it out. Orange fear spiked high in his aura, and Astrea grabbed that, too. With a heavy grunt, Tovan collapsed to his knees.

"Fuck you," Astrea spat as she clenched her fists tighter. "Fuck you."

Tovan strained against her hold. The veins in his neck threatened to pop out from his skin. He stabbed his dagger forward again. Astrea pivoted, but it caught the edge of her calf. Blood trickled down her leg as rain began to splatter on the road and her cheeks.

Astrea pulled on her pain, pouring it into the colorful bridge connecting her to Tovan. He wheezed. Why wouldn't he go down? He'd gone down last time she'd done this to him, a lot of good it had done her.

"Gotta . . . try . . . harder . . . Souleater," he choked out, warm satisfaction pushing into Astrea's bones. What, did he think this was some kind of game?

Astrea's magic burned in her veins. It burned. Her leg burned. Behind her, Cressida cried out.

End this, Az. End it now.

Astrea yanked on the energy pouring off Tovan. She yanked so hard she stumbled. The cuts on her legs screamed in protest. Tovan fell forward onto his hands. Astrea wrenched that energy again. He collapsed onto his face, unmoving except for the subtle up and down of his back as he breathed.

Whirling, Astrea caught a glimpse of Solana disappearing in a billow of smoke. Cressida faced Astrea, chest heaving and dagger clutched in her hand. Behind Cressida, the street was a mess of metal and earth.

"Az—"

Hot rage flared behind Astrea. She spun back around, grabbing onto the crimson surrounding Tovan as he tried to push back to his feet. Solana appeared behind him, that strange dark shadow of emotion flaring around her head. Astrea grabbed at it, desperate.

Bone-chilling cold pierced Astrea's body, but something in that darkness shifted, like clouds parting after a storm. And there. There was rage there, rage and frustration and fear, all Astrea's for the taking.

Solana froze, choking as Astrea yanked back. Her arms shook with the effort of holding onto Solana and Tovan's energy. The cold surrounding Solana crept into Astrea's muscles, almost paralyzing her.

"Cress, do something," Astrea begged. Her whole body trembled, like trying to push a weight she wasn't strong enough to handle. "Can't hold—"

Tovan lurched forward again. Metal whizzed by Astrea's ear, embedding into Tovan's chest with a sickening squelch. Pain seared through every inch of Astrea's body, burning impossibly hot and cold. That night at the museum. That night in The One's office. Astrea's hold on the Paragons' energy broke as she staggered back.

Tovan stumbled, gasping for air as shadows crawled up his exposed skin. He reached for his mask and threw it onto the ground as more of that inky darkness consumed his face. Solana screamed something, drowned out by the crash of thunder and splatter of rain. With one last step toward Astrea, Tovan collapsed to the ground, then stilled. The pain in Astrea's veins shut off like someone turning off a light.

The dagger embedded in his chest flew back toward Cressida. Icy shock pushed against Astrea, cold and almost familiar.

Solana looked at Tovan, then at Cressida and Astrea. Behind her mask, her gaze hardened. With one last look at her fallen comrade, Solana disappeared. Shadows swirled in the air where she'd once stood, then dissipated as the rain fell harder.

"What the fuck was that?" Cressida hissed as she stared down at Tovan.

"Meteorite," Astrea whispered. Emperor Aelius had thought it might have some special property. But this wasn't about meteorite blocking out Lightbringers. It wasn't about void fire or dreamwalking.

That was it. Those shadows . . . *that* was what the meteorite could do.

"Shit." Cressida wiped the dagger on her trousers, then tucked it into the pocket on the side of her knapsack. Sirens whined in the distance. "We gotta go."

Astrea stared down at Tovan for another heartbeat, two. He was dead. *Dead.* There was no recovering from that. And Solana had just left him there. That was so . . . cold. Ruthless.

"Are you hurt?" Astrea asked as she and Cressida sprinted down the street, past cars whose sides were peeled off and fences half destroyed.

"A few burns but nothing to stop for," Cressida said, her words coming in quick gasps. "You?"

"A little." She'd heal it later. She'd heal both of them later. They had to get to the docks before Solana came back. Before the police got to the scene.

Rain pelted Astrea's face as they ran through Kalama's dark streets. Her whole body ached with the effort of pushing her senses out. She strained as she searched for any voids. Solana. Nazarov. The One. Any of them.

Nothing.

They turned down street after street, ignoring the sirens as they got closer. Why were they getting closer when they were running away from the scene of the fight and toward the docks?

"Go right, go right," Cressida hissed, half pushing Astrea down an alley as flashing red lights illuminated the main road. "Go, faster."

They had to be running short on time, whether to catch Magdi's ship or to outrun the authorities. Astrea's lungs burned as they ran. Behind them, myriad emotions began to congregate: confusion, fear, irritation, annoyance. But none of that energy followed them. The more they ran, the more distance grew between Astrea and all those emotions.

"How close are we?" Astrea asked.

The rain tapered to a light mist as they crossed another empty road. The salty smell of the sea grew stronger, and overhead, thunder rumbled.

"Just a few blocks," Cressida said between heavy breaths.

The shorter buildings made of tan brick became more familiar. The roads narrowed, and soon, Astrea recognized the very street corner they were approaching. It was where they'd rendezvoused with Marko a few days before. Which meant there were port guards nearby.

Cressida shoved Astrea to the left. They dipped into a shadowed alley between two buildings. A few more turns, and the port's high brick wall rose up in front of them. Four people loitered nearby, two dressed in all black and two surrounded by gray confusion.

Astrea could've collapsed right there on the ground as both she and Cressida slowed. Minty cool relief coated Astrea's tongue and skin, then Cressida bolted forward.

Sarsali and Balthazar caught Cressida as she flung herself into their arms. Astrea's chest and throat tightened. Tears pricked her eyes as she forced her tired, bleeding legs to carry her a little farther.

"What happened to you two?" Sarsali asked as she pulled Astrea into a tight hug.

Skies, Astrea wanted nothing more than to melt into Sarsali's arms, to revel in their reunion. But now was neither the time nor place. "Tovan and Solana found us," Astrea said, more to Marko and Zephyrine than the Nikaphoroses. She'd catch up with her family later, when they were on the ship and headed away from this city. Still, she leaned into Sarsali's embrace and breathed in her sage and lavender soap. "Solana got away."

"And Tovan?" Marko asked.

"Dead," Cressida said as she pulled away from Balthazar.

Astrea hugged him next, welcoming the scent of his familiar earthy cologne. He seemed taller than he had when she'd last seen him, but his dark brown eyes crinkled at the corners with the same warmth they always did.

"Where are the others?" Balthazar asked. "I thought we were meeting more people."

"I don't know," Zephyrine said.

"Should we wait for them?" Sarsali asked.

Zephyrine shook her head. "Stick with the plan. We're getting you on that ship."

Sucking in a steadying breath, Astrea pushed past the relief and concern spiking around the Nikaphoroses. *Focus.* To their right, where the port's gate was, were all sorts of emotions. But directly on the other side of the wall, Astrea sensed nothing of concern. No people at all.

"Clear, as far as I can tell," she said.

Cressida clapped her hands together, then pulled them apart. The port wall shifted and opened, creating a gap just wide enough for them each to fit through if they turned sideways. Marko went first, followed by Sarsali and Astrea. Balthazar went next, then Zephyrine and Cressida ducked in behind them. The bricks moved back to their original configuration as Cressida dropped her hands to her sides.

"This way, quickly," Zephyrine said.

Wind kicked up, making the misty rain swirl about in an almost disorienting pattern and obscuring the gas lamps flickering around the port. To their right, someone shouted, but it didn't sound angry. Confused, maybe. Keeping her senses pushed out so far for so long was making Astrea's head spin.

"Just up ahead." Zephyrine pointed. "That ship, right there."

The Starseeker bobbed up and down lazily in the water. Smoke puffed up from the smokestack at the rear of the ship, and a couple of lights on deck wavered in the stormy weather. As they got closer, Astrea focused on the three people on board. Only three. Magdi, Bek, and Nahta, most likely.

Where was Jin? Adi and Saros? The twins and Adi's sister? Astrea swallowed hard. Maybe they'd gotten there faster than expected. Maybe Cressida's watch had been wrong and they had more time before midnight.

As they scrambled up the ramp to the ship, Magdi emerged from the pilothouse. Her long black jacket billowed in the wind.

"Glad to see some of you've made it," she muttered, squinting against the mist. "These your civilians?"

"Two of the four," Marko said. "Sarsali and Balthazar."

"Go on inside," Magdi said to the Nikaphoroses. "We're leaving in two minutes. You cut it close, Marko."

Two minutes? No . . . no, that couldn't be all they had. Astrea strode toward the front of the deck, focused on the port wall in the distance. She broke her stare only briefly to look up at where the palace towered high above the bay and the rest of the city. Nothing seemed amiss. Maybe Jin and Adi were just running late.

When Cressida joined her, Astrea started to ask about her injuries, but intense, overwhelming panic washed over her. She leaned against the ship's railing. That panic burst bright white through the mist as someone appeared near the wall, and two dark-clad figures were with them.

And behind them . . .

"Oh, fuck," Cressida muttered.

That had to be Jin, Adi, and Saros. It had to be. The two clad in black were too tall to be the twins.

Cressida called for Astrea as she ran down the ramp back onto the pier. Marko followed her.

One, two, three, four . . . Astrea tried to count the red-uniformed guards running after Jin, Adi, and Saros. There were too many. *Eight, nine, ten . . .*

Fire blasted through the darkness, but it wasn't Jin's. He turned right into the flames, but instead of being overrun, threw them back toward the palace guards. Adi shouted for Saros to get to the boat.

"Astrea, get back on the ship," Marko hissed as he grabbed her forearm.

She shook him off. "I will not go back on that ship without them," she snapped over her shoulder. "I will not."

Annoyance scraped Astrea's skin as she ran for the end of the pier. Saros sprinted toward her, his dark hair hanging limp and soaked around his shoulders. Water swelled over the side of the pier, lashing out at him and grabbing his leg. Saros crashed to the ground as the water pulled him backward.

The docks were just a flurry of elements, fire and earth and water crashing together. Emotions flared in the darkness, and pain slammed into Astrea as the fight raged on. Above the noise, Jin yelled something to Adi.

Astrea would not let the Helosians stop her family from getting away. She would not let them get Jin and Adi. She'd just taken on both Solana and Tovan. She would not let the Helosians or the Paragon or her fear stop her.

Skidding to a stop at the end of the pier, Astrea grabbed onto the first flash of crimson rage she saw. To her right, rust red annoyance. She grabbed onto that too. Astrea reached out, snapping up color after color as the Helosian guards fought her friends. Rage. Annoyance. Mistrust. Fear. Pain.

Astrea's muscles trembled with the effort of holding onto it all. Her palms burned. Her joints ached. And when she pulled back, the first Helosian guard stumbled to their knees. Astrea poured in her pain, her desperation. She could not let the Helosians take Jin, Adi, or Saros. She couldn't. That could not happen. They had to leave. They had to get out of Kalama.

Another guard fell to the ground, then another. They toppled over like dominos as Astrea squeezed their energy, forcing the colors into one tight rope. It was like a game of tug-of-war, only she was alone on her team.

But she was strong.

She could do this.

As the sounds of battle drifted away, new emotions flared to Astrea's left. A lot of them, coming in hot.

"Ship," Astrea croaked as she strained against the magic coursing through her. There was too much. Too much magic. Too many emotions. Her entire body spasmed as she held onto that colorful, burning hot rope. "Can't hold them all."

Marko yelled for Adi and Jin, but it barely reached Astrea's ears. As more guards stumbled onto the scene, Astrea grabbed their emotions too. Tears burned her eyes. Her hands and arms, stretched out before her, shook violently.

The earth and pier rumbled as an entire section of the port's wall broke away. It flew toward the guards pouring in from the left. Panic and fear surged, and Astrea grabbed on to that, too. Her knees weakened. She dropped to the ground, but she didn't let go.

Jin shoved Saros past Astrea. Marko grabbed hold of him, dragging him down the pier even as Saros shouted for her. Adi ran by next.

"Let it go, Az," Jin said as he stopped next to her. "Get on that ship."

It was too much. She couldn't put it down. It was going to hurt too much. There was so much energy coursing through her, so much she was barely keeping contained. "Can't."

"You *have* to, Az. We have to go."

Good. She needed something good. Astrea focused on the fact that Saros and the Nikaphoroses were on that ship. They were waiting for her. They could get away from this place together. They would be okay.

Astrea pushed all the energy caught in her hands back toward the docks. It rippled out from her with a boom, painful and overwhelming. She cried out, but Jin yanked her up and half dragged her toward the waiting *Starseeker*. He pushed her up the ramp when her legs collapsed again. Jin shoved the ramp away from the boat, and it surged forward into the bay.

Astrea stared up into familiar silver eyes as Saros said her name, but it sounded wrong. Far off. Like she was underwater, or maybe he was. Jin called her name next, and she tried to respond, but darkness took hold and didn't let her go.

<h1 style="text-align:center">CHAPTER 39</h1>

Light drifted around Astrea, gentle and warm. She floated, her body caressed by something soft as she stared up at the blue sky and white clouds. The perfect spring afternoon in Kalama.

"Az?"

That sounded like Jin.

"Az, hey."

Astrea's eyes fluttered closed as she let the sunshine wash over her. She loved that sunshine.

"Az!" Rough hands shook her shoulders. "Az!"

Astrea startled, scrambling as the real world snapped into focus around her. Rain and mist splattered the deck. Fear, relief, anxiety, curiosity—it all pushed against Astrea's fried senses. She shrank back, right into the strong arms holding her.

"Skies, Az." Jin helped her fully sit up. "That was a lot of magic you used back there. A *lot*."

"Yeah," she croaked as she pulled her mental shield around herself. Little good it did; she could barely control it. She hadn't grabbed just one person's emotions. She'd controlled so much energy. A dozen people's? Two dozen? And she'd done it to Solana, too. She'd found a way to hold onto a void mage's energy. "I—"

Something slammed into the sea next to the ship, sending a wall of water crashing over the side of the deck. Jin hauled Astrea back toward the pilothouse, then helped her to her feet.

"What's going on?" Astrea asked, barely steadying herself against the slick metal wall. Another projectile slammed into the water, missing *The Starseeker* by a few dozen yards.

"Cress!" Jin shouted above the wind and water. "Next one that comes in, can you redirect it?"

Astrea squinted against the rain and building fog. Cressida and Balthazar stood down toward the end of the deck with Marko and Nahta. Magdi, Bek, and Zephyrine were nowhere to be seen. Neither were Sarsali or Saros. With the thick fog, Astrea couldn't even see Kalama anymore. How long had she been out?

"You got it!" Cressida yelled over her shoulder. A boom echoed through the air and water. "Next one incoming!"

A gray cylindrical object broke through the fog at the other end of the deck. Cressida swung her arms back as the object—a missile, Astrea realized—stopped midair. Balthazar copied Cressida's stance. Father and daughter strained as they brought their arms up over their head again, then moved like they were throwing something. The bomb shot back toward its origin point. In the distance, smoke and fire billowed up into the air, obscured by the storm again.

Attack. They were under attack.

The Starseeker surged forward, treading water at breakneck speed. Every wave and dip in the sea made Astrea's stomach turn. Flames zoomed toward the ship. Jin sprinted forward with sure footing and took control of the fire, sending it back to where it had come from. Even standing behind him, heat seared Astrea's skin.

She was going to be sick.

"Let's find a way to lose 'em!" Magdi shouted over the noise. "Quickly! Three of 'em are still on us!"

Astrea had no idea how to help. How could they lose Helosian ships—war ships, if the missiles were any indication—like this? The fog and rain might help, but behind the boat, headlights glowed in the dark.

"Take out their lights!" Jin called. "Turn ours off, then get us more fog!"

Taking out their lights was one thing, but would that really stop the Helosians? Astrea didn't think so. They needed something to fire back. Something to go on the offensive.

Steadying herself, Astrea ran around the pilothouse to where there had been crates upon crates last time. Maybe they could use those, set them on fire and fling them back at the Helosians?

As she rounded the corner, Astrea was disappointed to find far fewer crates than the night they'd been dropped off in Kalama. She slipped as she headed for one, catching herself on the rough wood. The lid slid back a few inches, and glass clinked.

Rum, Astrea realized as she shoved the lid back farther. Magdi and her crew transported rum. And rum was flammable.

"I've got it!" she shouted, her voice consumed by the roar of water and wind. With a huff, Astrea grabbed two of the bottles and carried them back around the front of the pilothouse. "Jin!" she shouted again. "The rum!"

He stared at her over his shoulder for one heartbeat, two. When a third passed, Astrea wasn't sure he'd heard her. But Jin ran toward her, Adi right on his heels.

"How much of it is there?" Jin asked as he took one bottle from her.

"One crate for sure, maybe more."

"We should just take the whole crate at once," Adi said. "Light it on fire, then shoot it at them."

"Good idea," Jin said, both to Adi and Astrea. "Adi, help get the crate out here. Az, see if there's another. I'll get Marko and Zephyrine."

Jin didn't wait for their response. He turned and sprinted back toward the others. Adi grabbed Astrea's hand and tugged her along so fast Astrea was sure one of them was going to fall and crack their heads open. But they didn't.

Adi went straight for the crate Astrea had opened. As he flexed his hands out in front of him, the crate shifted, then lifted into the air. Did it have earth in it for him to move? Astrea pushed the thought away. *Not important.*

Instead, she moved to the next crate and shoved its half-loose lid off. Inside, more bottles clinked. And the box next to it contained rum, too. So did a fourth, though Astrea hadn't found a fifth yet when Adi came back.

"These ones," Astrea said, gesturing to the ones with the rum. "I'll look for more."

"Don't need more," Adi said. "Those'll be enough. I'll move these, then you're with me. C'mon."

Astrea followed Adi back and forth as he moved the crates to the front of the ship where Jin, Marko, and Zephyrine were waiting. Cressida and Balthazar stood to one side, watching.

"Why have they stopped firing on us?" Cressida asked.

"Don't know and don't care," Jin said. "We just need to distract them. Buy ourselves some time to get out of here in one piece."

"Where are they, though?" Cressida asked, turning and staring out over the dark water. "I can barely see them."

In the distance, a light occasionally flashed. No other indication of where they were. The likelihood of missing . . .

"We need light," Jin said. "Where's Saros?"

"I can do it," Astrea said, though she wasn't sure how much she had left to give. One light show. She could do it. She'd done it before.

"I'll go find him," Balthazar said as he headed for the pilothouse. "You can do it together."

"Make it quick!" Jin called after him.

As Balthazar disappeared, another boom echoed through the night. "Fuck me," Cressida muttered, widening and lowering her stance.

Astrea pulled on the trickle of light still burning under her skin, willing it to pulse out bright and wide as she fed it her fear and pain from her still-bleeding cuts. It lit up the sky, revealing a missile headed straight for them. Cressida clapped her hands together in front of herself, straining as the missile stopped midair.

"More light, Az?" she asked, voice trembling.

Astrea's veins burned as she forced her light farther away from the boat. In the distance, three shadowy ships dipped up and down on the waves.

Cressida flung the missile back toward the lead ship. It made impact as Astrea's light died, the night engulfed in an explosion of red flames and black smoke. The other two ships surged past their fallen comrade.

Astrea and Cressida collapsed onto the deck as Saros and Balthazar returned.

"Just need light, Saros," Jin said. "Left first."

Saros widened his stance. "Ready when you are, Varojin."

Jin's flame shot toward the first crate as it hovered over the deck. Light built over Saros's palms. Starlight filtered out over the waves, revealing one ship's shadowy form. The ship Cressida had hit still burned in the distance.

"Go," Jin said.

Adi grunted, then strong wind gusted across the deck and carried the flaming crate across the sea. It crashed onto the ship's deck. Another crate was already flying in the air, exploding as it landed near the first fire.

"To the right," Jin ordered, fire burning over his palms.

Saros lit up the night again, and again, Jin set the rum crate on fire. Marko and Zephyrine shot it toward the ship on their right. It hit. They shot the second. Another direct hit. The two ships slowed significantly, though they didn't stop their pursuit.

"Fuck," Cressida whispered as she sprawled out on the deck.

"It's fine," Jin said. "It's enough."

The Starseeker lurched forward. Nahta, Zephyrine, and Marko combined the rain and wind together again, a heavy fog settling over the ocean as far as Astrea could see.

"Come on." Jin extended his hand to Astrea and pulled her to her feet. "Let's get out of here."

Jin herded Astrea and Cressida into the pilothouse, then below deck. Saros and Balthazar followed behind them. Astrea's legs barely handled her weight, and her chest was so tight she could barely take a breath. But as Astrea collapsed onto a cot next to Sarsali, she finally breathed.

Her family. Her family was there and they'd just outrun Helosian forces. Her family was there and she was about to pass out again from exhaustion. Her family was there but Adi's wasn't, nor were the twins. Raela was in Prince Kaius's custody.

Astrea pushed up on her elbows and stared at where Saros stood across from her. He stared back, a tangle of mint relief and midnight blue sorrow surrounding him.

"Astrea—" Saros started, only to be cut off by Jin.

"I'm guessing you can't heal right now," Jin said, setting his knapsack down on the floor near her feet. He kneeled in front of her just as Astrea shook her head. "There's an extra med pack in that knapsack right there."

Jin tilted his chin toward where Adi's bag sat on an empty cot. "If you want to get it for yourself, Cress."

"Let me," Sarsali said.

As Sarsali began rifling through Adi's pack and pulling out items to tend to Cressida's injuries, Jin did the same for Astrea. His fingers were quick but gentle as he ran antiseptic over her wounds.

As Jin worked, Astrea peeked up at Saros again. That same relief and sorrow undulated around him, unwavering and bright. Other than his rain-soaked clothes and hair, he looked the same. Hair loose around his shoulders, dark half moons under his eyes. He'd lost a little weight. No surprise. He probably hadn't been eating enough if he'd been as fixated on finding answers as Astrea had been.

"What happened?" Jin asked.

"Tovan and Solana found us," Astrea said.

"Who?" Saros asked.

Astrea swallowed. She couldn't explain that. Not now. Not to her family. She wasn't sure she ever could. It would hurt them so much to know what had happened all those weeks ago in Talmaris.

"They're members of the Paragon, an ancient group of void mages who believe Jin and I are a key to some old Stargazer's vision they follow as a prophecy," Astrea said. "Tovan's dead."

"What?" Jin asked.

"The meteorite," Cressida said. "I used the dagger, and it created those shadows on his skin like the murder victims in Kalama and Sezia. He died, and Solana fled."

"I don't like that Solana got away," Jin muttered. He wrapped clean bandages around Astrea's thigh. "But I'm glad Tovan's dead."

Only Jin and Cressida really knew what Tovan had done to her. But Astrea was glad he was dead, too. He couldn't touch her. Never again.

"I was able to take control of Solana's emotions before we killed To-van," Astrea said, mostly to Jin.

"And all those guards," Jin said quietly as he peered up at her. "That was quite the feat."

"I had to do *something*."

"And you did," Cressida said. "Fucking skies, Az."

"What was it you did, exactly?" Saros asked. There was no malice to his soft words, just genuine curiosity. "I didn't know you could do that."

Astrea half smiled at her uncle. "I found someone to teach me."

"And I'm very glad, my dear." It was the first genuine smile she'd gotten from Saros in months. "I'm very, very glad."

She explained how she was able to take hold of emotional energy, then said, "The Paragon called me a Souleater after they found out I could do that." And after what she'd just done on those docks, it seemed like an appropriate title to Astrea. She hated doing it. Truly hated it. But skies, was it effective. She wasn't sure they'd have gotten out of Kalama if she hadn't held off the guards like that.

"Souleater?" Saros murmured.

"Perhaps we should talk about that later," Balthazar said. "Let the girls rest."

"What about Adi's sister? Lennor and Civan?" Blue sadness wavered around Cressida. "They didn't make it."

"They didn't." Jin's voice, though hard, betrayed no anxiety. "But they'll be alright. They know what to do to get back to Talmaris. Backup plan."

Astrea scrubbed at her face. Fatigue pulled at her mind, begging her to give in. Then she could heal anyone else's injuries. Stay alert in case the Paragon somehow managed to track her to this ship. She didn't doubt it was possible considering Tovan and Solana's appearance.

They may have slowed the Helosians down for now, but Emperor Aelius wasn't likely to just let them go, nor were Victor Nazarov or The One likely to let Astrea keep Theo's manuscript. No, this was certainly not the last time she'd hear from any of the three of them.

"You should get some sleep, Az," Cressida said.

Astrea wanted that more than anything. "I just need something to eat. I'll be fine for another hour."

Cressida pinned her with a look that suggested she didn't believe Astrea at all.

"I'll go find you something," Sarsali said. "And you too, Cress. Where's the galley?"

"I'll take you." Cressida pushed to her feet on mostly steady legs. "I've got dry clothes for you too, Ma."

"And Adi and I have dry clothes for you both," Jin said to Balthazar and Saros. "Take our packs. There's an empty room next door."

Saros hesitated, but Balthazar scooped up several knapsacks and motioned for Saros to follow him. "Thank you, Jin," he said. "We'll be back."

As Saros, Sarsali, and Balthazar shuffled out the door, Cressida paused near the threshold. She smiled at Astrea, though it was almost sad, then followed their family out into the hallway. The moment they were gone, Astrea collapsed into Jin's waiting arms.

Chapter 40

After letting Jin finish bandaging her up, Astrea slid her knapsack off and fished the book out from inside. The corners of the black cloth cover were a bit damp, but otherwise, it was in fine condition.

Astrea blew out a harsh breath. She finally had this book. *They* finally had this book. And now she had to keep it safe.

She forced herself to set it aside to change into dry clothes of her own, just her training pants and a loose black shirt. Jin rebraided her wet hair for her next; her limbs were shaking too much for her to do it herself. Not long after, Cressida and Sarsali returned with a meager snack, just a few apples, bread, and water. Astrea forced herself to eat. It did little for her stamina, but the tremors plaguing her muscles finally subsided.

Saros and Balthazar came into the room next, and Balthazar passed Jin an extra set of clothes. Jin excused himself to change but was gone for barely a minute. He stood next to Astrea's bed, where she still sat eating the rest of her apple. It hardly seemed real, getting to look at Saros, Sarsali, and Balthazar again. Seeing them right there, right in front of her. Seeing and feeling their anxiety, their relief, their fear and love.

"What's been happening in Kalama while we've been gone?" Cressida asked. "What's the emperor up to?"

"What isn't he up to?" Balthazar replied. "Things have been devolving rapidly since you fled. He stopped military pay, started spreading the word that *he'd* sent his children away for their safety, and made Kalama's residents even more paranoid."

"Nothing about void magic?" Jin asked.

"Not a whisper," Sarsali said. "Not as far as we've heard, anyway. Nobody's mentioned it at Lodestar, nor have any of the Greenkeepers I work with."

"And do you know if Kaius and Apelo are actually out of the city?" Jin asked.

"Apelo hasn't been back since before you left, and nobody's seen Kaius publicly," Sarsali said.

"We did tonight," Astrea said just before Cressida explained what had happened at the library with Raela. Jin's shoulders tightened.

"Prince Kaius has been holed up in the palace," Saros said. "To my knowledge, that's the first time he's left the compound in . . . oh, a week or two? Trying to play into your father's lie, I guess. He's not been attending council meetings, but I've run into him coming and going from your father's office at odd hours."

"My father didn't suspect you of helping Az and me, then?" Jin asked.

"Oh, he certainly did." Saros sighed as midnight blue grief swirled around his body. "I told him the truth, Astrea, about your magic. I didn't see any other choice. And he said he understood, that he would do anything to save his children, too."

Jin scoffed. Astrea knew exactly why. All Jin's years at war, forced there by his father. Emperor Aelius might save Apelo, Kaius, or Eliana, but not Jin. And with that threat his diplomats had delivered to the Talmaran palace days before, Astrea wasn't so sure he'd save Eliana, either.

"And because I told him the truth about that, he kept me in his employ," Saros continued. "I've been helping him try to access the void powers locked within the meteorite. The ones you have apparently dis-covered, Cressida."

"We were both brought on to help," Balthazar said. "Even got sent to the Badlands to examine what he's found."

"We had our suspicions and delayed him as long as we could," Saros said, "but he'll start trying other avenues now that we're gone. He's found more meteorites in the Badlands but is keeping them in place for the time being until he decides how to proceed."

Astrea plucked at the corner of the book now sitting in her lap, rolling a fraying string from the cloth cover between her fingers. What were they supposed to do with that information? Nothing, Astrea supposed. She was surprised that Saros and Balthazar had been able to delay the emperor's findings for that long, though. That was good. They had a small advantage, at least against Emperor Aelius.

"May I have a moment with Astrea and Varojin?" Saros said to the Nikaphoroses. "There's much we need to discuss."

"It can't wait?" Sarsali asked. "We're barely out of the city, Saros. Let them rest."

"I've waited fourteen years to explain myself," Saros said. "I think I've made Astrea wait long enough. I'd like to talk to her now."

"Can you check on the others?" Astrea asked Cressida. "See if they need any healing."

Cressida glanced at Saros, then Astrea, and nodded. "Sure."

After the Nikaphoroses shuffled out of the room, Saros closed the door, then he motioned for Jin to sit down on one of the cots. Jin sat right next to Astrea, so close that their thighs touched.

"How'd you get caught?" Astrea asked. "Leaving the palace, I mean."

Jin sighed. "We broke into my father's office."

"Again?" Astrea asked, earning her a small smile from Jin. Months before, at that dinner party, they'd broken into his father's office. And they'd gotten away with it. Mostly.

"Yes," Saros said as he leaned against the wall opposite them. He looked so strange, swallowed up by Jin's too-long clothes. "I had to get something." He reached into his pocket and pulled out a familiar trinket.

The bejeweled egg Astrea had seen several times during her visits to the emperor's office. The one he'd toyed with during their meetings. Its shiny black exterior caught the low lights of the room, as did the rubies studding its silver filigree accents. Saros popped the egg open and pulled out a rolled up piece of parchment. Water spots stained the creamy paper.

"This," Saros said. "This is what we needed."

"And you still haven't told me what it is," Jin said. "What we nearly derailed the mission for. We would've missed the fucking boat if it wasn't for Az."

Saros shifted his weight from foot to foot. "You said this Paragon group thinks you two are part of a prophecy, yes?"

They both nodded.

"Well, then you might be interested in seeing this." Saros unrolled it, then passed it to Astrea.

"The sun, moon, and earth will restore balance," Astrea read aloud. The ink was long faded and the parchment fragile under her fingertips. The edges of the paper were blackened and rough, like it had survived a fire. "The Paragon's version says the sun and moon will restore balance, and we found another in Talmaris that said the earth and stars would restore balance."

Was this it, then? The original Stargazer's prophecy? This one measly, tiny sentence?

"Turn it over," Saros said.

Delicately, Astrea turned the paper over in her hands. The void language was there, printed in much smaller font than the modern language had been. Some of the letters ran off the page, likely destroyed in whatever fire had burned it away.

How long might the original prophecy have been? Surely longer than this scrap they had left. What would it have revealed about why Astrea and Jin were supposedly connected to all of this? How much information were they missing? And how much of the full version did the Paragon know?

She showed it to Jin, then he looked at Saros and asked, "Where'd my father get this?"

"I don't know," Saros said. "But he showed it to me and asked if I knew what it meant or if I'd had any visions about it. I didn't know, and I hadn't had any visions of it, but it stuck with me. After what Victor Nazarov said that day in the gardens, the day you left, and then what you told me earlier tonight, Varojin . . ."

At least Emperor Aelius didn't seem to know what it meant. But was that true, or was it just an act? Was he just trying to get information from Saros instead? Did the emperor have someone who could translate the void words?

Her pulse roared in her ears. Astrea was so, so tired. Tired of the questions, the secrets, the mission.

Yes, Saros had said he wanted to talk to them, but she just . . . couldn't. Someone else could deal with whatever this paper and egg were. At least, for tonight, someone else could deal with it. She would get back to work in the morning.

"And that's not everything—" Saros started.

"I need to sleep." Astrea's voice was flat. Exhausted.

"But—"

"I pushed myself too far." Now, her words were sharper than she intended. But Cressida had been right; she needed to rest. "I need to sleep. We . . . we can talk later."

Saros's anxiety and regret, his grief and fear, pushed into her body. They lit up the small room with orange and blue. The colors made her nauseous. Bile crawled its way up her throat.

"Here." Jin stood, cutting off Saros's next words. He snatched the blanket off his cot and draped it around Astrea's shoulder. "You sleep. I'll go check on everyone."

"You're sure?" she whispered.

"I'm sure." He kissed the top of her head. "*You* got us out of Kalama. Let me worry about what comes next."

Astrea flopped back onto the bed and curled up with the thin blanket. Regret still pushed against her, rough and cold. She peeked over her shoulder just in time to see Jin ushering Saros out the door. Her eyes began to close even as her mind ran circles around everything that had happened. She really just needed some sleep . . .

Light pierced through Astrea's impossibly heavy eyelids. Every bone in her body felt like they weighed a thousand pounds. Her head pounded. Her tongue stuck to the roof of her mouth.

The boat swayed underneath her. Astrea blinked. It was like Solstice Night all over again. Too much magic. Only a hundred times more draining.

"Hey," Cressida whispered.

Astrea's body protested as she rolled over and found her best friend lying next to her. Mint relief and heavy fatigue pushed against Astrea's skin.

Cressida didn't look much better than Astrea felt. Dark circles tinged the usually bright copper skin under her eyes. Her curls had frizzed up more than usual in the rain. Her eyes were half closed. She'd used a lot of magic, too, redirecting those missiles like she had and fighting Solana.

"What time is it?" Astrea asked.

"Don't know."

Astrea needed to get up. Somewhere on the ship, anxiety and understanding tangled together. Upstairs on the main deck, maybe?

"Where is everyone?" Cressida asked.

"Upstairs."

"Are they alright?"

"Think so." Groaning, Astrea forced her aching bones to move. She pushed up on her forearm, then swung her legs over the side of the bed. "I'll go check."

"I'm coming, just give me a moment."

As both Astrea and Cressida managed to stand up and make their way to the door, Astrea could barely focus on anything other than the pounding in her head. She was fairly certain it was her own head, too, and not ghost pain, though the exhaustion clouding her mind made her question her own judgment. They stumbled together down the two hallways that led them to the stairs, their sea legs returning with each step.

As soon as they reached the top, Cressida forced the metal door open with nothing but a wave of her hand. It creaked as it swung out, and cool night air rushed through Astrea's hair that had long since come out of its braid. Stars sparkled high above them, the only light on the dark, dark sea.

Six people stood in a loose circle halfway down the deck. Jin, Adi, and Zephyrine in their dark clothes. Saros and Balthazar in dark grays, greens, and blue. Sarsali, wearing a beautiful lavender blouse and black pants. Marko was noticeably gone, as were Magdi's crew.

Cressida stumbled forward first. Astrea followed. Sarsali and Saros met them immediately, and the others weren't far behind. Astrea hated feeling so weak. *Being* so weak.

"Any sign of the Helosians?" Cressida asked.

"No," Adi said.

"I don't like that."

"Nor do I," Jin said. His gaze flicked over Cressida's form, then Astrea's. "You two should sit."

The only problem with that was that there was really no good place to sit out here on the deck. A couple of low crates were pushed up against the side of the pilothouse. Sarsali led both Astrea and Cressida that way.

Saros tried to catch Astrea's eye as she sat down. Of course he still wanted to talk. And she knew she should talk to him. But her mind was fractured. Beyond exhausted. If he'd already waited fourteen years to tell her these things—as he'd earlier claimed—then what would be a few more hours while she collected herself?

"I don't think we should go back to Thasia," Jin said when they were settled.

"What about getting back to Talmaris?" Astrea leaned her head against the cool metal wall behind her. That was the plan, going back to Novaria.

"Important, but Kaius probably has airships headed to Tornama right now. I'm sure he's figured out Raela helped you, Az, since we got caught at the palace. Records of this ship will be easy enough to confirm with Thasian officials, even if Magdi's been careful. He'll put it together."

Astrea's eyes fluttered closed. Raela . . . "Do you think he's going to punish her?"

"I wish I could say I didn't. I'm sorry."

She tried to force her tears away, but a few slid down her cheek. She wiped them away.

"So, no Thasia. We just . . . what?" Cressida gestured out to the dark sea. "Try to sail all the way to Novaria from here? That'll take forever."

They'd have to circle around Tornama's southern peninsula, then travel all the way up the continent's eastern coast before arriving in the northern seas and heading west to Talmaris. Assuming they could do that without getting caught. Astrea scrubbed at her face.

"Kaius will tell your father, right?" she asked Jin. When he nodded, she asked, "What about Ellie and Ysabel? What's he going to do about their meeting?"

"I don't know. Marko's working on a way to get Lucian a message to warn them."

"He wouldn't attack Novaria, would he?"

"He might."

Astrea slumped against the wall. She should've just stayed asleep, let the others figure this out while she regained her strength.

Silence settled over their group, the only sound that of the water lapping against the sides of the ship. Not even Magdi came out to speak with them. Hopefully Marko would have a little luck in getting in touch with Lucian. They needed to warn the Novarians about the emperor, and they needed to warn them that the twins had been separated from the team.

"We could go to the Taipoli Islands," Zephyrine said quietly.

The Taipoli Islands were south of both Helosia and Tornama, a small nation made up of one large island and multiple smaller ones. Astrea had never been, but half of Sarsali's family was from the Islands.

"But isn't that the same issue as going to Thasia?" Adi asked. "Magdi runs rum from the Islands to the continent."

Jin scratched at his beard, then sighed. "I think it's our best bet. We might be able to charter an airship from there to get back to Talmaris. If nothing else, it buys us a little time and better ways to contact Lucian."

"What do you think, Saros?" Zephyrine asked. "Have you had any visions of the Islands?"

"None," Saros said. "Though that doesn't mean much, Lady Kanakos. You know that."

"Maybe not, but I'll take it." She smiled at the group. "What do you say we get the skies off this ship?"

Chapter 41

The midmorning sun sparkling on the ocean made Astrea squint. Seagulls circled overhead, and a few dolphin fins peeked up from the water every so often.

Though Magdi hadn't been happy about the change in course, Marko had supported the decision to head for the Taipoli Islands. Astrea pulled at the straps of her knapsack, shifting her weight from foot to foot as the land in the distance grew larger, closer.

She'd spent most of the night asleep, and still, exhaustion tugged at every inch of her body. The farther they got from Kalama, the less she could believe what she'd done to all of those Helosian guards. She could hardly believe Raela had just walked into Kaius's custody and that the twins had never made it to the boat.

But she'd have to think about all that later. Now, she needed to focus on the book and getting it back to Talmaris. Standing on the open deck helped clear her mind a little; her room had become very claustrophobic overnight.

"You've really caused me quite a mess, Marko," Magdi said as she strolled out of the pilothouse right behind the Tempest. "Rami's going to have a fit when she hears about this."

"So will my man back in Talmaris," Marko said. "Just know you're doing the entire continent a service by getting caught up in all this."

As they stopped in front of Astrea, Magdi set her hands on her thick hips. "And what, exactly, might that be? What the skies have you gotten up to that'd make the Helosians chase us like that?"

"I thought you didn't ask questions," Marko replied dryly. The captain pinned him with a look. "Let's just say there are some very bad people we've gotten ourselves mixed up with, and them achieving their goals would be very bad for business all across the continent."

Magdi grunted. "Right. Well." She extended her hand to Marko for a shake. "We'll drop you at Katavena, but then we've got to get out of here. I wish you the best of luck."

"We'll need it. So will you."

As Magdi headed back to her post, Astrea asked Marko, "You think it's going to be hard?"

"No harder than what we've come up against so far." He stared off toward Katavena—the capital of the Taipoli Islands—where a tan skyline jutted into the blue sky. "You good?"

"I'll be perfectly capable of checking for the void when we get into the city."

"I don't doubt that, but I know magical burnout when I see it. What you did . . ."

"I'd rather not talk about that right now, Marko."

His lips tugged up into a wry smile. "Just wait until Lucian hears about it. I think he'll be jealous."

Astrea actually laughed. "Skies, I hope not."

Would the commander be envious of her apparent strength? Astrea had no idea what Lucian was truly capable of, how much magical strength he really had. She was fairly certain he'd shown just a fraction of his actual power in their lessons.

As *The Starseeker* moved closer to land, Astrea's friends and family trickled upstairs one by one. Cressida joined her first, and her fatigue pressed heavily against Astrea's skin. Astrea hadn't been the only one to burn herself out. Cressida's strength with those missiles was something else, not to mention their earlier fight with Tovan and Solana. Not to mention *killing* Tovan.

Zephyrine arrived next, followed by Sarsali and Balthazar, then Saros. Adi joined them, and though he started teasing Marko about something, all Astrea could focus on was the dense orange anxiety and steel pain surrounding his body.

Jin joined them last. She hadn't had a chance to speak with him alone yet. She needed to, though. After deciding to head for the Islands, Astrea had simply gone back to sleep. She'd woken up to find Jin's body curled around hers.

"Well, there it is," Jin said as he came to stand next to Astrea. "Katavena."

"There's only one place I can think to go when we get to the city," Zephyrine said. "A place that won't ask too many questions."

"Do you think their border patrol will be looking for us?" Balthazar asked.

"Unlikely." Zephyrine ran a hand through her hair, the long white strands flowing freely around her shoulders. "Regardless of what he tells Ysabel, Emperor Aelius will be trying to clean this up quietly. Putting out an international alert for us will just make others question why he's looking for Jin. That'll blow up his whole story about sending his heirs away."

That was it, then? Trust Zephyrine to get them someplace safe in Katavena and hope they'd eventually get back to Talmaris? It wasn't exactly the most solid plan, but it was better than taking their chances in Thasia, Astrea supposed.

As soon as *The Starseeker* stopped at one of the piers, Magdi shooed them off the ship. Astrea followed closely behind Cressida and the others, Jin right at her back. Endless rows of piers stretched out into the bay, a variety of vessels already at port. Throngs of people milled about preparing to either enter or depart the city.

Everything under the sun reached out for Astrea's magic as their group joined the crowd: anger, excitement, annoyance, pain, fatigue, joy. She kept her barrier loose; she'd just have to sort through it all as best she could, even if her skin ached from the intensity.

The fake papers Rami had given them ended up getting them through Taipoli customs with little incident. But when it came time for Saros and the Nikaphoroses to present their travel papers—their *real* travel papers—Zephyrine had offered the guards several handfuls of gold coins and a thick stack of paper bills in return for no further questions or identity checks. And that had been that. They'd made it through.

"Now where?" Jin asked Zephyrine.

The corner they stood on near the port's entrance offered them little in terms of privacy. Tall palm trees lined the roads, all of them matching almost perfectly in height. Pedestrians moved up and down the crowded sidewalks, stopping to buy food from street vendors and chat among themselves. Astrea's stomach rumbled.

"This way," Zephyrine said before turning and heading west up the crowded street.

Motorcycles, cars, and trolleys congested the road, so much like Kalama that way. The buildings had both Helosian and Thasian architecture: a unique mix of pastel colors, ornately carved archways and columns, and wide windows. People around them babbled mostly in Taipoli, though Astrea heard some Helosian and Tornamian, too.

The deeper they got into the city, the taller the buildings became, though they didn't look overly modern. They stopped outside one light green building, easily a dozen stories tall. Its arched windows were covered in stained glass, each one trimmed in silver and gold. The rotating front door was flanked by two doormen, both dressed in crisp white and blue uniforms.

Zephyrine said something to one of the attendants—a man with a thick mustache and light brown skin—in Taipoli. He said something to his colleague, a pale man with red hair. They waved Zephyrine and everyone else toward the doors.

The cool interior was not what Astrea had expected. Well, she hadn't known what she was expecting, but it wasn't the clean, high-end hotel lobby spreading out before her. Some kind of safe house, maybe? Or another front like Rami's place. But not this.

To Astrea's left, a few guests were seated on a large sofa facing a two-person band. To her right, a wide check-in counter stood empty except for six tellers wearing blue. The building was as beautiful inside as it was outside, with smooth tiled floors covered by thick rugs and colorful artwork hanging on the walls. The stained glass windows cast a rainbow of colors on the floor.

"Astrea?" Zephyrine asked.

"Seems fine," she said. There was no void. Nothing to suggest the Paragon or Nazarov were around, nor anything to suggest Helosian soldiers might be lying in wait. Other than the few guests and staff, the only activity was the distinct ding of the elevator bell echoing near the back of the lobby.

Astrea paid little attention as Zephyrine went to the front desk to talk to the staff. She surveyed the lobby again, watching as peach amusement sparkled around two of the women watching the band. Their companion, a man with dark brown skin and a head just as bald as Balthazar's, chuckled, but Astrea couldn't sense anything beyond his wall.

Before long, Zephyrine returned with a handful of keys. Where had she gotten the money to pay for a place like this? Astrea didn't ask; all she really cared about was the fact that they might be able to rest for a few hours. Get some real food, not rations on the boat. Sleep on a real bed, not some stone-hard cot.

One of the elevator doors chimed as it opened, revealing two men dressed in fine linen suits. The first rolled his wheelchair out of the elevator and greeted the group in Taipoli. The second man strode out after him. Sarsali returned their greeting, but the men were already heading away.

Everyone crammed into the elevator. The inside was mirrored on three walls, the fourth plated in gold and covered in buttons. Zephyrine pushed the button for the twelfth floor as the doors slid closed.

"I was able to get us six rooms," Zephyrine said. "I figured we can take today to regroup, then start looking for a ride tomorrow."

"Not today?" Saros asked.

"I suppose we could," Zephyrine said, "but skies damn it, I'm exhausted. I'll see how I feel after a nap and something to eat." She began passing out room keys: one for Sarsali and Balthazar, one for Astrea and Jin, one for Adi and Marko, then the remaining three split between her, Cressida, and Saros. "Call down for room service. It's all taken care of."

The elevator stopped its ascent. The doors slid open, revealing an empty, carpeted hallway beyond. A plaque on the wall across from the elevator showed the direction for different room numbers, the digits painted in gold. Zephyrine turned right.

They walked single file down the hallway until she finally stopped at the end. They all split off toward their own rooms. Jin unlocked the door for room 1216, then flipped on the lights as he entered ahead of Astrea. The room wasn't as spacious as where they'd been staying in Talmaris, but it was nice. Soft gray linens covered the canopy bed. There was even a settee and two side chairs separated by a coffee table. Sage green wallpaper decorated with a vine pattern and the warm-tone wood furniture made it feel cozy rather than luxurious.

Astrea locked the door behind her, then peeked into the bathroom. It was bright, made with marble floors and fixtures. The faucets in the sink and shower were gold.

"Well," Jin said as Astrea joined him near the bed. "We're here."

Stepping closer to Jin, Astrea wrapped her arms around his waist. He relaxed into the embrace as his arms circled her shoulders.

"Do you think Saros is going to kill me for sharing a room with you?"

Astrea actually laughed. "Maybe. I don't know with him anymore." She sighed and rested her head against Jin's chest. Despite him having changed into dry clothes on the ship, he smelled faintly of sea water. "I need to talk to him more."

There was a lot she needed to do, actually. She needed to finally check out Theo's book and figure out what was so important about it that everyone wanted it. She needed to check in with Cressida and Adi both. She needed to talk to Saros more about this prophecy he'd stolen from Emperor Aelius's office.

"How about you start the shower?" Jin suggested. "I'll make the rounds to make sure Zephyrine was serious about taking time to regroup. I think we all need a moment."

A moment sounded good. Besides, even through the walls, Astrea could feel everyone's fatigue. It had been an incredibly long night.

As Jin slipped back into the hall, Astrea started the shower. Its water remained cool for the first couple minutes, but by the time Jin returned, it had heated up to pleasantly warm.

"We'll regroup after we all clean up," Jin said.

"Not listening to Zephyrine's suggestion to take the day, then?" Astrea asked as she wiggled out of her clothes.

"No, and I don't think she'll follow through on it, either. There's too much to do."

Jin stripped down to nothing at all. As they stepped under the warm water, he pulled her close again. They said nothing, just held onto each other for a few moments before they began to clean up. The hotel's soap and shampoo both smelled of clementine and nectarine, a welcome replacement to the sea and salt stuck to Astrea's skin.

By the time they were done, the bathroom mirror had begun to fog over. Holding her towel with one hand, Astrea wiped some of the condensation away with the other. She'd just started gathering up her wet hair when Jin appeared behind her.

"Let me," he said, already reaching around her shoulders to pull her hair to her back again. "One braid?"

"Yeah, thanks."

As Jin combed his fingers through her hair, working through tangles gently, Astrea watched him in the mirror. Dark circles had made their home under his eyes. His wall was tight. Impassable.

"Jin."

He met her gaze in their reflection.

"Are you alright?"

"Tired." Jin went back to his task, arranging her long hair into three sections. "It's not that I expected any of that to go smoothly, but . . ."

"Yeah." Astrea played with the edge of her towel, rolling the fluffy blue fabric between her thumb and pointer finger.

Jin sucked in a deep breath as he started twisting her hair into a braid. "Do you think we're really these people from this prophecy?"

"No," Astrea said. "I think there's some reason the Paragon have pinned this on us, but I don't believe in prophecies." She never had. "Saros has always told me that people's choices change every day, and that's what influences the future. That's why some visions don't come to pass. And I think that's what's happening. The Paragon are trying to force us down this path . . . to force their prophecy to come true."

Jin nodded. "Me too." His fingers worked the last stretch of hair into the braid, then he draped it over her shoulder. "Should we eat now?" Jin asked as they returned to the bedroom in search of clean clothes.

"I just need to do one more thing."

Astrea was hungry, but she also still hadn't healed her wounds from the fight in Kalama. She sat on the edge of the bed, then loosened her grip on her towel and let it fall. The wound on her thigh wasn't the worst, mostly shallow and superficial. Soft white glow emanated from her palm, weaving between her fingers and around her thick thigh. Mirror healing and pain warred on her skin for just a few heartbeats. She did the same on her calf.

When she looked up, she found Jin staring at her. Her face heated. "What?"

"Just thinking that I'm really glad you're alright."

"Because I'm sitting here naked?"

As he laughed, sweet amusement coated Astrea's tongue. "While that's certainly not bad," he said, circling the bed to join her, "no, that's not why. I've never had to work so hard during a mission to stay focused on the task at hand. I was so worried."

She pulled her towel back around herself, not out of shyness but it seemed entirely inappropriate to be naked with what she was about to bring up. "Cress and I handled it."

"I know, and I'm so proud of you."

Astrea's heart flipped, then sank. "I'm sorry we had to leave without Lennor, Civan, and Adi's sister."

"They'll be alright . . . I'm sure they'll have gone to Rasa for help."

"That's your old teammate, right?" Astrea asked, trying to recall some of the stories he'd told her over the last couple of months.

"Yes, and she eventually took Zephyrine's spot and became our commanding officer for a while. She knows the twins well, and she shares Zephyrine's politics. Lennor and Civan know to go to her."

Astrea nodded. If Jin trusted Lennor and Civan and this Rasa, Astrea would trust them, too.

"We'll see them again when we get to Talmaris. Just might take a while," Jin said. She nodded again. "Now, should we get dressed and call down for something to eat?" he asked, voice teasing. "Or are you going to just sit there like that all day?"

"I'm pretty certain you'd like it if I sat around in nothing but a towel all day."

"And I'm certain I'd like it even better if there was no towel." Jin kissed her cheek. "Come on."

Jin pulled her off the bed, and as Astrea began pulling clothes out of her knapsack, she tried to let Jin's words sink in. Not about her in no towel but about the rest of the team.

They'd get back to Talmaris one way or another. They had to.

Chapter 42

Though Astrea didn't want to get out of bed, she couldn't stay there all day. She'd slept for just an hour while they waited for hotel staff to bring up the food they'd ordered. As someone knocked on the door, Jin pressed a sleepy kiss to Astrea's neck, then rolled out of bed.

Sitting up with a sigh, Astrea smoothed wrinkles out of her skirt. Jin cracked the door open, and it wasn't hotel staff waiting in the hallway. He opened the door wider, revealing Cressida. Heavy fatigue and anxiety pulsed against Astrea's skin.

"Can I come in?" she asked.

Jin stepped to one side and waved her in. "You don't have to ask us that, Cress."

"Yes, well, skies knew what was going on in here." Cressida's somber tone made the joke fall flat. "I don't want to intrude."

"It's no intrusion. Come sit." Astrea gestured to the settee. "Food should be here soon."

Jin yawned as he locked the door and followed Cressida over to the small sitting area. He flipped on the floor lamp nestled in one corner, then the one on the bedside table. They'd kept the drapes drawn tightly shut for their nap, and he didn't move to open them.

Sitting next to Cressida, Astrea reached for her hand. "Let me see your arm."

"I already cleaned them up again," Cressida said as Astrea unwound the bandages.

A few gashes marred Cressida's otherwise smooth skin, but the worst of the blood had been washed away, and they looked to be healing already. Still, Astrea tugged on her light, just a faint, stubborn trickle of energy under her skin. It glowed softly as it sank into Cressida's skin. The mirror pain wasn't even that bad.

Flashing a weak half smile, Cressida said, "Thanks, Az."

"I take it that wasn't what was bothering you," Astrea said as Cressida deflated.

"No, but I still appreciate it."

"Then what's wrong?"

"I just . . ." Cressida rubbed her eyes. "I don't know. I don't feel very good."

"In what way?" Astrea sensed nothing from her best friend other than the fatigue. It overwhelmed everything else in the room.

"I didn't . . ." Cressida peeked up at Jin, then Astrea. "I didn't expect to kill anyone yesterday, and I really didn't expect . . ."

"The meteorite to do what it did?" Astrea offered. Cressida nodded as mint relief and deep blue regret twined around her. "You didn't know it would do *that*."

"I know it's good he's dead, and I did what I had to do, but I keep seeing . . ."

"On my first mission with Zephyrine's team years ago, I had reservations about taking lives," Jin said. "I didn't think I could do it, even if I had to. But I did. And it was awful. It's still awful, every single time."

Cressida swallowed hard. "Really?"

"Two things can be true at the same time. You can regret taking another person's life while also knowing you had to do it to save your own.

Although frankly"—Jin's voice hardened—"I'm glad Tovan's dead. He was at the top of my list with Nazarov."

A choked laugh escaped Cressida. "Yeah."

It was strange, being glad that Tovan couldn't hurt her ever again while also feeling bad that he'd suffered like that woman behind the museum in Kalama months ago. Astrea still couldn't forget the way that strange void magic burned in her veins, either on that night so long ago or when Tovan died the night before.

Skies, how had it been just one night?

"Right, well." Cressida nodded. "It does make me feel a little better knowing that, Jin. Thanks."

"Adi feels the same," Jin said. "He and I have talked about it a lot over the years. Never truly gets easier to deal with. Take it one day at a time."

"When did you get so wise?" Cressida asked.

"War does that to a man, I suppose." He smiled wryly just as someone else knocked on the door, then announced room service in heavily accented Helosian. "At least lunch is here."

Not only did Jin roll in a two-tier cart laden with food, but Adi strolled in behind him. All things considered, he seemed okay. Quieter than usual, that was for sure. But he walked with his head held high and shoulders back. Astrea wasn't sure she could look so confident if part of the mission involving her family had failed.

The two men brought over several dishes covered by silver domes and set them on the small coffee table. Astrea hadn't even really paid attention when Jin had been ordering, but whatever he'd chosen, it smelled good. Her stomach growled.

"Does Marko want to join us?" Jin asked Adi as they both sat down in the chairs across from Astrea and Cressida.

Adi shrugged. "He was sleeping when I left the room. Figured you and I needed to debrief."

"I don't know what there is to say," Jin replied.

"You think your father will go after Rasa now?"

"I sure hope not."

Cressida lifted the dome off the nearest dish as she asked, "Who's Rasa?"

Astrea began uncovering the dishes closer to her. Her stomach rumbled again as she spotted the potato fritters Sarsali sometimes made. She loved those potato fritters. She couldn't remember the last time Sarsali had made them.

"Our old teammate who eventually became our commanding officer," Adi said. "She's still in the military. Oversees a special unit. Civan and Len would go to her in the event something like this happened."

"And she's trustworthy?" Cressida asked as she took a helping of fritters for herself.

"I'd trust her with any of our lives," Jin said.

"Are you alright, Adi?" Astrea asked. "I know it must be hard . . ."

In the months Astrea had known Adi, she'd rarely see his smile falter. He was always finding the bright side and making the most of bad days. But now, despite his shoulders being pushed back, orange anxiety twined around his body in thick, tight knots.

"Honestly, no, but if I think about it, I won't be able to focus on what we need to do." He sighed. "Anything in that book you two got?"

"I haven't looked." Astrea had *wanted* to look through it, but trying to escape Helosia had seemed more important. So had sleeping. She'd be no use to anyone if she was burnt out like she had been. "I was going to after this."

As they ate, Astrea relaxed a little. Cressida quizzed Jin and Adi about the safety of this new plan—particularly staying in a hotel, to which the two men had no objections. She then recounted some of the fight with Tovan and Solana to them.

"You could control Solana?" Adi asked. "I thought you couldn't do that to void mages."

"Lucian and I thought we might be able to with an opening," Astrea said. "And I guess we were right."

"That's good, then." Adi popped a piece of chicken covered in spicy green sauce in his mouth. "I mean, that gives you another tool."

"That Nazarov will know I can do," Astrea said. "Solana got away."

What if Solana told Nazarov and then he found a way to completely block her out? It wouldn't be that hard, or at least she didn't think so. Jin kept her blocked out most of the time without even consciously doing so. A little effort on Nazarov's part would surely have him untouchable again.

"Nazarov's not that levelheaded," Jin said, a faint sheen of red rage blossoming around him. "He'll slip up."

Astrea wasn't so sure, but she nodded. "Well, either way." She finished the last of her meal, the perfect bite of leftover sauce with leftover potatoes. "I should get to work on that book."

After passing her dirty dishes to Jin, Astrea went to the bathroom and washed her hands, then grabbed her knapsack off the floor where she'd tossed it before her nap. The inside was mostly empty, as she now had on the last of her clean clothes and had dropped the dirty ones in a pile on the ground. She pulled Theo's book out, running one hand over the black cloth cover.

"What do you think it says?" Cressida called from her spot on the settee.

"I have no idea."

That was the question. What could one volume, one that wasn't even that thick, tell them about the void? What could it possibly say that the Paragon would torture her over it? That the emperor would go to such great lengths to get?

Smoothing out the blankets, Astrea climbed back onto the bed and pulled the book in front of her. As she flipped open the front cover and began examining the title page, someone knocked on the door.

"For skies sake," Jin muttered as Adi went to answer it.

"Oh, Zephyrine." Adi stepped to one side to let the general into the room.

"I just wanted to let you know I'm going into the city." Her gaze flicked to Cressida, then Astrea. "Sarsali, Balthazar, and Saros are going with me to get some supplies."

"Do you want me to join you?" Astrea asked. She hadn't felt any voids since Solana the night before, but . . .

"Quite alright." Zephyrine flashed a quick smile. "We're just going to a market a few blocks away. I've been there many times; it won't be an issue. I actually came to see if anyone had special requests."

"Not really," Jin said. "Maybe an extra set of clothes if you can find them."

"Already on my list. What else?"

"If there are any jewelers at the market, could you look for more meteorite?" Cressida unhooked her necklace, then guided it through the air with her magic. It landed in Zephyrine's palm. "Ask Saros to look at this, too."

Zephyrine closed her hand around the necklace, and when they all agreed they didn't need anything else, she said, "Alright then. We'll reconvene in a couple hours."

Once the general was gone, Astrea asked, "Where'd she get the money for all this?"

"She's not the first Helosian noble I've known to have a bank account in another country," Jin said.

"Right, well . . ." Astrea supposed it didn't really matter. Zephyrine Kanakos didn't seem like the type to draw attention to her true identity or the rest of them if she could help it. "I need to look through this."

"I'll call down for coffee," Jin said.

"Mind if we stay?" Cressida asked.

"No," Astrea said. "No, I'm sure this is something we all need to see anyway."

As her friends settled down, Astrea took a deep breath and flipped to the first page of the book. This was it. It was time for her answers.

By the time Astrea was just halfway through Theo's book, her mind was a jumbled mess. So much information. It was so much information, almost like the Paragon's doctrine and history mixed together.

First, there'd been a story about a mountain king, just like the one Astrea had found back in Talmaris. Only this one told a different version, one that mixed the myth and history, just as Theo had promised. The Novarian version said the mountain king had been looking for his lost daughter in the mountains and eventually fought a "monster of darkness" to bring her to safety.

The Paragon's version, though, said the mountain king was an invader on void mage lands, and the various clans of the time banded together to fight back against him. The mage who united them? Tytas Ramkas, the first One of the Paragon. He had armed the clans with powerful weapons and brought together both void mages and other types of mages, all to stop the mountain king from encroaching on their territory more than he had.

Tytas Ramkas was heralded as a hero in all the stories about him in this book. Not just for pushing back against that mountain king, but for pushing back against the Fireweaver king and Novarian queen Astrea had already read about back in Talmaris. In this version, the Paragon called that Fireweaver the Sun King, though. And just like the version from the history book back in Talmaris, the united Fireweavers and Novarians did ultimately decimate Ramkas's forces once they allied. He'd died in that battle, and the mantle of The One had passed to his eldest daughter, Silya, who was a Dreamwalker.

Small annotations in the void language popped up in the margins every now and then, but Astrea couldn't make sense of them or find any pattern in how frequently they appeared. And beyond all of that, there was everything about void magic, which she was just starting to dive into.

"Look at this." She barely breathed the words as she pointed to a subsection in the chapter she'd started a few minutes before.

Jin, Adi, and Cressida had all piled on the bed with her at some point. They all leaned in to get a better look.

The passage detailed dreamwalking, which Astrea already felt confident she understood. It didn't offer much new information about that branch of void magic. It also talked about the void mages' ability to jump from location to location, confirming what they knew about long jumps being impossible. But none of that was all that important. What had Astrea's bones buzzing unpleasantly was the next bit.

"Lifestealers are able to pull the life out of others." Adi stared at the rest of them, mouth agape. "Are you fucking kidding me?"

"Keep reading," Astrea said.

"Lifestealers are able to pull the life out of others," he repeated. "And this energy they take is granted to themselves."

"Like . . . like healing themselves," Cressida said. "At the expense of another person."

"Balance," Astrea whispered. "It always goes back to balance. I'm a healer, and they're . . ."

"Something else," Jin said quietly from next to her.

"Have we met any Lifestealers yet?" Cressida asked.

"I don't think so. I mean, maybe I have, but they obviously didn't kill me. I don't know." Astrea ran a hand over her face and sighed. "But if they're Lifestealers, why did the Paragon call me a Souleater? How is my magic different from lightbringing?"

"Maybe it's not," Jin said.

"Yours is," Astrea retorted. "You're a Sunreaper. That's different, right?"

"What's different?" Cressida asked.

"I know why they call me a Sunreaper, Cress." As Jin explained his ability to create immense explosions with his magic, a nauseating mix of horror and curiosity pulsed out from Cressida. "But you don't know you're different, Az."

"And this lightbringing ability Lucian taught me?" Astrea asked. "You don't think that's what classifies me as a Souleater instead?"

"Could it be some kind of subtype of Lightbringer?" Adi asked. "I didn't realize such a thing existed, but if Jin's fireweaving is . . . fireweaving *and* the other thing he can do . . ."

It was the only thing Astrea could think of. So if that made Lucian a Souleater, too, was he wrong? He'd theorized that some people forgot about or hid Lightbringers' strength, but perhaps many Lightbringers didn't know about the ability because they truly couldn't do it.

"Let's just move on," Astrea said. Debating the origins of Souleaters didn't seem particularly useful, especially without any more data points.

The next dozen pages dove into the specifics of void magic, things they'd already seen firsthand. The ability to swallow a Lightbringer's light, jumping locations, the vast reach of dreamwalking with powerful mages. There was more about how the void mages could manipulate shadows, too, and how the ancient void mage armies used to cover their faces in shadow—like masks—before going into battle during the Great Wars.

The next chapter dove into Silya Ramkas again; the book was a little disorganized, but it was also hand-written and very, very old. Some first-hand account, most likely.

"Silya Ramkas, like her father before her, was a powerful mage," Adi read out loud. "After their ranks were decimated thanks to the Sun King's efforts, Silya enacted a new tactic. Her dreamwalking was so powerful that she could drive people mad, and so she targeted the Sun King, sending him nightmares full of monsters and terrible visions that convinced him to betray his Novarian allies."

"To be fair, I would do the same if someone decimated my army and was trying to take over my territory," Cressida said. She glanced at Jin. "This was the start of the Helosian Empire, right? So he was, what, your great-great-great . . . well, your ancestor?"

"I assume so," Jin said. "The Aurises have been ruling since the Great Wars."

"Sorry about him going mad."

"Don't be. I'm sure he deserved far worse."

"Wait," Adi said. "Look."

Astrea blinked hard, her eyes growing heavy with so much reading. "Silya knew her father had bestowed powerful weapons to their greatest warriors, weapons of aetherium."

"Aetherium?" Cressida asked. "What the fuck is that?"

"Silya had her smiths create more weapons with these gifts from the void, promising her people that her father, the great Tytas, had been chosen by the stars to receive such favor," Astrea continued. "These weapons, though rare, granted wielders the power of Lifestealers, though it could not grant the user the strength they stole."

"Fuck," Cressida whispered. Cold horror bled into the room. "Oh, shit. Shit, that's what's in my room, isn't it?"

"Only—" Astrea shuddered. "Only the strongest Metalli, with aid from the strongest Sunreapers, could create the conditions necessary to forge aetherium blades."

"Oh, fuck me." Burying her fingers in her hair, Cressida said, "Fuck, Jin, I didn't realize—I didn't *think* that— We made a fucking Paragonian weapon! By *accident*!"

"How could you ever have known that?" Jin asked. "That's not your fault."

Astrea flipped through the next few pages. The story continued, explaining that Silya never was able to recoup the Paragon's lost numbers, nor was she able to defeat the Sun King even once he lost his Novarian alliance. The Paragonian ruler retreated with her people to the mountains, hiding away from those who sought to conquer them. Silya became paranoid that the new governments forming would grow too powerful, or that perhaps worse, they would somehow capture some of these aetherium weapons. She eventually ordered them destroyed to prevent such a fate.

"Maybe that's where the tunnels came from," Adi said. "And the ruins. The old weapons."

"I mean . . ." Cressida trailed off, orange anxiety sparking around her. "I just can't believe it. My tests, Mariya's test . . . they didn't point to a new element."

"Maybe aetherium is something found in certain meteorites," Astrea said. "Not all meteorites."

"And that long ago," Adi added, "I doubt the Paragon or anyone would've separated it out from the ore. They probably discovered its power and just named it."

"So what we thought was meteorite was actually this aetherium?" Jin asked.

"Seems so," Cressida mumbled.

That would explain why the meteorite felt strange to Saros and Mariya. To Astrea and Lucian, too. Aetherium.

"We should assume my father knows all of this," Jin said. "Assume he's already read through this whole book multiple times."

But what did they do about that? What *could* they do about that?

In that moment? Not a damn thing.

Still, Astrea asked, "What now?"

"We need to talk to Balthazar and Saros," Jin said. "And we need to figure out where we're going next."

CHAPTER 43

Detailing the findings of the void magic book to the rest of the group was the easy part of what Astrea had to do. What concerned her most was the fact that Saros and Balthazar had never heard of aetherium ore.

"My father really didn't ask you about it, Balthazar?" Jin asked, arms folded tightly across his chest.

They'd gathered in Jin and Astrea's room once the others had returned from the market and Marko had woken up. The space certainly wasn't large enough for all eight of them, and they were all crammed into the sitting area and bed. Astrea fidgeted with the folds in her skirt.

"He mentioned nothing of the sort," Balthazar said. Next to him on the settee, Sarsali played with the end of her long braid. "Didn't ask me about it, nor did he suggest I look into it."

"Could that be what he's looking for in the Badlands?" Adi asked.

"He sent us to Fort Blackrock and a ways away to look at another piece of meteorite he'd dug up," Saros said quietly. "Nothing that would suggest a new metal."

"The book said that only the strongest Metalli and these . . . Sun-reapers"—Balthazar glanced at Jin—"could create the conditions to craft aetherium weapons. The heat and pressure generated between those two probably trigger these properties somehow."

"Perhaps," Marko drawled from his spot near the hotel room door, "I should get a message to Commander Lucian sooner rather than later. Tomas and Mariya can begin looking into this."

"Should we go to the Badlands and try to find this aetherium?" Cressida asked.

"I think we'll have to, especially since my father seems to have found a lot of it," Jin said, "but I'd rather not be running around the desert with no real direction. Let's keep looking at this book."

Astrea ground her teeth together. What else was there in the book? In the last few chapters, there had been information about other tactics both Tytas and Silya Ramkas used during the Great Wars, their dwindling army, and their decision to go into hiding. Silya and her successor—her son—ultimately began installing spies in royal courts around the continent as the Great Wars died down, all in hopes of influencing the larger powers and keeping void magic as much of a secret as possible so they could live in peace and privacy.

It was a shame that the early Paragon had felt the need to do so. Just how much devastation had the other armies wrought to lead to Silya Ramkas making that decision? For the Paragon to *remain* hidden for so long? Surely it was to ensure their survival, at least for a while. So what had happened to lead them to their current creed, the one about chaos, balance, and destruction? The ancient Stargazer's vision? Some long-simmering desire for revenge after their losses in the Great Wars?

Astrea sighed. Ultimately, all of that information, while helpful context in piecing together more about the Paragon, didn't exactly lead them to this aetherium ore the emperor—and surely the Paragon—was after.

"I still think we should try to get back to Talmaris," Marko said. "As soon as possible."

"We will," Zephyrine said. "Get another message to Commander Lucian about this, and do let him know we're looking for a way back."

"And ask him for any updates about my father," Jin said.

Marko nodded. "I'll need a day or two to get it all sorted."

"I'll need that time to make travel arrangements for us anyway," Zephyrine replied.

A day or two. That seemed reasonable to Astrea, even if she hated delays. Maybe this would be good. The Helosians would certainly be sniffing around, and if they could lay low here in Katavena for a bit longer, it might throw Emperor Aelius's people off their trail.

"But stay ready to leave at a moment's notice, as I may be able to get us passage sooner if I grease enough palms." Zephyrine pushed out of her seat and gestured to a few jute tote bags on the floor. Astrea had some just like that back at the observatory in Kalama, ones she'd always used when she went to the market or shopping with Cressida. "Some extra things for everyone. Marko?"

"Right behind you," he said as he followed Zephyrine out into the hallway.

Jin had just started to speak when Saros said, "Astrea, Varojin, may I speak with both of you?"

Astrea stiffened. Though there was no malice in his words, she felt like a child in trouble, one who was about to be scolded. But she couldn't put off their talk any longer. This was the second time he'd asked in half a day.

Hesitating, Astrea pushed herself off the bed, then she and Jin followed Saros out the door. He headed for the room two doors down and unlocked it with a small brass key.

Its interior was identical to Jin and Astrea's room, though some of the bed linens were white instead of gray. Another shopping tote sat in the middle of the untouched bed.

Astrea loitered near the settee but didn't sit down, not even when Jin tried to nudge her that way. She folded her arms across her chest. "What do you want to talk about, Uncle?"

"Everything I should've told you a long time ago," Saros said. "Do you remember when we moved to Kalama and I had the vision of you dying on the battlefield?"

"Yes." Astrea had never forgotten it. "And then you made me hide myself away from my friends and all the people I loved—"

"For your safety."

Staring at Saros now, hearing him try to justify everything again without thinking about her feelings . . . all the anger and frustration that had been building in her since the start of summer simmered just under her skin. "I understand that. But did you ever stop to think about what that would do to me? All of that hiding? Years spent terrified the emperor was going to come and throw us in his dungeon? I was just a child, and you put an impossible task on my shoulders."

"Of course I thought about it!" Saros folded his arms across his chest, his voice softening as he said, "Not a day goes by that I haven't regretted all this."

Astrea sucked in one deep breath, then another. Leaning into that anger felt . . . good. And wrong. Nice to finally say it to Saros's face, but awful and sickening at the same time.

He'd taken great care of her, provided everything she needed . . . except for the space and safety to be herself as she fully was. A Lightbringer—or Souleater, apparently. Yes, it was to save her, but to never have that freedom . . . Her head and heart hurt.

"Before you left Kalama," Saros said quietly, "I told you I'd had visions of you."

"It wasn't fair of you to tell me that." Astrea's voice cracked on the last word as fresh anger rolled through her. "You should've told me what that meant. Was it about this prophecy? The one you found in the emperor's office?"

"I know I should have." Saros stared down at his wingtip shoes. "But it was not about this prophecy. At least, that was never how it seemed to me."

"Then what was it?" As Astrea's voice cracked again, Jin took her hand in his.

"Varojin was in them, too," Saros said, his gaze flicking to their joined hands. A ghost of a smile crossed his face. "The first vision of the two of you came when Astrea was fourteen. It was you two as adults. You, Astrea, surrounded by mages with reddish eyes. Varojin among *them*. All I knew was you were in danger in that vision, Astrea. I thought that perhaps, because I'd had you hide your magic, it wouldn't happen. The vision ended with Varojin fireweaving."

"So?" Astrea asked.

"So I didn't know if he was attacking you or the other mages. I couldn't tell."

"You truly thought Jin would attack me even after all the years we were friends?" Astrea asked.

"I know he's always cared about you—"

"And yet you still thought he would turn on me?" she snapped.

"I wasn't willing to take that chance!" Saros exclaimed. "Skies, Astrea, I could not risk it. I could not risk losing you." He sighed. "Right around when you turned eighteen, Varojin . . ." Deep blue shame exploded in the room, cold against Astrea's skin.

"What?" Jin asked. "What about it?"

"Right around then, your father told me he was going to send you away and asked if I'd foreseen anything. Selfishly, I wanted you away from Astrea because of that earlier vision. I told him you were destined to win wars."

"You what?" Astrea nearly choked. Hot anger pooled in her belly. Saros . . . had influenced the emperor's decision to send Jin away?

"He was going to send me away regardless." Jin squeezed Astrea's hand slightly, and she glanced up at him just long enough to see lavender surprise and crimson anger flash around him. It was gone a moment later, replaced by his heavy wall. "It wouldn't have mattered what you said, Saros."

"And yet I cannot help but feel responsible for that," Saros said. "I certainly didn't help your situation."

Jin pressed his lips together.

"I thought everything was fine for years," Saros admitted. "Until I had another vision of you fireweaving, Varojin. Only this time, the destruction . . . I had no idea what it was, but I knew no mage should be that powerful. I told no one. But your father kept poking me for information about you for years, and I always lied."

"Sunreaper," Astrea whispered as she stared at Jin. Saros had foreseen Jin unlocking that aspect of his magic.

"And when you came home this summer, of course I wasn't pleased to see you," Saros said. "But with everything going on, it was obvious your father was up to no good. I didn't know what to do. Even with those visions . . . well, as I said before, I know you've always cared about Astrea, and this summer, it became clear you still resented your father. After Solstice Night, when you said you didn't think her hiding her magic was a crime, asking for your help getting her away from Kalama seemed like the only acceptable risk."

"You hoped to avoid those first two visions of Astrea on the battlefield by sending her away," Jin said.

Even if that was all true. Even if Saros had thought he was trying to protect her and save her life . . .

"You should have told me," Astrea said. "I had a right to know all that, Uncle. At least about the visions with me in them. I could've . . ." Well, she didn't know what she would've done. But she had a right to know. "What about that note you left me?"

"I've made so many mistakes over the years, Astrea. You have to understand," Saros pleaded. "I couldn't even foresee your mother's death. My own sister's death. I thought that because I had seen yours, if I kept the truth hidden—and you as hidden as I could—it wouldn't come to pass. I couldn't let you die. I couldn't fail you the way I'd failed her."

"And the note?" Astrea asked again. The note still tucked away somewhere in her belongings up in Talmaris.

"I wanted to apologize to you when you got back from Sezia," Saros said. "And, well . . . everything just got out of hand."

"But you said your visions of me were true. How are they true?"

"The red eyes. What you saw in Sezia told me that was not the end of those red eyes. Which means you and Varojin will be facing them—"

"We already have." Astrea had come so close to Victor Nazarov and The One and those red eyes. Maybe not exactly in the way Saros's vision played out, but she'd still faced them. She'd barely made it out.

"And you haven't had any other visions of us since then?" Jin asked.

"No." Saros's mouth set in a hard line. "I'm sorry."

"Sorry for what?" Astrea asked. "That you didn't tell us or that you haven't had another vision?"

"All of it!" Saros ran a hand through his dark hair. "I'm sorry for all of it, Astrea. I became blinded by my own obsession with . . . with all of this! But you have to understand, Astrea. I thought I was doing what I had to."

Astrea's chest heaved as she swallowed the words on the tip of her tongue. Saros shouldn't have kept any of that from her. He shouldn't have. But was it that simple? Could she really claim she would make different choices if faced with the same dilemma? She liked to think she would, but she couldn't say for sure.

"And I'm sorry, Varojin," Saros said. "I'm sorry I told your father to send you away. Trying to protect Astrea shouldn't have come at the cost of throwing you under the streetcar."

Astrea sucked in one deep breath, then another. She needed to be calm. She needed to stay in control. Blowing up at Saros would do neither of them any good. And besides, frustrated as she was with his secrets, she'd missed him. She was so glad he was standing there in front of her. How was it possible to both want to yell at him and hug him at the same time?

"I appreciate you being honest, Saros," Jin said, "though, as I said earlier, what you did or didn't tell my father was never going to change his course of action. I'm fairly certain he always intended to put me on the battlefield, even if I hadn't ended up with Auris magic."

"Yes, well, that doesn't make what I did right." Saros cleared his throat as he stared at her. It was like he was asking her some silent question, something Astrea didn't fully understand.

"I should go check in with Adi," Jin said quietly. He untangled his fingers from Astrea's. "Do either of you need anything?"

"No," Saros and Astrea said at the same time.

Jin smiled tightly at Astrea, then headed out the door. It closed behind him with a soft thunk.

She would need to check in with Jin later. He might've said Saros didn't have much of an effect on the emperor sending him off to war, but it didn't sit right with Astrea. He'd been through so much. And that tiny hint of surprise and rage she'd gleaned from him said enough.

"Astrea." Saros's voice was somehow firm and gentle.

"What?" Swallowing hard, she forced herself to look him in the eye.

"I was going to ask if you're alright. All that magic last night . . . all you've learned . . ."

"I'm fine."

"You're not."

Tears burned Astrea's eyes and throat with such suddenness that she almost choked. Of course she wasn't fine, and of course Saros could see that. He'd raised her. But she couldn't tell him. How could she tell him about all that had happened? How could she tell him about the Paragon and that house, the way that heartache followed her like a shadow?

She wasn't strong enough to bear the pain it would cause him. Because Astrea may have been upset with him, but she knew Saros so well. He'd blame himself. He'd start to question all his decisions—more than he already was—and wonder what could've been different. He'd start to question all of it, just like she was. And Astrea couldn't bear it.

But if she didn't tell him, would someone else? Would Cressida tell her parents? Would Commander Lucian or Grand Duchess Ysabel eventually reveal what had happened? The information would get to Saros somehow.

And she deserved to tell her own story. She deserved to tell it on her own time, when she was ready and when she wanted to.

"I'm not," Astrea whispered.

"What happened?"

Astrea wiped at her wet cheeks. "It's just been a lot," she said, a half-truth. She would tell him everything someday. "It's been hard being away from home, and it's been hard trying to figure this all out. I'm exhausted."

"I'm sorry. If I had just made different choices . . ."

"But you didn't." Astrea's words were sharp, quick. That anger from earlier surged forth, heating her entire body. "I know it must have felt impossible for you to navigate, Uncle, but you should have told me. You should have found someone to train me in case your visions did come true. But you didn't, and it's too late. I don't need more apologies or for you to feel sorry for yourself."

"Astrea—"

"I can't believe you tried to send Jin away," she whispered. "Skies, I always knew you didn't like him, but trying to get him sent off to war . . . Did you know he almost died during the Delian-Helosian War?"

"No, I didn't."

"Well, he did."

"That's not my fault."

"Maybe not directly, but I just—"

"You're right that I'm not faultless," Saros said with a huff. "But—"

What right did Saros have to be huffing and puffing about this? "But nothing."

"*But*," Saros continued emphatically, "what did you expect me to do? Not put your life ahead of his? You're my niece. You're like a daughter to me! Of course I prioritized you."

"I wish you'd told me. I wish you'd told me all of it."

Because, Astrea reasoned, maybe if she'd known for years that some of this might come to pass, she could've been prepared. If she'd known Saros had seen her surrounded by void mages, perhaps she could've found someone in Kalama to train her. Maybe then she wouldn't have been so unprepared when it came time to face them. Maybe then Nazarov wouldn't have hurt her the way he did. Maybe he never would've been able to take her in the first place.

Somewhere deep down, Astrea knew thinking that way wasn't going to fix anything. What had happened had already happened. There was no changing it. Just as knowing this potential future could've helped her be prepared, it was just as likely she wouldn't have been able to find someone willing to teach her in secret, and it was just as likely that even if she had, the emperor could've found out about it. Even if she'd been highly trained, who was to say the Paragon still wouldn't have captured her?

There was no life without risks. There were no guarantees of anything, no matter how prepared one was. Jin had been highly trained but, in the chaos of war, had still almost lost it all. Astrea couldn't let herself get stuck on the what-ifs.

That didn't make her any less angry with Saros, though.

"All my life, you've hidden things from me," Astrea said. "Ever since Mom died. And while I understand you thought you were doing what was right, it's only left me at a disadvantage, so I need you to start being honest with me today."

"I will be," Saros said. "I promise."

"Then I need to ask you something."

"Anything."

Astrea sucked in a steadying breath. "Did Mom know about void magic?"

"What?" Gray confusion burst to life around Saros, heavy and oppressive. "Why?"

"Jin's mother's family was tied to the Paragon. We think she seduced the emperor to try to have Jin and fulfill this prophecy, so we thought maybe Mom—"

"I truly don't think your mother knew about the Paragon or void magic, Astrea."

"Then do you know who my father is?"

"We've been over this before," he said gently. "I don't know."

"You weren't just keeping it from me?"

"A fair question, I suppose, but no. Your mother never told me, and I was just preparing to go off to university when she had you. I never pushed the subject; it seemed like an invasion of her privacy."

"Do you know anything about him?"

Saros regarded her, his silver eyes dull in the room's low light. Outside, the sun had begun to sink lower in the sky. Soon, night would fall.

"Why is this so important to you?" he asked.

Why was it important? Hadn't she *just* told him why it was important? That they'd figured out Jin's mother had been trying to fulfill some prophecy. And if Astrea's mother hadn't gotten pregnant with that goal in mind, how had the Paragon connected Astrea to this ancient vision? Her father was the next obvious link. It was so clear to Astrea. How could Saros not see it?

But he hadn't seen those visions The One had sent her. Hadn't seen any of it, just like Astrea didn't know the exact details of Saros's visions. In fact . . .

"What do your visions feel like?" she asked. When his eyebrows furrowed, she said, "It's important."

"Well . . . they often come suddenly. It's difficult to know when I'll get one."

"Do they hurt?"

That wrinkle between his brows deepened. "Hurt? No, why?"

"And nobody speaks to you? You can't talk during them?"

"No . . ." Gray confusion pulsed around him in slow, steady beats. "What does this have to do with your mother?"

"When the Paragon send me visions with their dreamwalking, it's painful. I didn't know if any of your visions might have actually been the Paragon dreamwalking to you."

"Me?" Saros asked. "Why would they target me?"

"They have . . . suggested to me that they had something to do with Mom's death. But if she's not connected directly, then I assume my father was. It's the only thing that makes sense."

Steel pain spiked around Saros. Astrea gritted her teeth, desperate to pull her barrier back but unwilling to let her guard down for even a second.

"They what?" Saros barely whispered.

"I don't know," she said. And that was still the truth. "That's why I asked you."

"I truly don't know, Astrea. If I did, I would tell you."

Saros may have kept much from her over the years, but as that pain and confusion continued to dance around him, Astrea believed her uncle. He didn't know about that any more than Astrea did.

"How did she die?" Astrea asked. "Was she covered in shadows?" The One had suggested he had been the one to kill her mother. So was it with void magic? Was it one of these Lifestealers? Or with aetherium, perhaps?

"There were no shadows. She looked like herself. Like you," Saros said. "She simply got sicker and weaker over time, and she never recovered. She said it couldn't be healed."

There was very little that Lightbringers—and Purifiers, for that matter—couldn't heal. Some wounds were too big, especially if the victim started bleeding out too fast. Some illnesses and poisons spread so quickly to the whole body that even magic couldn't outpace the damage. And then things like lost limbs, of course, couldn't be repaired with magic, though Lodestar and other companies had begun developing prosthetics.

So what was it that had killed Roxana Sovna? One of these quick-acting illnesses or poisons? Poison seemed like something The One might use. He didn't seem like the kind of person to get his hands dirty. In all the days the Paragon had held Astrea under that house, The One had only injected Astrea with blue lotus one time. And they still didn't know exactly how lifestealing worked.

"I'm sorry I don't have more answers, Astrea," Saros said. "I know I've screwed up so many times, my dear, but I'm here now. I'm going to help you stop these people if you'll let me."

Astrea nodded.

"How about you go to bed?" he suggested. "You should be well rested when we get back to work."

Astrea nodded again. She didn't know what else to do with herself. Saros's answers, while they didn't provide new information, at least confirmed what Astrea had hoped: that Roxana hadn't been involved with the Paragon. Not willingly or knowingly, anyway. And Saros was right; she really needed to rest if she was going to continue this mission.

When Astrea returned to her and Jin's hotel room, Adi, Cressida, and the Nikaphoroses were all gone. The bathroom door was closed, and water splashed quietly inside.

Astrea padded to the bed and kicked her shoes off. Jin had unpacked two of the shopping totes, which now sat folded up on the floor near their knapsacks. A few stacks of new clothes were on the bed, mostly undergarments, a couple of pairs of sporting clothes, and street clothes for both of them. Astrea sifted through her new things, thankful that Sarsali had been there. She knew exactly what Astrea liked and had gotten her just that: three loose linen dresses and five new pairs of cotton bloomers.

As Astrea set their new clean clothes on the settee, the bathroom door opened. Jin strode out in nothing but his underwear. His hair was slightly damp in the front.

"How'd the rest of your talk with Saros go?" Jin asked. "Did he say anything about us sharing a room?"

"No, actually," Astrea said, the realization washing over her. Saros had mentioned no such thing. Hadn't even alluded to it. He'd been so hostile toward Jin all those months ago in Kalama and for so many years, and now he just . . . wasn't. Maybe Saros knew there were bigger things at stake. Maybe he was finally over his hostilities. "I asked him about my mother."

Jin's eyebrows rose. "And?"

"And he doesn't think she was connected to the Paragon knowingly," Astrea said. "He told me she had no shadows on her body when she died. She told him it wasn't something that could be cured."

"Mysterious," Jin murmured.

Astrea shrugged. "I asked Saros if he knew my father, but he has no idea who it might be. He must be connected to the Paragon."

"It would make sense."

"It makes my head hurt."

"We'll figure it out," Jin said as he rounded the bed and pulled the covers back.

The sun had barely even set, and the clock on the bedside table said it was only the eighth evening hour. But skies, Astrea wanted nothing more than to sleep. She went to the bathroom, cleaned up, and changed out of her dress. By the time she got back to the bed, Jin's breathing had slowed.

Astrea slipped in next to him, but he didn't move. "Jin?" she whispered.

"Hm?" Snaking his arms around her waist, Jin pulled her front flush against his.

"Thank you for getting him out of there."

"Anything for you, Az. I've already told you that."

"I know. I just . . . Thank you. I know he hasn't been the best to you."

"Maybe he hasn't, and maybe I should care, but I just don't."

"How can you not? Part of me is so angry with him. I hate that he kept so much from us. From me."

"I do, too. But he was just trying to keep you safe, Az. And I certainly can't hate the man for that. I don't want you to hate him for that, either."

"I don't *hate* him." Far from it. Astrea loved Saros, and that was part of why it hurt so much. "He just frustrates me. I'm just . . . I'm angry with him."

"I know." With gentle hands, Jin smoothed some of her hair back. "And you have every right to be. I'm not saying you have to forgive him or become the best of friends, but I hope you find a way forward with him."

Astrea didn't know what the future held with Saros. But maybe Jin was right, that she could find a way forward with her uncle despite everything. Her eyes fluttered closed, and her body relaxed. At least now that they were reunited, she'd have the chance to figure it out.

CHAPTER 44

Little Lightbringer.

Astrea's eyes cracked open, only to be met by darkness. It pressed in against her, oppressive and overwhelming. She couldn't breathe. Couldn't see. Could barely think.

Little Lightbringer, The One drawled. *Wake up, Miss Sovna.*

I'm awake. Blood roared in her ears. Somewhere far away, Jin's warm hands brushed Astrea's bare shoulders. Not brushed, gripped. Was he here, too? Seeing this? Hearing this?

Good.

An image not of her hotel room or even Katavena came into focus. In front of Astrea were Solana, Nazarov, and Theo, all huddled around a body. Tovan's body. Red rage exploded around Nazarov while Solana remained steadfast. Theo didn't react at all. Astrea couldn't hear them, but skies, was Nazarov angry. He whirled on Solana, jabbing a finger in her face as he shouted. Astrea couldn't hear anything he said.

You've made him very angry. The One sounded . . . pleased. Proud, if Astrea wasn't mistaken. *You've done the impossible.*

Killed one of his own?

Controlled a void mage.

How do you know that?

I have people everywhere, Miss Sovna, The One said. *And I know what you did at the Kalamian docks. Most impressive. Those of us who follow the true path still want to work with you and the sun. You are touched by the void, after all.*

Was it some thinly veiled threat? Did The One know where she was now?

I also know you've finally gotten the book, The One continued. *It seems you were telling me the truth after all. My apologies.*

Fuck you. Apologies? The One wanted to pretend to apologize after all he'd orchestrated? All he'd put her through?

My, my. A sardonic chuckle echoed in Astrea's mind as the image of Nazarov and the others faded to black. *Fine. Then be warned. Victor Nazarov will not rest until he finds you and Prince Varojin. He will not rest until he has that book, and he will not rest until you are back under his control.*

What do you mean—

If you want protection from the likes of such Wanderers, you know where to find me, Miss Sovna. You've been to our ancestral home before. Visit me near the Path of Ruin.

And just like that, that heavy, cold darkness pressing in around Astrea receded. Her muscles seized up as she blinked rapidly.

"Az?" Jin asked. "What was that?"

Panic lodged in Astrea's throat. She squeezed her eyes shut. *Jin's worry. The bedsheets. My hair in my face.* There was nothing she could smell, but in the next room over, something thudded against the floor. Annoyance flickered over her skin.

"The One." She huffed, pushing hair out of her face as she glanced over at Jin. Orange anxiety vibrated around his entire body. "He's back. He knows we have the book, and he knows what I can do to void mages."

Jin's eyebrows furrowed. "He dreamwalked to you again?"

Astrea nodded. It was the first time she'd heard from The One since that time under the house, when he and Nazarov had fought for control in her mind.

"Nazarov's irate that we killed Tovan. The One warned me that Nazarov won't rest until he finds us and the book. He offered us protection if we meet him at the ruins in eastern Novaria."

"That's not happening." Jin ran his hands through his curls, detangling a few with his fingers. "Alright. We need to talk to the team. We should assume all the void mages know where we are now."

Astrea had been hoping for a quiet morning. A slow morning, just this once, before they were back at it. She'd hoped to get another half hour alone with Jin and enjoy the first real semblance of privacy they'd had in many days. She'd hoped to sit with Sarsali and catch up over coffee before they had to run again.

It simply wasn't meant to be.

Astrea and Jin worked like a well-oiled machine. After waking up the others, they got to work. As one took a short, quick shower, the other brushed their teeth and tidied up the hotel room. In just a quarter of an hour, they were both clean, dressed, and packed. The new clothes Zephyrine had bought for them barely fit in their packs, but they were just going to have to make do.

In another quarter of an hour, they'd gathered with the rest of their team in Zephyrine's room. As they finished explaining what The One had told and shown Astrea, wariness settled in her bones. For a moment, nobody said a word.

"There's someplace we can go," Zephyrine said. "My husband owns a small property on the southern side of the island, very remote"

"Some of my extended family lives—" Sarsali started.

"We aren't bringing your family into this, Sarsali," Jin said, the words both gentle and commanding. "As much as I appreciate the thought, I won't put them in harm's way."

"How do we get to your property, then?" Sarsali asked Zephyrine.

"A car can only take us so far," Zephyrine said. "But we can get there if you're all willing to hike."

Sarsali chuckled as she gestured to her long, loose skirt, linen blouse, and sandals. In fact, with her hair in its usual long braid, she looked like she was ready for another day in her garden in Kalama. The rest of them had dressed casually as well; Astrea's armor was packed in her knapsack, and she'd put on a linen skirt and blouse similar to Sarsali's. Even Jin and Adi were in street clothes.

"We're hardly prepared for a hike," Sarsali said. "General Kanakos—"

"Zephyrine."

"*Zephyrine*," Sarsali said. "How far will it be?"

"Two miles."

"We'll make it work, darling," Balthazar said as he set a large hand on Sarsali's shoulder. "We must. How soon can we get a car?"

"Half an hour and I should be able to secure us two," Zephyrine replied. "Adi, with me. The rest of you, stay here."

As Zephyrine and Adi headed for the hallway, Sarsali turned to Jin. "Now what?" she asked.

He sighed as he watched his mentor and best friend leave the room. "We stick to the plan."

Zephyrine had been right about getting two cars. Where she'd gotten them, Astrea wasn't sure, nor did she care to ask. She was in one with

Adi, Marko, Cressida, and Jin, Marko firmly planted in the driver's seat. Zephyrine drove the other and had Sarsali, Balthazar, and Saros with her.

Making their way through Katavena's crowded streets proved time consuming, but it gave Astrea time to look at the city. She'd been right in her earlier assessment that the architecture was a mix of Helosian and Thasian styles, but comparisons stopped there. The streets here were more crowded, more ancient by the looks of them. Astrea liked the added character to the buildings, and she loved the tropical gardens flourishing on side streets and in public parks they passed.

As they finally made it to the outskirts of Katavena and continued south, the buildings grew sparse and were replaced by rolling fields and orchards. By the time they'd been driving for over two hours, the farmland had changed to dense tropical forest. Any side roads they passed were clearly meant for estates high up in the hills. Some of the large houses peeked over the trees, only to disappear again as Marko followed Zephyrine down the winding roads.

By the time the third hour rolled around, the sun was high above them. Zephyrine finally pulled off on the side of the road, and Marko followed suit. As the engines shut off and everyone stepped out, the only sign of life was a bright red and blue bird gliding from tree to tree. Besides their group, Astrea sensed no people for as far as she could spread her magic.

"What's this, Zephyrine?" Jin asked as he gestured to the dense forest. "I know you said there'd be a hike, but this . . ."

". . . is exactly where we need to be," Zephyrine finished for him. "Anjou owns property here, but there's no access by vehicle, just small boat or even smaller airship."

"And you didn't think we should take one of those instead?" Jin asked.

"No. This is still faster for us. We hike from here, our two miles, then we'll be at the property. I'll find us a way out of here, even if we have to go back to Katavena. We just need to buy ourselves a little time."

Trekking through the Taipoli forest—which was more like a jungle, really—was less than ideal, even with Sarsali's magic nudging the worst of the flora and fauna out of the way. Seeing Sarsali work always amazed Astrea. Her sweeping hand movements and gentle direction of plants was almost like watching an artist work. And Sarsali's gardens back home were certainly art. This place, though? Not so much.

Rocks and tree roots littered the soil, and besides that, it was damp and slippery. Astrea was just glad she'd thought to change into her boots partway into their drive out here. It certainly made the difficult terrain a bit easier.

"You good?" Jin asked as he and Astrea fell behind the others.

"Well, not really." She stepped over a large tree root, grabbing onto Jin's hand as she did. "I don't like that The One is trying to get me back to the ruins in Novaria."

"Nor do I."

Part of Astrea wondered, though, if they should go. Not to actually work with him, but to capture him or stop him somehow. Or was it just a trap? If they could gather Grand Duchess Ysabel's army, would that be enough to stop him and the Paragon?

Up ahead, Sarsali swept her hands out to her sides. A thick collection of bushes covered in wide flowers bent away from their path. Sarsali ushered everyone past, and only when they were in the clear did she follow them and let the shrubs go back to their natural state.

"You know, Balthazar," Sarsali called from just behind Astrea, "when I said I wanted to travel more in the coming years, this wasn't what I had in mind."

Peach amusement danced around the large Metalli. He was at the front of the group with Zephyrine and Marko. But before he could say anything, Cressida cut in and said, "Way worse than the time we were camping in the Novarian mountains."

"You, camping?" Sarsali scoffed. "I don't believe it."

"Oh, you should," Astrea said. "Cress complained all night."

"And you were there?" Now, peach bubbled around Sarsali's carefully plaited hair. "If I were a betting woman, I'd be out a good chunk of money because I would never in a million years have imagined that *or* this." She gestured to the tropical forest, and overhead, a large green bird cawed loudly. "Unbelievable."

"Anjou's property isn't much farther," Zephyrine called over her shoulder. "Let's focus, yes?"

Astrea, Jin, and Sarsali hurried to catch up with the others. The sloping terrain began to flatten out for stretches, though there was still one more hill ahead of them. Astrea shook out her arms, unused to the sticky heat and midday sun. It was more humid here than Kalama.

When they finally reached the peak of the hill, Astrea's breath caught in her chest. Blue sky, dark storm clouds, and green sea spread out far to the horizon. And closer, still on land, was what most of the aristocracy in Kalama would call a modest vacation house. Astrea didn't think it was modest at all. The tan brick walls nearly melded into the forest, but the ornate windows and overall size of the building were just the first hint of extravagance. There would be more inside, Astrea was sure. The forest around the building had been carefully curated to look natural.

"Here it is," Zephyrine said. "Anything, Astrea?"

"Actually, yes." Just at the edge of Astrea's senses, far below in that house, were people. "There are three inside as far as I can tell. They seem annoyed."

"Three?" Zephyrine asked. A faint sheen of gray confusion wavered around her. "There shouldn't be anyone."

Astrea's chest tightened when a fourth presence moved into the range of her magic. "Someone's coming," she whispered. Down below, three people rounded the corner of the house, all dressed in Helosian red.

"Get down," Zephyrine hissed.

Everyone retreated down the hill as Astrea said again, "Someone else is coming. Not void."

That was the only consolation. But that didn't mean they weren't a Helosian soldier or one of the void mages' compatriots. Would the Paragon even know of Lord Anjou Lazzaro's property? Astrea was about to ask when the bushes to her right rustled.

Jin crept forward, Adi and Zephyrine on his heels and Marko not far behind. As that mysterious fourth presence drew nearer, it wasn't Helosian red or a Paragon mask that stepped out of the thick Taipoli jungle.

A middle-aged man with tan skin and long black hair moved toward them. Smiling at Zephyrine, he said, "At last, my wife's decided to join me."

Chapter 45

Zephyrine's entire body relaxed. "Your wife's finally decided to join you? Really?"

"This is him?" Jin asked.

"Yes, this is him," Zephyrine said. "Lord Anjou Lazzaro, my husband."

"At your service." Anjou Lazzaro flashed another grin. He wasn't the most handsome man in the world, but his dimpled cheeks and slightly crooked, narrow nose gave him a certain charm. Besides, his light brown eyes were kind. Friendly. "Balthazar! You're the last skies damned person I'd expect to see out here."

"What the skies are *you* doing out here?" Zephyrine asked her husband. "I thought you were missing."

"Got knocked a bit off course and decided to come here for a while."

"And what are the Helosians doing down at the house?"

"That's why I'm . . . you know . . ." Anjou gestured to the jungle around them. "Saw their ship come in early this morning. I assume they're looking for you. Interrupted my nice tropical retreat."

"How would they know to look here?" Zephyrine asked. "You bought the property under a fake name."

"And even that isn't foolproof, I suppose." Anjou's gaze flicked over their group, lingering on Jin a beat longer than necessary. "At last we meet, Varojin. My wife's told me all about you."

"And yet she's told me nothing about you," Jin replied.

Anjou's eyes narrowed, then he laughed. "Fair enough, I suppose."

"Not to distract you all from this lovely reunion," Cressida said, "but what are we going to do about the Helosians? We can't go down there."

Anjou sighed. "No, but we can wait a bit longer. They should be done with their search soon. Not much for them to find down there. The only person who comes here besides me is the housekeeper, and we needn't worry about him."

"Where's your crew?" Zephyrine asked.

"Out at sea, safely away from any Helosian patrols," Anjou said. "Instructed to lie about me falling overboard if they get questioned."

Jin edged closer to the crest of the hill again, staying low as he ascended. Astrea watched him carefully, waiting for any sign of distress or warning. Nothing. His tight shoulders loosened a fraction before he turned around.

"They're leaving," Jin said. "You think they'll come back?"

"Hard to say," Anjou mused. "Seems there's a reason they'd bother coming all the way out here to look for you."

"You think?" Zephyrine replied dryly.

"It should be safe to make our way down to the back of the house, on the side hidden from the inlet," Anjou said. "And then we can discuss why you're really here."

As Anjou led them to the northern edge of the hill behind his house, Astrea focused as much attention as she could on her magic. This far away, she could no longer sense the three Helosians. Aside from their group, there didn't seem to be anyone around. Maybe Anjou was right and the Helosians would simply leave after not finding evidence.

They half slid down the hill toward the back of the house. A small fountain bubbled near a wide back patio, revealing tall windows and double doors leading into the building. Zephyrine, Adi, Jin, and Astrea went to check the front of the house, circling around the gardens and toward the front door. There was nothing other than the swaying palm trees standing guard near the covered front porch. No Helosians. No void mages. Nobody.

Zephyrine led them in through the front door, which the Helosians had left ajar. As Astrea had expected, the inside of the house was fit for a Kalamian business mogul and aristocrat. Dark and light wood furniture mixed with colorful accents. Wallpaper patterned with trees, flowers, and birds. Even the ceilings were painted to look like the afternoon sky.

Deeper into the house, simmering annoyance bounced around. Anjou's voice carried complaints about the Helosians going through his belongings. What had he expected? They were probably looking for something about Zephyrine, anything small the emperor might be able to use to track her down.

"Anjou?" Zephyrine yelled.

"We're in here!"

They made their way to a large open kitchen, where everyone else had congregated. Sweat beaded their brows, and both Saros and Balthazar's shirts were soaked with perspiration. Astrea wrinkled her nose.

"There's much we need to tell you," Zephyrine said to Anjou. "I've been in Talmaris with Eliana, Varojin, and their friends."

"Why?"

"Grand Duchess Ysabel is tentatively supporting Eliana's claim to the throne, among other reasons. We need to find a way back to Talmaris as soon as possible."

"That doesn't explain why you're here." Anjou moved past where they'd all gathered around the kitchen island and headed for a wide refrigerator on the other side of the room. He pulled out several carafes of water, then brought those and glasses to the island.

"I wouldn't be here if I didn't have to be," Zephyrine replied coolly. "We need your help."

"With what, the rebellion?"

"It's bigger than my father," Jin said. "Far bigger. Far worse."

Chuckling, Anjou poured himself a glass of water. "What could possibly be worse than your father, Varojin?"

"Void mages," Zephyrine said. "Void mages think Varojin and Astrea"—she gestured to where they both stood—"are key to some ancient Stargazer's vision they're following. These void mages have attacked Grand Duchess Ysabel, and Emperor Aelius has void mages in his service and is looking to exploit meteoritic ore that contains void magic properties."

Slowly, Anjou lowered his empty glass to the counter. He looked each one of them in the face, solemn and entirely unreadable. If it were possible, his wall grew even tighter than Jin's.

And then Anjou laughed. He laughed a deep belly laugh, peach amusement flashing brightly around him. "Skies, Zephyrine, you almost had me going. Void magic?" When all of them remained quiet, Anjou's thick eyebrows rose. "You're . . . you're serious?"

"Why would we lie about this?" Zephyrine asked. "Have you ever known me to be a liar?"

"Not exactly." Anjou pulled at the collar of his dress shirt. Like the rest of them, his skin glistened with sweat. "Skies. Well, that still doesn't explain why you're here."

As Zephyrine explained the last couple months, and particularly the last two days, in detail, Astrea finally poured herself a glass of water. She was thirsty, sure, but the weight of the cold glass in her hands was almost comforting. They may have dodged the Helosians for the time being, but what were they going to do about the void mages possibly showing up? What if the Helosians doubled back? Her mind went round and round in circles, coming up with dizzying possibilities.

"And when the void mages sent Astrea this vision, I knew we needed to go someplace off the books," Zephyrine said. "Hence being here."

"And hence returning to Talmaris," Anjou finished. He scratched at the stubble on his chin, then sighed. "Ten people to go to Talmaris without anyone finding out. That's quite the fucking job, Zephyrine."

"Couldn't your crew sail us there?" Zephyrine asked. "You said they're somewhere offshore."

"It won't be the fastest trip," Anjou said, "though I don't see much of a choice. The airship isn't big enough to accommodate all of us. I'll need some time to get everything arranged."

"Then arrange it," Zephyrine said. "It's imperative we get that book back to Talmaris as soon as possible."

Anjou surveyed the group again, almost studying them. He didn't seem distrustful, but Astrea certainly didn't think the shipping magnate was thrilled to be pulled into their mission. "While I try to get in contact with my crew, how about you all go get cleaned up?" he said. "No offense."

"None taken." Balthazar flashed his usual easy smile, the first time Astrea had seen it in months. She'd missed that smile.

"Guest rooms are down the first hallway to your left when you leave the kitchen," Anjou said. "Make yourselves at home."

While the rest of them shuffled out of the kitchen, Zephyrine stayed behind and began speaking with her husband in hushed tones. Astrea trusted the general, but her husband didn't seem as enthusiastic about the whole thing as Astrea had hoped he'd be. Maybe she just wasn't getting the right read on him.

The hallway with the guest bedrooms was the same as the rest of the house: dark wood finishes and bright accents. The artwork hanging on the walls—just paintings of sunsets and tropical settings—betrayed nothing about the owner. The guest bedrooms were similarly impersonal, more like a hotel than someone's home. The one Jin chose had sage green wallpaper and an ornate four-poster bed.

"Anjou didn't seem pleased to see us once Zephyrine started explaining it all," Astrea said as soon as Jin had closed the door.

"It's probably just a lot for him to wrap his mind around."

"Yeah, probably." Astrea dropped her knapsack on the ground, then wandered into the bathroom. Smaller than what she'd expected given the rest of the house but luxurious nonetheless. "Do you want to go first or shall I?" she asked Jin over her shoulder.

"Why not be efficient and take one together? Just something quick."

"Quick," Astrea mused as she strode over to the shower. It was hardly bigger than her old one at home, barely large enough to fit both of them. But being close to Jin sounded nice. "I don't think I've ever seen you take a quick shower."

"Me?" he asked, sugary amusement coating Astrea's tongue. "I'm very efficient, thank you."

True to his word, their shower was efficient, and Astrea was sweat-free and dressed again in just ten minutes. As Jin gathered their dirty clothes, Astrea pulled the book out of her knapsack again. An idea tickled her mind, not quite fully formed but starting to take shape.

"Jin," she said.

"Yes?"

"I don't think you and I should be around this book."

A faint whisper of surprise danced over her skin. "What?"

"I don't think you and I should be around this book," she repeated. "The One obviously wants it and us. So does Nazarov. They know we have it, and Nazarov knew we were in Kalama. It's only a matter of time before one of them finds us."

To have either The One or Victor Nazarov catch up with not just Astrea and Jin but the book would be disastrous. Astrea knew that much deep in her bones. When Jin said nothing for several moments, Astrea peeked over her shoulder. He'd paused at the bathroom door, his muscular body leaning against the frame.

"Well?" she asked.

"Risk mitigation . . . I get it. Just thinking." Jin huffed, then nodded. "You're right. But what, we split the group up and get back to Talmaris a different way?"

"I guess. Do you think it's a good idea?"

"Yes. We just need to figure out exactly what we're going to do."

"Then let's go talk to the team," Astrea said.

Jin's lips quirked up as he watched her, that faint sheen of pink love mingling with his vermilion pride. He held his hand out to her, and she took it. "Alright," he said. "Let's go talk to the team."

When Jin and Astrea returned to the kitchen, it was empty. Frowning, Astrea clutched the book to her chest. Not everyone had been in the guest rooms. A burst of anxiety made Astrea pivot. She followed that tingle, letting her magic guide her from room to room. Jin trailed behind her, stopping only when she did in an ornate parlor.

"Oh." Sarsali peeked up from where she was fidgeting with her white skirt. "Astrea. Jin. We didn't want to bother you, but . . ."

"But we also didn't know what else to do," Balthazar said. "Zephyrine and Anjou were gone when we came back out."

Both of Cressida's parents were seated on a narrow sofa, its yellow-gold upholstery clashing with Sarsali's purple blouse. Balthazar ran a hand over his bald head.

"I'll go look for them," Jin said. "We all need to talk. Wait here."

Astrea dropped into one of the formal armchairs across from Sarsali and Balthazar, wincing at its lack of decent cushioning. "Are you two alright?" she asked as she watched the Nikaphoroses. Both sat with too-straight posture.

"It's all just a lot, my dear," Sarsali said gently. "We didn't wake up a couple of days ago thinking we'd go on the run. Not that we aren't relieved to see you and Cress. It's still . . ."

"Still a lot," Astrea finished for her. "I know. That's how it feels all the time, honestly."

"Now that the initial shock has worn off . . ." Balthazar's voice trailed off. "I feel like I've run all the way across Kalama in twenty minutes."

That was how Astrea often felt, too. Bone-deep weariness followed her wherever she went, never letting up even when she managed to get a full night's rest. Which wasn't often, but *some* relief would've been nice.

"Can I do anything?" Astrea asked.

"If you're inclined to do something," Sarsali said with a smile, "you can give me a proper hug."

Laughing, Astrea pushed herself to her feet. Sarsali met her halfway between the sofa and chair, then pulled Astrea into a tight embrace. Astrea melted into her arms. Relief pulsed against her skin, cool and light, just before a third joined them. Balthazar. Being here with the Nikaphoroses—two of the most important people in her life for so long—nearly made Astrea weep.

But she didn't. Instead, as she pulled away, she said, "Can I ask you something about Mom?"

"Roxana?" Sarsali asked, gray confusion dancing around her head. "Of course, sweetheart."

"Do you know if she was involved in . . . in anything like what we've told you about the Paragon?" Astrea swallowed hard as the question hung in the air between them.

Sarsali's narrow eyebrows furrowed while Balthazar's thick ones shot up. "I've never really thought about it," Sarsali said. "Nothing jumps to mind, but let me think. That was so long ago."

"Or anything about my father?" Astrea asked. "I think he might be, you know . . ." She gestured vaguely to the room. "Involved?"

"Now that's a secret she never told us," Sarsali said. "I tried to figure out who it was, but she wouldn't tell me, just that he didn't live in Irvina."

"How'd she meet him?"

"She told me they'd met in town while she was making her healing rounds," Sarsali said. "That he'd been charming and polite and she'd been lonely, and it just . . . happened."

That didn't exactly sound like someone connected to the void. Could it be that only Souleaters, like Astrea and Lucian, could sense the cold that surrounded void mages? No . . . that wouldn't make sense. Plenty of Lightbringers at the palace back in Novaria could sense the void mages.

Unless . . . that cold was just a barrier, like the wall Jin put up. Could the void mages let their emotions open up past that? Would that have disguised her father's true identity?

Or maybe he wasn't a void mage at all. Plenty of people who weren't void mages were connected to the Paragon.

Astrea wished she knew. More than anything, she wished she knew. Maybe that would give her some answers about why the Paragon thought *she* was this moon in this prophecy.

Or maybe not. Maybe her father had just been a kind stranger passing through town. Perhaps he hadn't been connected to any of this at all.

"She met him just after we moved away," Sarsali said. "Just before I got pregnant with Cress. I wish we'd still been there so we could've met him."

"Why did you move, anyway?" Astrea asked. She'd never really thought to ask for specifics; she'd just known that the Nikaphoroses had lived in several cities around the continent before settling in Helosia.

"Better opportunities for us to start Lodestar in Kalama," Balthazar said. "Guessing by the look on your face, you were hoping we knew more about him. Sorry."

Astrea forced herself to smile. "Honestly, that's the most anyone's ever been able to tell me. It's helpful, thank you."

As Sarsali and Balthazar both gave Astrea one more hug, Astrea tucked away that piece of information about her father for later. The rest of the house's inhabitants moved closer to the parlor, a mix of nervous energy and fatigue. Astrea settled back down in her chair as the Nikaphoroses returned to their sofa, just in time for everyone else to arrive.

Everyone moved into the room, either standing or sitting, but Saros stayed on the far end near the door.

"Well," Zephyrine said as she surveyed the group, "Jin, you said you have a plan to propose. Would you like to fill us in?"

"It was actually Az's idea," he said, taking the book from Astrea as she passed it to him. "But we think it's best for us not to be with this. We don't think we should be the ones to take it to Talmaris."

"What, you think the void mages are going to come after it?" Cressida asked.

"Obviously Nazarov didn't intend for us to keep it, Cress," Astrea said. Cressida nodded. "And after the dreamwalking, I just don't want to take any chances."

"Or if my father's people catch up to us and he's realized the Paragon think the two of us are key, that could be equally bad," Jin said. "No matter which of the three groups finds us, they can't have us *and* the book."

"If they realize you do not have the book," Sarsali said, "don't you think they'll just figure out who does?"

"Maybe," Jin said. "They very well could. But if they think Az and I have it and catch up to us first, that buys the rest of you time."

"Should you two even travel together?" Marko asked.

"I won't split us up." Jin's firm answer left no room for argument. "Besides, if we're split and they come for us, it'll just make it that much harder to fight them off. Some strength in numbers, right?"

"I suppose," Marko murmured.

Astrea took the book back from Jin, turning it over in her hands. Another half-formed idea tickled her mind as she stared down at the book's dark cover. "We should take it apart."

"Destroy it?" Cressida asked. "Az, after all that, we can't just—"

"Not destroy it," Astrea said. "Take it apart. Send it off to Talmaris in a new binding and put something else in the old binding. Which Jin and I can keep."

"Trick them, you mean," Adi said. "If they catch up to you two, they might think you actually do have the real thing."

"At least for long enough to buy the rest of you some time," Astrea said.

Saros cleared his throat. "I do have experience rebinding books. I haven't in many years, but . . ."

"I used to help Raela fix bindings sometimes at the library, too," Astrea said.

"Would it be possible to split the actual book up into two volumes?" Jin asked. "And then we split up that way? It would make it less likely that any one faction would get both volumes."

"We could make it work," Astrea said. She'd find a way to make that happen.

"And who would split up?" Zephyrine asked. "Do you even have enough transportation for us to get to Talmaris, Anjou?"

"I do not, but I think it's a good idea. I've got contacts in Katavena. We'll be able to split up."

"And how will we split up?" Zephyrine asked.

The general didn't sound entirely convinced. Astrea fidgeted in her seat.

"I think Sarsali and Balthazar should go with Anjou," Jin said. "Saros and Zephyrine, you can take the other half. Adi, Marko, Cress, Az, and I will take the decoy."

Splitting up again. Astrea could barely stomach the thought even though this had been her idea in the first place. It just hurt, looking at Sarsali, Balthazar, and Saros and knowing it was in everyone's best interest to split up again. Two months she'd been separated from her family, and after just two days of being reunited, they'd have to go their separate ways again.

"How do we begin with this plan?" Zephyrine asked. "What supplies do you need to deconstruct the book?"

"Scalpels, glue, boards, something to wrap the covers in . . ." Astrea trailed off, thinking back to what Raela often used. "Linen's easiest, probably. And extra paper, or we'll need another book to take apart to use for the decoy."

"I have none of that here," Anjou said. "Well, other books, sure, but none of the rest. I can go to town and get some supplies if you think we have time to spare. Besides, I need to meet with my contact about the third route off the island."

Astrea didn't really see much of a choice unless they wanted to abandon this plan. Would taking an extra day or two be worth it?

"We should do it," Zephyrine said. The others echoed their agreement.

"Then I will leave for town right now," Anjou said. "I can be back tonight with the supplies if you can get me a list."

Chapter 46

Despite Cressida and Balthazar cooking a delicious dinner, Astrea barely had an appetite. Anjou, Zephyrine, and Saros had set off for Katavena hours before to get the supplies they needed to rebind the void book. It sat on the credenza on the dining room wall opposite where Astrea sat, almost beckoning her to leaf through it again.

Dinner had been less awkward than she'd expected. Sarsali had taken an immediate liking to Adi and Marko both, and Balthazar had appreciated Adi's knowledge of some of the mage athletes working their way up the professional rankings back in Kalama. It had been entirely unimportant conversation, but Astrea wouldn't take that comfort away from any of them. Some of the anxiety pulsing around both the Nikaphoros parents had finally died off.

"So, what do we do while we wait for the others to return from the city?" Balthazar asked. "Wait up all night for them?"

"No," Jin said. "We'll take shifts and stay up on watch. Adi, Marko, take the first shift. Az and I will take the second. And you three"—he smiled at the Nikaphoroses—"should take the third shift. Cress can walk you through it. Rotate every four hours, even when the others are back."

"Shall we do the dishes and get to it?" Sarsali asked.

"Cress and I can clean up," Astrea said.

Already pushing out of her seat, Cressida said, "Yeah, don't worry about it, Ma. Go get some sleep. I'll wake you up when it's time."

As Sarsali and Balthazar headed back toward their room, Adi, Marko, and Jin helped Astrea and Cressida bring the dishes to the kitchen. Then the three men headed out of the house. A window over the wide kitchen sink revealed the setting sun. Hints of red and orange still clung to the horizon even as the dark night sky threatened to consume them.

For the first few minutes, Astrea and Cressida worked in silence. They put food scraps outside to compost, then started in on washing and drying the dishes. Cressida took the spot in front of the sink, just as she always did back home.

"You think this is the right decision?" she asked as she handed Astrea a freshly washed plate.

"Nothing ever feels like the right decision anymore, Cress," Astrea said. "Not fully. But I think it's our best choice."

"Yeah." Cressida slid another dish under the water and began scrubbing it clean.

"We shouldn't be split up for too long at least. We'll all get back to Talmaris in, what, a week? A week and a half? And then we'll all be there with Ellie."

"You're right."

"I often am."

Peach amusement flashed in the air as Cressida nudged Astrea's ribs with her elbow. "Shut up."

"And by the time we get back, I bet Civan, Lennor, and Adi's sister will be in Talmaris, or close to it," Astrea said.

A faint sheen of blue wavered around Cressida. "What if they don't come back?"

"They have to." Astrea couldn't let herself think of the alternatives. She had to believe that Jin was right, that they'd find Jin's old commander and get her aid. "They will. You'll get to see Len again."

Cressida half smiled. "And finally tell her I like her."

"I think she knows. She certainly likes you."

"You know," Cressida said as she handed Astrea the last plate to dry, "it's a bit unfair that you get to read people like that. I mean, how is anyone supposed to stand a chance when I have you as my wing woman?"

Laughing, Astrea set the final dry dish on the counter. Over the years, she'd helped Cressida in all kinds of romantic situations. There'd been several women she'd had crushes on in their university days, plus a couple of men in recent years. But Cressida certainly had a type, and that type was Lennor. Smart, strong, funny people with dark hair. That was who Cressida was always drawn to the most.

"I'll always help you, Cress. In life and in love."

"Now look who's getting emotional," Cressida teased. She dried her hands off, then pulled Astrea into a tight hug. "I'm lucky to call you my sister."

Heavy guilt settled in Astrea's bones as she wrapped her arms around Cressida. A few rooms away, Sarsali and Balthazar's relief and anxiety threatened to bury Astrea with renewed intensity.

"I'm sorry, Cress."

"What? Why?"

"You—your parents—got dragged into this because of me and Saros. Maybe if we *hadn't* been friends—if he hadn't brought me to Kalama—"

"Then we would both have had lonely lives," Cressida whispered. "We can't change who our parents were friends with or what Saros did, but I'm glad to be here, Az. Even when it's scary and awful. There's no one whose side I'd rather fight by than yours."

"I don't say it enough, but I hope you know how grateful I am for you."

"Don't worry, I know."

"And I love you. I don't say that enough, either."

"I love you, too." A half laugh left Cressida as she pulled away and wiped at her eyes, her jade irises bright with tears. "Skies, just imagine if Ellie were here. I don't know if she'd poke fun at us or join us."

"Both," Astrea said. "She'd do both."

"Hopefully she's not driving Nicos too mad."

"You know she is."

As they both began putting the clean dishes back into the cupboards, Astrea hoped she was right. That Lennor and Civan and Adi's sister were alright. That they'd all get back to Talmaris soon.

By the time Astrea had cleaned up for the night and climbed into bed, nearly an hour had passed. She tried her best not to stare at the clock. Where was Jin? And how long would Zephyrine, Anjou, and Saros be?

She rolled onto her side so she faced the windows, staring at the sliver of moonlight she could see through the semi-sheer curtains. She'd often stared out at the moonlight just like this back in Kalama, watching its glow through her bedroom window as her mind raced. It raced now, too, her thoughts jumbling together as sleep pulled her eyes closed and worries forced them back open.

Had Eliana gotten anything sorted to dethrone her father? What if Saros and the others ran into Helosian soldiers or the Paragon while in the city? What if Nazarov showed up tonight? Would Sarsali and Balthazar be alright? They *had* been pulled from their home with little warning, even if it was ultimately for their safety. Where were Lennor, Civan, and Adi's sister?

Astrea's eyelids drooped again, the glow of moonlight flickering as she tried to fight the fatigue. Burrowing into the soft blankets didn't help, yet she still burrowed deeper.

The bed dipped behind her. Familiar warm hands touched her waist, somehow heavy and soft at the same time. Longing shot through her core. Astrea turned halfway over to find molten golden eyes staring down at her.

"Go back to sleep," Jin whispered. His bare chest and shoulders glowed in the faint moonlight still streaming in through the crack in the curtains.

Astrea missed that silly Talmaran guest house and that base. They'd barely had any rest in recent days. Any rest or any privacy. So much time spent on cots and in cargo holds and nightclub basements, so little time with those hands on her waist.

Angling herself toward Jin, Astrea reached for his face and pulled him down into a kiss. He melted under her touch, groaning softly as she nipped at his lower lip.

"That's not sleeping," he whispered against her mouth.

"Sleep soon," she murmured. "Touch me, please."

Tart lust coated Astrea's tongue as Jin moved his mouth down her jaw and throat. He continued sucking the delicate skin there as he unbuttoned her nightshirt, only pulling away when he'd accomplished his task. He cupped her left breast, massaging it gently as he kissed the right. His journey down her body continued as he trailed kisses along her soft belly and down to the waistband of her bloomers.

"Can I take these off?" he asked, voice low.

Sleep and lust tugged at her mind, an internal war. She just wanted to feel good. She just wanted Jin to make her feel good for a while. Make him feel good. "Please."

Jin pulled them off her slowly, then kissed the insides of her thighs. Astrea squirmed as he touched her exactly how she liked. And when his mouth was on her and his tongue flicked every sensitive spot, Astrea fisted his curls in one hand.

Her legs trembled, but she didn't want to climax. Not yet.

"Wait." She tugged on his hair, and Jin pulled away. "Come here."

As soon as Jin's face was nearly even with hers, Astrea fumbled with his underwear. He shucked it off, fucking into Astrea's hand as soon as she'd wrapped it around his warm, hard length. As she pushed him onto his back, surprise danced over her skin. It was quickly replaced by approval and even stronger lust as she brought her lips to his erection.

Jin groaned as she took just the head into her mouth, but she barely had time to do anything at all. "Need to be in you," he rasped, tugging her onto him so she straddled his waist.

Astrea lifted her hips. As soon as Jin positioned himself at her entrance, he slammed into her. Pleasure jolted from Astrea's belly straight up to her head, coating her limbs in pleasant, buzzing warmth. Placing her hands flat on his chest, Astrea ground against him.

His hands slid from her waist down to her ass, fingers digging into her tender skin. "Fuck, Az."

When she kissed him, he tasted like her, and Astrea didn't care. That spring inside her coiled tighter and tighter. Every part of her tightened. Her skin burned in the best way. Release came, and she gasped, trying to pull away from his kiss. But Jin held her there, kissing her as she fell apart on top of him.

"Done?" he asked.

"Not until you are."

He flipped her onto her back. Wrapping her legs around his waist, Astrea held onto him as he pushed back into her in quick, strong thrusts. She reveled in the feeling of his skin on hers. Her fingers in his hair. His lips on her neck. Warm bliss exploded in her chest, and Jin collapsed on top of her. She held him there as he kissed her neck again.

Eventually, they disentangled from one another, half stumbling around the bathroom as they cleaned themselves up. That sunshine warmth, ever present on Astrea's skin, nearly doubled as they settled back into bed, face to face but all lust gone. Fatigue pulled at Astrea's mind and eyes again. But it was nice, getting to connect.

"I didn't mean to wake you," Jin said, smoothing her hair away from her face.

"I don't mind."

"No, I suppose you didn't."

Astrea burrowed down into the blankets again, sighing contentedly. It wasn't the same as the relative safety of Talmaris, but for tonight, this would do. She breathed in the smell of Jin's soap and shampoo; it smelled like oranges. It didn't suit him quite like eucalyptus did.

"Az?" Jin murmured.

"Hm?"

Electric anxiety pulsed against her skin as he said, "I'm really glad I got recalled home this summer."

She let out a soft laugh, her eyes still closed as she reached for Jin's cheek. "Me too."

"Even with all the shit I went through, I think it was worth it because it led me to you."

"I don't know if it was worth all that, but I'm glad you came home."

"It was. I don't think we'd be here if I hadn't had to leave." Jin sighed as he tucked his head close to hers, his breath warm on her skin. "Still, someday, when I have children of my own, I'll make sure they don't go through all the things I have."

Astrea's face warmed as she heard herself ask, "You want children?"

"Someday." Jin was quiet for a long moment, then he asked, "Do you?"

It had never seemed like a possibility for Astrea when she was still in Kalama. None of this had seemed possible—void magic, being with

Jin—but especially not the thought of a future with a spouse or children or both.

"I think so," she said. "Maybe."

"Maybe?" Jin hedged.

"I just never thought I'd have the option for that or even to get married." She forced her eyes open. Jin was watching her carefully. "It's hard to commit to someone when you can't tell them who you really are."

Jin knew who she was, though. He knew who she was, and he knew what she'd hidden, and that didn't change what he felt for her. He knew what she'd been through, what she was still going through, and he still held that safe space for her. He'd stood by her side from the very beginning, no matter how bad things had become.

Astrea didn't think one had to get married or have children to be happy, but she'd always admired Sarsali and Balthazar, the way they were partners not just in love but in life. Deep in her heart, she'd always held onto a shred of hope that it might be possible for her to have a future like that if she found the right person.

The image of Jin as a father flashed in her mind's eye. Jin holding a little baby with her dark hair and his beautiful golden eyes. Her stomach fluttered. Could that really be a possibility? The more she thought about it, the more Astrea realized that yes, she could imagine that future. Someday, far in the future, when they were older and there wasn't a war on the horizon. But she could imagine it nonetheless.

A scrape of jealousy brushed Astrea's skin, but it was replaced by something gentler. "I suppose that would make it difficult," Jin said before clearing his throat. "Do you want anything else in the future?"

"A vacation."

He laughed. "I'd like that too."

"I know there's more I need to figure out," she said, "like what I'm going to do when we go back to Kalama someday, but . . . it seems so far away from now."

"You'll figure it out. There's plenty of time."

"What about you?"

They hadn't talked about it before, what Jin's responsibilities would become if they were successful in overthrowing his father and stopping the Paragon. When he'd first come home to Kalama at the start of the summer, Astrea had assumed he would be returning to the Corsycan front, but Eliana planned to end Helosian involvement in that war.

"I promised Ellie I'd help her during the transition, but I'd really like to just . . . be normal. Not royalty. Not an army officer."

"What about . . ." Astrea ran her fingers along the soft sheets. "Even with your Novarian status?" Her pulse doubled. What would that mean for their future? She hadn't wanted to consider it too closely before, but now?

"I really don't care about that. I just want to be me, but I don't know what that looks like. These last few months are the closest I've ever gotten to that."

"I'll help you figure it out . . . If you want me to."

"I'd like that very much. We should take that vacation first, though."

Astrea's heart fluttered. "You want to go on vacation with me?"

"I want to do everything with you, Az." Jin tugged her close so their bodies were flush, and her heart fluttered again. "Everything." He kissed the end of her nose. "Now go back to sleep. I'll wake you up when it's time for our shift to start."

CHAPTER 47

Rebinding a book—deconstructing and rebinding several books, really—was not going to be as quick as Astrea hoped. She'd known that hope was far-fetched, but staring down at the supplies Saros, Zephyrine, and Anjou had retrieved didn't make it seem any easier. Just harder.

Marko had officially gotten a message to Lucian, warning him not just of what happened in Helosia but that the Talmaran palace should expect not one but four groups to begin returning. The Nikaphoroses and Anjou. Zephyrine and Saros. The twins and Adi's sister. And then Astrea and the rest of them. Though they hadn't heard back from Lucian specifically yet, Marko at least had confirmation from another guard that his message was received.

Now, Jin was with Zephyrine, Anjou, Marko, and Adi, discussing routes to get back to Talmaris. Astrea would leave that planning up to them. The book was her task. Hers, Saros's, and the Nikaphoroses.

"You've really done this before?" Cressida asked as she helped Astrea spread their supplies out on the long formal dining room table. Its deep mahogany wood shone in the early morning sun filtering in through the windows.

"Well . . ."

"Oh, here we go."

"No, it's just that I never fully deconstructed something like what we're planning. I helped Raela repair bindings and even watched her change them before."

It wasn't something Raela had done often, but when she hadn't been able to send the tomes off to an actual specialist, Raela had brought out her tools and done it herself. Sometimes, as the library's budget had shrunk more and more, she'd done it just to save money.

Just the thought of the library made a knot form in Astrea's stomach. She couldn't dwell on it.

"We'll be fine," Astrea continued as she picked up the void book. "It doesn't have to be a perfect job. Just enough to get it up to Talmaris in one piece."

"Wow, Astrea Sovna foregoing perfection?" Cressida mused as she set a few bottles of glue at the far end of the table. "Imagine that."

"Oh, hush."

Sticking her tongue out, Cressida circled the table and picked up one of the large metal clamps. Saros really had thought to get everything they would need.

"I probably could've just made this," Cressida said as she examined the clamp.

"Probably," Astrea agreed. She was just glad to have it either way.

Striding into the dining room, Saros asked, "Is everything set?" He looked better than he had in months. Some of the color had returned to his cheeks, and his dark circles weren't as prominent. "Did I forget anything?"

Astrea shook her head. "I don't think so." It was all there. Books from Anjou's home office to use in the process. Glue and clamps. Boards and new linen. Scalpels and scissors. Fine-point tweezers and knives. "Should we get started?"

Rolling up the sleeves of his white shirt, Saros nodded. "Let's."

At Saros's direction, both Cressida and Astrea helped set up the long dining table. They decided to create one section for each book they needed to work on. One area to deconstruct the void book, two more sections to split the void book up into two volumes, and a final area to craft the decoy. Given their limited time and space, it would have to do.

Once Sarsali and Balthazar joined them, they got to work. The plan was simple. Saros would take the void book out of its binding, then he and Astrea would split it into two volumes. Sarsali and Cressida would work to set the pages, then Balthazar would bind them in their new covers. While the Nikaphoroses did that, Astrea and Saros would put together the decoy.

As Saros opened the void book and carefully cut the glue holding the binding together, Astrea held her breath. The cover and spine pulled away from the manuscript in one piece. Good. This was good. They'd be able to put the decoy together.

Astrea took the dark cloth cover from Saros and set it at the far end of the dining table. She needed to find a book that matched the thickness and length. The options Anjou had brought in earlier in the morning weren't quite right, but she'd just have to make one of them work.

She rejoined Saros, who had begun pulling the binding's threads with tweezers. The pages loosened and loosened until finally, Saros began pulling them apart.

"What do you think about re-ordering these?" he asked as he carefully split the manuscript in half.

"As in mixing up the order of the pages?" Cressida asked.

"Wouldn't that make it hard to put together again in Talmaris?" Balthazar fidgeted with one of the strips of cloth they were going to use on the new binding. "What if we lose one of the books? Then we won't have all the information."

Uncertainty rolled over Astrea's skin, but she pushed back against it. "It's better than the Paragon or emperor having all the information. Let's mix them up."

Balthazar wasn't wrong; it would certainly make more work for them in Talmaris, and it would also certainly add risk. They *would* be in trouble if they lost random pages. But they'd be in more trouble if the Paragon or Emperor Aelius got even half the book in order.

And so she and Saros set about detaching every page, mixing them up over and over again until they had nothing that resembled a readable book. The page numbers scrawled at the bottom would help them re-organize everything in Talmaris. Once satisfied, Sarsali and Cressida began re-stitching the pages together to make their two new manuscripts. It was tedious work, as was Balthazar's job of getting the covers and spines the right size for the new volumes.

As the Nikaphoros family worked, Astrea and Saros started on the decoy. By early afternoon, all three new books were sitting in clamps, which they'd need to sit in overnight until the glue had dried. Only then would they be ready.

"Never thought I'd see the day the five of us would work together on a project," Balthazar said as he checked one of the clamps. "It was almost fun."

"If you discount all the glue stuck to my fingers," Cressida said, sighing as she picked at her skin.

"As if that's worse than all the times you came into the house with gunpowder and chemicals on your hands and clothes," Sarsali said. "I prefer the glue."

"Your mom's got a point, Cress," Astrea said. "Remember that time in university, you were coming out of the lab and ran into your—"

"My friend!" Cressida exclaimed, cutting Astrea off. "We used to run into so many people on campus. I doubt any of them would believe what we've been up to nowadays."

Balthazar arched an eyebrow, and Astrea couldn't help but smile. This felt good. It felt right, being with her family and working together, even if Cressida was keen on keeping old crushes on professors secret. Not that anything had ever happened between them, but it was one of the few times Astrea had ever seen Cressida truly flustered around another person.

"Are we done?" Sarsali asked, gesturing to where Balthazar and Saros stood with the books. One had been bound in blue, the other in green, while the decoy void book had the original black cover.

"All we have to do is wait," Saros said. "They'll be ready tomorrow morning."

"I'll go tell Jin," Astrea said. She wanted to check in on their plans anyway.

Cressida joined her as she left the dining room and made her way to the kitchen. Adi, Jin, and Marko's voices carried out into the hallway. And that wasn't the only thing. The smell of frying potatoes and grilled meat wafted out from the kitchen.

"You made us lunch?" Cressida cooed as she strode into the kitchen. "How sweet of you."

"Jin and I made lunch," Adi corrected from his spot near the stove, where he was busy pushing fried potatoes around a large pan. "Marko has no interest in cooking."

"Oh, for shame!" Cressida made a beeline for Adi, immediately leaning around him to see what he was doing. "Skies, it smells good."

"I didn't say I had no interest," Marko replied. "Just that I don't know how."

"And you declined my offer to teach you," Adi said over his shoulder. "That means you have no interest."

That wasn't true at all, at least as far as Astrea could tell. The curiosity and desire she sometimes saw around Marko had grown in recent weeks, always popping up for brief moments when Adi teased him or cracked jokes. Both were things he did often, and he was wearing down Marko's tough exterior. But would they ever act on their mirrored desires?

"You should take him up on it, Marko," Jin said as he joined Astrea near the kitchen island. "Adi's a very good teacher. Best teacher at Fort Ironwing, really. Very hands on."

Deep red flooded Marko's pale cheeks. "I see."

"The best kind of teaching," Astrea said as Jin wrapped an arm around her shoulders. "I agree with Jin."

"And that's the kind of support you just can't argue with," Adi said. "At least help me get all this plated, would you, Marko?"

As Marko and Adi began final preparations for lunch, Cressida said, "Books should be ready to go in the morning. Are we clear to leave?"

"As clear as it'll ever be," Jin said. "We were actually thinking Anjou and your parents should leave before the rest of us. Spread out our departures."

Orange anxiety blossomed around Cressida and scraped over Astrea's skin like tree bark. She flinched.

"If you all think it's best," Cressida said.

"We do. Zephyrine and Saros will leave last."

Putting as much space between their groups as possible, as much space between the books as possible. Astrea traced patterns in the stone countertop with her finger, swirls of gray amid white and black. "So we leave, what, tomorrow afternoon?" she asked.

"Tomorrow night," Marko said as he brought a platter of fried potatoes to the counter. Steam curled up from the crispy golden slices. "We'll leave after sunset, then Zephyrine and your uncle will go to Katavena at sunrise the following morning."

"Let's just eat," Cressida said as she took a platter of grilled meat from Adi. "I'm starving."

As her friends settled into the kitchen and began serving themselves lunch, Astrea followed their lead. She wasn't sure she'd be able to rest until they all arrived in Talmaris. Until the whole team was safe.

Being on watch duty three hours after midnight wasn't exactly the most pleasant way to spend a night. Jin had woken Astrea up just a few minutes before so they could start their shift with Marko.

Astrea shuffled into the kitchen, where Marko chatted with Adi. His shift was over, but he'd just started a pot of coffee, and skies, did it smell good. When Adi offered her a cup, she took it with a grateful smile. One thing she wouldn't miss were watch shifts. At least back at the Novarian palace, she had the opportunity to sleep through the night. Not that she ever really did anymore. But she could try.

"I should go talk to Jin," Adi said as he picked up another mug filled to the brim. "Then I'm going to bed. See you two in the morning."

Adi disappeared through the wide kitchen doorway, his footsteps silent despite his large frame and boots. Only as the distance between her and his fatigue grew was she sure he was actually gone.

"Is this something you're used to?" Astrea asked Marko. "Being on watch, I mean. Besides at the fort for those few weeks."

His spoon clinked against his ceramic mug as he stirred sugar into his coffee. "It was part of my duties working for the grand duchess, yes."

"Was?"

"Well, considering the turns things have taken, I don't exactly consider that my job anymore."

"Right." Fair enough, Astrea supposed. "Do you think Magdi and her crew are safe?"

A surprised chuckle escaped Marko. "What could possibly make you ask that at three in the morning?"

"Just thinking about it."

Astrea hadn't *not* been thinking about Magdi's safety. Raela's safety. Would the Helosians have caught up to the smuggler? And what about Raela? Had Kaius punished her for losing the void book? As much as Astrea knew getting that book had been crucial, part of her couldn't help but feel guilty.

"Magdi and her crew seemed to know how to take care of themselves," he said. "I believe they'll be just fine."

"I hope so."

When Marko was finished preparing his coffee, he left the sugar and cream on the counter. He brought his cup over to the kitchen island and set it across from Astrea. "I believe this is the first time you and I have been on a shift together before. I usually patrol."

"Jin does, too," Astrea said. "I don't really need to."

Pushing a few strands of blond hair from his eyes, Marko said, "Must be nice."

Astrea shrugged one shoulder. "And overwhelming at times."

"I imagine so, although Lucian never speaks of such things."

"He doesn't?"

"No." Marko chuckled again, a deep, throaty sound. "He never admits to anything being difficult. That was one thing he and Rami always disagreed about. She was willing to admit to hardship while Lucian always wanted to pretend it would all work out."

"Sounds about right," Astrea murmured before taking a sip of her coffee.

"What sounds right?" Jin asked as he strode into the kitchen. As he approached, his hand found its usual spot between Astrea's shoulder blades.

"Just discussing Lucian's inability to admit to all sorts of things," Marko said. "Do you want to get started on patrols? I can take the western and southern sides if you want east and north."

"I don't particularly want to be out there at all, but sure," Jin said. "Az, with me?"

"I just want to check on the books first," Astrea said. Nobody had examined them since dinner, and though she was sure they were fine, Astrea just wanted to make sure everything was as it should be.

Marko headed outside while Jin followed Astrea to the dining room. There sat all three books, held together under the pressure of the large clamps. Totally undisturbed. Astrea handed Jin her coffee, then squatted down to look at the tomes. Everything looked fine. No warping. No fraying cloth for the new covers.

Satisfied, she and Jin headed out into the night. Overhead was nothing more than a smattering of clouds that occasionally obscured the brilliant blanket of stars. The night's sea breeze drifted through Astrea's hair and cooled the humidity already sticking to her skin.

"I've been thinking more about this aetherium ore my father's apparently after," Jin said, "and my gut is telling me we need to go to the Badlands."

"You think that's where it is?" Astrea asked, coffee cup clutched between her hands as they walked. Nothing changed in her magical awareness; everyone was where they were supposed to be.

"Maybe," Jin said. "I don't know why else he'd be there, unless he's just trying to mine as much meteoric material as he can before he finds this aetherium. Honestly, I wish I could ask Theo."

"You do?"

"Well, yes and no," he said. "Of course not knowing what we know about him now, but back before all this . . . I don't know. He was always helpful. I see why now. He must've always connected me to that vision somehow."

"You don't think the Paragon know the true vision, do you?" Astrea asked.

"The sun, moon, and earth will restore balance," Jin murmured. "I doubt it. If they knew the true wording, I think they'd follow it. They care too much about balance to purposefully change it."

"Or the version written in the void language? Do you think it's different?"

"Maybe."

Astrea sighed. "I wish we knew who the Stargazer was who had that vision. I wish I knew exactly what they saw."

But wishes didn't come true. Astrea knew that. She was going to have to work hard to find those answers, if they were even out there. An ancient Stargazer's notes could easily have been lost to time. Even the small scrap of paper Saros had stolen from the emperor had almost been lost to time or some long ago fire. What were the odds that the rest of those notes existed somewhere?

"I don't think it's just about you and me," Astrea said as they turned to the eastern side of the house. "Or it doesn't have to be. If that Stargazer said it would take the sun, moon, and earth to restore balance, then it's not just you and me. It's all the elements."

"Fire," Jin said quietly. "Celestial. Earth. Air. Water."

"And void," Astrea said. "I think it will take them, too."

"Too bad there aren't any we could work with."

"Maybe they don't need to work with us. Maybe we just need to start playing the Paragon's game. They obviously wanted to try to force the vision to come true by getting the two of us. What if we can try to force it to come true, too?"

"By bringing the elements together." Gazing up at the stars high above them, Jin sighed. "Is it selfish that I wish this hadn't fallen on our shoulders?"

"No, of course not," Astrea said. "I wish that, too."

"Do you think it really is some kind of destiny?"

"No," Astrea said again. "I think it's been thousands of small decisions people have made since the Great Wars. Thousands of small decisions, all in pursuit of their own goals. And that's led to this, unfortunately."

Astrea doubted the generations of Paragon had really known it was her and Jin specifically they were looking for. She doubted she and Jin were truly the key to this, anyway. Swap out any powerful mages for the two of them, and it would likely still play out like this.

"And I think now we have to make our own decisions," Astrea said. "Stop reacting to them and start taking control."

Warm pride radiated off Jin. "Taking control," he mused. "When we get back to Talmaris, let's start making a thousand decisions of our own."

Chapter 48

Before dawn, Astrea, her family, and the rest of the team gathered on the pier jutting out from the beach as they awaited the arrival of Anjou's crew. Waves lapped against its sides, steady and unyielding.

"And you have the book?" Cressida asked her parents, the third time she'd brought it up.

"Skies, yes, we have the book," Sarsali said with a laugh. "And it'll stay in our bags until we arrive in Talmaris."

"Should take over a week if we run into no problems," Anjou said. "Though the seas do tend to get a bit stormy this time of year off Tornama's coast."

"Be careful," Cressida said.

Sarsali set her small hands on Cressida's shoulders. "We'll be fine, my dear. Stop worrying so much."

"Boat's coming in." Zephyrine lowered the binoculars she'd been looking through. "Should be here in a few minutes. Let's wrap this up, yes? We need to get you all out of here."

Adi, Marko, and Zephyrine said goodbye to the Nikaphoroses first, then moved off to one side with Anjou. Jin stepped up next, surprise dancing over Astrea's skin as Sarsali pulled him into a hug.

"Take care of our girls," she said as she released him. "The best care of them."

"I wouldn't dream of doing anything less, Sarsali," Jin said. "I promise."

"Take care of each other," Balthazar said as he, too, pulled Jin into a quick embrace. "Just as you have been these last couple of months. We'll see you soon."

With one last smile, Jin left the Nikaphoroses and went to speak with Anjou and Zephyrine. As he did, Sarsali's gentle hand on Astrea's forearm brought her back to her family. Tears pricked Astrea's eyes as Sarsali pulled her into an embrace.

"I love you," she whispered before Sarsali could pull away. "I missed you so much."

"We missed you too, my dear," Sarsali said. "We'll see you soon, alright? You and Cress take care of each other. And make sure Jin doesn't get into trouble."

Astrea laughed as Cressida said, "And make sure Dad doesn't get into trouble. He's the one we really need to worry about."

"You do not," Balthazar teased as Astrea hugged him next. He smelled like leather and coffee, as he often did when he wasn't fresh out of his workshop back home. It was a smell Astrea had grown fond of over the years, a promise of hugs and fresh-baked cookies and stories to keep her and Cressida entertained for hours. "Not even a bit. Right, darling?"

"I think your daughter has a point," Sarsali mused. "You do like to find trouble."

Smirking, Balthazar pulled away from Astrea. "And you, old friend," he said to Saros. "We'll see you in a week. Get Talmaris prepared for us."

"I will," Saros said from where he loitered behind Cressida and Astrea. "Safe travels."

Despite their banter, blue sadness and orange anxiety wavered around Sarsali, Balthazar, and Cressida. The colors twined around Saros, too, and Astrea was sure her aura would reflect the same. For fourteen years, they'd spent so much time together, one family under two roofs. For fourteen years, they'd been inseparable. Weekly dinners. Frequent lunches. Sleepovers for Astrea and Cressida, even into their twenties. Shopping dates with both Sarsali and Balthazar. Simply tagging along for mundane errands.

And now, here Astrea was, separating from them for a second time. *At least I get to say goodbye.* When they'd fled Kalama, Astrea hadn't had the opportunity. *It was temporary then, just as it's temporary now,* she reminded herself. *Just a week.*

With everyone exchanging one last hug, the small boat from Anjou's shipping vessel pulled up to the dock. Astrea, Saros, and the Nikaphoroses stood back as Anjou stepped up to greet his crew. He introduced them to everyone, but Astrea didn't pay much attention to their names, just the fact that they weren't void mages. She hardly paid attention to anything except the sight of Sarsali and Balthazar waving to them as the boat pulled away from the dock and into the choppy waters.

Cressida slung one arm around Astrea's shoulders, so Astrea wrapped her arm around Cressida's toned waist. And together, they watched the Nikaphoroses until the little boat was out of sight, swallowed up by the predawn sky.

"And with that, final preparations are complete." Adi snapped a small notebook closed and gestured out the window overlooking the front of the property.

There sat one of the smallest airships Astrea had ever seen, smaller even than the one they'd taken to the ruins and back. That seemed so long ago, at least in Astrea's mind, and yet it had just been a few weeks. The airship waiting for them was painted a mix of light blues, grays, and whites. A sort of camouflage, at least according to Adi and Jin. Astrea didn't see how it'd work, but they assured her it would, that the Helosian military used similar paint techniques.

"*All* the preparations?" Marko asked. "You remembered to check the—"

With a triumphant grin, Adi waved the notebook in front of Marko's face. "I remembered to check everything because, unlike you, I write everything down."

Marko's hand snapped out, grabbing hold of the notebook and yanking it from Adi's grasp. "Let me see that."

After the Nikaphoroses and Anjou had left for their leg of the journey, Astrea and Cressida had fallen asleep in Cressida's bed for a couple of hours. Only when Zephyrine roused them with promises of breakfast did they get up, and once they were up, they'd been dragged into helping Adi, Marko, and Jin prepare the airship. Not that Astrea minded; she was exhausted after staying up most of the night on watch, and it wasn't like she exactly knew all that needed to be done to prepare an airship for such a journey.

"Engines have been checked," Marko murmured as he scanned a page of Adi's notebook.

"By me *and* Adi," Cressida said.

"I trust you more than I trust Adi."

"Hey!" Bright peach amusement burst around Adi as sugar coated Astrea's tongue. "I'd trust you with my life, Marko. You have to have some level of trust in me after all the nights we've spent in the same bed."

"Skies . . ." Marko turned red from his neck all the way to the tips of his ears. "And then I see we've double-checked the other systems as well."

"There's always time for a third check if you want me to go back in," Cressida said.

"Engines checked, systems checked, flight path checked," Jin said as he strode into the front sitting room of the house. "It's all been checked, Marko. We're ready to go as soon as the sun sets."

"Yeah," Adi said. "If you don't trust me, trust Jin. He wouldn't dare take Az in an airship he didn't deem safe."

It was Astrea's turn to flush red. But all Jin did was smile and wrap his arm around her shoulders as he said, "No, I wouldn't. I—"

"Can we move on before Jin starts getting disgustingly cute?" Cressida asked.

"I was just going to say," Jin continued, "that I wouldn't take *any* of you in an airship I didn't deem safe."

"Nice to know we're included," Adi said, "though I'm sure Az—"

"*Anyway,*" Astrea said, "I need to finish packing."

"And I'd still like to go over this ship one more time," Marko said.

Jin shook his head. "Adi and I will go over it with you."

"And me?" Cressida asked.

"Spend the afternoon however you want?" Jin suggested with a shrug.

"Taking a nap it is." Cressida turned on her heel and strode out of the room, orange anxiety and mint relief both trailing in her wake.

Astrea wandered after her. A nap sounded nice. But there'd be plenty of time to sleep on the flight back to Talmaris, and now, she wanted to be sure she had everything packed up. She returned to her and Jin's room. The bed was neatly made, just as Jin always made it. His pack sat on his side of the bed, though Astrea's was still open. A few of her clothes were still on the bed, too.

Folding them carefully, Astrea stuffed each piece into her bag. Once those were settled, Astrea grabbed the decoy void book. *Novaria: Myths and Other Legends* was stamped on the cover in what had surely been silver leaf at one point. Now, just faded remnants of that silver remained. Saros's work rebinding it had been good, though it wasn't exactly as it should be. Without examining it too closely, one might think it was just worn with time and age. Of course, looking inside would reveal the true contents, some random astronomy book pulled from Anjou's personal library.

Good enough, Astrea thought as she nestled the book at the top of her knapsack. As she began securing the top flap, a knock sounded on the bedroom door. Whoever was on the other side was calm. Steady. Certainly not Jin; he no longer knocked.

Astrea padded over to the door and pulled it open, expecting perhaps Marko or Zephyrine. Saros stood in the hallway, his hands clasped behind his back.

"May I come in?" he asked.

"Sure." Astrea stepped to one side and motioned for her uncle to enter.

He shuffled by her, and only when he was halfway into the room did Astrea close the door and return to the bed. Saros's gaze flicked to Jin's bag several times.

"Do you have everything you need for your trip?" he asked.

"Everything," Astrea said. "The book's the only truly important thing."

"Mine is packed as well."

As she fiddled with the buckles on her knapsack, Astrea chanced a look up at Saros. His mouth was set in a thin line, as it often was this last half year, and he looked more serious than she'd seen him in days. As if that were possible. That same steadiness permeated the air around him. Astrea sensed no worry, nor did she sense any kind of physical discomfort.

"Is that all you came here for?" she asked. "To see if I had the book?"

"No."

Alright . . . so if he hadn't come to ask just about that, then what had he come about? Astrea remained quiet. Saros was going to have to spit it out if he wanted to talk.

"You've been sharing a room with Varojin."

Astrea couldn't help it. She laughed. Actually laughed, mostly in disbelief. Saros's eyebrows furrowed.

"I'm grown up, Uncle," she said despite the unpleasant warmth flooding her veins and stomach twisting in knots. Though Astrea loved Saros and appreciated all he'd done for her over the years, they didn't talk about this type of thing. Romance. Sex. Relationships. Those were conversations Astrea had always limited to just Eliana, Cressida, and Sarsali. "I'm allowed to share a room with a man."

"I just want to make sure you're being careful."

"Oh, skies," Astrea muttered. She scrubbed at her face and sighed. "Uncle . . . Sarsali already talked to me years ago about safe—"

"What?" Saros interrupted. "No, skies, no, not *that*."

"Then what?"

"Can we sit?" Saros asked, gesturing to the bed.

After setting both her and Jin's knapsacks on the floor, Astrea joined Saros as he perched on the edge of the mattress. What would he possibly have to talk about? More visions? Or had he left something out the first time? She hoped not, but it also wouldn't surprise her if he had.

"You've been sharing a room with Varojin," Saros repeated. "And I want to make sure you're being careful with your heart, my dear."

"Where is this coming from?" Astrea asked. "You never cared about things like this in the past."

"Varojin is not his father's son, but he is still an Auris, Astrea. Aurises aren't known for . . ."

"Known for what?"

Keeping his attention trained on the ground, Saros murmured, "Loy-alty, for one. Discretion for another."

A knot tightened around her heart. "You said it yourself; Jin isn't like his father."

"I want to make sure you aren't moving too quickly."

Astrea folded her arms over her chest. Was that any of Saros's business? Astrea didn't think so, nor did she think she'd moved into things with Jin too quickly. It wasn't any faster than how Kalamian couples typically moved. Sure, the world seemed to be falling apart around them, but did that matter? She saw how clearly Jin loved her. Felt everything he felt for her. Those strong, genuine feelings, a mirror to her own. He'd been nothing but kind and supportive these last months.

"I don't think we are," Astrea said, though it sounded lame. "We're doing what feels right."

"That was what your mother said about your father, too."

"What?" She stared at Saros, but he focused on his hands and picked at his nails. "I thought you didn't know who he was."

"I don't, but I cautioned her against moving too quickly, as she often did. Always jumped into things with her heart, not her head. And look what happened. He abandoned both of you."

"Jin's not going to do that to me."

Astrea wasn't sure of much anymore, but Jin would not abandon her. It didn't matter what the world threw at them. Void magic. Kidnapping. Torture. Victor Nazarov screwing around with them at that night club. Dreamwalking. None of it had made Jin falter for even a moment. If those weren't a test of his commitment, what would be?

"Did you see something?" Astrea asked. "Is that why you're bringing this up?"

"No, I've had no visions of you two," Saros said. "But all our talk of your mother, and seeing you and Varojin together . . . it just reminded me of Roxana and how she was. And while I admired her ability to let her heart guide her, she also should've used her head sometimes."

"That's not fair. You don't know what I've been thinking or feeling." Nor did he know what she and Jin had been through. Not really.

"No, I don't," Saros agreed.

"You know I'm careful."

"I know. I just worry about you, and I see so much of your mother in you. You have a big heart, just like she did. And I want to make sure someone worthy has earned their spot in it."

"You think Jin isn't worthy?"

"After all that happened in the past between you two, I just hope he's proven himself."

Astrea had never really told Saros about what happened all those years ago, though she'd certainly been upset for months. He'd never said anything to her at the time. Sixteen-year-old Astrea had thought she'd kept that sadness hidden from Saros, but apparently not.

"He has," Astrea said. Not that it was really Saros's business, but still, she added, "He really has, Uncle."

"Alright, well." Saros smiled tightly. "I just had to give my two cents. I've always wanted you to be happy, my dear. That's all I've ever wanted for you. And if Varojin makes you happy . . . well, I guess I just have to trust you, don't I?"

"Yes, you do."

Saros cleared his throat and nodded. "I do, Astrea. I trust you. And I'm sorry if I've crossed any sort of"—he gestured toward the floor—"line. You know I'm not very good at this parenting thing. I never have been."

"I'm grown, Uncle. I don't need you to parent me anymore."

Saros laughed, the first time Astrea had heard the sound in months. "Oh, my dear," he said with another chuckle. "Someday, if you have children of your own, you'll understand. We always need our parents, even as we grow and age." He patted her knee, then stood. "I've taken up enough of your time. Finish packing. I heard Adi saying you'd be leaving soon."

As Saros headed out the door, Astrea sighed. He meant well; she was sure he did. But why did he feel he could step in now, especially after all the ways he'd hurt not just her but also Jin?

Saros was trying to make things right, or at least, that was what Astrea thought he was trying to do. All the truths he'd finally given her. Getting that document from the emperor's office. Helping with the books. He was trying, even if he didn't know what lines to not cross.

Astrea sighed again and ran a hand over her braid. Someday she'd figure out how her uncle's mind worked. Until then, she had an airship to catch.

By the time night fell, Adi, Cressida, and Marko had completed another final engine check at Marko's insistence. All their bags were in the airship. Zephyrine had even ensured they all had one last decent meal.

The night's breeze played in the loose hair Astrea hadn't been able to capture in her braid, then twirled around the skirt of her dress. High above, just a sliver of the moon was visible among the brilliant stars. Astrea's magic buzzed in her veins.

"We're leaving for Katavena in a few hours," Zephyrine said to Jin. "We'll only be about a day behind you."

Jin nodded. "Then we'll see you soon."

Zephyrine extended her hand to him, but he pulled his commanding officer into a quick hug. She pushed away from him with a laugh. "Don't even think about it, Adi," she said as the Earthmover grinned at her. She pulled at her shirt and rolled her neck. "You kids and your sentimental-ities."

"See you in a few days, Zeph," Adi said instead, to which she rolled her eyes.

Saros embraced Cressida, then Astrea. Even with his poor choice in conversation topics earlier in the day, Astrea leaned into the hug. It reminded her of years long past, all the hugs he'd given her when she was much younger.

"Take care of yourself," Saros whispered to her. "See you in Talmaris."

"You too," Astrea said as she pulled away.

She joined Cressida near the airship as Jin went to speak with Saros. They were so different: Saros's shorter stature and smaller build com-pared to Jin's tall, muscular one; Saros's pale skin to Jin's light tawny; even Saros's dark hair to Jin's warm chestnut. The two men exchanged a few words in low voices, then shook hands before Jin joined both Astrea and Cressida.

"Ready?" he asked them. Adi and Marko were already climbing into the ship.

"Ready," Cressida said. "Let's get back to Novaria. I never thought I'd say it, but I think I actually miss it up there."

Cressida boarded the ship first, and Astrea followed. As Jin climbed up behind her, Astrea took one last look over her shoulder at where Zephyrine and Saros stood in the darkness, watching. She waved, and they both waved back.

Astrea pushed her shoulders back as she entered the ship. They'd been away from Novaria for long enough. It was time to return.

CHAPTER 49

The first leg of the trip on the airship was tense. Not because of the company but the simple stress of avoiding detection by the Helosians.

And Astrea couldn't escape the tense atmosphere. The ship was so small that there weren't any bedrooms or a second level. Just one cabin, one bathroom, and something that couldn't even be called a kitchen. The only place for Astrea to sit was in the main cabin with Cressida and Jin, and Marko or Adi whenever they switched off flying. Their route wasn't even direct; they were trying to avoid common Helosian flight paths Adi and Jin were familiar with.

So when Marko took off his headphones and yelled over his shoulder that he was going to land north of Thasia to refuel with Rami's people, Astrea couldn't help but be grateful. It might mean a few minutes of fresh air.

As the ship began its descent, Astrea watched the clouds and midafternoon sun out the small window to her left, then the tropical foliage as they drew closer to the ground. She counted back in her head, trying to remember when they'd arrived in Thasia that first night. It had been nearly a fortnight since. Not long by most standards, but they'd deviated so far away from their original plan.

"You alright?" Jin asked, nudging her shoulder with his.

They'd spent most of the flight taking turns sleeping whenever he and Cressida weren't checking on the engine or helping Marko and Adi with something. Astrea hated feeling useless up here in the sky, but there just wasn't anything for her to do. Now, both Cressida and Adi were half asleep on the row of seats adjacent to where Jin and Astrea sat together.

"Just thinking about everything."

"Your family?"

"Them," she admitted, "but . . . everything else." Astrea finally tore her gaze from the window and glanced up at Jin. "What did Saros say to you when we left last night?"

His expression softened. "He asked me to take care of you."

That was better than she'd imagined, at least. She wouldn't have been surprised if Saros had whispered some kind of useless threat against Jin.

"And what did you tell him?"

"That he didn't have to worry. That not only will I take care of you, but that the whole team will take care of each other. That seemed to settle his nerves."

And it was true, too. Astrea had never had that many close friends or that many people she could trust. But over the last few months, she'd seen what a team could do. How they had to take care of each other.

"Landing in two!" Marko yelled over the hum of the engines.

Cressida yawned and stretched as Adi sat up with a groan. The airship landed with a small jostle and clunk of metal on pavement. Outside, Astrea could make out the same airfield where they'd first landed in Thasia. A few people approached their ship.

"Should be Rami," Marko said as he climbed out of the pilot's seat and headed for the door.

As three figures outside drew closer, anxiety grated across Astrea's skin, rough and unwelcome. "Rami's anxious about something."

"Well, shit," Marko muttered.

Cressida clambered out of her seat, running one hand over her sleepy eyes and waving the other at the ship's sealed metal door. The locks began tumbling free, and Marko grabbed the wheel to speed up the process. They all pushed out the door and into the warm Thasian air.

Rami was indeed waiting just outside along with Talin—her Light-bringer friend—and a third person Astrea didn't recognize. The third was armed to the teeth, several guns and knives strapped to their lean body.

"What's going on?" Marko asked.

"What kind of greeting is that?" Rami asked, voice teasing despite the heavy tangle of orange in her aura.

"We know something's wrong," Marko said. "Astrea says you're anxious."

"Indeed, I am," Rami said as Talin flashed Astrea the smallest of smiles. Rami pivoted her entire body to face Jin and Jin alone. "There's talk of a Helosian prince being here with a fleet of airships."

"That's definitely not Apelo." Jin sucked in a heavy breath, then swore. "When did he arrive?"

Kaius? Kaius was in Thasia? Astrea's blood chilled.

"Last night. He's trying to meet with our government officials about your little stunt in Kalama."

"Stealing valuable information from my father is hardly a stunt," Jin said. "We got what we needed."

"How soon can we refuel the ship?" Marko asked Rami.

"Not long, maybe thirty minutes to get everything set," she replied. "We need to get you out of here. The Helosian airships are at a field on the southern side of the city."

"See if you can cut that thirty minutes down," Jin said.

"I'll try, Prince Varojin."

As Rami, Marko, Talin, and their well-armed friend strode off in search of Rami's airfield workers, Astrea forced her shoulders to relax.

Kaius wasn't *here*, at this airfield. But he was around, and that was bad enough.

"I'm surprised your father would let Kaius leave the country considering what he's been telling the public," Cressida said.

"Me too." Tugging at his curls, Jin stared out at the rest of the mostly empty airfield. "Maybe my father doesn't even know, if he's still out of the country." He sighed. "I suppose over two months without so much as a peep from him meant this was overdue. I crossed the line with that mission. I can only imagine how my father's going to take it."

"We had to, Jin," Astrea said.

"I know."

What would this mean for Eliana, Jin, and the rest of them moving forward? What would this mean for not just them but Helosia? Novaria?

"Should we stay here?" Cressida asked. "Plead our case to the Tornamians? Surely they'd want to hear what we have to say . . ."

"I think it would mean more coming from Ysabel," Jin said. "Her and my sister, both. My word's never held much weight."

"Would Rami be able to get in touch with Lucian again?" Astrea asked. "Maybe she can warn them faster than we can get back. If she can tell Ysabel now . . ."

"I've already got a message to Lucian," Rami said as she rounded the airship's corner. "Talmaris knows what's going on."

Marko rounded the ship next, jerking his chin toward the door. "We should stay on board. We'll be refueled in twenty minutes."

Astrea had hoped for fresh air, sure, but not with Kaius lurking around Thasia. Twenty more minutes on the ground seemed like twenty minutes too long.

As they all started to reboard the ship, Rami said, "Wait, Marko." She pulled a small envelope out of the pocket of her wide-legged trousers and passed it to the Tempest. "For Lucian. Please get this to him."

"I will. Thanks for everything."

"Better not bring the Helosians down on my ass next time I see you," she said.

He flashed her a grin. "Wouldn't dream of it."

After stuffing the envelope in his pocket, Marko ushered the rest of them farther into the ship. He and Cressida sealed the door, then Marko half dragged Adi toward their seats.

"What do you think about this, Jin?" Marko called over his shoulder.

"It's like I already told the others," Jin said as he followed the two men. "We went too long without hearing from my family. Kaius is angry, and if my father isn't aware of the situation, he will be soon. We can certainly expect some kind of retaliation."

"Like them going after Novaria?" Marko squeezed past Adi and dropped into the pilot's chair. He flicked a few switches on the dashboard. "Like the Helosians declaring war on Novaria?"

"Troops are spread too thin with Corsyca still being an issue," Adi said. "Your father wouldn't divert attention away from that to focus on you and Ellie, right?"

"Honestly," Jin said with a sigh, "I don't know anymore. I think he's willing to do anything to get that book back. That might mean abandoning Corsyca. He might not declare war on Novaria, but he'll certainly be declaring war on me."

Astrea set a hand on Jin's shoulder. He tensed for a moment, then relaxed. "Let's just get back to Talmaris," she said.

Marko nodded. "No use deliberating over something we're not going to solve. Best to see what the grand duchess has to say."

As Astrea settled back into her seat, she tried to rein her wild imagination back in. But she couldn't. All she could do was picture Kaius's fleet of Helosian war airships. Him approaching the Tornamian government about some kind of alliance against Novaria. Him finding Lord Anjou

Lazzaro's ship, along with Sarsali and Balthazar. Finding Zephyrine and Saros.

No. That could not happen. She couldn't let herself think the worst. Not when they were so close to getting back to Talmaris.

The airship jostled to one side, then back the other way. Astrea startled awake from her doze, muscles tensing. The floor underneath her was hard, cold.

After leaving Thasia, she and Jin had bunked down on the airship's floor while Cressida and Marko took the padded benches. Adi was at the helm. The airship jostled again, its metal body creaking. But Astrea's magic brushed up against nothing other than Adi's steady focus and fatigue. Everyone else was asleep.

Turbulence, she told herself as the bumps continued. *Just turbulence.*

How much longer until they crossed into Novarian territory? They might be getting close; Jin had asked Adi and Marko to fly as fast as they could on as direct of a route as they could considering the development with Kaius. And last Astrea had been awake, she'd heard Marko talking about how the winds were working in their favor.

Jin twitched as the ship bumped and bounced again. Only instead of waking, terror pushed against Astrea's skin, cold and somehow distant. A faint sheen of white blossomed around Jin's body. His muscles flexed and relaxed, flexed and relaxed, as that white terror pulsed over and over again.

"Jin," Astrea whispered as she rolled toward him. When he didn't wake, she pressed a gentle hand to his chest and shook him. "Jin, wake up."

His eyes cracked open. The white undulating around him dissipated, replaced by minty cool relief on Astrea's tongue.

"You were having a bad dream," she murmured.

Jin pulled Astrea into his arms and cradled her to his chest, then he tangled one hand in her hair at the base of her neck. Slowly, his body began to relax. "Just a dream," he whispered, so low Astrea barely heard him above the engines.

"Just a dream," she repeated. "I'm here."

His pulse slowed. He relaxed more. She thought about asking exactly what that dream was, but with the way his energy calmed and slowed, she didn't want to upset him again. So, she buried her face in the crook of his neck.

"Sorry if I woke you," he said.

"You didn't."

When the ship bumped again, Adi called out, "Anyone awake?"

Jin finally disentangled himself from Astrea and, with a grunt, pushed to his feet. He half stumbled toward where Adi sat. Astrea forced herself off the floor and followed as orange lit up the front of the ship.

"How bad is it?" Jin asked, voice rough with sleep.

"Bad," Adi said.

"What's wrong?" Astrea asked.

"Storm ahead, hence the bumps."

Astrea peered out the front windows. There, distorting the clouds and dark sky, were massive clouds.

"Can we make it through?" Jin asked.

Adi shook his head. "I wouldn't risk it."

"And going around it?"

"We can either fly up the Tornamian coast and try to take the long way back to Talmaris," Adi said, "or we can fly over Helosia for . . . about two hours, then we'll cross into Novarian territory."

"Can we make it the long way?"

"We can, but I wouldn't advise it. Don't know how big that storm system is. It could extend well beyond where we want to go."

"Fuck," Jin muttered. He rubbed at his face and let out a harsh, heavy sigh. "Alright. Cut over Helosia."

"Is that really a good idea?" Astrea asked.

"This part of the country is barely populated anyway," Jin said. "Just push us fast, Adi."

Adi flipped several blinking switches on the control panel, then the ship lurched left. "You got it, Captain."

Jin tugged on Astrea's arm, but she couldn't look away from the storm even as the ship pitched and turned in the opposite direction. "Something about it doesn't look right," she said.

"Could be a Stormchaser," Adi said. "Skies only knows who's down there in the mountains."

Astrea pressed her lips together. What would a Stormchaser be doing down there to create such a magnificent, enormous storm?

"Wake Marko for me, would you?" Adi asked Astrea. "My eyes hurt."

"Let him sleep," Astrea said. "I can take some of the fatigue."

Lavender surprise bubbled up around Adi. "What?"

"It's fine, Adi. We need both you and Marko in good shape. We've still got a ways to go. Let him rest for now."

"Well, if you're sure."

"I'm sure."

Astrea placed her hand on Adi's shoulder. A faint trace of starlight glowed from her hands as Astrea's eyes grew heavy. Skies damn, that was a lot. She hadn't realized Adi was *so* tired.

"Better?" she asked, sucking in a sharp breath as she pulled her hand away.

Adi straightened in his seat. "A lot better, actually."

"Good. Wake me up if you need it again."

Astrea left Adi to navigate them past the storm. She crossed the short distance to where Jin had lain back down on the floor. A few blankets were spread out beneath him, and as Astrea joined him, she let her eyes fall closed.

"Is he okay?" Jin asked as he tucked another blanket around them both.

"Fine," Astrea said.

"And you?" Jin pressed a kiss to the back of Astrea's head.

"Fine," she repeated. She was going to ask Jin about his dream, but before she could, sleep took her.

"Az."

Astrea groaned as she turned in the arms wrapped around her. She buried her face in a warm, hard chest.

"Az, I really need you to wake up."

"Can't," she whispered.

Skies, she was so tired. Bone-deep tired, like a thousand weights were dragging her to the bottom of the ocean.

"You have to."

Jin. It was Jin she was snuggled up against. He jostled her, gently at first then harder.

"Az, you have to wake up. Please."

With a huff, Astrea rolled away from Jin's warm body and forced her eyes open. The airship ceiling—industrial gray metal—stared back at her. Around her, voices carried and bounced off the walls. Cressida. Marko. Adi. The airship rumbled beneath her. Anxiety grated on her skin.

"What's wrong?" Astrea asked, tilting her stiff neck to look at Jin.

His mouth was set in a hard line. "Someone's following us."

"Who?"

"We don't know."

What was she supposed to do about that, exactly? Astrea tugged at her consciousness, begging it to wake up. She might not be able to figure out who was following them, but Jin was right. She needed to be alert.

"I'm awake," she said, voice rough. "I'm awake. I'll get up."

Jin helped her to her feet. She needed water or coffee or something, anything to help clear the fatigue from her mind. But Adi's exhaustion was still stacked on top of hers. Outside, dawn barely lit up the sky.

"Is there any way we can get a better look at that ship?" Jin asked as he moved around Astrea and toward where Adi and Marko sat at the helm.

"Not unless they get closer or we try to circle around them," Adi said. "They're holding steady speed as far as I can tell."

Marko peered at one of the dials on the dashboard. "Steady is good."

"Yet the fact that someone is following us is bad," Cressida said. "Is it Kaius?"

"How would he even have known we were in Thasia?" Adi asked. He leaned to his right, toward what looked like the eyepiece of a telescope. With a sigh, he straightened again. "I can't tell if the ship's Helosian or not. It's too far away. And I think there's more than one."

"Can we go any faster?" Jin asked.

"Not much," Marko said. "But we can try."

"Then we need to try," Jin said. "Get us back into Novarian airspace as soon as possible. And radio to whomever you can once we're in range, Marko."

With a nod, Marko began flipping switches and pressing buttons. Adi joined him, his fingers flying over the various controls. It made Astrea's head spin, or maybe that was just everything else going on inside her body.

"What can I do?" Astrea asked Jin as she followed him to the windows at the back of the cabin.

"Nothing for now, I suppose. You either, Cress. Just be ready."

"For what?" Cressida asked.

"Anything. Everything."

Astrea plopped onto the bench next to Cressida, then leaned against her best friend. They settled in together, and Astrea let her eyes close again. She didn't sleep, though. She listened to Adi and Marko's indistinguishable chatter, and Cressida offered theories to Jin. Maybe it was Zephyrine and Saros's ship, or maybe it was the Helosians, or maybe it was just a coincidence and it wasn't anyone important at all.

The two of them argued in circles about it, and Astrea almost told them to stop when Marko finally called out over his shoulder, "We'll cross into Novaria in just a few minutes. Closest place I can radio is a fort near Irvina."

"Do it!" Jin called back.

"On it."

Jin paced back to the window, his shoulders tight, but he said nothing, nor did Cressida. *At least they aren't arguing anymore.* The ship bumped and rumbled as it went along.

"They're putting too much stress on the engine," Cressida said, her fingers twitching where her hands rested on her thighs.

"How can you possibly tell?" Astrea asked.

"I can feel it." Cressida hesitated for just a moment before she yelled, "You need to slow down!"

"We're not even two miles from the border!" Adi called. "We can make it."

"Not if you keep pushing it."

"Slow down!" Jin yelled. "No use getting us to the border if we crash before we make it. But only slow down as much as we absolutely have to."

"Or the other ships are going to overtake us instead," Adi said. "They're gaining."

"Fuck," Cressida muttered. "Fine, don't slow down. I'll go try to keep the engine in one piece."

"Be careful," Astrea said as Cressida pushed to her feet and stomped to the door in the floor that led to the engine room. Cressida yanked it open, then disappeared as she climbed down the ladder.

Marko grabbed the mouthpiece for the radio, speaking in frantic Novarian. He paused, then started speaking again. If he was getting a reply, Astrea couldn't hear.

"Oh, it's definitely the Helosians," Adi yelled over his shoulder.

"I see them," Jin said.

Astrea scrambled to where he still stood near the window and peeked out behind him. Sure enough, the airship in the distance was painted red. Several more trailed the lead ship.

After months of nothing, after waiting for this day, the Helosians had finally caught up with them.

Chapter 50

"What do we do?" Astrea asked.

"We get over that border as fast as we can and hope the Novarians are ready to get in a fight," Jin said, grabbing Astrea's hand and pulling her away from the window. "Tell Cress, then both of you need to get back up here."

As Jin dropped her hand and strode toward where Adi and Marko still sat steady at the helm, Astrea yanked open the hatch to the engine room. She poked her head inside and yelled, "Cress!"

"What?" The roar of the engine nearly drowned out Cressida's voice.

"It's definitely the Helosians! Jin says to get back up here."

"Can't or this skies damned engine's going to fall apart!"

Astrea's gaze flicked back up to Jin, Adi, and Marko, who were all hunched over the radio. With a huff, Astrea climbed down the ladder into the engine room. Warm air coated her skin, drawing perspiration straight to her brow. Cressida wiped at her own forehead with the sleeve of her blouse, her attention focused solely on the engine in front of her.

It was similar to the one Adi and Marko had found some issues with back at that base, but Astrea still didn't understand what she was looking at. Wheels, knobs, long arms, lots of steam. Cressida's fingers twitched as hot air shot out from a valve. Astrea flinched.

"What's wrong with it?" she asked.

"Getting way too hot," Cressida said.

"Can we cool it?"

"Maybe if Civan were here, but I can't do anything other than try to keep everything working."

"Jin said we just need to get over the border, then we can slow down."

"Well then." Cressida's hands settled on her hips. "I guess I'd better stop talking and just focus."

"You said we could cool it if Civan were here," Astrea said. "Would water help?"

"It's probably going to damage it, but yeah, it might get us the last of the way."

"I'll go get some."

"We need a lot!" Cressida shouted after Astrea as she scrambled back up the ladder.

As soon as Astrea pulled herself out of the hole in the floor, she yelled, "Jin, we need water! A lot of it!"

Then she went to the so-called kitchen, which was really just a small sink and several cabinets. She found a glass jar and a few cups; none of them would hold much, but if she could just fill up enough of them . . .

"Take one down to her," Jin said, reaching around Astrea to take several of the containers. "I'll fill up more and hand them down to you."

As Jin went to the washroom with his empty cups, Astrea filled the jar as much as she dared and hurried back to the ladder. She managed to only spill a little as she climbed down, then passed the jar to a waiting Cressida.

"This is it?" she asked.

"Jin's getting more. It's all we have."

"Fuck me." Cressida jogged toward the engine, jar in hand, and yelled over her shoulder, "Bring me more!"

Astrea started back up the ladder only to Jin waiting at the top, ready to hand her a tall glass filled with cool water. They repeated the process a few times, with Astrea bringing back empty containers for Jin to refill. The engine room grew hotter by the second.

"It's not helping," Cressida said as she joined Astrea at the bottom of the ladder. "How close are we, Jin?"

"Adi?" Jin shouted. Astrea couldn't hear Adi's response, but Jin looked back down at them and said, "We're in Novaria."

"Then tell him to slow the fuck down," Cressida said.

"The Helosians are right behind us—" Astrea started, only for steam to start pouring into the room.

"Adi, slow down!" Jin yelled. He paused. "What do you mean?" Another pause. "Well slow down anyway!" Then he started climbing down into the engine room. He rolled up his sleeves as soon as his feet hit the floor. "What can I do, Cress?"

"What the fuck is going on?" Cressida asked him instead.

"Helosians coming from the southwest, too. Farther away, so we'll worry about them later. What can I do to make sure we even make it to this base Marko's bringing us to?"

Just how many people had Emperor Aelius sent after them? Astrea swallowed hard and wiped at the sweat beading across her forehead.

"Shit," Cressida muttered. "Can your fireweaving take some of this heat away?"

"I've never tried."

"Well, now might be the perfect time to figure it out, Your Highness."

Jin shot Cressida a glare over his shoulder as he strode toward the engine. At first, it didn't even look like he was doing anything. But his hands slowly raised toward the metal block in the middle of the room.

"Well?" Cressida asked. "Anything?"

"I feel it," Jin said. "Let me try."

His wide shoulders heaved with a deep breath. He lifted his hand again, only to stagger forward.

"Jin?" Astrea asked. "What—"

Pain exploded in Astrea's body, stabbing her sternum and the spot between her shoulder blades. It doubled, tripled, quadrupled as her vision went dark. Cressida cried out.

Oh, Souleater, The One mused. *You've brought your friends back with you, I see. Have you thought any more about my offer?*

All Astrea could feel was that pain. Ghost pain throughout the ship as The One dreamwalked to all of them.

We're midair, Astrea said. *Let us go and I'll meet you at the ruins.*

And how is that my problem? The One asked.

Because you're dreamwalking to the people flying our airship.

Am I? The One chuckled as the ship pitched down. Astrea stumbled forward even though the ship leveled again. *Don't worry, Miss Sovna.*

The hairs on Astrea's arms prickled as bone-chilling cold replaced the oppressive heat of the engine room. The darkness crowding her vision dissipated just long enough for Astrea to make out the masked figure in front of her. Grabbing her wrist, they pulled her into the void.

They didn't land. Wind slapped at Astrea's face, tears clouding her vision as she tried to take in the cotton candy sunrise. High above them, their airship sped forward, a second one painted black flying right alongside it. It veered left, away from their ship.

"Az!" Jin yelled, barely audible over the roar of air.

Whoever held onto Astrea's wrist jumped them again. Void swirled around them, heavy and disorienting and so freezing cold. The next time the sunrise came into view, they were still free-falling. Astrea struggled against her captor, but they held tight and jumped a third time.

Vomit crept up Astrea's throat as they landed on hard, solid ground. Branches and rocks scraped her skin as she tumbled again and again. Nearby, Jin grunted, and the pain in Astrea's body doubled.

"Az!" Jin yelled again.

Astrea forced herself to her feet, vision blurring. She straightened just in time to see the void mage headed straight for her, their obsidian mask glinting in the early morning sun filtering in through the trees.

Her shield burst to life. The void mage lunged forward. Astrea shoved into them with all the strength she could muster. They fell to the ground, crying out as their head slammed into the forest floor.

They rolled over and staggered to their feet. Astrea took half a step back, throwing her shield up again as they came at her with void fire.

In front of her, Jin battled with the second void mage, nothing but a flurry of red flames and gray shadow. Jin stumbled as the void mage landed a blow. Astrea's muscles tensed. That strange, wrong power charging up in front of her forced her attention back to her opponent.

They moved in, shadows flaring to life over their hands. Astrea willed more light into her shield, pulling on the panic running through her veins. Every time the void mage advanced, Astrea retreated.

"Can't keep this up forever, Souleater," they sneered as they circled her.

Astrea's whole body dragged with each movement, impossibly heavy and slow. She wasn't usually this slow.

Astrea let her shield drop. "Then let's finish it."

She swore that mask smiled a mean smile as they stalked forward. Astrea took several steps back, lowering her center of gravity as she did.

The void mage charged. Brilliant starlight lit up the forest as Astrea summoned her shield again and slammed into them. They fell again, harder this time.

Ghost pain of bone fracturing whispered through Astrea's body, but she couldn't even focus on that. Something sharp and burning hot pinged in Astrea's chest. Blood and flesh squelched behind her, and the cold pulsing through the forest lessened.

"Get back, Az!" Jin called.

She pivoted. Jin strode up to her, circling around the disoriented void mage. Grabbing them by their collar, he shoved a blade of fire deep into their chest. The cold pressing into Astrea's senses flickered out completely as Jin dropped the body and his fire disappeared.

Dead. They were dead.

Jin had killed both of them.

"Come on," he said, grabbing her hand. "We need to go."

"Which way?" Astrea asked, her breath coming in short, harsh gasps as they sprinted through the thinning forest.

"This way," Jin said, adjusting his trajectory the slightest bit. "Adi was headed northeast, toward that base. They're probably already coming back to look for us."

Sure, they would be if The One hadn't locked them in some kind of dreamwalking state. But Astrea didn't say that. They had to keep going.

They sprinted through the forest hand in hand, Jin guiding the way as Astrea focused on her senses. Nothing. No void mages lying in wait. None of that oppressive cold.

The farther they ran, the more Astrea's body was ready to give out. Taking that fatigue from Adi just an hour or two before had seemed harmless. *Foolish,* Astrea chided herself. Her bones may as well have weighed a million pounds.

"Can we stop?" she asked. "Just for a moment."

As Jin slowed to a walk, he said, "We need to keep going."

"Yes, well, you didn't take a day's worth of exhaustion from Adi."

They stopped. Astrea leaned forward, hands on her knees, and breathed deeply the way Adi had taught her weeks before. Her lungs loosened. "Where'd they come from?" she asked as she straightened. "How'd he find us?"

Jin grabbed her hand, forcing her to walk again. "Don't know." He scanned the forest, but he didn't have to. Astrea sensed nothing. "Probably knew we were in the Taipoli Islands or someone in Thasia told him."

"Who? We only saw Rami's people."

"Maybe Rami or one of them is compromised."

Would Lucian's ex-wife be working with the Paragon? No, that didn't seem right. Talin, the Lightbringer? But what would he gain? Or maybe that stranger who'd been with them, the one armed to the teeth? It didn't matter at that moment; there wasn't anything they could do. They were hundreds of miles away from Thasia.

Ahead, the forest began to thin out. The distance between soaring trees grew, and the colorful bushes and flowers became sparse. And ahead, far in the distance, was a road.

"Come on," Jin said, breaking into a jog.

They kept pushing, farther and faster until they were sprinting again. Trees passed them by in a blur, and some distant part of Astrea's mind was surprised she hadn't tripped on the thick brush.

As the trees cleared, their steps finally slowed. They had eyes on the sky again, but there was no sign of their airship. No—yes? Something soared past high above them, a mix of blue, white, and gray. Yes, that was their airship. That damn paint job Jin and Adi had said the military used for camouflage.

And it was headed right toward the red Helosian ship flying north. Where was the rest of the fleet?

"What are they doing?" Jin muttered. He tugged Astrea closer to the road. "Adi, ascend. Don't get close."

Their small airship swung around above the trees, then headed north again. "Did they see us?" Astrea asked.

"I don't think so."

The ship zoomed past overhead, smoke trailing out of the bottom.

"They're heading toward town and the base," Jin said. "Come on."

Though the road was next to them, Jin led them back into the edge of the forest. They followed the road for at least a mile, every so often leaving the cover of the woods to check the skies again. Their airship had long since disappeared, but the Helosian one crept closer. It had slowed down, almost like they were hesitating to be in Novarian territory.

"Why would they follow us across the border?" Astrea asked.

"The better question is where are the Novarian airships?" Jin asked. "The base commander should've sent them in to help once Marko contacted them."

"Did he contact them?"

"He said they responded."

"Did Ysabel give them orders not to engage?" Astrea asked. "She hasn't exactly been thrilled with us lately."

"Not liking our plans and letting Helosians shoot a member of her family out of the sky are very different things," Jin said. "I doubt she'd give orders like that. Besides, she's never let Helosian aggression go unchecked before."

They started around a bend in the road. It curved away into the forest, but far down the stretch, were several buildings. More in the distance. No gates. Town, maybe?

That strangely painted airship zipped past again, smoke still trailing from its back. It headed for the Helosian ship again, which had stopped moving.

"What are they doing?" Astrea asked. "Why didn't they go to the—"

A projectile exploded from the Helosian ship and slammed right into the smaller one. The ship burst into flames as it flew underneath the Helosians and slammed into the ground in a mangled mess of fire and metal.

Astrea screamed. She sprinted for the ship, wiggling out of Jin's grasp when he tried to haul her back. Cressida was in there. Adi and Marko were in there. She could not let them burn.

"Az!" Jin shouted, though the footsteps and panic surging right behind her told her he was following. "Wait!"

The burning wreckage exploded again. The ground rocked, sending Astrea tumbling back. Jin caught her. He steadied her, then pushed her forward.

"They're hurt," Astrea cried. Pain overwhelmed her, broken bones and bruised skin and skies, the fire. "They're hurt."

Jin sprinted ahead of her, each stride steady and strong. He skidded to a stop not far from the burning airship, and with one sweep of his arms, the fire snuffed out. Like it was nothing, like he'd blown out a single birthday candle.

Astrea hurdled past him. She pushed and pushed until the heat from the smoking debris snapped out at her exposed arms.

"Careful!" Jin yelled. "It's going to be hot!"

She didn't care. Astrea didn't know where to look first. "Where are they?" she asked Jin. "Help me find them."

"There." Jin pointed to what had to have been the front of the ship. Adi was pushing up to his hands and knees, a sputtering, barking cough exploding from his chest.

"Find Cress," Astrea said. Marko, too, had popped his head up, his blond hair streaked with dark ash.

Astrea hurried to where Adi and Marko were both trying to pull themselves from the wreckage. Pain washed over Astrea again and again and again, pulsing through every inch of her body.

"Hold still," she said to them. "Hold still, just stop moving. Let me see."

"Az?" Adi asked.

"Where's Cress?" she asked as she sank to her knees. Hot debris pressed into her skin. "What's hurt?"

"My leg," Adi wheezed. "I think it's broken."

"And Marko?" Astrea asked.

"I'm fine," he said. "Just bumped my head."

"You're not fine. I can feel it."

"Take care of Adi," Marko said, voice strained. When she hesitated, he rasped, "Please."

Astrea helped Adi sit down on the pavement just away from the destroyed ship, then pulled on Jin's growing panic and her own thundering fear. They surged into her light. Astrea gritted her teeth as mirror healing and pain warred on her left shin, as her bone seemed to piece itself back together in time with Adi's. He slumped back and groaned.

Marko crawled toward them and rolled onto his back. Despite everything pressing into Astrea, she forced herself to move to him. "What's hurt?" she asked him again.

"Head, shoulder, knee."

Astrea pulled and pulled on her light, pushing it deeper into Marko's body. He sighed in relief. Tears sprang to Astrea's eyes as the pain in her body doubled. *Skies damn it.*

"Where's Cress?" she asked. "Where was she?"

"She was in the engine room," Adi said. "Was trying to find something to hit the Helosians with. Flew to the base but it was under attack."

Astrea risked a glance skyward. The Helosian ship had drifted past them and was now descending. Smoke rose over the trees in the distance. Much closer, Jin was moving large pieces of metal. Every time he touched them, Astrea's palms burned.

"Can you two fight them?" she asked Adi and Marko. "Can you fight them off?"

"Give me thirty seconds and I can get up," Adi said.

"We don't have thirty seconds, Adi."

"Ten seconds." He sucked in one deep breath, then another. "Alright."

Astrea shoved to her feet and ran to where Jin was still picking through the wreckage. Her knees almost gave out as pain overwhelmed her. The closer she got to Jin, the worse it grew. That couldn't be him. It had to be Cress. Panic and pain and . . . and annoyance, of all things.

"She's here," Astrea said. "She's around here, I can feel her."

Metal shuddered and whined as it unfurled like a flower blooming on a spring day.

"Cress," Astrea breathed.

There she was, curled up under all that metal. Cressida's entire body trembled and shook. A thin piece of metal jutted out from her abdomen. It wasn't long, just enough to pierce the lower right side of her torso. Blood stained her white shirt, bright red and awful.

"Az?" Cressida asked with a cough. "Thank fuck."

Astrea fell to her knees, barely noticing the pain of metal and rubble digging into her flesh. "Hold on, Cress. I'm going to get this thing out of you. Just lie still."

"Can't move even if I want to." Cressida wheezed. "*Fuck*, that hurts."

Jin dropped to the ground beside Astrea. "Shit, Cress. Just hold on."

Astrea sucked in one shallow breath, then another, as she stared down at the short rod rammed into Cressida's torso. She just had to get that out, then she could heal her. It would be fine. It would be fine if she had enough time, but the Helosian airship's door hissed as it unsealed.

"Can you pull it out?" she asked Jin. "I'll be ready to heal it."

He pushed his shoulders back. "On the count of three."

Astrea set her hands on either side of Cressida's wound as Jin gripped the metal.

"One," he said. "Two."

Light built around Astrea's palms.

"Three."

Jin yanked the metal out with a sickening squelch. Cressida screamed, and Astrea screamed with her as she pushed every ray of light into her that she could. Everything. She pulled on Cressida's growing panic. Her own growing panic. The fear swirling around them as Adi and Marko headed for the Helosians. But she thought of Sarsali and Balthazar too, of their gentle hugs and banter before they'd gotten on that boat.

Her light grew and grew until it blinded her. She screamed as pain tore through her, as muscle and flesh stitched themselves back together in Cressida's body and her own. Tears leaked down Astrea's cheeks even when she pulled her hands away and even as Cressida coughed and groaned.

Astrea slumped back, finding Jin's hard body right behind hers.

"Skies damn me." Cressida groaned. "Don't ever let me in an airship again."

With Jin's help, Astrea sat forward. Cressida's warm copper skin lacked its usual glow, but there, where that metal rod had been, was solid flesh and dried blood.

"Fuck," Jin muttered.

As Astrea helped Cressida sit up, they both looked toward where Adi and Marko waited a dozen feet away. The Helosian airship door was open, and a handful of guards dressed in Auris red lined up on either side of the stairs.

As the last guard descended, there was just one person left standing in the airship doorway.

Victor Nazarov stepped out of the ship and raised his hand in greeting. "Souleater and Sunreaper. So lovely to see you again. Now tell me, where's my book?"

Chapter 51

Victor Nazarov.

Nazarov was there, stepping out of a Helosian airship. With ten Helosian royal guards.

Not necessarily, Astrea realized. Their uniforms didn't fit quite right, not the way Helosian guards uniforms always fit. Always perfectly tailored to their bodies. Never a hair out of place. The sleeves were too long on some of the so-called guards, while the pants were too short on others.

Not all of them were void mages. While some were surrounded by heavy walls, anticipation seeped out from others.

"Well?" Nazarov called. As he moved farther away from the craft, Solana exited behind him. Cold blistered Astrea's skin.

"Why'd you shoot us down?" Jin shouted, then gestured to the wreckage. "Everything's gone. I thought you needed us, and yet you're trying to kill us."

"Because we saw you two get jumped out of your ship by The One's lapdogs," Nazarov said. "Speaking of, where are they?"

"Taken care of," Jin snapped. "Want to join them?"

Nazarov chuckled as he took another few steps forward. Adi and Marko shifted, both of them looking slower than Astrea had seen them in all their time training together.

"You couldn't kill me even if you tried, princeling." Nazarov smiled. "Where's the book? Solana tells me my favorite little Lightbringer found it."

Astrea swallowed hard, her hand still on Cressida's shoulder as they crouched near the ground. "You shot us down," Astrea said. "Everything on the ship was destroyed."

"Is that so?" Nazarov asked.

"You mean to tell me you can't see the wreckage?"

"Watch the tone, Miss Sovna."

She pressed her lips together. Beneath her hand, Cressida shivered. Astrea desperately wanted to check her over with her magic, but even if Nazarov weren't standing so close, she wasn't sure she had anything left to give. That fatigue, the kind when she'd overused her magic, pulled at the edges of her consciousness, weighing her down.

"Tell you what," Nazarov said. "You give me the book, and I'll tell The One I have it. He should leave you alone for a little while. You'd like that, wouldn't you? Or . . ." He laughed, low and deep. "If you don't, I'll just keep following you two across the world until you give me what I want. I think I've proven just how persistent I can be. And I'm fairly certain whatever's in that book will help me restore balance and leave you two out of it."

Astrea didn't believe that even for a second. Nazarov wouldn't have been so insistent on getting her to cooperate when he didn't actually need her for his plan, whatever it might be. He wouldn't have tortured her under that house.

As Jin began to speak, cold swept over Astrea's skin. Not cold from Nazarov and Solana. New cold. So much cold, moving toward them faster and faster.

"Jin," Astrea whispered. "More are coming."

They needed to leave. Find a way to get past Nazarov and Solana and away from The One.

"You want the book?" Jin called to Nazarov. "Then give us a few minutes to find it in this mess you've made."

"Don't take too long, princeling."

As Jin pivoted and surveyed the wreckage, Adi and Marko slowly joined them. They positioned themselves just so, keeping their attention on Nazarov and his followers.

"Cress," Jin said quietly, "can you help Adi and Marko?"

"I can try, though I don't think I'll be a good shot right now. Why?" she asked as Astrea helped her to her feet.

The faintest light twinkled around Astrea's fingers as she pressed her hand to Cressida's abdomen. Everything was healed; it didn't mean Cressida would feel *good*, though.

"Stall them. If we find that book, Az and I are going to run."

"Why?" Cressida asked again. "We might be able to hold them off until the—"

"Not with all of them coming." That cold moved closer, coating Astrea's limbs and seeping into her blood. "There are too many."

"Stall whomever you can until the Novarians arrive," Jin said.

"Jin, the smoke—" Adi started.

"They should get someone here regardless," Marko said. Black smoke rose above the tree line, higher and higher. "Someone will come."

Jin began picking through the wreckage again, slowly and deliberately. "Az and I won't go far. You think the Paragon leader is here, Az?"

"I can't tell, but I think so." The One wouldn't have sent just two of his lackeys to nab them. Even if it wasn't The One himself, surely they were Paragon. The One's Paragon, not Nazarov's.

"If it is, we'll try to turn them against each other. Now let's look for this book."

"This is foolish, Jin," Cressida said. "Just stay here. Now's not the time to gamble."

"Az and I can take care of ourselves," Jin said as he kneeled down. "Marko, you're sure your people are coming?"

"I'd bet my life on it."

Jin pushed a piece of metal away, revealing several half-burned knapsacks. "Let's hope both our gambles are right, then."

"I'm waiting, princeling!" Nazarov yelled.

"I think I found it!"

Astrea's hands shook as she helped Jin open the bags. Sure enough, inside one was the book, looking a little worse for the wear but mostly intact. "What if he looks inside?" she whispered.

"Then he'll be distracted enough for me to kill him," Jin said.

Skies, she hoped he was right. This was barely a plan at all. But the voids pressing in closer would have them backed into a corner. What else could they do? Let Nazarov or The One take them? They had to try something.

Book in hand, Jin stood and waved it in the air. "Found it!"

"At least you two aren't totally useless," Nazarov said. "Just think of what we could do if we actually worked together."

"Not a chance!" Adi called.

"Nobody asked you, Earthmover."

Jin clutched the book in one hand, then took Astrea's in the other. "Don't let go of my hand no matter what," he said as he peered down at her. "Ready?"

Astrea was far from ready. Her gut ached from where she'd healed Cressida. Her head, knee, and shoulders ached from where she'd healed Adi and Marko. But she had to go.

"Ready."

"Well?" Nazarov stretched his arms out to both sides. "I'm waiting."

Adi, Marko, and Cressida shifted, their boots scuffing the tiny pieces of debris scattered across the pavement.

Jin passed the book to Astrea. She held it to her chest. Her lungs tightened, and her muscles tensed. She shivered. The voids approaching were so close now.

"I forgot how little patience you have, Nazarov," Jin replied. "But I'm a little slow after, well." He gestured to the ruined airship. "You get the idea."

"Just—" Nazarov paused, turning to look around as cold swept through the area like a winter breeze.

One by one, masked members of the Paragon emerged from the forest. Masks of gray, white, red. Dark gray uniforms. A small army.

Nazarov's glare shifted from the forest to Solana and back again. "What is this?"

One tall, familiar form stepped out onto the road. That white mask trimmed with obsidian. The crisp, dark suit. The carefully coiffed hair.

The One.

"You didn't really think you'd killed me, did you, Advocate Nazarov?" The One called. "I won't be put down so easily."

"I knew you were still lurking around here somewhere," Nazarov snapped. "Back off. The book's mine."

"Don't you mean you retrieved the book for me?" The One asked. "I am your king, Advocate."

"Maybe in your dreams. You preach balance and taking down the continental powers, yet you call yourself a king."

"As if you wouldn't crown yourself if you had the opportunity. I know you, Advocate." The One chuckled as he strolled closer. "Don't be so self-righteous."

"Self-righteous?" Nazarov turned toward The One. "As if you aren't? Going on and on about our history and duty and blah, blah, blah." Black spiked around him, there one heartbeat and gone the next. "But you never wanted to *do* anything, *Your Highness.* I'm willing to take action."

"You call the last few months action?" The One barked. "You've done nothing but create problems for me. I never should have listened to you. You have no plan, Advocate. You're taking our creed of chaos a bit too literally."

"As if *you* have a plan?" Nazarov gazed out at the group of Paragon. "You really want this pathetic, weak, indecisive man to be your leader?" With each word, he jabbed his finger in The One's direction. "Is that really who you're going to follow? Is that really who you think can lead you into the new age?"

A few low murmurs came from the group.

"Enough!" The One bellowed. His followers quieted as Nazarov just crossed his arms over his chest. "You will either fall in line behind me, Nazarov, or I'll deal with you today."

"You're nothing but an old man who won't get his hands dirty," Nazarov spat. "I'd like to see you try."

Cold spiked in the air as The One disappeared in a puff of shadow. He materialized behind Nazarov, black flames dancing over his palms. Pivoting, Nazarov withdrew a knife from his belt.

"Go, Az." Jin pushed her to their right, east toward the forest on the other side of the road.

Astrea ran. Jin stayed right behind her, a shield, as Nazarov roared, "Now look what you've done!"

Metal groaned, and the earth under their feet trembled. She so badly wanted to look back over her shoulder at the sounds of fighting and elements clashing, at the pain flowing toward her, but she kept her eyes trained on the trees as they ran.

"Souleater!" Nazarov shouted. "Sunreaper! Get back here!"

Astrea ran faster, propelled by Jin's intense speed. He guided them around trees as they moved deeper and deeper into the forest, occasionally changing directions but always heading north. The farther they ran, the closer Nazarov and another void seemed to grow.

As shadows snaked up from the ground just a dozen feet ahead, Jin pulled Astrea to the left. She risked a glance over her shoulder and found The One staring at them, that strange inky darkness spiking around his head.

"Jin," Astrea said between breaths. "I can attack them. Their auras—"

"Save it for when we really need it."

Brush crunched underfoot. The morning sun disappeared behind the thick canopy of leaves high above. Astrea's lungs burned. Her muscles screamed. But they could not stop. She willed one foot in front of the other as she clung to Jin with one hand and held the book in the other.

Cold pressed in so close it made the hairs on the back of Astrea's neck stand on end. And as someone yanked on her hair, Astrea cried out.

The void sucked her and Jin in, their hands still tightly clasped. They landed, slamming against the ground with a loud thwack. Jin rolled them over, shielding Astrea with his body and not letting her go. That cold sucked them in again, spitting them out near the edge of the forest. Beyond the shadows crowding Astrea's vision, she could just make out a town.

"Come on, Az," Jin whispered. "Gotta get up."

He yanked her off the ground so hard she thought her arm might dislodge from its socket. They both swayed on their feet.

"Always with the running, eh, Souleater?" Nazarov cooed as he strolled toward them. "Do I really need to teach you this lesson again?"

Frost pierced Astrea's limbs just before Solana appeared behind Nazarov. "Your little Metalli friend shouldn't have killed Tovan like that," she said. "Now you've just made me angry, Souleater."

Before Solana could take a step forward, pain exploded in Astrea's back. Shadows took over her vision, and through the roaring in her ears, she heard Nazarov and Solana both curse. Astrea clung to Jin's arm as they stumbled.

Cold flooded Astrea's veins. Brush crunched. But she couldn't move. She couldn't do anything, not even as someone tore the book from her arms.

"Thank you for finding this for me, Miss Sovna," said The One. "I knew you could be helpful."

Astrea tensed, the words she so wanted to scream at him lodged in her throat. The rage. The anger. The fear. She hated that man. Skies, did she hate him for all he'd put her through and all he planned.

The darkness receded as The One strolled toward where Nazarov and Solana were crouched on the ground, chests heaving. "See, Advocate? Not everything has to be a fight."

With a growl, Nazarov lunged at The One. They fell to the ground in a tangle of limbs and dark fire, ghost pain and freezing cold air. The book landed somewhere among the brush.

"Do we get it?" Astrea asked Jin.

"No," he said. "Run."

And so they ran.

Chapter 52

Trees and bushes filled with colorful flowers whizzed by in a blur as Astrea and Jin sprinted away from the fighting void mages. Cold rippled through the air in continuous waves, never diminishing even as Astrea ran away from them.

Jin tugged Astrea along at breakneck speed, so fast she kept tripping over herself. He pulled her up every time she stumbled, helping her stay steady enough to find her footing again.

"We should get back to the team," Jin said through gasping breaths.

"Void," Astrea said. It was all she could say. All around her, as far as her senses would stretch, void magic surrounded her. It was impossible to escape.

"We'll deal with them."

"What's the plan?"

"Steal Nazarov's airship."

That was Jin's plan? Outrun Nazarov and The One, outrun the void mages no doubt still crawling around? On a stolen Helosian airship?

"I don't think—"

Cold pulsed painfully against Astrea's exposed skin. She yanked Jin back just as shadows spun through the air, both of them nearly falling with her change in direction. The One's masked face appeared just in front of them.

"Thought you could trick us?" he snarled, void book in hand. He chucked it at their feet. "You truly thought you could convince me this was real?"

"Fuck you," Astrea snapped. But where was Nazarov? The One hadn't killed him, had he? Or maybe he had. At least that would just leave one zealot to deal with.

His eyes bore into Astrea's, that icy blue the most terrifying thing she'd ever seen. "But I suppose I shouldn't be too surprised. You are, after all, your father's daughter."

Astrea's heart thundered in her chest and all the way up her throat. "What?"

"My brother never was easy to deal with, always trying to pull one over on me."

"What?" she asked again. She didn't know why, but . . .

The One scoffed as he took half a step forward. "Your father was my brother, little Lightbringer. I was going to tell you sooner, but you keep running away." He moved closer. "He could have had all of this, our legacy"—another step, just an arm's length away—"and yet he chose—"

Jin lunged. His free hand snapped out, fire dagger forming just before it stabbed into The One's left arm. It burned straight through his suit jacket and flesh. He roared, and Astrea tried not to cry out as ghost pain flared to life on her body.

"Stupid little brats." Grabbing Astrea's hand, The One dragged them through that disorienting and suffocating darkness. When they landed, darkness wavered around The One. The forest's shadows seemed to stretch and move, almost like they were alive. "Tell me where the book is."

"No," Jin spat as he tugged Astrea closer.

They jumped again. Astrea landed on top of Jin, all breath leaving her lungs. He rolled them over, then he shoved to his feet, fire blazing over his palms.

"Oh, good," cooed The One. "The Sunreaper wants to fight."

Jin advanced, rage and determination blending with the red and orange flames of his fire. Quick, efficient, brutal. That was the only way Astrea could describe his movements. The One stumbled back, stuck on defense.

"You'll have to do better than that, Sunreaper," The One called before disappearing. Shadows snaked up from the ground as he reappeared a dozen feet away.

"I've waited long enough to kill you," Jin snarled. "I can be patient for a little while longer."

Astrea rolled one shoulder. The very core of her bones ached. But she tracked The One and Jin as they danced around the forest, red flames and dark shadows blurring together. Jin landed blow after blow, but The One didn't relent. Didn't even seem fazed except for the ghost pain burning all over Astrea's body.

She needed that shadow in his aura, the one she always seemed to find around Nazarov.

"The Paragon will not be stopped, Sunreaper!" The One shouted as he reappeared closer to Astrea. "The prophecy will come true! You are touched by the void!"

Jin and The One sprinted toward Astrea at the same time. Just like that morning after the night club in Talmaris, when Jin had taken Astrea to the lake and tackled her dozens of times.

Just like that night, when she'd felt so small.

She was not small, and the Paragon would not take her again. This man, her uncle, would never take her again.

The One reached her first. Bright, hot starlight exploded in front of her. And as The One grabbed for her, Astrea shoved. She shoved with all her might, every ounce of strength left in her body.

Cold pulsed behind The One as shadows swirled up, sucking in some of Astrea's light.

Metal glinted, and a sickening squelch was followed by a spray of blood. The One had fallen right into a long, curved dagger. Straight through the heart.

Blood and shadow mixed on his pale skin. Hot and cold ate him from the inside out. Ate Astrea from the inside out. She stood frozen in horror and pain, watching as his body thumped against the forest floor.

That pain snuffed out in an instant. Gone, like it had never been there.

The One was dead.

And Victor Nazarov was the one pulling the dagger out of his back. Nazarov yanked the blade out, then seized Astrea's forearm. The void began swirling around them both.

Jin reached Astrea, grabbing her other hand so hard she thought he might actually pull her back out of those swirling shadows. But he tumbled in after her, and the void disappeared almost as quickly as it had come. Nazarov swore, then swore again as his magic swallowed the three of them whole.

They jumped again and again. The forest passed by in flash after flash. They even jumped close to the road, close enough to see a flurry of magic and hear the clash of the fight. Wind swirled around them, and Jin's hand on Astrea's was gone. She reached for him, but Nazarov jumped farther and farther up the road, closer and closer to those buildings that had once been distant.

Finally, the shadows stopped. The only thing above Astrea now were the clear morning skies, colored light pink and lavender and dusty blue.

Around them, small, well-kept buildings lined both sides of the road. A few cars were parked nearby.

"Thank you so much for your help, Astrea," Nazarov purred as he stalked toward her. "Though it doesn't make up for you trying to trick me about my book. Really, I thought we were past all that."

Black flashed through his aura once, too quick for her to grab.

"Don't know where you got that idea," Astrea said as she pushed to her feet. Jin was nowhere in sight. None of her friends were.

Nobody was at all. No civilians. No Novarian soldiers. Not even Paragon members.

"What you and I need is a chance to start fresh," Nazarov said. When Astrea remained silent, that black flashed above his head again. "Skies above, you're fucking stubborn."

"You don't exactly make me want to cooperate."

Nazarov's eyes narrowed. He started forward. And when that darkness spiked in Nazarov's aura again, Astrea grabbed it.

She grabbed it so violently that both she and Nazarov cried out. It was like reaching through the void itself, cold and harsh, until finally, there, underneath that shadow. There. Rage and annoyance and pain and fear, all hers for the taking. All hers to control.

Nazarov's eyes widened.

Astrea squeezed her fists and yanked back. With a strangled cry, Nazarov fell to his knees. Astrea pulled on his rage. She pulled on hers, that rage boiling deep within her. She hated The One, and she hated her father, whoever he was, for whatever he'd done to cause all this.

Nazarov cried out, then hissed, "How the fuck—?"

She hated herself for not pushing Saros more over the years. For not fighting back harder, sooner. For not trying to escape the Paragon sooner, for letting them keep her for days.

But most of all, she hated Victor Nazarov. Astrea hated him, so much so that fire burned under her skin. She hated him. She hated him for all the things he'd done to her and all the things he planned to do.

She hated him, hated him, hated him.

And Astrea poured all that fire into him, making him cry out again.

But even that inferno raging within her couldn't sustain Astrea much longer. Her arms trembled. Her entire body shuddered.

Nazarov pushed to his feet. His body shook, too, like he had to fight against her hold. Gritting her teeth, Astrea squeezed her fists tighter until her knuckles turned white.

"Not so strong now, huh, little Lightbringer?" Nazarov whispered as he took one stiff step toward her.

Astrea took one unsteady step back.

"Where's your princeling when you need him, hm?" He smiled that nasty, predatory smile of his. "He would burn the world for you, you know. I still think Tovan's plan to kill you might get me what I want. Prince Varojin, the Sunreaper, tearing down these pathetic rulers for not protecting you. The revenge he'd seek . . . the destruction he could bring . . ."

Astrea took another unsteady step back. Her knees faltered as her magic burned through her, as every ounce of hate in Nazarov's body flowed from his aura and into hers.

"You cannot have me," Astrea whispered as Nazarov inched closer.

"Oh, I think I can. There's no one here to save you today, and it seems you're all tuckered out." As Astrea's tight hold on her magic slipped, Nazarov smiled. "You poor, foolish girl. All that training hasn't paid off?"

Astrea scanned the street behind him. No one came out of their homes. No shopkeepers were opening their stores. The town may as well have been deserted. No Jin, either. No Cressida or Adi or Marko.

Nazarov would not take her. He could not have her, just as she'd promised herself so long ago. She would be in control this time. She would fight back.

Astrea let her hold on his aura go. As all that hate bled away, she could breathe again. Cool morning air filled her lungs.

"See, you're finally learning," he said as he shook out his limbs. "Smart girl."

Not even a dozen feet separated them. But it was enough.

Astrea bent her knees.

"Skies, that little trick hurts, I'll give you that, Souleater."

She braced herself.

"Would you like to go back to the airship? Solana and I will take you someplace to rest."

"Fuck you," Astrea whispered.

She launched herself at him.

Just like she'd practiced with Jin. Just like she'd practiced with Adi. Astrea ran toward Nazarov at full speed. That black shot through his aura again, and Astrea grabbed onto it with one hand while she summoned her light in the other. She yanked on that darkness, on that hatred burning beyond the veil, as she slammed into him with the full force of her shield.

Surprise and rage flitted across her skin, and Astrea grabbed those, too. She clenched her fists as she pinned Nazarov to the ground with her weight, and she did what Adi and Cressida taught her.

She punched Nazarov so hard her own head spun.

She punched him again and again and again, not stopping even as her face ached with the ghost pain. Not stopping even when blood covered her fists.

Nazarov shoved her off him in a fit of swears and rage. "You bitch," he hissed.

Astrea scrambled to her feet faster than he could sit upright. She kicked him in the crotch. He groaned. She'd almost kicked him again when he grabbed her leg and pulled her back down. Astrea's head slammed into the pavement so hard she saw stars.

"I don't even care about the book." Nazarov hovered over her. Blood covered his face, almost burning the way his eyes did. "I'm done with you, Souleater. I'll find another way. You aren't worth the trouble."

"Nazarov!" Jin bellowed.

Warring relief and rage danced over Astrea's skin. As soon as Nazarov glanced up, Astrea grabbed his hair and pulled to the right, throwing him off balance. She kicked up, her knee jamming into his stomach.

Boots pounded against pavement, then heat burned the air. Nazarov rolled off Astrea and to his feet. He wiped the blood off his face and nose.

Jin advanced toward him, a fire dagger burning in each palm. He lunged. Nazarov barely dodged. They continued in a dance of flames and pivots. One of Jin's daggers caught Nazarov's shoulder. He maneuvered away, but Jin caught him on the other side, right in the thigh.

Shadows drifted by overhead. Astrea didn't know whether to look up or focus on Jin.

The stench of burning flesh filled the air as Jin drove his dagger into Nazarov's forearm. As he roared in agony, Astrea cried out too.

Stumbling back, Nazarov clutched his arm to his chest. Jin lunged—aiming for Nazarov's chest—just as cold rippled through the air. A bloody, bruised Solana appeared. She grabbed Nazarov's arm, and then the two of them disappeared into the void.

"Skies damn it!" Jin yelled. "Fuck. Fuck!"

They didn't reappear. No voids were anywhere as far as Astrea could sense. The only thing she could feel was the heat of Jin's anger and the pain pulsing through her body in time with her heart.

Everything hurt. Her head, especially, hurt. And as she reached behind herself, all she could feel was blood in her hair.

The faintest trickle of light pulsed under her skin. She pulled on it, letting it soak into her scalp. Mirror healing and pain warred for just a moment, then flickered out. Astrea pressed against her skull, satisfied that the wound was closed and nothing but a dull ache remained in her head.

"Az?" Jin asked gently as he crouched down in front of her.

"I tried everything," she choked out. "I did *everything*—"

She'd done everything. Jin had done *everything*. And Nazarov had still managed to escape.

"I know."

"Were those more void mages on those ships?" she asked. The other Helosian ships were nearly out of sight, headed northeast.

"I don't know," he said. "Can you walk? We need to go."

"I think so."

Jin helped her to her feet. With his help, she managed to stay upright. Her muscles trembled with fatigue and magical overuse.

"This is as fast as I can go," she said as she and Jin hobbled down the road.

"That's alright. We'll just go as fast as we can."

"What if Nazarov comes back?"

"I don't think he's coming back. Not for a while, anyway."

That was all Astrea could hope for now. That Nazarov was gone, at least for a little while. "Are the others alright?"

"Banged up, but I think they're fine considering everything."

"Where'd the other void mages go?"

"Dead."

The empty road stretched before them as they exited the town. Neither of them said anything as Astrea limped along, battered and beaten and so, so tired. Neither of them said anything as they found where their small airship was nothing but bent metal and the stolen Helosian airship sat amid a sea of bodies.

Cressida, Adi, and Marko loitered nearby, orange anxiety twining between the three of them. Only when Jin and Astrea arrived did that orange fade even the slightest.

"What happened?" Cressida asked.

"The One's dead," Astrea said. "Nazarov's gone."

"And it looks like more airships are heading northeast," Jin said.

Marko nodded. "We saw them, too."

"Is it more void mages?" Adi asked. "Is it Nazarov's people?"

Jin shook his head. "I don't know."

"Then we need to get back to Talmaris now," Marko said. "I need to radio Lucian."

"See if you can get the radio in the stolen ship to work," Jin said. "I want to go make sure The One's actually dead this time."

"He seemed dead to me," Astrea murmured. She'd felt the life drain right out of him.

"Better safe than sorry. Adi and I will go check. You and Cress help Marko."

As Jin and Adi headed off into the woods, Astrea tried to look anywhere but the dead bodies littering the ground. Skies, there had to be nearly two dozen, most of them Paragon but some of them Nazarov's people dressed in Helosian red.

"Did you—" she started to ask, but Cressida shook her head.

"We took out some," she said, "but they honestly did a lot of the work for us. I've never seen anything like it. Void magic . . ."

"It's a lot," Astrea whispered.

"A couple of them may have been those Lifestealers we read about," Marko said as he gestured to the road. "Look at some of the marks on the impostor guards' skin."

Swallowing the bile in the back of her throat, Astrea followed Marko's gaze. Sure enough, some of the mages dressed like Helosian imperial guards were covered in those faded shadows.

"They seemed to grow stronger after killing," he continued. "As Cressida said, I've never seen anything like it."

Familiar cold settled on Astrea's skin, not like when the void mages appeared but that awful cold she always felt after a fight. "You said you need to radio the palace?" she asked Marko. "What about the other Novarians?"

"It seems my gamble didn't pay off," Marko muttered. "Though judging by that smoke, they have their own problems to deal with."

Thick, dark smoke still rose above the trees, high into the sky. Astrea stared up at it, trying to find the question bouncing around in the back of her mind. "Is that where Nazarov went?"

"I'll get the radio working," Cressida said. "Hopefully we can find out."

As Cressida headed for the red ship, Marko said, "Maybe you and I can gather what's left of our things from the wreckage?"

Astrea didn't really see the point. Their fake book was gone, and they'd just be going back to Talmaris. But she nodded and followed Marko. They picked through the debris, finding two of their five knapsacks mostly unscathed. They took those back to the Helosian ship.

Cressida's muttered curses filtered out from the pilot's area as soon as Astrea stepped aboard. The interior was exactly as she imagined a Helosian airship would be: red. Red, gold, and white everywhere, just as Emperor Aelius liked.

"If this isn't gaudy, I don't know what is," Marko muttered as he passed Astrea.

As Marko and Cressida fiddled with the radio, Astrea stumbled to one of the sofas in the middle of the cabin and collapsed onto it. Fatigue weighed heavily in her bones, like she couldn't move even if she wanted to. Even her senses wouldn't spread as far as normal, and they almost wavered back and forth around her.

When she closed her eyes, all she saw was The One's mask as he fell back into Nazarov's blade. *You are your father's daughter, after all.* All she saw was the hate twisting Nazarov's face as she attacked him. *Where's your princeling when you need him?*

Astrea sucked in one shaky breath, then another, as her body sank farther into the sofa. Even when Jin and Adi returned, she couldn't make herself sit up.

"The One's definitely dead," Jin said.

"Good." It was the only thing Astrea could say. Good. She was glad he was dead. Her uncle. Her paternal uncle was dead, and she was relieved.

"That doesn't explain where Nazarov went," Adi said.

Jin sighed. "We'll figure it out soon. Marko?"

The Tempest turned around from the radio and nodded. "Lucian's aware of the situation. He's getting on an airship to meet us midflight and escort us back. He said to get going."

"Give me two minutes and we'll take off!" Cressida yelled over her shoulder. A door shut somewhere behind Astrea, and soon, the floor trembled as the engine kicked on.

"What about the base?" Adi asked.

Marko's lips pressed together before he said, "Lucian said to leave it be. It's been handled."

Astrea lay down on the sofa and closed her eyes. Footsteps tracked all over the cabin, two sets slow and the other hurried. A soft, warm hand brushed Astrea's cheek. She forced her eyes open, and familiar golden ones watched her. Jin was crouched next to her.

"Are you hurt?" she asked him.

"A little bruised, but I'm fine."

"And everyone else?" She couldn't pick out ghost pain from her own.

"The same." He smoothed hair back from her face. "Can you heal yourself?"

"I did a little already."

"Then sleep," Jin said as the ship lurched into the air. Cressida whooped. "I'll wake you when we rendezvous with Lucian."

"You'll stay?" she whispered.

"Always."

It was only as Jin settled on the floor next to her that Astrea let her fatigue win and darkness pull her under.

CHAPTER 53

Talmaris was just a speck of light on the horizon as dark settled over the world. Astrea couldn't help but stare at it. Talmaris.

Some time while Astrea had been asleep, they'd landed at another Novarian base to wait for Commander Lucian. He'd arrived with four Novarian war airships to escort them back to the capital. She'd also learned that Anjou Lazzaro's ship had been found and was being escorted by the Novarian navy. Zephyrine and Saros had contacted a Novarian base and were scheduled to arrive in Talmaris the next morning. All was well.

But Astrea couldn't get Nazarov's hatred out of her mind. She couldn't get The One's words out of her mind. *You are your father's daughter. He could have had all of this, our legacy.* What would The One's death mean for the future of the Paragon? Would a new Dreamwalker king rise? Would Nazarov take his place? It wouldn't surprise her in the slightest.

Or what about her father? Was he alive? Was *he* a Dreamwalker? Would he become the Paragon's new leader? Had he known what The One was doing?

"Hey." Jin's heat enveloped Astrea as he joined her near the windows. Cressida was dozing on the sofa behind them. "I'm really, really proud of you, Az. I hate that we were put in the situation, but you did great."

She leaned back into him as he put an arm around her shoulders. "Thanks."

"We'll be landing in a few minutes, and then we'll need to debrief with Lucian and Ysabel."

"Whatever we have to do." He squeezed her shoulders as she said, "I should wake Cress."

Waking up Cressida proved to be no issue; she jolted up as soon as Astrea said her name. They gathered what few belongings they had after the airship crash and waited for Marko and Adi to land. They weren't going to the airfield but instead to a spot just outside the palace.

The ship landed smoothly. The others moved slowly, like they were swimming through molasses. Their exhaustion piled on top of Astrea's. Yes, they needed to debrief, but skies, for a moment, all she could think about was the soft bed that awaited her.

As soon as the airship door was open, Lucian swept in, two Novarian guards at his heels. He looked as he always did: perfectly put together. "Are you hurt?" he asked as he surveyed the group.

"Nothing to slow us down, but not our best, Commander," Marko said. "Astrea's done more than she ever should have had to this mission. An outstanding job, but she needs a break. A trip to the infirmary and dinner before debrief would be great."

Lucian's eyebrows lifted.

"We've got a lot to tell you," Astrea said, cheeks burning. "The short of it is that I can attack void mages our way."

His eyebrows rose higher. For a moment, Astrea was sure he was going to quiz her then and there. But he just nodded and said, "Let's get you all patched up and fed, then we'll talk."

The trip to the infirmary didn't leave Astrea feeling any better, though she had a prescription from Ivy, the Purifier and head healer, to rest for a few days. There was nothing else to do after such magical overuse. Dinner had helped, though the food may as well have been ash in Astrea's mouth. She'd eaten whatever had been given to her while Ivy and Lucian checked out the rest of the group. Burns, bumps, bruises, and torn muscles—all healed.

That was all the time they'd gotten to rest, an hour at most. Now, Lucian led them through the palace halls, empty except for the soldiers and guards. The atmosphere was tense, worse than when they'd left for the mission. Everyone they passed stood rigid, worry lines marking their expressions.

Lucian went straight for the war room, which buzzed with life. Several members of the Novarian Grand Council, Grand Duchess Ysabel, Crown Prince Veiko, and most importantly, Eliana and Nicos, were inside. Astrea wanted to run to them both, hug them, but she refrained. Eliana remained seated, mint relief blooming around her. Nicos was a different story. He stood at one end of the long table in the middle of the room, unreadable and expression hard as he stared down at a map. He looked . . . so official. In command, though he was technically one of the lowest ranked people in the room.

"Commander." Ysabel stood and smoothed the front of her dark blue blouse. "Nobody told me you all were back. I would've come to greet you."

"Needed to get them healed up and fed, Your Highness," Lucian said. "There's much to discuss."

"Indeed, there is," Ysabel said. "I've received another update from Commander Tarkun down at Fort Silverpine."

"And?" Lucian asked.

"Casualties are lower than expected."

"Thank the skies," Lucian murmured as he moved farther into the room. Astrea and the others followed.

"That's the fort that was attacked, near Irvina?" Jin asked. He pulled out one of the last empty chairs for Astrea, and she dropped into it.

"Indeed," Crown Prince Veiko said. "I'm glad to see you all unharmed. It appears the Helosians have—"

"It wasn't actually the Helosians," Jin said, his gaze flicking from his cousins to Eliana, then Nicos. "Victor Nazarov appears to have several Helosian airships under his command. We got one back from him, but he escaped."

And with that, the floodgates opened. They were met with a barrage of questions: what happened near the base? What happened in Kalama? Where was the book? Jin, Astrea, and the others provided all the details they could, from Raela's self-sacrifice to the true prophecy to the contents of the book. They covered everything that had happened since they'd left Talmaris, and with each detail they added, horror, curiosity, fear, and even pride swept through the room, pushing against Astrea's tired mind over and over again. That pride had spiked highest around Lucian, Eliana, and Nicos when Astrea had explained how she not only attacked all the guards at the Helosian port but Nazarov and Solana, too.

"You aren't the only ones who've had a remarkable couple of weeks," Ysabel said once the questions had run out. "We did meet with your father, though it was short-lived."

"And?" Jin asked.

Eliana sucked in a deep breath. "He told me what his emissaries did. That if we stayed out of it, if we left him alone, he'd leave us alone."

"And if we don't?"

"Then he will wage war not just on us, but on Novaria. He only stayed long enough to tell me that."

Astrea barely swallowed past the lump in her throat. It was the obvious reaction from the emperor, sure, but hearing it didn't make it any less awful.

Tense, heavy silence fell over the room. Jin looked first at his sister, then across the table to Ysabel and Veiko. He sighed. "I'm sorry we've put you in this position."

"Varojin," Ysabel said, her voice steel, "your father was going to come after us one way or another. If he's really going after this . . . what was it? Aetherium?" Jin nodded. "If he's really going after this aetherium, then it was only a matter of time before he came for Novaria. It's only a matter of time before he goes after Tornama, too, and eventually the Islands."

"Still," Jin said. "I know war. It's never easy for anybody. Everyone suffers."

"We're going to shore up forces near the Helosian border for the time being," said Veiko. "We'll send Delfine and Katerina down to the Taipoli Islands to try to get their leadership into talks about an alliance. I'll head to Thasia next week for the same purpose."

"What of Zaikud and Delia?" Lucian asked.

"I'm not sure, quite frankly," Ysabel said. "I could very well see them trying to get this aetherium for themselves. Do we tell them and hope they see reason, that they join us? Or do we hold off and hope they don't discover it for themselves?"

To Astrea, it seemed like there was no good choice. Allying with Delia and Zaikud could give them strength, sure, but at what cost? They hated Emperor Aelius—hated Helosia—and would surely want to do more than just stop the emperor. And if they didn't agree to an alliance, they would surely go after aetherium for themselves. Was there even a right choice?

"Perhaps we can finish discussing that tomorrow," said Councillor Tarsaya, the one who had backed their mission to Helosia. He offered a tired smile. "It's been a very long day."

"That it has," Ysabel said. "Let's reconvene tomorrow. I should make sure Delfine and Katerina know their mission, anyway."

The Novarian royals and councillors left without much grandeur, just a few goodnights and well wishes to those who had just returned. Astrea didn't bother to stand as they passed.

"Do you need anything, Your Highnesses?" Lucian asked, the question directed at Eliana and Jin.

"No, thank you, Commander," Eliana said. "I think we're fine."

"Astrea, we need to talk when you're up for it," Lucian said. "I need to hear more about what you've discovered."

"In the morning?" she offered.

"Tomorrow," he agreed.

And then he, too, was gone. He closed the war room door with a soft thunk, leaving Astrea, Cressida, Eliana, Jin, Adi, Nicos, and Marko alone. For a few moments, nobody said anything. Exhaustion and worry pulsed through the room in relentless waves. Jin finally sat down next to Astrea.

"Are we ready for this?" Eliana asked.

"We have to be," Cressida said. "Nazarov's bad enough, if Emperor Aelius recruits Lifestealers or finds a cache of aetherium . . ."

"We'll find a way," Nicos said. "I don't know how yet, but we'll stop them both."

Though Adi and Marko murmured their agreement, and though determination rolled off both Eliana and Cressida, Astrea wasn't so sure.

They'd need resources. They'd need a plan. And those things required time, time they didn't really have.

Astrea ran a comb through her damp hair, barely taking in her reflection as she did. The bathroom was humid after her and Jin's shower, but skies, it felt so good to be free of the blood and dirt from the last few days.

After arranging her hair into a loose braid, she headed for bed. Jin was already under the covers, and Astrea's whole body melted as she climbed in next to him. A soft bed. Her nightlight, still on in the corner. And Jin, her partner, her love. Wordlessly, she slid closer to him, just grateful he was there with her.

"You alright?" he asked as he draped one arm over her waist.

"What's going to become of the Paragon?" she asked. The rest of the group hadn't discussed the implications of The One's death yet, nor had they touched on the fact that he was apparently her family. "You didn't feel what I felt, Jin. I reached beyond that void surrounding Nazarov, and there was so much hatred. So much. Directed at me."

He sighed. "I'm not surprised, if I'm honest."

"No, but it makes me worry about just how far he's willing to go," Astrea whispered. "I know he's willing to go far, but . . ."

"But it makes you think."

"Yes."

"Well, if we don't find him first, he always seems to find us," Jin said. "I'm killing him next time I see him. I'll be ready."

"And The One being my uncle?" Astrea asked.

"We don't know if it's true."

"I believe him." Something in Astrea's gut told her The One was telling the truth. "If he's alive, is my father going to inherit control of the Paragon? Is he going to come after me?"

"Hey." Jin's lips brushed her forehead. "We won't figure it out tonight. Let's tackle that in a few days, after we've had a chance to rest."

"I don't like waiting."

"Skies, don't I know it," he murmured, sweet and sour amusement bubbling up on Astrea's tongue. "Then we'll ask Tomas to pull some records, and we'll talk to Saros and the Nikaphoroses, and we'll figure it out. But you heard Ivy. You need to rest, otherwise you're never going to recover. No magic, no research. It's just a couple of days. Let other people take care of things until then."

"I know." She sighed. "Thank you for always being there for me."

"Always, Az."

She leaned into Jin's body, savoring the way his arm wrapped around her shoulders and his sunshine love coated her skin. She may not have had the answers, but together, they would finish this. They would stop Victor Nazarov, and they would stop Emperor Aelius.

Not just the two of them, but the team. Astrea, Jin, Cressida, Adi, Marko, and everyone else. They would face this, and they would find a way to put an end to it.

They had to. Together.

Chapter 54

The morning went by in a blur. Breakfast with Eliana had taken forever, especially because Eliana wanted every last detail Astrea and Cressida could remember about Kalama. Then, she'd had to meet with Lucian to discuss her magical developments. It was well past lunchtime, but her work was not done yet.

Saros, Zephyrine, Sarsali, and Balthazar had all arrived at the palace earlier that morning. And now that they were all settled in and had been introduced to the grand ducal family and Lucian, it was time to deliver their treasure to the people who might be able to help unravel the webs.

"I can't believe you've been living here," Sarsali whispered as they walked through the palace. "How has it been?"

"Fine, Ma," Cressida said, her mood noticeably lighter now that she was reunited with her parents. "It's been just fine."

"Feeding you enough, I hope," Balthazar said.

"The only bad part is that they won't let me in the kitchen," Cressida quipped. "I'm dying to get my hands in some dough."

"Maybe we can work something out with Ysabel's staff now that we'll be here for the foreseeable future," Jin said. "Surely they won't continue denying you."

"Or you," Adi said. Unlike Cressida, his mood hadn't lightened at all. But with no news about Lennor, Civan, and his sister, Astrea wasn't surprised. "Don't pretend you don't want to be in there, too."

Astrea smiled. "The infamous chocolate cake."

"What?" Saros asked. He had both volumes of the scrambled void book tucked under one arm.

"Jin's famous for his chocolate cake," Adi said, as if that were the clearest explanation in the world. Saros simply raised an eyebrow.

After following two more short hallways, they arrived at the library's familiar double doors. Astrea hadn't been here in so long; it seemed almost foreign somehow. But as she opened them and led everyone inside, she relaxed a fraction. The familiar ceiling, painted midnight blue and gold, almost like the night sky. The busts of past dukes and duchesses. Even Tomas's hurried footsteps.

Mariya was already seated at one of the tables, her cane resting against the side of her chair. As the group drew nearer, Mariya perked up, green curiosity swirling around her. Behind Astrea, a cool breeze swept in. She peeked over her shoulder to find the same green mirrored around Saros.

"Astrea! Cressida! Adi!" Tomas called as he ambled down one of the spiral staircases. "Prince Varojin! You're all back, I see."

"That we are," Jin said. "I hope you're ready. We've got a lot to show you."

"Please, sit, sit," Tomas said, ushering everyone to Mariya's table. "Sit, then introduce me to these new faces."

Cressida introduced her parents first, and just as Astrea started to introduce her uncle, Mariya cut her off.

"Saros Sovna," she said, leaning back into her chair. "I haven't seen you in the better part of two decades."

"Nor I you, Mariya Halara," Saros said. "This is the last skies damned place I expected to run into you again."

"What, like that's a bad thing?" Mariya smiled, a challenge.

"No, but you'd always vowed not to work for any crown." Saros smiled back.

"As did you. It seems neither of us could stick to our desired paths."

"It seems not," Saros agreed.

From across the table, Cressida shot Astrea a confused look. Astrea barely shrugged; Mariya had once said Saros wasn't fun at parties, but it hadn't seemed, at least to Astrea, that Mariya had known her uncle all that well. This suggested otherwise.

"You two know each other?" Tomas asked.

"From university," Mariya said.

If Tomas had any further questions, he didn't press. Instead, he said, "So, you have information for me?"

Saros set the two tomes on the table, sliding one to Mariya and one to Tomas as Astrea and the others began explaining the contents. The deeper they got into the explanation, the more gray confusion and green curiosity spiked around Tomas and Mariya, their emotions almost twining together as one.

"I must say," Tomas began once their explanation concluded, "you did an excellent job rebinding these considering the time you had. I'll get to work deconstructing them this afternoon. Hopefully we can get them put back together within the next few days. I'll need some help, though."

"I can help," Saros offered.

"I'd appreciate that very much," Tomas said. "The grand duchess explained a bit about what you found already, Astrea, but I'd like to take some time to read through myself."

"Sure," Astrea said. "There's actually something else, though."

"Yes?" Tomas asked, barely looking up from the second book Mariya had slid to him.

Astrea swallowed hard. She hadn't actually had a chance to tell Saros or the Nikaphoroses this yet, but she needed to. Privately might've been better, but they were here now. *Just get on with it.*

"I don't know how much the grand duchess told you, Tomas, but we"—she gestured to Jin, Cressida, and Adi—"fought the void mages again yesterday morning. One of them, the leader of the Paragon, told me something."

"Yes?"

Under the table, Jin twined his fingers with Astrea's. She took a deep breath. "He said he was my paternal uncle."

Shock exploded around the table. Saros, Sarsali, and Balthazar all radiated that cold, sharp energy and ice blue took over their auras. Astrea pulled her barrier toward herself.

"I really don't know anything else about him, and . . . well, he's dead now," Astrea said. "But I'm concerned about what this means. Do you think there's anything about him, somewhere, in Novarian records? Anything?"

"About your father or this dead leader?" Tomas asked slowly.

"Either one?" Astrea shrugged. "I was born in Irvina."

Tomas glanced at Saros, a silent question hanging in the air. "I don't know who he is," Saros said. "My sister never told me."

"How do you know this man was telling the truth?" Sarsali asked. "Your mother would never have knowingly been with someone from this Paragon. Roxana cared about helping people, not hurting them."

Pieces of the conversation Saros and Astrea had a few nights before stuck out in her mind. That her mother often led with her heart, not her head. That she didn't always think things through.

"I don't think she knew," Astrea said quietly.

"We believe my mother was brought up with the purpose of having me," Jin said. "Perhaps Az's father set out with a similar mission."

Sarsali pursed her lips. Saros slumped back in his chair and ran a hand over his face. Adi kept his eyes trained on the table, and both Cressida and Balthazar folded their arms over their chests.

"Perhaps . . . some records in Irvina could tell us something," Mariya said. "Or maybe someone there will remember her, and by extension, him?"

"I'll talk to the grand duchess and see what I can do about getting records," Tomas said. "Unless you want to go all the way down to the border. Nasty business down there, setting up the border patrol."

"Whatever it takes," Astrea said. And she meant it. Whatever she had to do, she would.

"Very well." Clearing his throat, Tomas pushed his glasses up the bridge of his nose. "Saros, perhaps you'd like to begin helping me? Let's not put this off any longer."

"Indeed," Saros murmured. As he stood, he set a gentle hand on Astrea's shoulder. She offered him a weak smile.

"Is there anything we can help with?" Balthazar asked.

"I don't believe so," Tomas said. "Please, go about your days."

"I'll see you for dinner?" Saros half stated, half asked. When everyone agreed, he gathered the books and followed Tomas upstairs.

"And I should go speak with the councillors," Mariya said. After saying her goodbyes, she headed out of the library, letting the door close with a heavy thunk.

"Now what?" Cressida asked.

"Maybe we could go back to our room?" Balthazar asked. "Didn't get much sleep on the ship."

"Sure, I'll walk with you," Cressida said.

"I could use some fresh air," Astrea said to Jin. "Adi? Want to join us for a walk?" With the tight tangle of orange anxiety around him, she hoped he'd say yes. A walk might help him relax for a few minutes.

"Sure, I guess."

The five of them got up from the table, then headed back into the hallway. When they got to a junction Astrea barely recognized, Jin herded her and Adi to the left. Cressida led her parents straight ahead, then disappeared out of sight.

Even though the palace gardens were still crawling with soldiers, the cloud-smattered sky and soft sunshine made some of the tension in Astrea's muscles melt away. That, plus the strong smell of peonies and roses, almost made it feel like home. The air had cooled significantly in the fortnight they'd been gone, a sign of the season to come.

She, Jin, and Adi walked a ways into the garden in silence, Astrea right between the two of them. The knot around Adi didn't loosen, but when Astrea gently touched his forearm and smiled at him, he smiled back.

"I'm fine, Az," he said.

"It's okay if you're not."

"It's just . . ." He huffed and shoved his hands into his pockets. "It's not knowing where they are that's the worst part. If I knew for sure they were with Rasa, it'd be a different story."

"Adi, I know—" Jin started, but Adi cut him off.

"Can we talk about anything else right now? Please? Or maybe we just don't talk at all."

Though Adi would need to talk about it eventually, Astrea didn't push him, nor did Jin. They continued on in silence, past guards and soldiers, until they finally arrived at the lake. The one they'd spent so much time near the last few months. While they'd been at the old base, Astrea had missed it, even running laps around it. And seeing it now, sparkling in the sun, helped more of the tension in her muscles bleed away.

But when freezing cold panic and worry exploded behind her, Astrea whipped around. She couldn't see where it was coming from, so she started back toward the palace.

"Az?" Jin called after her. "Az, where are you go—"

"Something's wrong!" she yelled over her shoulder. Both Adi and Jin were running after her. "I don't know what, but something."

They wound their way back through the gardens, much faster this time. Nobody stopped them, though confusion and fear still rippled through the ranks. They'd almost gotten back to the palace when Marko burst out onto the nearby veranda.

"Jin!" he shouted. "Come quickly!"

Astrea pushed herself to go faster as they followed Marko into the palace. He led them through the halls until they were once again emerging outside. The palace's long driveway and front gardens stretched out before them.

And there, a few dozen feet away, was a face Astrea hadn't expected to see.

Snow white hair and skin, and those eyes that looked almost red. Caliban. Two Novarian guards restrained him, though he stood calmly. So incredibly calmly as he stared right at Jin.

"What—" Adi started, but confusion and fear pulsed behind Astrea, drawing her attention away.

Eliana, Nicos, Lucian, and Ysabel all stepped onto the palace's front veranda.

"You know this man, Varojin?" Ysabel asked. "That is what he told the guards, that he knows you and has a message for you."

"Oh, I know him," Jin muttered. "That's my father's personal guard, the void mage we told you about."

"And what would he be doing here?" Ysabel asked. "He wasn't with your father when we met with him recently."

Jin started down the steps. Astrea hurried after him, as did everyone else. He stopped a dozen feet short of Caliban and crossed his arms over his chest.

"Prince Varojin," Caliban said, voice low. "Princess Eliana."

"What do you want?" Jin asked.

"I come with a message."

"From our father?"

"From your brother."

"What does he want?" Eliana asked.

Staring at Jin, Caliban said, "He wants you to know that he has something you're looking for. Three things, actually. And if you want them back, you will meet with him in a week's time."

"Why would I do that?" Jin asked, voice hard. But the fear pulsing around him gave away the truth.

"Because if you do not, he will dispose of them. Traitors, all three," Caliban said.

"He wouldn't dare."

"He would."

For five long heartbeats, Jin didn't move. Astrea didn't think he even breathed. Panic slowly unfurled around Adi, his gaze frantically darting between Jin and Caliban.

Finally, Jin asked, "And where would he have us meet?"

"He will send note of his location once I return to him," Caliban said. "If I do not return by tomorrow, there will be no meeting."

"Then go to him," Jin said, "and tell him that I'll see him soon."

"Varojin—" Ysabel started, but Eliana cut her off.

"Tell him that he'll see both of us."

Caliban inclined his head. "Your Imperial Highnesses." Cold spiked, then a swirl of shadow enveloped Caliban. He was gone.

Astrea didn't dare move a muscle. Prince Kaius had Lennor, Civan, and Noemi? How the skies had he found them? And where did he have them now? Close to the border, Astrea assumed. Maybe in the Antare Mountains, near Tornama. Skies, had they been in Thasia with Prince

Kaius, and he'd had their friends on his ship? Had they been so close to them, only to leave them behind?

"You cannot be serious about meeting with your brother, Varojin," Ysabel said. "You don't know that he—"

"I'm not even going to give him a chance," Jin said. "We go, and we get our people back. No conversations. No threats. Lennor, Civan, and Noemi deserve nothing less." As he turned to Adi, he said, "We'll get them back, I promise."

Adi nodded, but so close to him, Astrea could see the tears clouding his vision.

"Varojin—" Ysabel tried again.

"Whatever you need, Varojin, we'll go get your people back," Lucian said. "Just name it."

"I need Zephyrine, Adi, Cress, Marko, and Az," Jin said. "And we need a plan."

Astrea's breath hitched.

But they'd done it once. They'd gotten Saros, Sarsali, and Balthazar out of Kalama, into the Taipoli Islands, and all the way across the continent to Talmaris. And as she looked at the rigidness in Marko's shoulders, at the hope on Adi's face, and the set of Jin's jaw, she knew they'd do it again.

They left no one behind.

To be continued

Books by H.E. Bauman

Forged by Flames: A Darkened Skies Prequel

Under Darkened Skies: Darkened Skies Book One

Into Whispering Shadows: Darkened Skies Book Two

Amid Twisted Chaos: Darkened Skies Book Three

Darkened Skies Books 4 & 5 coming soon!

Acknowledgments

Continuing to tell Astrea's story is one of the great privileges I've had in recent years, and to know so many people are not only connecting with her but supporting my work is so special.

To Sarah, Kayla, Laura, and Michelle, thank you for helping me iron out this story and getting Astrea where she needed to be.

To Jeanine, thank you for your eagle eyes and editing expertise!

To my street team, thank you all for your ongoing love for this series and continuing enthusiasm.

To my husband, family, and friends, thank you for all your understanding and support as I keep working on these books.

And finally, to all my readers, thank you for loving the whole Darkened Skies crew just as much as I do. I can't wait to bring you the final books in the series.

About the Author

H.E. Bauman is a fantasy author fascinated with all things magical. After spending her childhood writing stories, she went on to receive her bachelor's in English and has continued writing ever since. When she's not reading or writing, she enjoys playing tennis, immersing herself in video games, and spending time with her family.

If you want to get in touch, visit H.E.'s website or follow her on social media.